CONVERSION

S.C. STEPHENS

Edited by Debra L. Stang

Cover photo © Toski Covey Photography
Cover design © Sarah Hansen, Okay Creations

ISBN-13: 978-1491008119

ISBN-10: 1491008113

Dedication

I dedicate this one to my fans who have followed me since my early days of writing. Your encouragement has meant the world to me, and I wouldn't be here without you!

A huge thank you to everyone who helped bring this book to life—Lori, Becky, Kyla, Nicky, Sam, Jenny, Nicola, Debra and Sarah. Your help was invaluable!

My heart goes out to the authors who have given me their time and support, the bloggers who have endlessly promoted my books, and the worldwide fans who have been so passionate about my characters. You amaze me! And a very special thank you to Mark at Smashwords, Christopher at Kindle Direct Publishing, Lauren at Createspace, my agent, Kristyn Keene at ICM, and everyone at Gallery Books, who have all been so incredibly helpful and supportive. I'm very blessed to be surrounded by such great people.

Chapter One – I'm Sorry, You're What?

I never thought I'd be dating a vampire. I never even considered it. Of course, up until a few weeks ago, I had believed that vampires were as mythic as the Easter Bunny and Santa Claus. That was, until the day I met one, or more accurately, collided with one. It happened in broad daylight on a crowded sidewalk. I had been running late getting back to work from my lunch hour and smashed right into him, dumping my venti, double, non-fat, soy, vanilla latte all over his shirt. I'd had it prepared extra-hot—I like my coffee sweet and searing—and he'd jumped back about a foot, holding his dampened shirt away from his skin like I'd just poured molten lava down the front of him. No, nothing about our first encounter had made me think he was supernatural in the slightest. That revelation came much later, and it shook me to my core. Now I'm starting to wonder about the Easter Bunny and Santa Claus…anything was possible.

Apologizing profusely on the outside, and cursing at the loss of my afternoon pick-me-up on the inside, I'd shoved my card in his face and told him I'd pick up the dry cleaning bill. His crisp, button up shirt had been white, of course, and had looked expensive. I was sure he was going to call me and demand that I replace it, for surely my sweet, yummy, ruined coffee would never fully escape that once pristine fabric.

I worried about his phone call when I got back to work. Sometimes I had a lot of time to worry at my job. I was an executive administrative assistant's assistant. In other words, I was the secretary's secretary—the gofer who got all the piss-ass jobs the secretary didn't want. I worked for a prosperous local accounting firm, so my job involved a lot of paperwork—filing, faxing, copying…daydreaming. While I worried, I hoped one of my assignments would involve a coffee run for my boss, so I would have an excuse to grab another one for myself; an hour after lunch, I could feel my eyelids drooping as I went through stacks of financial documents.

It was in this near catatonic state that the phone rang. I answered automatically with a comatose voice. "Neilson, Sampson and Peterson." I really hated how the firm name rhymed. "This is

Emma, how can I help you?"

A cool voice answered me with, "Is this the Emma that dumped her coffee all over my shirt?"

My heart started beating faster as I pictured the surely irate man on the other end of the line. I tried to remember what he'd looked like, but I was drawing a blank. The incident was overshadowing his face—although, I thought I remembered dark hair and tan skin.

"Yes…I'm so sorry about that. Do you have a bill for me already?" I twirled the phone cord in my fingers and waited for the surely exorbitant figure he was going to spout at me.

Taking me by surprise, he laughed. "No, don't worry about the bill." I wondered why he was calling, if he wasn't interested in repayment. I didn't have to wonder long. "I was just thinking…you gave up all your coffee for my shirt, maybe I could buy you another?"

That took me back a step. Did he seriously just ask me out? "Um…sure, I guess."

"Great. What time are you off work?"

It was at this point, that I had the briefest moment of *You're agreeing to meet someone who could be a serial killer* panic. If I'd only known… Quickly pushing that fear aside as irrational, I said, "Five."

"Want to meet at the same place? I'll have another venti, double, non-fat, soy, vanilla latte waiting for you…extra hot, of course." He laughed a little on end of that.

Caught off guard, I blankly stared at the prosaic wall of my cubicle. "Sounds great… I'll see you then." I hung up the phone and only then realized that I'd never asked him his name. I'd been too stunned by the fact that he knew what my drink was—exactly what my drink was. That was my first hint that something was not quite right with this man. It was not my last.

When I met him after work, he greeted me at the door in a non-coffee-stained light green shirt, with my perfectly recreated drink. He seemed as normal as they come…not vampiric at all, not that I was really thinking about such things yet. He was around six feet tall, medium athletic build, black hair in a traditional "guy" cut, a lovely shade of sky blue eyes, the I-don't-really-care-about-my-looks-but-I-care-about-my-looks perfectly light, facial stubble, and a delightful smile, with perfect, and normal, white teeth. Nothing odd about him at all—no fangs, no clammy, pale skin, no Slavic accent, and no aversion to crosses; I'd been wearing one. If I had been expecting to meet a vampire that day, I would have been highly disappointed.

As it was, I'd only been expecting to meet a possibly irate man, so the attractive gentleman before me was a very pleasant surprise. He held his hand out to me in greeting; it was as warm as any other man's hand. "Emma? Emma Taylor?" I nodded and he smiled. "Hello, I'm Teren. Teren Adams."

I blinked. His name was the oddest thing about him. "Teren? That's…unusual."

He laughed a little as he handed me my coffee. It was a delightful sound, slightly husky. "You should meet my parents…then you'd understand." He gave me an odd grin, like he'd just said something funny, that I wasn't supposed to understand. And at the time, I hadn't. At the time, I hadn't noticed anything beyond how incredibly sexy my surprise date was.

He grabbed his coffee from a nearby table and led me to a couple of comfortable chairs in the back. I think we spent two hours in that coffee shop before deciding we were hungry, and moving to a nearby restaurant for a nice dinner. We both ate. We both had wine. We shared a light dessert, along with hours of pleasant conversation. And after he drove me back to my car at the coffee shop, the only thoughts I had about him were pleasant. Well, there were a couple naughty thoughts too when he kissed me good night.

There was nothing at all that made me think he was anything other than an interesting human man that I'd literally run into. We saw each other pretty steadily over the next few weeks, and I grew even more attracted to him. Of course, I did notice oddities, but then, everyone has oddities and truly, vampirism was the last thing I'd suspected. But I did notice that he was strong. He once nearly pulled my front door off the hinges. It had rattled him almost as much as it had shocked me. With a nervous laugh, he'd explained the incident away as my mere presence had given him an adrenaline rush.

Yeah…I'd gagged a little at that too.

He also had disturbingly good hearing. I could whisper our conversations into the phone at work, so as to not get caught by my dried-up old shrew of a boss, and he'd hear every word perfectly. He said he had an Aunt who had been traumatized as a child and spoke very softly, so he was used to it. Uh-huh, sure.

At times, he was faster than someone ought to be. He'd be running late in meeting me, and then still end up there before me. He'd explained that as hitting all the lights just right. I would have believed him more, if he hadn't been biking while I'd been driving.

But then, one day, I saw his fangs. Those were a little harder for him to explain away.

We were on his couch. His long, white, comfortable, leather, sit down and you never want to get up again couch. Only we weren't sitting. We were lying. We were kissing. And I was really hoping we wouldn't be stopping at second base, that we'd be rounding home. I wasn't opposed to going slow, but I really liked this guy, and I was ready to take it up a notch. I'd been ready for a while now, but we still hadn't had our shining moment. I was beginning to get a little frustrated.

He was an excellent kisser, with the kind of kisses you could feel all the way to the bottom of your toes. His tongue was caressing mine, and mine was caressing his right back, when *it* happened.

"Ow!" I pulled away and stuck a finger in my mouth. My tongue felt like it had just been pricked by a needle. When I removed my finger, a trace amount of blood was on it.

Teren immediately flew off of me. Standing a ways from the couch, his hand pulled on his upper lip, effectively hiding his mouth in a nonchalant way. "I'm sorry. It's been a long day. Maybe I should give you a ride home now."

Still wishing for that home run, I shook my head. "No, I'm fine. It's still light out and I'm not the least bit tired." We'd gone out to dinner earlier at a nice Italian restaurant, and had come back to watch a movie on his big screen with a glass of wine…and promptly started making out instead; the movie playing in the background was all but forgotten. "Come back here and keep kissing me…" I raised my eyebrows suggestively, but he was having none of it.

His hand still hiding his mouth, he said, "I really do have an early day…rain check?"

Getting up, I walked over to where he was standing in the middle of his spacious living room. "You said you weren't working tomorrow? What are you doing?" I tried to keep my tone light and airy, but he was disturbing my nightly plans again, and I really wanted to share that intimacy with him. I'd even stuffed my toothbrush, a tank top, flip-flops, a fresh pair of underwear and yoga pants, into my satchel-sized purse, just in case our date turned into an impromptu overnight visit.

He rubbed his lip and I could see the gears turning in his head. That made me suspicious…then it made me mad. "Teren…what are you hiding from me?" My tone shifted to definite irritation.

He shook his head and shrugged his shoulders, looking very uncomfortable and sort of embarrassed. "Nothing. I have to…go to my parents' place tomorrow morning, that's all." His pale eyes were giving me the *Just believe me* look, and I wasn't.

"Your parents? Really." I huffed out an annoyed breath as I straightened my tight skirt and adjusted the red, lacy top that was clinging to my curves. With my outfit and my body language, I couldn't have given him a bigger green light if I tried, but he was still pulling away from me, and I wasn't sure why. I guess I'd just have to be blunt and ask him.

I shook my head, causing my brown locks to bounce around my shoulders. "I don't mean to be overly forward, but…is there a reason you don't want to have sex with me? I thought most men were all gung-ho for that, but we've been dating for weeks now and nothing." Knowing my question was coming out a bit rudely, thanks to my rising frustration and disappointment, I mentally cringed.

I could see his jaw drop under the hand still over his mouth and his eyes widened. "I…of course I want—"

A spark of anger at his mumbled response ripped through me. "Would you stop talking through your hand!" I jerked it away from his mouth and we both stared at each other in shock.

His mouth had been open from speaking, and his fangs were perfectly visible, and to me—perfectly new. I'd seen his teeth plenty of times. I'd run my tongue along them on several occasions. I sure as heck had never seen inch long canines on him before. At first, I didn't make the connection. I thought he'd slipped them in as a joke. Because really, how often in real life do you see something weird and automatically think—vampire! The brain will always go for the rational explanation first.

"What the hell? Are you role-playing with me?" I cocked an eyebrow and gave him a cautious look. "Because, I'm not into the whole Anne Rice fantasy."

He shut his mouth and blushed. That's right, he blushed. "No…I'm not playing."

"Then what? You had a sudden…dental emergency?" I scrunched my brow, still trying to understand what I was seeing.

He laughed. At the moment, I didn't find it amusing. "No, you got me a little…excited, and they kind of slipped out, and I'm so sorry. That's so embarrassing." He ran a hand over his stubbly jaw and I swear his blush deepened.

I furrowed my brow to a deep point, still hopelessly confused. "What slipped out? Teeth, even long ones, don't just slip out." I lost my train of thought as what he'd said finally registered with me…well, registered with my body, anyway. "Wait…I got you excited?"

He twisted his lips. The movement looked a little funny around his fangs. "You always get me excited." He lowered his gaze to my body and I flushed. Maybe we'd get to home base after all… But not until he fully explained this new development.

I shook my head and put my hands on my hips. "You're distracting me from this." I waggled my finger at his teeth.

He sighed. "I can't hide this from you forever, not with how close we're getting. I guess you should know anyway." He started to reach out for me and then seemed to change his mind. He let his hand drop back down to his side as he quietly added, "I want you to know."

I started tapping my foot—part nervousness, part irritation. "Know what?" I asked with forced patience.

His smile widened and I watched in shock as his teeth retracted to normal. My hands limply fell to my sides and my mouth dropped wide open—you could have parked a bus in there. "How did you do that?"

He indicated the sofa. "Have a seat. I'll explain it to you." I didn't sit, so much as fall. He clicked off the television and then sat down close beside me; his hands nervously ran up and down his gray slacks. He chuckled at my rapt attention to his mouth. "Well…to be blunt, I'm a vampire."

I couldn't help it. Any sane person would have had the exact same reaction I did. I laughed. I belly laughed. Pushing his shoulder away from me, I told him, "Be serious."

He didn't laugh with me, if anything, he looked a little offended. "I am."

My laughter slowly died down as I watched him watch me. His pale eyes relaxed as my giggles drifted off. "Okay." I bit my lip and forcefully stopped myself from chuckling. "You're a vampire. That's…wonderful."

He shook his head at my contained amusement. "Well, to be technical, I'm only a little bit vampire." He relaxed onto his elbows over his knees, seeming to be glad the hard part was over with…at least for him. I was still spinning with the absurdity of everything my, up until this point, seemingly normal, boyfriend was telling me.

"I'm sorry…you're what?"

Now he smirked and looked about to laugh. "I'm pretty sure you heard me." His grin mischievous, he leaned into my side. "But don't worry, I'm not hungry. You're perfectly safe." His tone was even more amused now.

I shook my head, hoping he was punking me. I decided to play along though. "Okay. Let's assume that you're not teasing me…or crazy. How does one become a 'little bit' vampire? Isn't that kind of like being a 'little bit' pregnant? Some things, you either are or you aren't."

He softly laughed. "Well, it's confusing…"

I pursed my lips and crossed my legs, as much as I could in my tight skirt, anyway. "Try me."

He raised an eyebrow and I startled as I considered the literal way my words could be taken to a vampire. He laughed in earnest at my reaction. "Really…I'm not going to bite you. Not unless you asked me to, anyway." He said the last part quietly, with a sparkle in his eyes and a small smile on his lips. I wondered if he was serious about that, and then wondered if I was just as crazy as he apparently was, for believing one iota of his tall tale. But then he started speaking, and I relaxed into the couch and listened to his smooth, deep voice. I tried to keep my mind as wide open as I could. He hadn't seemed crazy before this point. Maybe I should give him the benefit of the doubt.

"My great-grandmother was turned while she was nine months pregnant."

"Turned?" I asked, wanting to be sure of my vampire terminology.

He smiled at my interest and splayed his fingers out to me as he explained his heritage. "Made into a vampire by another vampire…just like in the movies. Anyway, the change induced labor, and the baby was born before being…fully changed. My grandmother was born half-vampire, a rarity for our kind." He paused and sat back on the couch, looking over at me with a thoughtful expression. "In fact, we know of no others like us." He seemed to contemplate that for a second, and then continued while I soaked up his story like a sponge. "Gran married a human and had my mother—"

"Who's a quarter vampire?" I asked, leaning into him and bringing my legs up onto the couch. His tale was sucking me in.

He put an arm around my shoulder and pulled me into him, as he smiled down at me. "Something like that. Anyway, my mother also married a human, and had me, so…" he held his free hand out to his side, "…little bit vampire."

"Huh."

He pulled away and gave me an odd, relieved-offended look. "That's all you have to say…huh?" He exaggerated the way I had said it, and I twisted my lips at him, a little annoyed.

"Well, assuming that your little fable was real, I was just thinking that you should marry a full-blood vampire if you want to keep the trait alive, otherwise you'll dilute it right out." That *had* been the first odd thought that had popped into my head after hearing his story. Well, second thought really…right behind, *Is he nuts?*

He blinked at me and then started laughing. Then he grabbed my cheek with his free hand and pulled me in for a heat-inducing kiss. My body forgot his crazy story, forgot his pointy teeth, and focused instead on the multiple sensations coursing through every cell of my now highly sensitive skin. Teren's reaction to me progressed beyond anything he'd shown so far, and before I knew it, he was lifting me up with those incredibly strong arms, and sweeping me to his room upstairs, where we went right on rounding the rest of those bases. I guess his lack of interest had more to do with his hidden secret, than anything else.

Afterwards, we lay close together in his cream-colored, silk sheets, our legs entwined and my arm over his muscled chest. My head rested on his skin and I could clearly hear his evening heartbeat. I looked back up at his face, at the strong, stubbly jaw, the relaxed full lips, and the perfect pale eyes staring back at me.

"I think you're wrong," I said matter-of-factly.

He laughed, deep in his chest. "Am I? I'm assuming we're still on the vampire thing."

I scoffed at his casualness. "Vampire thing. You say that like it's only as strange as having a sixth toe or something."

His eyes widened and he got a huge grin on his face. "Do you have a sixth toe?" He looked down at my feet loosely coiled up in his sheets and I gently kicked his shin.

"No! It was just an example." I raised my head off his chest to fully look at him.

He laughed again. "Well it's not strange to me. Everyone in my family is…well, the women are anyway." His hand on my bare back started tracing circles into my skin.

I shook my head, processing his statement. "Your father is human, but your mother is not?"

He nodded. "Yes." He said it so easily, like we were discussing his nationality or something.

"So…you drink blood and stuff?" I bit my lip, wondering if I really wanted the answer to that, and thinking maybe I should have asked these questions before sleeping with him. Oh well. I guessed I had survived it, and while mind-blowingly good, it was pretty standard stuff, so if he did sip a little O-positive, he could at least control it.

He frowned. "You really want to know this?"

I propped myself up on my elbows and stroked his chest. "Yes, I do." And I realized that I did. I wanted to know everything about him, the good and the bad.

He sighed and his hand stopped its circular motion and dropped to my hip. He watched me for a moment, perhaps judging if I would stay put on his chest once he told me his answer. Finally, he said, "Yes…I do, sometimes. It tastes good to me and I enjoy it, but I can eat regular food too and I enjoy that as well, as you've seen."

I cocked my head. I'd never heard of an omnivore vampire before. Of course, I'd never heard of a vampire with a heartbeat before. "Oh, that's interesting. So your body is…"

He visibly relaxed, since I hadn't bolted from the room. "Mostly human. I do everything…human males…do." He shrugged his shoulders and laughed. His hand returned to my back and he smiled at me.

"That's so weird. So, you drink blood on occasion and have fangs…" Remembering back to our little tumble not so long ago, I gave him a curious look. "Where did your fangs go?"

He blinked at me, a small laugh escaping him. "What?"

"When we were…you know…you were fangless. Why didn't they pop out when you were excited?" I probably shouldn't have asked him such a personal question, not that we weren't quite personal with each other now, but maybe his teeth were something really private that I shouldn't have brought up. Like him wanting to discuss tampons or something.

Amused, he shook his head. "And you say I'm casual about this." I twisted my lips into a pout and he grinned. "I can control it…most of the time. It's easier to do now, knowing that you know, and if I mess up, you won't go running or anything. It takes the pressure off."

"Weird." He seemed okay talking about it, so I continued my train of thought. "So…on the couch… You didn't mean to do that?"

"No…definitely no." His pale eyes looked down at my fingers on his chest. He still seemed a touch embarrassed about his slip-up.

I brought a finger to his cheek and stroked it; the light stubble grazing my skin was delightful to touch. He looked up at me, a warm smile on his lips. I held my breath, reluctant to ask my next question, since it was one that would probably embarrass us both. I really wanted an answer to it, though, so I sucked it up and said, "And, we've waited all this time, because you were afraid of that happening?"

He looked at me with a blank expression. I thought for a moment that maybe he didn't understand what I was vaguely referencing. Or maybe he did, and he just didn't want to answer me. But then he finally smiled and said, "It's only been three weeks. You make it sound like I've been holding out on you for years." His mouth twisted into a devilish grin. "I didn't realize you wanted me so bad. I was just trying to be a gentleman." He laughed again as the hand on my back tightened into a hug.

I playfully patted his shoulder. "Shut up."

The last rays of the sun sank all the way down as we talked and the room darkened to blackness. I laid my head on his chest and again marveled at his steady and strong heartbeat. *Vampire?* If I hadn't seen the fangs, I still wouldn't have believed it. He seemed too…human.

"Are you really sure?" I asked, as I looked back up to his eyes. My breath caught as I stared at his face. I believed. I fully believed. With the sun set and the heavy curtains blocking the street lights, the room should have been pitch-black. But it wasn't. There was light in his bedroom, and it was coming from him...from his eyes. They glowed, a phosphorescent glow, like someone had painted the whites of his eyes with glow in the dark paint. Aside from his teeth, it was the strangest thing I'd ever seen.

"Oh...wow. That's weird."

"What?" The glow narrowed as his eyes narrowed.

"Your eyes...that's just freaky." It was also a little hypnotic. I couldn't turn away from it, and I felt my head getting lighter and my face starting to relax. I could bathe in those eyes. I never wanted to look away. I'd follow those eyes anywhere...

"Oh, that. Right...yeah, that is kind of weird. It's like...you know those fish in the deepest parts of the ocean that use light to attract their prey? Kind of the same idea." I could see his shoulders shrug in the dim light emitted...by him.

I blinked and shook my head a little, forcing myself to look away from those hypnotic eyes, remembering that, technically, *I* was his prey. "Oh...well, it's weird and a little...creepy."

"Sorry, I can't shut it off or anything. Luckily, it's barely noticeable unless it's completely dark. There's usually enough light pollution in the city that people don't see it." He laughed, the glow bouncing with him. "It does make for awkward conversations when I try and go camping in the countryside though."

I turned on the lamp sitting on his nightstand to bring his eyes back to normal. Blinking in the now too-bright light, I looked over at him again. "You...camp?" For some reason, the thought of a vampire camping struck me as the oddest thing he'd uttered all night.

He smiled and shrugged again. "Sure...who doesn't love camping?"

"You're so weird." I plopped myself back down onto his wonderfully masculine chest. A fresh burst of his light cologne hit my nose as I inhaled a deep, contented breath.

His amused chuckle vibrated beneath me as he brought his hands up to play with the long strands of my dark hair. "Would you stop saying that. I'm starting to get a complex."

I smiled as his hand sweeping the hair away from my bare shoulder gave me goose bumps. "Sorry, I'm trying to process this. I've never met a vampire before." I nestled further into his chest, relaxing into his capable hands.

"That's a very good thing." There was an oddness to his voice. I looked up to his beautiful, pale blue eyes, and there was an odd look in them as well. I wondered if I wanted to know what he meant by that.

Instead I asked, "How old are you?" I propped myself on my elbows on his chest again, suddenly very excited at an idea that had popped into my head. "Are you a couple hundred years old? Have you seen the civil war, or the first cars, or thin Elvis? What have you seen? I want to know everything." I rested my head in my hands and waited for his surely fascinating answer.

He cocked his head at me. "I'm twenty-five."

I frowned. "You're twenty-five because that's my cover story and I'm sticking to it, or you're twenty-five because you were birthed twenty-five years ago?"

He laughed. "The latter...I really am twenty-five. I've seen what you've seen." I sighed and slumped a little on his chest. "Does that disappoint you?" He asked, a grin on his face.

I sighed again. "Yes...actually, as far as vampires go, I find you a little disappointing."

I was abruptly flipped over onto my back. The move was so fast, my mind couldn't even comprehend it; one minute I was on my stomach and the next I was on my back. My breath increased as I tried to wrap my mind around this new position. Teren was hovering over me and his fangs were out again. My mouth dropped open watching him.

"Am I still disappointing to you?" he growled.

I couldn't even answer him. His presence, his undeniable power—it took my breath away. He leaned over me and very lightly dragged his teeth along my skin. It did wonderful things to my body, but I wasn't about to let him hurt me.

My speech came back to me in a pant. "If you bite me, it will be the last thing your vampire ass does."

He laughed and retracted his teeth. "I wasn't going to. Remember…I said I wouldn't, unless you asked. I was just proving a point." As I relaxed underneath him, I brought my hands up his chest and laced them around his neck. "How exactly were you planning on ending me anyway?" he asked.

I twisted my lips as I pulled him closer to me. "I would find a way…you just keep that in mind, buddy. I'm no snack."

Smiling, he gave me a gentle kiss. "You might like it…"

"Why would I like you piercing my skin? Does that sound like fun to you?" Realizing what I'd just said, and who I'd just said it to, I rolled my eyes at myself. "Wait…don't answer that…"

He laughed again and kissed me a bit deeper. I pulled away, slightly breathless. "Does anything else…glow…on you?"

He flashed me an impish grin. "Why don't you shut the light back off and find out?"

I laughed and did shut the light off. I searched pretty thoroughly, but didn't find any other glowing spots on him. And eventually his creepy, glowing orbs closed, and the room was blissfully and naturally dark.

The next day, I studiously watched him over breakfast. He made us bacon, eggs and toast, and he ate it all like any normal guy. I kept waiting for him to do something unreal, turn into mist and slip under the door or mentally call forth rodents or bats. I don't know—something creepy and mysterious. But he didn't. He made espressos.

He walked around his spacious kitchen with stainless steel appliances at normal, boring human speed. He got food from his fully stocked refrigerator. He put spices away in his fully stocked cupboards. He kissed me on the cheek and asked me what I wanted to do on this sunny Sunday morning. I was a little disappointed again with my very unvampire-like vampire. I had kind of been expecting him to secret away to a coffin last night, after our rousing second romp. But he hadn't, he'd fallen asleep right afterwards and he'd even snored. It was so commonplace that I was beginning to doubt the entire thing ever even happened.

We sat at his metal kitchen table, sipping our espressos after breakfast. I was wearing my "just in case clothes" and was happy for the fact that I had planned for that little eventuality. I was even happier that the scenario had finally happened, although the night hadn't mapped out quite like I'd expected. I watched him sip his coffee and read a magazine, wearing a pair of perfectly faded blue jeans and a casual looking t-shirt. He was the perfect sight to wake up to—dark hair, pale eyes, full lips, strong jaw, sexy as all get-out stubble. Delicious…and impossibly human. Last night must have been a vivid dream. One way to make sure, I suppose.

"Let me see again," I said after another couple minutes of comfortable silence.

He looked up at me, a little confused. "See what?"

I pointed to his mouth as I set down my coffee cup. "The fangs…whip 'em out."

He looked a little embarrassed, his eyes darting back down to the cup in his hand. "No."

"Come on. You don't have to be shy." I reached over to him and stroked his forearm with my fingers. "I've seen everything on you. There's nothing to be embarrassed about. Show me." I smiled encouragingly.

He met my eyes again. "Why?"

I took my hand off his arm and gestured in the air. "Because I'm starting to think I imagined the whole thing last night." I gestured to the drink he was still holding. "I mean, you're drinking a cappuccino for God's sake."

He twisted his lips. "What's wrong with cappuccino?"

"Well, it's not blood for starters," I deadpanned.

He smiled wide, showing perfect, white, even teeth. "Well, I have some humans tied up in my underground lair, next to my coffin, being guarded by my hunchback assistant Igor." He pointed over his shoulder with his thumb. "Would you like me to have him bring one up so I can devour them in front of you?"

I smirked. "Funny." I sure hoped he was kidding about that.

He shook his head and went back to his coffee. Apparently, he wasn't caving to my request for a peep show. I tried a different approach. "You can bite me?"

Without looking up from the magazine he was reading (National Geographic, of all things), he calmly said, "No." He peeked up at me from under his eyebrows. "I thought that would bring about my end anyway."

Ignoring his one hundred percent accurate comment, I, as seductively as I could, said, "Oh, come on." I leaned my head to the side, exposing my vein, and stroked my neck with my finger. "It's a nice, juicy artery."

Teren smirked. Looking back down to his magazine, he pointed at himself. "Nearly all human remember? That isn't as much of a temptation as you seem to think."

Disappointed, I slumped back into my chair. "Fine, be all modest on me. I would have shown you mine," I muttered.

He exhaled loudly and looked at the ceiling for a moment. "God…" Making a fake growling noise like a five-year-old would, he looked over at me with his hands raised in the air like claws. Extending his fangs, he said, "I vant to suck your blood," in a horrible Dracula impersonation. Then he immediately retracted his teeth and went back to his magazine as if he hadn't done anything strange at all. "Satisfied?" he asked.

Laughing at his over-the-top display, I walked over and sat on his lap. He looked up at me with a semi-amused smile. "Yes…that was priceless. Thank you."

He shook his head. "However I can entertain the human."

I laughed some more and gave him a soft kiss. I was a little surprised at how well I was taking things. I never realized I was so…progressive. Well, good men are hard to come by, and I'd had more than my fair share of duds. If his only drawback was a pair of sharp teeth and a penchant for hemoglobin, well, I'd take it.

We decided to spend our Sunday afternoon doing the most vampire-like thing we could—we took his collie, Spike (as in stake—

har har), to Golden Gate Park. Teren and I lived in beautiful, sunny San Francisco, which one would think would make it a natural deterrent for vampires, but Teren seemed perfectly happy and un-crispy, walking hand in hand with me as Spike ran ahead of us for a few feet, before coming back and then running forward again. We walked through the green grass and under a few large trees and I watched the sunlight filter through the leaves to speckle my honey in shadow and light, a fitting metaphor if I'd ever seen one.

When Spike got too far in front of us, Teren put a couple of fingers in his mouth and let out an ear-piercing whistle. Spike immediately turned around, his shaggy, multi-colored coat bristling in the breeze, and loped back to us with his tongue extending and retracting as he merrily panted. Teren reached down and ruffled his fur, earning him a lick on the cheek.

"So, you don't chow on dogs?" I asked with a small smile on my lips.

Teren looked up at me and grimaced. "No…do you?" I laughed and shook my head. He smiled and stood, coming to my side and pulling me close to him. "Good, I don't think I could keep seeing you if you ate dog. That's just gross."

I poked him in the ribs while he laughed and Spike ran around our feet. He brought me in for a tender kiss as Spike's attention was diverted by a squirrel running up a nearby tree trunk. I relaxed into the comfort of his kiss—a wonderful mix of soft lips and scratchy stubble. Abruptly, he pulled back from me and I frowned as my comfort was ripped away.

"Come to my parents' place with me."

I blinked at him, startled. "I'm sorry…what?"

He half-grinned at my stupefied face. "Now that you know everything…and seem to be perfectly fine with it, you should meet my parents."

"Today?" My voice came out a little strained, and I tried to relax my throat.

"No, I wasn't serious about that. I do need to go up there soon though. Maybe in a couple of weekends we could go?" His pale eyes sparkled in the sunlight, and I had the odd thought that they were charging in the sun for another glow session this evening. I shook my head to shake away the strange vision.

"Um…I guess that could be fun. Where do they live?" *Please don't say a castle…*

He nodded vaguely to the right of us. "They manage a ranch about sixty miles from here, near Mount Diablo."

I nodded as I absorbed that. "Wait…your family are ranchers?"

He smiled, like he didn't see anything odd about that. "Yeah."

I pulled away to look at him better. "Your…vampire family…are ranchers?"

He laughed at the expression on my face. "Yeah, it kind of makes sense for us, if you think about it."

I blinked. "What do you mean?"

He took my hand and we started walking through the grass, catching up to his hyper collie that was chasing his tail, ten feet up the lawn. "Well, to the outside world, my family comes from a long line of successful ranchers, but to us…," he glanced over at me walking beside him and gave me a wicked grin—he only needed his fangs out to complete the look, "…to us, it's more of an open-air pantry."

I paled a bit as that statement sank into the ridges of my brain. I envisioned the teeth that he had dragged along my neck, plunging deep into some poor Holstein. "Oh…I'm never going to be able to look at a cow the same way again."

Laughing, he squeezed my hand. We watched Spike roll on his back and frolic in the sun, and I thought about meeting his family…his vampire family. Dealing with his weirdness was one thing—I mean, for the most part, he acted completely human. But he was only slightly vampire. The rest of his family would be even more foreign and his great-grandmother was a full-fledged mistress of the night. I had to admit that it intimidated me a little bit. Although, it was nice to hear that they snacked on livestock.

"We've only been dating a few weeks…isn't it a little early to bring me home?"

He smiled down on me as Spike ran up to him and licked his jeans. "You got so irritated by the abstaining you thought we were doing, I don't want to mess up again by making you wait."

I frowned at him and he pulled me tight. "I really do need to go up there…it's been too long. And I'd love for you to join me. I'd love for you to meet them, and for them to meet you." He looked down as we walked, seeming almost shy. "You're kind of important to me."

"Oh," I said quietly.

Before I could respond further, he added, "It's not every girl who would stick around after hearing what I really am." He nudged my shoulder playfully. "And you're really pretty."

I smiled as he bent down and clipped Spike's leash back onto his collar. We made our way back to his Toyota Prius (yes, my vampire drove a hybrid), and went over to a breezy outdoor diner for a late lunch. At the end of our day and a half date, he drove me home, walked me to my door, and kissed me goodbye like a perfect gentleman.

In the safety and solitude of my cute, Victorian townhouse, I analyzed how much things had changed in my life in the past twenty-four hours. Vampires were real. I was dating one. I'd slept with one—twice. He wanted to take me home to his…nest. He thought I was really pretty.

I had a dream that night, once I finally fell asleep, of being surrounded by beautiful, black-haired women with sharp fangs and glowing eyes, and a deep voice rumbled in my head, "Don't worry…they won't eat my girlfriend."

Chapter 2 – What's That?

Monday morning at work I was approached by my rotund boss, Clarice. She had gray hair, with streaks of brown, and she coiled it into a bun so tight that it pulled some of the wrinkles out of her face. She wore "professional" clothes straight from the fifties, which is when I think she started working here. A shapeless gray skirt that hit her mid-calf, with a basic white blouse tucked inside it and as the topper—June Cleaver pearls. She tended to look at my slacks, lacy camisoles and fitted jackets with her lips twisted in a small scowl, like she thought I looked inappropriate. I rebelled in my own small way by almost always wearing my hair loose and bouncy and leaving my jackets unbuttoned, so just a hint of my sublime cleavage showed.

"Emma."

I smiled warmly at her vapid face. "Good Morning, Clarice." As I smiled, I wondered if my boyfriend wouldn't mind draining her. If only just enough to keep her home for a few days, so I could try my hand at being Mr. Peterson's assistant. Being his assistant brought along the more prestigious assignments and of course, the yearly trip to Belize. Being his assistant's assistant…did not.

She harrumphed at me and handed me a half-foot stack of papers. "I need these copied and collated in triplicate by lunchtime."

On second thought, I didn't want her vile blood swimming around his system.

I kept up my fake smile. "Sure thing, Clarice." Anything for the sea hag. Eventually she had to retire, I kept repeating to myself.

She started to leave, then almost as an afterthought, she turned her thick neck and said, "Gate Magazine sent flowers for you. They're in the break room."

My smile became real. "Oh, thank you."

She twisted to face me. "If you're going over there to work for that Adams man, you should put in your notice."

"I'm not going anywhere. Thank you, Clarice." I kept up my smile until she left my cubicle.

My friend Tracey popped her head over the short wall separating our "offices". She was blonde and beautiful and spunky as could be. Clarice couldn't stand her, but didn't have to talk to her much, since she was the assistant for Mr. Sampson's assistant. Tracey had started working here a week after me, and since we shared a thin wall in our cubicle hell, we'd become fast friends.

"Hey, Emma, Teren send you flowers again? He's such a good man." She looked over my desk to Clarice's office, which was right outside of Mr. Peterson's office. "The witch had them sent to the break room instead of leaving them on your desk. I think she's hoping someone tosses them." She shook her head of blonde hair. "I'm surprised she didn't toss them herself."

I smiled as I set the papers Clarice had handed me down on my desk. Teren worked at Gate Magazine, a regional monthly magazine specializing in San Francisco life—places to go, places to eat, events in the area, local news, and stuff like that. He wrote articles for the life and style section which now I actually found a little humorous. I let Clarice think he was trying to woo me away for a job so she wouldn't complain about my personal life intruding on my work life. She was irritating that way.

I sighed with contentment as I answered her. "He's the best, Trace." I left out that he was slightly more than just a man. "We finally had our night." I winked to indicate what I meant.

Her blue eyes widened at me. "All right, 'bout time." Her pixyish face relaxed into an *Isn't he sweet* look. "Oh, and he sent you flowers afterwards. Ugh, if you don't marry that man, I will."

I laughed as I wondered what Tracey would think about him, if she knew as much as I now did. I nodded my head towards the break room. "I better go retrieve my flowers."

She ducked her head back down as I made my way down the hall to the communal room used for coffee and food breaks. A few men that I passed subtly checked out my chest as I walked by, and for a moment, I wondered if I was setting womanhood back by showing off my "rack". Or maybe I was showing empowerment—I am woman, hear me roar. Sometimes it was a fine line to walk. I pushed the odd thought away as I reached the room and stared at my arrangement of calla lilies. Teren did have good taste.

I reached inside for the card and pulled out the small envelope from a local shop. Inside, Teren had written, "Thank you for a surprising weekend". On the bottom he'd drawn a smiley face with fangs. I chuckled at his sense of humor and shook my head—his weekend couldn't have been anywhere near as surprising as mine. I tucked the card into my pocket and, grabbing the vase, headed back to my desk. I placed them right on the edge, where Clarice would see them every time she walked by.

Monday nights were kickboxing at the gym, so after work, Tracey and I headed over there and sweated out our cubicle frustrations by envisioning our bosses as we kicked and punched the air. The music-laden class was being subbed tonight by an extremely hot guy named Ben. The usual instructor was a peppy girl named Lita, who made the class amusing with her anecdotal comments, as well as difficult.

Hot Ben didn't do much for me (my guy was hot *and* supernatural) but Tracey found his highlighted hair, bulging biceps and chiseled, model-like features distracting. Eventually, he had to come over and help her position her feet correctly for a side kick. As he adjusted her hip, Tracey looked over at me and winked really fast. I rolled my eyes at her as he walked away from us.

They were chatting after class as I waved goodbye, Tracey putting a hand on his shoulder and laughing at something he was saying. I was pretty sure that he'd have her number by the time I got to the dressing room. I showered at the gym, politely averting my eyes from the flock of eighty-year-old women who no longer cared who saw them buck naked, and changed into date clothes.

After drying and restyling my hair, I redid my makeup and grabbed my gym bag. Slipping into my car, a cute little yellow VW Bug, I headed over to Teren's house for a late dinner. He met me in his half circle driveway and opened my door. Must have heard me coming. I'd have to remember that his hearing was probably not just good but "enhanced," and I'd have to be careful what I muttered around him, or within a block radius of him. Who knew how enhanced he was?

"Hello," he said, with a sweet smile and an even sweeter kiss.

"Hello to you, too," I replied, slipping my arms around his

neck. "I loved my flowers."

"Good. I was wondering about that." He grabbed my hand and we started walking to his house. Teren lived in a modern, two-story home, with panoramic views of the Pacific. Unlike my house, which was firmly sandwiched in-between my neighbors, his home was spaced from the houses surrounding it. It was a very nice spread.

I squeezed his fingers as we walked up his steps. "Tracey's going to marry you, if I don't."

He laughed as he opened his wrought iron and wood front door. "Oh good, as long as someone is going to. How do you think she'd feel about...?" He made a prong-like motion with his forefinger and middle finger, indicating fangs.

I put my purse and jacket in his entryway closet, nestled right in-between his heavy winter coat and his "only for special occasions" dress jacket. "You'd still be able to hear her screams," I said, laughing. Spike padded up to me, wagging his tail in clear merriment at seeing me again. I scratched behind his ear while I continued chuckling over the image of Teren fanging Tracey.

Teren laughed with me, and then grabbed both of my hands and pulled me through his formal dining room into the kitchen, where the incredible smells emanating from the stove started making my mouth water. Spike obediently followed us and lay down on the cool tiles in front of the fridge.

"That's why I like *you* so much," he said, pulling me tight to him in front of the oven.

I giggled and twisted away from him to sneak a peek at a saucepan bubbling on a burner—it was thick, white and smelled delicious. "Is that why your weekend was surprising? Because I didn't scream?"

He came up behind me and slipped his arms around my waist as I stirred the creamy goodness and then took a lick from the spoon. It was an Alfredo sauce and it was incredible. My stomach rumbled. "You only screamed when I wanted you to..." he whispered in my ear. I elbowed him in the ribs and he grunted softly. It astounded me a little, that I could make a vampire grunt. He laughed, then more seriously said, "You have taken everything surprisingly well."

I turned in his arms and laced my hands around his neck again. "Maybe I'm just freaking out on the inside."

He chuckled and gave me a soft kiss, then he seemed to remember something. "Oh hey, I talked to my parents today— they're really looking forward to meeting you. They want us to come up *this* weekend."

My face went blank…and surely pale white. "Now I'm freaking out."

He kissed my nose. "You'll be fine. It will be fun, I promise. You should have heard how excited they were—"

I cocked an eyebrow as I cut him off. "Excited our son is bringing home a girl, or excited we're having a tasty snack delivered?"

He twisted his lips at me in obvious displeasure. "My family is not going to eat you. That would be pretty rude."

"Right…well, why are they so excited to meet me then?"

He paused for an inordinately long amount of time…that worried me some. "I've never brought a girl home before," he finally said with a warm expression. Even though his soft smile was genuine, I couldn't help but think that there was more to the story. "So, what do you think? This weekend?"

"Sure…why not." If I'm going to be an Adams family snack…might as well get it over with.

Releasing me, he finished making our Chicken Fettuccini Alfredo dinner, handing a forkful of sauce-coated chicken to me to test, and tossing a bare chunk of chicken down to Spike, who thumped his tail on the floor appreciatively. As we sat down at his candlelit formal table with our meal and a glass of chilled wine, I forgot all about the upcoming weekend and raptured in the flawless food. For a man who only ate because he chose to, boy could he cook!

He offered me a nightcap at the end of dinner but I politely declined. It was getting pretty late and I did have to work tomorrow. He walked me to my car and gave me a final hug and a kiss at my car door. I narrowed my eyes, intensely studying his. It was late and very dark outside, but we were close to a streetlamp and we were bathed in the amber light. Since I was looking for it, I noticed the faint glow of the whites of his eyes, but a person not expecting it, really wouldn't notice it at all.

He slowly shook his head at me and my fascination. "Do you want to do something tomorrow night?"

"Sorry, can't. I'm having dinner with Mom and Ash. Rain check?"

"I have an editor's meeting Wednesday night, but can you come by Thursday for dinner? We can work out the details for Friday night." I frowned and he laughed as he gently pushed me into my seat. "It will be fine. Promise." He cocked his head at me as he leaned against my open door. "When do I get to meet your family?"

I sighed. "Let's just get your family out of the way first...then we'll talk."

Smiling, he nodded, then leaned in to give me a final, final kiss before he closed my door. I watched him in my rearview mirror as I pulled away. It was a bit startling that I could see his reflection— that particular myth must not be true then. Of course, my vampire didn't seem to conform to any of the traditional vampire lore. What a rebel he was. He waved at me with one hand, the other casually stuffed into the pocket of his slacks, and I smiled at my tall, dark and pointy-teethed boyfriend.

I walked into my gray on gray cubicle the next morning and smiled at the arrangement of calla lilies still on my desk. I sat down at my ergonomically correct chair, opened the bottom drawer of my desk, and stuffed my heavy purse inside. I had to shove and rearrange the purse a couple times to be able to close the drawer all the way. Apparently, I was becoming a bit of a pack rat. I'd have to dig through the purse soon and toss out all the old receipts, empty packages of gum, out of style lipsticks and semi-melted tubes of Chapstick, that were collecting in there.

I adjusted a picture of my mother and sister next to my computer and wondered if I should bring in a photo of Teren. That would dispel the myth that he was trying to woo me away for work, if Clarice ever figured out who the man in the picture was, but it would be nice to look at his handsome face while I went about my day.

I flicked my computer on and opened my emails. I just about shut my computer back off. There were thirty-six emails requesting old P&L statements that I'd have to dig through piles and piles of paperwork to find. And each email had the dreaded red flag of urgency. Well, of course, everyone believed their problem was the most urgent thing in the world. Sighing, I started writing down the information that I would need.

Tracey walked up to my "home away from home" and leaned against one of the walls. She looked blissfully happy, a peaceful smile on her peach stained lips, and I was pretty sure why. "So, did you get a date with Ben?"

"Of course!" She shook her blonde head, like it was a ridiculous concept that she wouldn't.

I smiled and shook my head at her, in awe that she felt completely comfortable hitting on someone, while dripping with sweat. Personally, there was only one way I wanted a cute guy I liked to see me all sweaty, and by that point, I usually knew him pretty well. Usually—there might have been some poor decisions made in college.

"We're going on a date Friday," she finished.

"That's great!"

She told me all about the fancy restaurant they were going to, and the club she wanted him to take her to afterwards. When her story dwindled down, I told her my plans for the weekend. "Teren is taking me up to his parents' place for the weekend."

"Already? That's fast, he must really like you." Her blue eyes sparkled at me with genuine happiness for my relationship that was going quite smoothly, and as she had correctly pointed out, was starting to definitely pick up speed.

"Yeah, I think he's been bitten by something." My lips curled a little at the corners over my dumb vampire reference that Tracey didn't get at all.

"And you? What do you think of him?" She walked over to my flowers and smelled one, her blonde hair leaning forward with her and brushing against the lengthy stems.

My smile widened. "He's like no one else I've ever met." *Quite literally.*

She straightened and pulled her hair back behind her shoulders. "Are you heading to the gym tonight?"

"No, I'm having dinner with Mom and Ash."

She nodded. "Oh that's right…Tuesday." She put a slim hand over her heart. "Give Ash a great big hug and a kiss for me. I miss that girl."

"I will."

I smiled as I continued on with my tedious task, and Tracey disappeared behind her adjoining wall. My smile faded after an hour, and by lunchtime, I was craving a pick-me-up. I skipped out and rushed to get my coffee treat—making sure I didn't dump it on any potential bloodsuckers this time. Then I settled back into my monotonous work in the records room—finding files, copying them and then replacing them—all with my caffeinated secret weapon tight in hand. Even though by five o'clock, the very backs of my eyes ached, I still managed to get every single piece of paper sent out that was requested of me from my urgent email list by quitting time. I was quite pleased with my productivity as I strolled out the front doors.

I smiled as I walked into the quaint café that was Ashley's favorite place to eat. She always ordered the butternut squash ravioli, no matter what time of year it was, and the staff always added extra gorgonzola crumbles on the top, just for her. They sort of loved her here, which is really the reason why we came here so often. My sister tended to attract attention…and not the good kind.

The hostess greeted me and motioned to a table in the back, where we preferred to sit. I nodded thanks to her and started walking in that direction. The café was quiet tonight and soothing contemporary jazz played over the sound system. The tables were all set up with a small vase of wild flowers, and the hand painted lamps, lightly swinging above each table, lit the area with a soft glow. It was a cozy, comforting place.

I approached a table where a woman with chin-length,

graying brown hair, was sitting with her back to me. She was plump in the *I don't care, I'm going to fully enjoy this life I was given* sort of way, and she had a deep, earthy laugh that echoed down the aisle to me. She was laughing with a woman who was facing me. A woman who had the most horrific face you could image. A woman I deeply loved.

The woman stood as I came up to the table. Half of her head and half of her face were covered in a thick patchwork of scars. The side of her head that could still grow hair was a deep brown that bounced in the exact same way that mine did.

"Hey, sis," she said, as she hugged me warmly.

"Hey, Ash." I hugged her right back, ignoring the imperfectness of her face. It was irrelevant anyway—her beauty was her heart. It always had been, it always would be.

She sat back down stiffly; some of the scarring over her joints made some movements a little difficult for her. Scooting over, she patted the seat so I would sit beside her. I giggled and snuggled into her side. My sister had been horribly burned when she was nine years old, in a house fire that had claimed the life of our father. My mother had gotten out of the house safely, but Dad had rushed back in to save Ashley; it was the last thing he ever did. I was at a friend's house that night and had missed the whole disaster. I was equally regretful and grateful for that. But that was ten years, and for Ashley, several surgeries ago.

Her body was a variegated mix of layer-upon-layer of discernible scarring. It covered over two thirds of her, but that didn't dampen her spirit. She took the teasing and ridicule she received from the uneducated idiots we often encountered, with grace and aplomb. She was my best friend. She was my hero.

Her light brown eyes sparkled at me playfully as she grabbed my arm. "So, how's the boy?"

I playfully nudged her back. "The *man* is wonderful."

My mother across from the table from us laughed. "When do we get to meet this mystery man?"

I smiled at my mom as I held Ashley's hand. My mother had never remarried, in fact she still wore her wedding ring—to chase away the would-be suitors, she said. Whenever I hinted about her dating again (she was only fifty-two after all), she would sniff and say that she had a husband and he was waiting for her in Heaven. I would always sigh at that and let it go. You can't make someone do something they don't want to do. But she was a vibrant, happy woman. Her face had deep laugh lines around her eyes and the corners of her lips. She was quick to smile and even quicker to laugh.

I chuckled at my mother's question. "That's kind of funny. Just yesterday, he asked when he'd get to meet you."

She leaned in, her expression curious. "And you said…?"

"All in due time."

We ordered our "usual" from the waitress, Debby, who lounged at our table for a few moments, chatting away, catching us up on her life—funny stories about her kids, a fight she'd had with her husband, a horrible weekend at the in-laws, which was the precursor to the aforementioned fight. We came to this café weekly. It was our way to stay together as a family and fill each other in on the aspects of our busy, daily lives. We'd been coming here for over five years now, and most of the staff was the same as our first night here. It sort of became a way for us to be filled in on their lives too.

After a few moments of friendly chit-chat, Debby left to get our drinks and place our orders. Our food arrived only moments later; the cook was well aware that we were here, and what we were going to order. Debby talked with us a few minutes longer while she set down Ashley's ravioli, my smoked ham Panini and Mom's raspberry-stuffed French toast. Then she moseyed on to other customers and we ate our meal and talked about what had happened during our week.

Mom and Ashley laughed as they discussed Mom's ongoing battle with her neighbor's yappy dogs that kept her up at night. Mom was considering secreting them away to the vet to get them debarked. I told her to go for it, but Ashley stuck up for the dogs and convinced Mom to try earplugs first. I smiled inwardly that I could always have Teren stop by for a little midnight snack…but then I remembered his aversion to the very idea of eating dog. Honestly, who'd imagine a vampire being squeamish?

Ashley caught us up on school. She would only say it was going well. I took that to mean that her classes were going well, but as per usual, the relentless staring and whispering wasn't stopping. She was in the last semester of her first year at San Francisco State University. She was taking the nursing course, and had noble dreams of working in the burn unit ICU at San Francisco General Hospital. The students weren't used to her yet, and she was a constant source of wonderment for them. I was grateful that college students were slightly more mature than high school students, and at least the relentless teasing that used to bring her home in tears had stopped. Well, mostly stopped. She had run into a group of frat boys once that had acted like they ran the school…and were still thirteen. I'd received a tearful phone call after the encounter, and spent the night comforting her with a quart of Haagen-Dazs. Maybe I'd sic my vamp on the frats? Surely he had no compunction about assholes.

I briefly considered telling my family about Teren, about what he really was. Ash would think it was cool…she wasn't one to chide anyone on being different. Mom…would act like a Mom though, and panic about me dating a man who, like some rabid dog, could turn on me at any moment and drain me dry. I was pretty sure Teren would never do that. But I'd never be able to convince Mom, and she'd only see his vampirism after that, not the amazing, smart, funny, brilliant man that he also was. I decided that maybe I'd tell Ashley later, but we'd have to keep it a secret from Mom. Much like the time I'd dated a member of Hell's Angels. At the time, he'd been thirty-five, covered head to toe in tattoos, and had some questionable extracurricular activities. Like I said, I had made some poor choices in college.

At the end of the evening, I gave my mom a big hug, and she rubbed my back and told me to be safe in the generic way that I knew meant, *I love you too much to handle anything happening to you, so lock every door, never go outside after dark, and don't eat the unlabeled tin can in the very back of your pantry.* I hugged her back and wished her well, then turned to Ashley and gave her an even bigger hug, and a big wet kiss on her bare scalp.

"Oops, I almost forgot." I gave her one more hug and a kiss. "That's from Trace, she misses you."

"Oh, she's so nice. Tell her we'll get together soon, maybe next week." She kissed my cheek and then grabbed Mom's hand and walked stiffly from the café.

I lingered a few steps behind them, watching the amazingly strong women of my family. That thought brought up thoughts of my upcoming weekend. I hadn't mentioned it to Mom or Ashley. I'd tell them later…after I'd survived meeting the amazingly, and supernaturally, strong women of Teren's family.

Teren had his meeting the next evening, so when I got home from my second kickboxing class of the week, after a long day of Clarice scolding me for not exactly lining up the corners of the pages I'd copied before stapling them (she was a little OCD), I drew a nice warm bubble bath and picked up a nice long book—an Anne Rice novel, no less. I may have lied about the whole vampire fantasy thing. I did not lie about the disinclination towards pain though, and biting was still a no-no.

The next morning, I felt refreshed and recharged—and lusty as all get out for some vamp loving. It made the day go by achingly slowly, but it had been two days since I'd seen him, and I missed him. The jet-black hair that set off his startlingly pale blue eyes, the just right fitness of his athletic frame, the strong capable hands, the set of his stubbly jaw, the smell of his cologne, the curl of his full lips as he smiled at me…and yes, even his pointy fangs, that he so very rarely let me see.

By the end of the day I was a little riled up, so I had Tracey cover for me and snuck out of work thirty minutes early. Teren usually left, and started, work an hour before I did, so I wasn't too worried that he wouldn't be home. Maybe I'd even catch him in the shower. Geeze, I really had missed him.

I pulled into his drive and wondered if he'd heard me. If he did, he didn't come out. Maybe since he thought I was at work, he assumed I was a neighbor pulling into their drive. I approached his door and, since I felt like after we'd been intimate, I had the right to—and honestly since I was a little anxious to be intimate again—I opened it as I was knocking on it.

"Teren?" The house sounded empty as my voice bounced back to me.

"Come on in. I'll be there in a minute." His voice was calling to me from a distance. He had heard me and responded, but I still didn't know where he was.

I took a couple steps into the entryway and closed the heavy door behind me. The wrought iron and glass door had matching windows on both sides of it, and there were solid looking brass pots before them that were holding sculpted, three-foot-high mini trees. If Teren ever strung lights on them, the light would show through the windows and the effect from the outside would be quite pretty.

I put my jacket and purse in the closet to my right and wondered where my boyfriend was in this large spread he called a home. An archway to my left led to a formal dining room with a massive mahogany table, complete with six intricately carved high-backed chairs. The chairs at the head and foot of the table had padded arm rests, and sitting in them made you feel like the King or Queen of this tiny fiefdom. Continuing on through that room led you to the kitchen.

An archway on my right led to a smaller room with a baby grand piano tucked in the corner. Teren didn't play, I'd asked, so I wasn't sure why he had one. Maybe someone else in his family did. I wasn't too excited about the fact that some vampire in his family frequented so often, that he had brought in special furniture to appease them. Or maybe a house this large was just expected to have one...like an extra bathroom or something, it was just built right into the floor plan.

I decided to go straight through the entry way, or was it a foyer in a house this size? It did have a chandelier swinging high above me in the vaulted ceiling. Anyway, I walked straight through the room (passing the first of his four bathrooms) into the living room. The west wall of the living room was glass and all you could see was the ocean, you could even just make out the Golden Gate Bridge through the very right window. The sunsets from this room were spectacular. In the middle of the glass wall was a sliding door that led to the backyard. The slider was designed in such a way that it seamlessly matched the windows, and until you saw it opened, you wouldn't even realize it was a door. Teren's house was on a slope and you couldn't actually see his yard unless you went outside and looked off the decked patio. There were a couple of chaise lounge chairs out there, for relaxing, and a six-foot long metal table, with a set of matching, padded swiveling chairs, making a comfortable spot for an evening meal while enjoying the amazing view. Maybe we'd eat outside tonight?

Not wanting to search for him, since he knew I was here and he'd find me, I sat on his long, leather couch to wait. I looked over at the spiral staircase in the corner of his living room that led to a loft upstairs that he used as his office. I wondered if he was up there, working late on an article. His office was positioned over the kitchen and it had bookcases that lined the far wall and looked down into the living room. Following the wall of bookcases took you to another glass wall, with a slider that led to a second-story patio that slightly overhung the first, creating a nice shaded spot on the table below. That patio had a couple more chaise loungers for sunbathing. That's right, my vamp liked to sunbathe.

As my eyes were still on his office above me, Teren surprised me by coming in through the living room slider. He was still in his nice work clothes—light khakis with a black leather belt, matching black dress shoes and a crisp, navy blue shirt that looked amazing against his dark hair and tan skin. They'd look even more amazing, crumpled on the floor next to his King-size bed. But I was too entranced by what he was holding, to tackle him like I'd wanted to all day.

"What is that?"

He lifted up what he was holding. "It's dinner."

"It's a chicken."

His smile widened. "Yes…we're having chicken for dinner."

"It's alive."

The small, white chicken clucked stupidly at me in the mesh cage Teren was holding up. Teren twisted his lips and walked through the open space in the wall that led into the kitchen. Insanely curious, I followed him. He set the cage down on a granite island in the center of the spacious area. He looked up at me with his lips still pursed.

"This is how I prefer to buy them. I picked one up last night after my meeting."

I was fascinated. I didn't even know there were stores where you could "pick-up" live chickens. This city really did have everything. He was still looking at me oddly and I finally realized why he bought them alive.

"Oooooohhhh. You're gonna…" I pointed at the doomed chicken and he nodded.

"You're not usually here for this part…you're early." He seemed a little disappointed, like he'd have to forgo his snack or something.

I crossed my arms over my chest and leaned back against the counter. "Don't stop on my account…go ahead."

He furrowed his brow at me. "Are you sure? You might think of me differently after you see this. It's not the sort of thing you can un-see." He pointed over his shoulder with his thumb. "I could go somewhere else. You don't have to watch."

I shook my head and smiled. "I want to see all of the different pieces of you…and this is a pretty big piece." I made a go-ahead motion with my fingers. "Go on…just don't spoil your dinner."

He rolled his eyes and then smiled with just one edge of his lip. It was a cocky, self-assured look that made my heart speed up a little. Then he opened his mouth a little wider and his fangs snapped down into place right before my eyes—my heart sped up a lot. I wondered if he could hear that, but got distracted by the thought from him opening the cage door. The stupid chicken didn't move, other than to flick its head rapidly here and there. What it was looking at, I had no idea, for it certainly was unaware of the danger approaching from behind it. I had a sudden, strong desire to shout at the dumb animal—"Don't you know that death is stalking you? Run!"

I watched in silence though, too fascinated with the hunter versus prey scenario playing out before me, to make a peep. I held my breath at what the poor chicken didn't know was coming, but I did. Then, lightning-quick, Teren grabbed the chicken and sunk his teeth into its neck; it feebly clucked once. He drained it in three seconds. I counted. I didn't breathe for any of those three seconds.

He pulled the chicken away from his mouth and set the lifeless carcass on a chopping block set on the counter. He wiped just a spot of blood from his lip and stared at the dead beast. Then, very slowly, he turned his head to face me. He looked very worried.

"That was…" I struggled for the words to summarize just what I was feeling at that moment, "…kind of hot."

He blinked at me. "What?"

I shook my head. "Yeah, I know…right? I'm a little surprised too…but, yeah, that kind of turned me on."

He gaped at me as he slowly moved his head back and forth. "You're so weird," he said, as his fangs retracted back to wherever they went when they were hiding.

"Said the vampire who just drained our dinner," I wryly replied.

"Touché," he laughed. A burner on the stove had a large pot of water sitting on top of it, and he turned the knob to hot.

I stepped over to where he was now washing his hands, of all things. "You did that so fast."

Drying his hands on a towel, he gave me a serious look. "There is no point in needless suffering. I'm not cruel."

Still morbidly curious, I asked, "How long would it take to drain a human?"

His jaw clenched and he frowned at my question. "I will never drain a human."

I shook my head and brushed aside his concern with my hand. "Just in theory…how long?"

He looked at me a long time before answering. "I've heard it can be done in seven seconds."

Holy…dang…

"Wow…you'd never even know what hit you."

He looked over at the chicken, almost like he now felt sorry for it. "Yeah."

Wanting to lighten his mood, and perhaps actually being serious with my request, I playfully tossed out, "Will you drain my boss?"

His head snapped back to mine and the corners of his lips lifted. "What?"

I slipped my arms around his neck and, relaxing, he curled his around my waist. "The shrew I work for. Just a smidge. Just enough to knock her on her ass for a few days."

He kissed my nose. "No."

I ran my hands suggestively down his shirt, and then started un-tucking it. "I'd be most…appreciative."

He laughed as he watched my hands pull up the fabric. "Are you offering yourself to me, if I suck on your boss?"

I husked out a laugh and kissed his neck. "Hmmmm…is it working?"

He pushed me back and stopped my hands from unbuttoning his shirt; his grin was wide. "No…I'd rather go back to abstaining."

I smacked his chest. "Some vampire you are. I can't even get you to nibble on a human for some lovin'." I shook my head and dramatically sighed. "What is the supernatural world coming to?"

Teren laughed and walked over to the chicken. "You should be grateful I'm not more inclined to 'nibble on humans,' as you put it." Holding the feet with a silicone pot holder, he immersed it in the boiling water for a few seconds, then set it back on the counter. When it cooled enough, he grabbed a leg and started removing feathers.

My stomach churned at the sight. "Ugh, see-ya. I'll be in the living room."

He stopped his hands to look over at me. Pointing at the chicken carcass he was plucking, he said, "This…this makes you squeamish?"

I pointed to the feathers in his hand. "Yes. That…that is gross."

He was chuckling at me as I turned the corner into his magnificent living room and plopped onto his super soft couch. He finished preparing the chicken and then brought us out a glass of wine—blood red, of course—to enjoy while the bird cooked. We snuggled on the sofa and talked over our couple days apart while we sipped our drinks. He talked about his meeting, and how impressed his boss was with his last article—a feature on how to enjoy the city on a tight budget, which, as I looked around his incredible home, made me wonder how he'd known what to write about. I didn't think he had to "budget" for anything. I told him about my mom and sister wanting to meet him and he gave me an *Anytime you're ready* look. That brought the conversation around to this weekend, and meeting his parents.

We decided…well, he decided and I grudgingly agreed, that he would pick me up at my place after work Friday night. I had a feeling he was mainly picking me up, just so I wouldn't bail on the whole event. He said he could make the sixty mile drive in forty-five minutes, if we hit the traffic just right, so we'd be arriving just in time for dinner. I didn't know what unsettled me more—how fast we'd be going to get there so quickly, or the getting there just in time for dinner part. Was that arriving in time to join his family for a meal, or arriving in time to *be* the meal?

The majority of my brain really wasn't worried about his family killing me…after all, he was right, that would be a pretty rude way to meet your son's girlfriend. But I'm only human, and there is an intrinsic fear of knowingly walking into a predator's den. Like the fear you get when you go to the zoo, and the only thing separating you from the field where the lionesses are basking in the sun, is some vegetation, a ditch and a short fence. I don't know, but I'm pretty sure, given the proper incentive, that really wouldn't pose as much of an obstacle as the zookeepers would have us believe.

We finalized our plans and talked over some details, like, they have a pool, so bring your suit. Then we ate our roasted chicken on the patio and watched the sun set, the burnished reds and oranges rippled across the sky and reflected in the water below it. When we were full and satisfied, Teren proceeded to satisfy my other hungers as well…and I'd been right—his very nice dress clothes looked much, much better crumpled up along with mine beside his very spacious and luxurious bed.

Chapter 3 – The Adams Family

I tried to make Friday night come as slowly as possible. I stayed up late Thursday night, once I got home from Teren's. I woke up early and took my time getting ready for work. I drove five miles under the speed limit. I took an inordinately long time lining up the corners whenever I had to staple something. I looked over every page I was researching three times before filing it away. I walked to the Starbucks at lunch for my pick-me-up. I actually held a conversation with Clarice—and that was out of pure desperation.

But nothing worked, time betrayed me and surged forward at a quicker-than-possible pace, and before I knew it, I was hugging Tracey goodbye, almost willing her to beg me to stay home this weekend for some friend-emergency. But her Friday had been the opposite of mine. Hers had dragged on and on and she briefly returned my hug, before pushing me back and nearly skipping out the door to get ready for her date with Hot Ben. I sighed as I left to go get ready for my date...with the whole Adams clan.

I was stubborn though, and when Teren arrived on my doorstep I sputtered that I wasn't ready, that I hadn't even packed yet, and that I was really sorry, but we were going to be late. Looking casual in faded blue jeans and a layered t-shirt, Teren smiled at my attempt to delay us and phased from my sight with inhuman speed. I blinked at the spot in my small living room, where only three seconds ago he had been. I'd never actually seen him move blurringly fast and I was a little stunned that it was physically possible. I wondered why he moved at regular speed at all. If I could zip around like a human hummingbird, I'd get so much more done during my day.

When I slowly trudged up my steep steps, he was in my room, zipping up a bag he had lightning-quick packed for me. I sighed at my half-hearted attempt to postpone the inevitable and then grinned. "I need to double-check what you packed."

In ten seconds, he rattled off everything he'd put in there as he flopped the bag over his shoulder. He had forgotten nothing...even my cosmetics and an extra swimsuit were in there. He did a better job than I would have. He smiled as he headed for my door. I sidestepped in front of it. I had other ways to slow him down.

At least I could make it so we'd miss this elusive "dinner" that I still wasn't entirely sure about.

Teren twisted his lips and cocked his head as he looked at me. "We really should get going, Emma."

I put my hands on his chest and bit my lip suggestively. I slowly started running my hands down to his jeans. "What's your hurry?"

He frowned and slightly shifted his stance. "I told my parents we'd be there in time for dinner. I don't want them waiting for us."

I slid my fingers under his waist band and brought them around to the button. I slowly unfastened it and gazed at him with some serious bedroom eyes. "But I want you...now..."

He dropped my bag and for the briefest moment, I thought I'd actually won. But then he grabbed my fingers and stopped them from unzipping his jeans. He held them in one hand while he fixed his clothes with the other. "Would you stop trying to delay us? Everything will be fine."

I sulked. "I'm not trying to delay us. I'm..." I looked up at him from under my brows and half-smiling, gave it one last shot. "I'm incredibly turned on by your...speed packing...and I want you," I growled in a low voice.

He smiled at me in an equally seductive manner. "You can have me..." he turned me around so I was facing the door and then he lightly pushed me through it, "...after dinner."

I made an affronted noise and looked over my shoulder at him while I trudged back down the stairs. "I'm not being intimate with you at your parents' place. Consider yourself cut off this weekend, buddy."

I turned back to the front and only his laughter answered me. Irritated, I looked over my shoulder again and saw him still chuckling. "What?" I asked, a little bit of heat in my tone.

"Nothing...I'm just trying to picture *you* telling *me* no." His attractive face looked a little smug now.

I stopped at the bottom stair and he stopped a step behind

me. The smugness faded as he frowned. "Come on, Emma, let's go."

I half-grinned up at him. "I need to change."

He eyed me up and down. "You look fine. You look great. Let's go."

My smile widened. "Nope, I want to change out of my work clothes. I'll be just a minute." I gave him a sweet peck on the cheek as I snuck past him on the narrow stairs. This was one thing he really couldn't deny me and he couldn't rush me either. I took twenty minutes, changing my pantsuit into more comfortable jeans and a fitted top, and what I deemed were appropriate ranch-wear boots. He was sitting on my bottom step, twiddling his thumbs and looking irritated, when I was finished.

I blew past him on the stairs. "Come on, Teren, we don't want to be late." He exhaled in a heavy sigh as he followed me out of the house.

Almost instantly, I realized my error in taking my time getting ready. For one thing, I had not succeeded in causing us to arrive any later. No, the only thing I had succeeded in doing was causing Teren to drive faster. He pushed his little Prius to an alarming speed and, since it apparently was not my day, there was little traffic to deter him and zero cops to slow him down. He made the supposedly 60-mile drive in forty minutes.

Teren looked over at me with a wide smile as we made the final right turn into their seemingly endless gravel driveway. "I think that's my new personal best. Thank you for pushing me."

Ignoring him, I looked out the window at the acre upon acre of long, waving blonde grass and the occasional brown and white cow head, peeking up before poking back down. I had the sudden image of a fanged, black-haired woman draining one of those cows, and shuddered. I looked straight ahead as we passed under a huge, white, wooden arch, boldly bearing the family name in large black letters—ADAMS. My previous cow thought jogged a memory, and in my nervousness I started laughing almost hysterically.

Teren gave me an odd look, like he thought I was losing it. "You okay?"

I wiped some tears from my eyes. "Yeah, I just got the name...Adams."

His expression shifted to blankness. "Yeah?"

"Your family name is Adams." I started laughing again.

He was looking at me like maybe he should have packed a straightjacket, and I laughed even harder. I pointed back at the sign. "The Addams Family."

He sighed and shook his head at me as I kept right on laughing. "Oh yeah...this should be interesting," he muttered.

My laughter died down as the bumpy road opened out into a parking area as large as the lot of our local grocery store. He pulled right up to the front of the house, next to a sports car of European design, a black luxury sedan, a simple two-door coupe, and an oversized 4x4 truck. I could only stare in awe, mixed with a trace of horror, at his parents' home. It was massive. It was impressive. It was as close to a castle as modern vampires in California could get.

The ranch was a couple miles from the base of Mount Diablo, nestled among the rolling foothills. Green trees dotted the valleys between the hills, and tan grass hugged each hill like a second skin. White wooden fences separated different areas of the pastures, and cows of various colors were standing or lying in the fields, enjoying the last minutes of daylight. The drive inclined to the top of one of the larger foothills and the main house sat atop it.

The house was an interesting mix of ancient and new. The upper half of the walls were white plaster and stucco, and the lower half looked like someone had painstakingly pressed individual river rocks of varying sizes right into the home, creating a perfect wall of stone. The roof was red Spanish tile and gleamed in the fading light of the setting sun. The ranch consisted of three buildings, forming a U-shape around what I would bet money on was the pool in the back. The center dwelling was a huge two-story building that was maybe twice the size of Teren's place. At the top of the home, in the center, the roof was raised, maybe twenty feet above the roof around it. There didn't appear to be anything up there, just an empty space, like a covered patio on top of the roof, but I swear, if these were medieval times, that was where the belfry would be.

Huge one hundred-year-old timber, stained in warm honey, supported a thirty foot overhang in front of the main doors, which were also in warm honeyed wood. The two buildings on either side were long and narrow with low, red roofs. The buildings were all connected by covered breezeways with graceful, open arches formed into the sides of the stucco walls. Spacious windows were placed everywhere along the home, the warm light from inside glowing in welcome to us, as if they were trying to calm my nerves along with Teren, who placed his hand upon mine on my lap.

"Ready?" he asked softly, with a smile on his lips.

"No." I shook my head at him and looked back at the intimidating house. "You said your family had a ranch, you didn't say they were the Rockefellers of ranching."

He laughed. "I wouldn't exactly go that far, but we do all right."

I sighed. "Should we honk or something? It probably takes ten minutes to get to the door."

He looked down and smiled. "No. They know I'm here." He leaned over to me and pointed to the front door. "My mom is pacing the entryway, waiting for us to stop talking out here and come in the house." He pointed over to a corner of the main house. "My grandmother is in there, finishing up dinner." He pointed down to what must be a basement level. "My great-grandmother is down there. She'll be up in a few minutes."

I stared at him with what had to be the blankest expression on my face. How could he possibly know all that?

Seeing my face, he explained. "We can all sense each other. Usually, it's just a vague feeling of 'he's in that direction', but the closer we get to each other, the more pronounced it is. While we're staying here, I'll know exactly where they are at all times."

I didn't even know what to say to that. "Just when I think you can't get any odder."

He laughed. "Yeah…inconvenient at times, too. It was impossible to sneak out as a kid, and don't think I didn't try."

I laughed with him, my nerves slightly calmed at hearing a

childhood anecdote. It made him seem more like me. "What about your dad? Can you sense him?"

He shrugged. "No. He's pure human, like you, so I have no idea where he is. Knowing him though, he's probably near my mom. They're kind of inseparable."

I smiled and squeezed his hand. "Oh, that's so sweet. Still in love after so long together."

"Yeah, we vamps tend to…stick to what we like." Smiling, he leaned in to kiss my cheek. "We should go inside and say hi. My mom's about to come out here and get us."

I looked back at the door, slightly alarmed. "Oh, can you sense her…intentions?"

Laughing, he moved to open his door. "No, I just know my mom."

He opened his door while I stared at the behemoth of a home ahead of me. I felt like I was entranced by the massive, iron banded double doors looming before me. I couldn't stop staring. I couldn't get out of the car. I couldn't move. Teren's hand caressed my cheek and I started, looking up at him standing in front of my now open car door. His eyes were glowing slightly as the sky around us darkened; without the city lights to mask it, the glow was quite perceptible to me, and I felt myself relaxing into the white depths. I stood without realizing it and he took my hand and pulled me away from the car. Still staring into his eyes, in a trancelike state, I calmly followed him up the granite steps that led to the timbered overhang.

We passed some lights attached to the heavy wooden supports and his eyes returned to normal, their enchanting hold on me momentarily broken. I blinked and looked around at the massive covered entrance to the front doors. Heavy, wooden support beams showed through the underside. There were tiny lights wrapped around them, twinkling in the approaching darkness.

I stopped walking and looked over at Teren; he was eyeing me with a curious expression. I smacked his arm in irritation. "Don't do that to me."

He laughed and backed up a step. "I told you I couldn't turn it off, and it *was* calming you down, so I just let you feel mellow. Wouldn't you rather have it that way?"

I smacked his arm again. "No! It's designed to make your prey feel mellow." I pointed at myself. "I'm not prey. I don't want to mellowly walk into certain death!"

I clamped my hand over my mouth as I realized that we were only twenty feet or so from the front door—from his mother. His mother with the vampire-acute hearing. He laughed again and grabbed my hand, pulling me the rest of the way to the door.

He raised his hand to knock, but the doors swung inward before he even had a chance. A blurring flurry of arms and hair encircled him and I stepped away; a surge of fear sliced through me at the suddenness of the movement.

"Mom," he muttered, sounding very much like an average human guy embarrassed by his mother's over-the-top affections.

"Sorry. You've just been gone so long and…we worry."

His mother pulled away from him and I felt my mouth opening in surprise. I took another step away from them and tried to process what I was seeing. She was beautiful, but I had been expecting that—Teren was unbelievably attractive. She had long, black hair that, except for the two pieces in the front braided down the back, flowed around her with a life of its own. Her eyes were the same pale shade of blue as her son's and her skin had the olive tone of someone who didn't quite tan, but spent a lot of time outdoors. She wore deep blue jeans with a green and blue checked button-up shirt tucked into them. She looked very much the picture of a rancher's wife. That wasn't what had me gaping though. It was her face—her flawless, lineless, perfect face. She looked no older than Teren; she could have been his sister and not his mother.

I suppose it shouldn't have shocked me, given the fact that she was even less human than Teren, but it did. I was sure, as that perfect face turned to regard me, that I looked a lot like a deer caught in headlights. That thought did not thrill me, as I considered how appetizing that look probably was to her. I forced my mouth closed and jerked the corners of my lips up into a tight smile.

As she pulled away from Teren, an older man approached her

from behind. Placing a hand upon her lower back, he reached his other out to Teren. "Hi, Dad," Teren said warmly as he clasped his hand and then gave him a swift hug.

Teren's dad surprised me too. He was a tall, middle-aged man with dark brown hair, speckled with gray, and intelligent brown eyes. He was attractive in a distinguished way, but he really looked nothing like Teren. It would seem that more than just vampirism was passed along by Teren's mother; Teren looked just like her. Teren's father pulled away from his son and joined his wife in studying me. He was still a big, strong-looking man with a sturdy frame and a mostly-still-fit body, although his stomach had a slight paunchiness to it. He wore faded jeans with a basic blue shirt tucked inside, and a belt buckle the size of my fist. He looked very much the role of a successful rancher.

The older man and his impossibly young looking wife, waited patiently for Teren, who slipped his arm around my waist and introduced me. "Mom, Dad...this is Emma Taylor. Emma, these are my parents, Jack and Alanna."

"Hello," I said quietly as they both looked at each other for a second. Then Alanna's arms were around me and she was hugging me tight. She was cool to the touch and a shiver went down my spine. I worried, for just the slightest second, that she was inhaling me and imagining sinking her teeth into the exposed area of my neck. I instantly berated myself for pulling my hair up into a ponytail before we left. I quickly dismissed the concern though. If she was thinking that, I couldn't stop her, but I was pretty sure she wouldn't take it any further than a thought with her son standing right beside her, so, no point in worrying about it.

Alanna pulled back to gaze at me with that flawless, young face and her pale eyes danced with un-concealable merriment. "We're so happy to meet you, Emma," she gushed, as she clutched my upper arms. She swooshed a hand behind her at the open front doors. "Please come in and make yourself at home." I murmured a thank you and glanced at Teren; he was beaming at me. He nodded his head in encouragement, clapped his dad on the shoulder, and entered the house. His mother wrapped both of her arms around one of mine and ushered me into the house after them.

It was not the vampiric ranch house I'd been imagining. It was idyllically beautiful—classic, but modern. The large entryway was as big as Teren's living room and the focal point of the room was a marble statue of a naked woman in the center. Looking at it more closely, I could see it wasn't just a statue, it was a fountain, only the water was coming from the woman's eyes and flowing down her body to the basin she was standing in. It was breathtaking.

Alanna pulled me past it, and I gazed at the numerous paintings of Californian vistas on the walls. Most were rolling hills, or mountain ranges with cattle in the foreground, but the most impressive piece was on the far side of the magnificent statue. It was a huge painting, taking up almost the entire wall, depicting a glorious sunrise, or perhaps it was a sunset? Either way, there was a longing in the painting that pulled at my heartstrings.

We walked past the painting, following Teren and his father, Jack, as they talked animatedly over something. I thought I heard fishing and baseball, and figured his dad was probably pleased as punch to have a little testosterone back in his house overflowing with women....vampire women.

Alanna's chilly hand patted my arm. "We have a beautiful room made up for the two of you upstairs. Mom...well, Teren's grandmother, is finishing up a wonderful dinner, so I hope you're hungry." She gave me a charming smile, but I couldn't help but wonder about this dinner again. Did she eat regular food, like her twin-like son? What exactly would they be serving us?

"Yes, I'm starving. Thank you," I said politely.

She rubbed my arm again as we walked through a hallway with worn, wooden floors and even more paintings. I was a little disappointed to not see any dark, mythical art. No Bram Stoker reenactments of virgins being devoured by hungry beasts. No bats dangling from high steeples, blood dripping from their tiny fangs. No graveyards drenched in moonlight with a chalky, white hand reaching up out of the grass. No, nothing dark or sinister at all in the décor. It was very warm and friendly and inviting. On second thought...I wasn't disappointed at all.

I was feeling more at ease in this warm home, both because of Teren's musical laughter drifting back to me and Alanna's reassuring pats on my arm, like I was a frightened animal that needed constant encouragement...and maybe I did. Then we stepped into the formal dining room. I'd nearly forgotten that I'd only met one of the female vampires in the house. I remembered immediately, when I saw the next one. She was setting the table with fine china, crystal wine goblets and gold silverware, so her back was to me. She knew we were there though, thanks to the odd blood connection that all the Adams vamps seemed to share, and she immediately turned to face us. I felt my jaw drop again.

She could have been Teren and Alanna's twin sister...or would that be triplet? Whatever the technical term, she looked strikingly like Teren and an almost carbon copy of Alanna. She was wearing a long skirt with a neat, white blouse tucked into it, and her long, black hair was done up into a loose bun at the nape of her neck. Her eyes were the exact same shade of blue as the others, her skin, a pale ivory, and her face...was young and beautiful and no older than Teren's. I had to remind myself that this woman was his grandmother.

I forcibly shut my mouth again as Teren walked over. Extraditing me from his mother's grasp, he introduced me to his grandmother. "Gran, this is Emma. Emma, this is my grandmother, Imogen Teren."

I blinked at her name and looked back at him. "Teren?"

He smiled. "When Mom married Dad, the family name changed to Adams. They wanted to keep the old family name alive somehow, to honor my grandfather, so they named me Teren."

I smiled at the warmth in that. "Oh, that's really beautiful." I turned back to Imogen and she gave me a soft hug; her body was as cool to the touch as Alanna's. "Hello," I said as I gently patted her cold back. She seemed no older than me, but for some reason, she had that grandmotherly vibe and I felt almost instantly relaxed in her presence.

She pulled back and looked at me with her deceptively bright eyes. "Hello, child. We're so happy to meet you." She looked over at Teren and raised an eyebrow.

Teren coughed once. "Yes, well...she's here

now…so…maybe we could eat." He looked at the floor and stomped once. "If someone would stop hiding."

Instantly, a figure blew into the room. "I was not hiding. It wasn't perfectly dark yet."

"It's been dark for three minutes, forty-five seconds and you know that. You were hiding."

"I was making an entrance. There's a difference, boy."

I think my mouth was scraping the floor. Before me was a one hundred percent, pure vampire and I could feel her very presence across my skin. There was an instinctual warning ringing through every cell in my body to run. I felt like that stupid chicken that Teren had drained in his kitchen. Too dumb to know how dangerous a position it was in, until it was too late. If Teren hadn't come over to put an arm around me, I probably would have bolted, screaming foolishly all the way back to the car. As it was, it took a conscious decision to stay in the room with her. I clutched Teren's arm hard and he looked down and gently squeezed me.

"Emma, this is my great-grandmother, Halina. Great-Gran this is Emma." He nudged me a little, like he wanted me to hug her too, but I clung close to his side.

Halina was also a spitting image of Teren and the others, or I suppose, they were recreations of her, since she was the first. Her jet-black hair was long, well past the middle of her back, and was wild and free around her body. Her eyes were an ice cold blue and her skin was snow white, like it had never seen the light of day. She cocked her head as she regarded me and a slight smile touched her lips, like she was enjoying my obvious unease at her presence. Her body was lithe and graceful as she strolled towards me. She wore a tight, deep blue fitted dress that left none of her curves to the imagination. It was not the sort of thing you'd expect to see on a woman who, if she were human, would probably be approaching the centenarian age. Of course, her face also looked nothing like a woman of her age. She was the youngest looking woman in the room, maybe twenty, if even that. Her deceptive youth did not match the intelligence in her eyes, or the worldliness of her soft smile. As she walked around Teren and me, she lightly trailed a finger along our bodies. Against my will, I shivered at her icy touch.

"She's a pretty one, Teren. She'll do quite well."

I had no idea what she meant by that and I started shivering even more. It was embarrassing how much I was shaking, but I couldn't stop doing it. Teren slipped both his arms around me. "Just ignore her. She's all bark...no bite." He glared at her, as she finished her circle around us.

She smiled. "No bite?" Her fangs slid instantly into place and I gasped and backed up a step. "I know a few who would disagree."

"Mother! That's quite enough. You're scaring her...be nice."

Halina turned to face her daughter, Imogen. "Fine." She exaggerated a deep sigh and then turned back to me. "Welcome to our home. We're very happy you're here." Her tone was polite, even warm, but her fangs were still extended and it kind of spoiled the sincerity of it.

Swallowing, I forced composure into myself. I was safe, I was perfectly safe. Teren wouldn't let anything happen to me.

"I'm going to go get our bags. Why don't you have a seat at the table? Mom could get you some wine?" Teren smiled as he let go of me.

I clutched at him with all the strength I possessed. "What? No...stay here." I lowered my voice to where even I couldn't really hear it. "Don't leave me alone in here with them."

"Oh, honey, you're fine here. Don't mind Halina, no one will harm you." Alanna, obviously having heard my near-imperceptible speech, which meant all the vampires had, came up to me and swept her arms around my shoulders.

"I'll get you some wine, dear," Imogen added, walking over to a wall-sized wine rack and picking out a deep red one.

Halina crossed her pale arms over her chest and leaned against the table, laughing heartily...at me. Teren scowled at her and then kissed my forehead. "I'll be back in a minute. You'll be fine," he whispered in my ear, before he kissed it.

Reluctantly, I watched him leave. I frowned when his father left with him, and not just because the only other pure human had left, but also because, if he was walking with Teren, then Teren couldn't do his super-speedy thing, and at the moment, I'd rather have him back at my side in mere seconds. I could hear their continued joyous conversation down the hall and I gulped as I turned back to where Teren's grandmother was handing me a glass of blood red wine.

"Thank you, Imogen," I said politely as I immediately took a long draw.

The young-faced woman patted my arm. "Call me Gran. You're practically family." The joy on her face was strange to me, but I ignored it as she led me to an intricately carved, solid oak chair at the most impressive oak table I'd ever seen. She plopped me in the chair and went back to the kitchen, which I could see through the archway in the wall separating the two rooms.

"Would you like anything else, dear?" Alanna asked as she hovered at my side, looking like an anxious hostess eager to calm her spooked guest.

I smiled at the remembered warmth of her greeting and the sincerity in her excited eyes. "No, I'm fine. Thank you."

"All right. I'd better help Mom in the kitchen." She glanced at Halina, who was casually sliding into the chair directly across from me. "I'll be in the next room if you need anything, sweetheart." Her voice carried a clear warning to the eldest vampire to behave. Then, with a reassuring pat on my shoulder, Alanna left me alone with the one vampire that kind of freaked me out.

Halina leaned forward and put her head in her youthful hands. "They worry too much, don't you think?" She smiled, and it pleased me a tad that her fangs were gone. "It's not like I'm going to nibble on you, since Teren's claimed you." She rolled her eyes. "Like I would do that to my great-grandson." She gave me a very pointed look. "You're too important, anyway."

"Important?" I asked, taken aback by her strange word choice.

She ignored my question and stretched her hand out to stroke my arm. I made an effort to not jerk my body away from her cold touch. After all, she had just said that she wasn't going to...nibble on me. What did she mean by important though? And what exactly did "Teren claimed you" mean? I didn't like the idea of being referred to as property. I had a million questions for this pure vampire in front of me, but not nearly enough wine in my system to ask them. I gulped from my goblet in silence as she regarded me with her timeless blue eyes.

Our silent stare down lasted until Teren and Jack reentered the room. Halina smiled warmly at Teren, and he cocked an eyebrow at her. She smiled even wider, but said nothing. I scrunched my brow again, feeling like I was missing an entire conversation. Teren turned to me and smiled as he sat beside me.

"I put our things away. We're in a guest room at the end of the hall upstairs." He gestured with his head somewhere above us.

I discreetly looked around, but Halina was having a quiet conversation with Jack, and I figured all the vampires were otherwise occupied. "Are we really allowed to…share a bed?" I asked him as softly as I could. Not even my mom would allow that to happen under her roof. Not that she was old fashioned or anything, but still, a certain…decorum was expected.

Before Teren could respond, Halina turned her head and answered me. "We practically insist on it, my dear."

Teren shot her a look and she smiled. "You are lovers…are you not?"

I instantly flushed and stared at the table. Teren ignored her and answered my question. "They are okay with us staying together, but if you're uncomfortable, I can sleep in another guest room."

"Don't be silly. Of course you two will room together." His mother beamed at us as she entered the room with his grandmother. "We're not strict on that sort of thing here. You may do…whatever you like while you're under our roof."

I suddenly wished I'd never brought it up in this house of super-acute hearing. I made a mental note to not bring up any more delicate topics until we were miles away from here.

Teren cleared his throat and grabbed my hand, looking a little flushed himself. "Okay, now that we've all discussed that…"

His father laughed and clapped Teren's back as he sat at the head of the table, to my left. Imogen sat next to her mother, Halina, across from me. Alanna squeezed my shoulder. "Dinner's ready," she said in a bright voice. My stomach clenched.

Forcing a calm breath, I pushed back my chair. "Here, let me help you, Alanna."

She patted my arm. "You can call me Mom, dear, and you're a guest, you just sit back, relax and let me take care of everything."

With one hand, she shoved my chair back under the table and my eyes widened at her strength. "Okay…I'll just sit here then."

Imogen asked Teren about work, and they pleasantly talked back and forth for a few minutes, with Jack and Halina interjecting now and then. Alanna blurred back and forth between the kitchen and the dining room, bringing out warm platters piled high with mashed potatoes, green beans, broccoli crowns with almond slivers, and lastly, a tray of perfectly just-cooked-enough steaks. I wondered if the steaks were from one of their cows, but then decided that they must be; they seemed the self-sufficient lot. After she blindingly fast brought out salt, pepper and full water glasses, she started preparing plates for everyone.

I felt a little guilty watching her, knowing that I was perfectly capable of making a plate for myself, but everyone else was letting her serve them without comment or complaint, so I figured it was something she just liked to do. Not wanting to be rude, I kept my mouth shut and waited patiently. It smelled incredible and I prayed my stomach didn't rumble while I waited; even if my gurgling tummy was virtually silent, I knew almost every ear in the room would hear it. Alanna handed her husband a heaping plate of food and gave him a warm kiss.

"Thank you, dear."

Jack started eating his meal while Alanna blurred to Teren's side and started preparing his plate. Her speed made me a little nauseous as she, in record time, set a heaping plate in front of Teren. Alanna gave him a warm kiss on the cheek while rumpling his hair.

"Thank you, Mom," he said, rolling his eyes as he looked over at me.

I smiled at his embarrassment while Alanna prepared a plate for me just as blazingly fast. I barely had time to hope she didn't pile my plate as high as the boys', before she was done. She placed a more respectable sized meal in front of me and gave me a quick, cool kiss on the cheek as well.

"Thank you, Alann...Mom." It felt weird to say that, but she smiled so wide when I did, that I was happy I had. Plus, Teren gave my hand an affectionate squeeze, so I knew it made him happy as well.

Alanna blurred into the kitchen and I wondered if she'd forgotten something. Teren dug into his food, elbowing me and nodding at my plate. It felt strange to start eating when only half the table had food, so I picked up my fork and waited for Alanna to come back. She returned in a few seconds with a stainless steel coffee carafe. I looked over at Teren, but he was focused on his plate and ignoring his mother; almost studiously ignoring his mother.

I watched Alanna stop at Halina's side and pour coffee into her glass, which I thought was odd, until I realized that the coffee was red...and that it wasn't coffee. Her goblet quickly filled with a thick, steaming, deep-red liquid that could only be blood. My mouth dropped and my stomach tightened. Halina sniffed at it, frowned and then took a large gulp. Alanna filled Imogen's glass next. Imogen smiled warmly at her daughter and took a more reserved sip of her steaming beverage. Alanna then turned to Teren and filled one for him. He finally looked up at her and nodded a brief thanks, making her beam. She poured a glass for herself, and set the carafe down by Halina, before sitting at the foot of the table, on Teren's right.

My stomach twisted into a knot. No food then for the vampire women...just deep-red plasma that even I could smell. It turned my stomach a bit. I watched Teren eye his still steaming glass. He seemed to be debating whether or not he should drink it with me sitting right beside him. I had no idea if I wanted him to or not. Watching him drain a chicken was one thing, and that had been pretty bloodless. This, watching him down a clear glass of viscous cow blood—and I was really hoping it was from a cow—was quite another thing. He finally cast a quick glance in my direction and reached across his plate for his drink. It did unpleasant things to my already churning stomach, watching him tilt the goblet back to his lips. He took a long draw, swallowing a couple times before pulling the glass away.

His fangs had extended when the blood hit his mouth, and they were clearly visible as he closed his eyes and made a deep, soft noise—almost a purr. I tore my gaze away from him and finally noticed the other vampires at the table. Every mouth had fangs. Every face looked elated. Every tongue was red. Halina was licking her lips and pouring another glass of warm liquid from the carafe.

What happened to me next wasn't voluntary. It was pure instinct. Fear surged through my body and I could *not* stay calmly seated at that table, surrounded by creatures higher up on the food chain than me. A tiny part of my brain knew I wasn't in danger, but every other single impulse in my head was screaming at me to get the hell out of that house! I felt like the dumb, busty chick in the horror flick that runs up the stairs, instead of running outside, but I wasn't going to be the dumb girl any longer. I was getting out of there. I would run the sixty miles home if need be, but I was finally leaving this family of monsters.

I was just about to bolt for the door, and wondering if I could make it against four super-speedies, when a light touch on my arm startled me; I jumped nearly a foot.

"I just about peed my pants, the first time I sat down and ate with them. You're doing very well." I looked over at my saving grace, the only other human in the room and currently, the only other person without fangs—Teren's dad. "What?" I squeaked.

He nodded over to the vampires curiously watching me. I flinched when Teren grabbed my hand. "It's instinct…the desire to run. It's perfectly normal, so don't feel embarrassed. Your body's just telling you that they're dangerous." He laughed while I tried to swallow with my dry throat. "Which is pretty humorous, since they're all basically giant kitty cats."

I gaped at him and then let out a short laugh. The tension eased from me as the knot in my stomach started to loosen and the fear slowly started to leech from my system. Teren put his arm around me and kissed my cheek; his fangs were still out.

Halina scoffed at Jack. "Kitty cats?" She hissed at him, baring her sharp teeth.

Jack laughed at her and I stared at him with a surely bewildered look on my face. That was one woman I would never laugh at. "Don't even bother you old bat. You don't scare me anymore."

She twisted her lips and pointed a finger at him, while looking at me. "Don't let his bravado fool you. He nearly fainted when he watched how we really feed." She flicked her crystal glass with her fingernail, making a musical clink. "Not this dainty, eating at the table crap."

"Grandma," Alanna scolded her. "Manners. Emma is our guest this weekend and we would like her to visit again sometime."

Halina raised her glass in answer and downed it in one long gulp. She immediately smiled, displaying her red-tinted fangs.

Chapter 4 – Inappropriate Dinner Conversations

Somehow, and I'm still not sure how, I managed to make it through the rest of dinner. I even managed to eat my meal, which was sinfully good. Imogen could cook as well as Teren, maybe better. I supposed she'd probably taught him or taught his mom, who taught him. After dinner, I yawned in exaggeration a couple of times, and was all but ushered upstairs to the bedroom by Alanna, who insisted that I rest, since we had plenty of time to chat this weekend. Real exhaustion swept over me as I stared at the king-sized behemoth of a bed before me in the "guest" room. The room was so large and elegantly decorated that it made my room back home seem about as nice as a pantry under the stairs.

I plopped down on the satin sheets, closed my eyes and threw my arms over my head. I considered falling asleep like that, nearly buried in decorative pillows, when I heard a deep voice chuckle at me. I opened my eyes at Teren, who had closed the door and was pulling off his shirt. I sat up on my elbows and watched him undress. Normally, the sight would have had me biting my lip in anticipation of a rousing love fest…but I'd had a long night, and that really was the last thing on my mind. That and there was no way we were doing anything remotely intimate around super-hearing vampire ears.

"So…what do you think?" he asked with a soft smile, as he slipped his jeans off.

I sighed, not knowing where to start. "They aren't what I expected. They're very…welcoming."

"Of course they are. They want you to be here, Emma." Once in his boxer briefs, he sat down on the side of the bed and put a hand on my knee. "I told you there was nothing to worry about. They like you."

I sighed and sat up. "Why are they all so young?"

He cocked his head, looking like he wasn't sure how to answer that. "Great-Gran was turned at nineteen, so she'll always look nineteen. Mom and Gran…just don't show their age anymore, but none of them are exactly young. Mom's in her fifties, Gran is over seventy and Great-Gran is up in the nineties by now."

"Oh…why don't your mom and grandmother age? Isn't that kind of odd, since they're only partially vampire?"

He looked away and quietly said, "At twenty-five we just…stop aging. We don't know why."

"Weird." I put my arms around his shoulders and hugged him tight. "What about you…you're twenty-five. Have you stopped aging?"

He grinned in an odd way as he looked back at me. "No…not today." His eyes examined my body. "It's been a long day. We should go to bed."

"Yeah, you're right." I stood and started undressing as he slipped under the covers. Glancing around the room, I asked him, "What's up with the honeymoon suite?"

He laughed at me as I took my shirt and jeans off. "What do you mean?"

"Well, the satin sheets, candles everywhere, fresh flowers on the nightstands, crackling fireplace…it just needs a little mood music, and I'd think you were trying to get fresh with me." I gave him a suggestive look and he laughed again.

Looking down he paused for a moment, then said, "All the rooms are like this. It's just my mom's style."

"Oh…" His expression was very odd as he chewed on his lip. "Are you okay, Teren?" I asked.

Releasing his lip, he looked back up at me and smiled. "I'm fine."

He was silent after that, so I began rummaging in my bag for my pajamas. I found my favorite silky pajama shorts with a matching pink camisole—the boy was such a good packer. I quickly threw them on and found my toothbrush and cleanser. As I was walking towards the adjoining bathroom he softly asked me, "Did I freak you out with the cow's blood?"

I turned back around to face him and inwardly sighed with relief that it *was* cow's blood. I regarded his worried expression for a minute, then I went back to the bed and sat next to him. "To be honest…yes, a little. I'm still getting used to this and that was a lot to take in." I stroked his cheek while he frowned and stared at his hands in his lap. I moved his chin up so he'd look at me. "I *will* get used to it though…okay. Just give me a little absorption time…and maybe a heads up too."

He smiled. "Yeah, I can do that. Sorry, I should have been clearer about dinner."

I stood back up, then leaned over and gave him a light kiss. "Yes…yes, you should have."

I awoke early the next morning to a pale shaft of sunlight streaking across my eyes, and the undeniable aroma of bacon wafting through the door, even all the way up here. My stomach let out a loud rumble and I pressed a hand against it. I felt Teren laugh beside me and then he raised his jet-black head to gaze at me, blocking the light from my eyes in the process.

"Hungry?" he asked, as he shifted in bed to turn towards me.

I giggled as I massaged my belly. "I shouldn't be after that meal last night, but apparently, I am." I sighed. My scale wasn't going to thank me for this. "I'm gonna gain ten pounds hanging around your family this weekend."

Teren stroked my hair in a soothing, repetitive pattern. "It's all part of our plan to fatten you up," he whispered. My eyes widened and he laughed at the look on my face. "I'm just kidding, Emma."

"Funny."

He smirked. "Your weight doesn't change the flavor of your blood anyway."

Offended, I smacked him on the shoulder over and over. He blocked a few hits, but that only made me try and hit him harder. In a defensive move, he brought the bulk of his body over mine. "Would you stop," his fangs slid out as he hovered inches from my face, "hitting me."

I instantly stopped provoking the vampire above me and held completely still. He cocked his head and stared at me in an inhuman way. Then, quicker than perceptible, he lunged for my neck. Before I could scream, he clamped onto my skin. As the sound of my terror bubbled up from my chest, I waited for the impending pain of my throat being sliced open.

It didn't come.

I stopped the approaching wail and struggled through my labored breathing to understand what was happening. It was then that I realized he was only kissing my neck, not sucking me dry. I had felt the tiniest prick of a fang, but he must have retracted them perfectly upon impact with my skin, and only his normal, much less threatening teeth were playfully nipping at my neck.

My heart painfully stuttered, and I smacked his shoulder again and pushed him away from me. He gave me an impish grin while I took deep breaths. "Don't you ever do that again! You scared the life out of me!"

Grunting, he shook his head. "Do you honestly think I'd do that?"

Feeling calmer, I shrugged my shoulders. "You looked pretty convincing…"

He leaned back in to kiss my neck. "Silly human," he breathed across my skin. "I keep telling you…I won't bite until you ask."

His lips across my throat were starting to do wonderful things to my body, and my breath quickened again for another reason. "Don't get your hopes up on that one," I muttered, as I closed my eyes and savored the feel of rough stubble, soft lips, and a warm tongue against my very sensitive skin.

He shifted his position on top of me and pressed his hardening body against me. I made a soft, satisfied noise at the intimate sensation of our bodies touching each other, and ran my fingers up his bare back. His breath increased as well as he shifted his mouth to mine. A deep noise escaped his throat, thrilling me, and I eagerly kissed him. Wrapping my legs around his, I imagined him ripping my silky pajamas off and taking me on this oversized, satin bed. The oversized, satin bed that belonged to his family. His vampire family…with the uncanny hearing, that right now, was listening in on every moan, lip smack, heavy breath, and squeak of the bed, as if they were standing at the end of said bed.

I immediately broke contact and pushed his shoulders back. "Get off, get off, get off!" I whispered intensely.

He rolled over and looked confused…and disappointed. "What? I was just teasing about the whole neck biting thing."

I sat up and gathered the sheets around me, like his family *was* actually in the room. "I know. That's not why… We can't… I am not…" I didn't know how to explain it to him, without explaining it to everyone. Eventually I just whispered, "Super ears."

He looked at me confused for a minute more, and then he understood and started laughing. "Emma." He couldn't say more than that since he was laughing so hard, so I got up and went to the bathroom to take a cold shower.

After I had finished with my chilly shower, I went back to the bedroom, where Teren was still just lying on the bed. He started laughing again as I approached my bag on the dresser and I scowled at him. He made a concentrated effort to stop laughing and quieted to soft chuckles. Eventually, he sighed and held his arms open to me. I ignored him and rummaged through my bag for fresh clothes— faded jeans and a fitted, button-up shirt that looked very ranch-like. Teren could pack my bag from now on, I decided, since he was so good at it.

Not letting me ignore him, he sat up on his knees and blindingly quick, removed my towel. I gasped at the sudden surprise of being naked, and at the cooler air swirling around my skin. I modestly tried to cover myself with my hands. "Teren!"

He lay back on the bed and grinned at me. I couldn't even see where the towel went; he could have put it back in the bathroom and I wouldn't have seen it, he was so fast. He opened his arms for me again.

I didn't ignore him this time. "No," I said firmly.

He pouted. "Why not?"

I threw on my bra and underwear before he could blur them away as well. After I was successful with that, I slid on my jeans. "I'm hungry," I said, sliding on my shirt.

"So am I."

He grinned, and I rolled my eyes and pointed to the bathroom. "Go take a shower…now!"

This time *he* rolled his eyes. "Fine."

I dried my hair and threw on some makeup essentials, mascara and lipstick, while Teren took his cooling shower. While he dried off, I lightly curled my hair with the provided curling iron. Not only did our fancy guest bathroom have a dual headed shower, a jetted tub, and a private room for the toilet, it came with a fully stocked vanity, complete with a plush, cream-colored, cushioned bench and a three-by-six foot mirror. I just might move into this bathroom, I mused.

After toweling off from his shower, Teren dressed in his most lived-in pair of jeans with a blue button-up shirt that he left loose over the top of them. The jeans did wonderful things to his backside, and the shirt did wonderful things to his pale blue eyes. He slipped on a pair of work boots and I hoped that somewhere in his bag, he'd tucked in a cowboy hat; it just would have completed the outfit. He looked incredibly handsome. This life suited him.

Hatless, he grabbed my hand and we made our way down the elaborate staircase to the foyer with the naked woman statue. We took the hallway to the right that led to the kitchen, and the smells of breakfast made my stomach rumble again. You'd think I hadn't eaten in years by my body's reaction to the amazing hickory and maple scented bacon that was filling my nose. We walked into the cheery, sunlit room and spotted Teren's dad reading the paper and sipping on a mug of coffee. He looked up at hearing our approach.

"Good morning, kids. Sleep well?"

I smiled as Teren answered, "Yeah. Thanks, Dad."

We sat across the table from him, and just as I was wondering if I should help out in the kitchen, Alanna came out with a tray full of food. She set it in the middle of the table and gave me a warm smile. "Good morning, dear. Hungry?"

Knowing that every vampire in the house had probably heard

my gurgling stomach…among other things…made my cheeks heat. I cringed as I answered. "Yes…thank you."

Alanna looked over at Teren with an odd glint in her eye. Teren looked away for a second, seeming almost embarrassed, but then he calmly returned her gaze. "Good morning, Mother."

She looked at him for a silent second, flicked a quick glance to me and then back to him. "Good morning, Son." She smiled brightly and so did Teren.

Alanna blurred back to the kitchen and returned almost instantly with plates, silverware, mugs and glasses. Disappearing again, she returned with milk, orange juice and a carafe. I ignored the carafe and eyed the overflowing platter of bacon, scrambled eggs and toast, with my mouth practically watering. Jack started helping himself and Alanna gave him a swift kiss before blurring out of the room. I figured it was all right to load up our own plates, so I grabbed a spoon resting in the eggs and started piling.

Teren grabbed the carafe and I tried very hard not to notice. He held it out to me and I glanced at him out of the corner of my eye. "Coffee?" he asked, as he grabbed a mug.

"Coffee?" I asked quietly.

He smiled. "Yes…just coffee this morning."

I relaxed and nodded as he filled my cup. I wondered where the rest of the vampires were in this huge house as Teren set down my steaming mug. I supposed they didn't need to eat breakfast, so there wasn't much point in them idly sitting at the table and watching the humans, and the mostly-human, eat regular food. As I watched Teren fill his plate with bacon, I wondered why he ate regular food and they didn't appear to. Maybe their more vampiric nature just made regular food not taste as good to them. Teren certainly appeared to be thoroughly enjoying the slice he'd popped in his mouth though. I stopped worrying about it and focused on the incredible meal before me. It tasted just fine to this one hundred percent human.

Once breakfast was out of the way, Alanna lickety-split cleared the table. She removed almost everything while I went from a sitting to a standing position. I was instantly a little jealous; being super-fast was one vampire trait that I really wouldn't mind having. While she finished cleaning up, Teren held his hand out to me, to show me the rest of the expansive home.

We walked through the five star kitchen, where Alanna was already washing the breakfast dishes. I marveled at the double oven, a walk-in freezer, the ceramic, smooth-top burner-less range on an island in the center of the room, that also had its own sink, and a refrigerator that was built right into the wall and resembled cabinets, until you looked closer and spotted the handles. All the countertops were thick, green-speckled granite and all the wood in the various cabinets and cupboards was a deep mahogany. For a home where only one person appeared to eat, they sure spared no expense on the kitchen.

Walking through that room, we swung around to the living room that seemed to take up the entire back of the house. A wall of glass on one side of me had French doors that opened up to the foyer and the set of elegant staircases that led to the rooms upstairs. A wall of glass on the other side showed me that my earlier assumption was correct; a large swimming pool was nestled in-between the three buildings.

The living room itself was an homage to a comfortable ski lodge. Plush chairs, throw rugs and ottomans were scattered in clusters around the massive room. A couch that looked as if you could live in it was opposite an antique, claw-footed coffee table, scattered with oversized books filled with glossy looking pages featuring ranches around the country. I wondered if this ranch was in one of those books and decided that if it wasn't, that was purely by the owner's choice—this spread was amazing.

The couch and coffee table were in front of the single most impressive fireplace I had ever seen in my life. I stopped in front of it and just stared and shook my head at the innate beauty of it. It was large, taking up a good chunk of the wall it was positioned on, and it protruded into the room with a semi-circle ring of stones that commanded attention. But that was pretty standard for a fireplace of its size. What made it intrinsically breathtaking was the flue. It was shaped in a semi-circle, much like the hearth, and, like the outside of the home, river rocks in various sizes and colors were pressed into the wall. While that would have been impressive enough, it was the fact that the rocks were formed into what was clearly a flame design that had me still marveling.

"Beautiful, isn't it?" Teren asked, as he watched me examining every flawlessly placed stone.

I nodded as I looked over at him. "It's amazing. Your parents' home is pretty…impressive."

He smiled nonchalantly and shrugged. "It's all right."

I laughed as he pulled me through the rest of the living room to the other side of the house. He showed me the mandatory "piano" room and explained that both his mother and grandmother enjoyed playing. He pulled me through a library packed with leather-bound editions of just about every classic novel the world had ever seen. He showed me the main bathroom downstairs; it rivaled the penthouse suite bathroom in any five star hotel in California, and, because I was a curious girl, I couldn't help but wonder if vampires even needed a bathroom?

Next, he showed me the rest of the rooms upstairs, including the oasis his parents called a bedroom. It was about the size of my mother's entire house, and probably included all the same amenities. Everything was cream, gold, burnished reds and oranges. It reminded me of the sunrise painting downstairs. Fresh flowers were in every room and spaced evenly along the hallway, so that the entire upper floor smelled of freesia. There was nothing in this home that wasn't meticulous and magnificent.

At the opposite end of the hallway from our room, Teren stopped in front of a closed, heavy-duty, white door. He softly knocked twice. A soft voice replied with something I couldn't make out through the thick door, and Teren gently opened it.

We walked into a spacious room with thick, beaded curtains covering every window. The air was perfumed, and light vibrated and danced by the dozen or so lit candles. I felt like tiptoeing into the near sanctuary of this quiet place. Teren's grandmother was sitting on a padded, antique rocking chair, knitting at lightning speed. She gently rocked herself as she knitted, and the odd mixture of her slow moving feet with her quicker-than-humanly-possible hands was causing some small part of my brain to melt, I was sure.

"Good morning, children." It was a little disconcerting, to be referred to as a child from someone who looked younger than me, but I ignored it and smiled politely at her.

"Good morning, Gran," Teren said. "I was just showing Emma the house."

Not stopping from her work, her young face beamed at her grandson. "That's good, dear. You could show her the ranch hand's home down the road as well, if you like? No one's staying there right now." She crooked a smile as she raised an eyebrow.

Teren coughed and looked around the room. "Yeah. Maybe we'll do that...later."

She stopped knitting for a moment and motioned to a plush chair beside her. "Have a seat."

Teren grabbed my hand as I was halfway to a seated position, and I straightened. "Maybe another time, Gran. I still have a lot to show Emma." He smiled at her as he started leading me away.

Imogen raised her lips slightly at the corners as she replied, "Yes, I suppose you do. We'll catch up this evening, I'm sure."

I waved goodbye as we exited her room, Teren shutting the heavy door behind him.

Knowing there was only one vampire we hadn't seen this morning, I hesitantly asked him, "So...where's Halina?"

Teren nodded at the floor. "Her rooms are in the basement levels."

"Oh. Will we be going down there?" I hoped my voice didn't betray my reluctance at that prospect. Entering her "lair" wasn't exactly an appealing thought to me.

Teren's expression turned thoughtful. "She tends to sleep through most of the day. Waking her up really isn't...a good idea."

"Oh...okay." I breathed the word in case she could hear it.

He laughed at my attempt to be quiet. "She's asleep right now. She's actually the only vampire who can't hear you. And she's a pretty solid sleeper once she's down, so you don't need to worry about waking her up."

I relaxed. "Oh," I said again, but at normal volume. "So, she's…nocturnal?"

He nodded, his eyes amused. "Yeah…it kind of goes with the whole vampire thing."

I twisted my lips and gave him a meaningful onceover. He laughed, understanding. "I'm mostly human, remember."

My mouth shifted into a wry smile. "Right. I don't know how I keep forgetting that. What about your mom and Imogen?"

Grabbing my hand, he started leading me back down one side of the dual staircase. "They are more human in that respect. They sleep at night and are awake during the day, although sometimes Gran will stay up all night with Great-Gran, and sleep during the day as well."

"Oh."

The thought of a vampire roaming the halls while I obliviously slept didn't sit well with me, but I kept my irrational fear of that from Teren. He would just say that I had nothing to worry about and that his family wouldn't eat me. I had the sudden thought that everyone was going to keep reassuring me that I wouldn't get eaten, right up until the day I did. Hopefully, I would at least get an "oops" or "sorry" before I was completely consumed.

He showed me around the side buildings that housed more guest rooms. I wasn't quite sure what they needed so many rooms for, maybe it just came with the spread, but there were two libraries, three offices, more bathrooms than I could count, a laundry room with the single largest washer and dryer I'd ever seen, an indoor greenhouse that smelled wonderfully of ripening tomatoes and made me damp with sweat before we left the room, a formal dining room that put the area by the kitchen to shame, and an informal lounging area with televisions, board games, a plethora of movies, including a slew of modern and classic vampire movies, which I found pretty amusing. There was even a three-hole putting green, because what self-respecting vampire doesn't like to practice their putt?

Really, all it needed was an indoor bowling alley, and I'd have been convinced that Teren's family was some sort of vampire royalty.

He ended the home tour by leading me to the courtyard out back. It took my breath away. The sun was approaching its zenith and its rays sparkled along the ripples of water in the Olympic-sized swimming pool basking below it. The entire family could swim laps and not bump into each other. A diving board on the far end indicated where the deep end was, and a few feet on the other side of that was the one thing I was actually really looking forward to…a hot tub—what looked like a twenty person hot tub, with jets everywhere and areas that conformed to a lying person's shape, so you could nearly nap in the slightly-below-boiling water.

Flat river rocks formed a patio, stretching from the glass wall of the living room, all the way around the pool and hot tub, to a large area behind that, where covered tables and lounge chairs rested in the sunshine before a barbecue grilling station. That huge grill swept up out of the river rock floor so naturally, that you'd expect to come across its twin while hiking in the Grand Tetons.

We walked across the flat stones while Teren pointed out various aspects of the land that we could see. The summit of Mount Diablo was positioned perfectly in the open area of the courtyard, creating a stunning backdrop for the already stunning view. These vampires sure knew how to pick a place.

On the far side of the patio were granite steps that led to a granite pathway. We followed the pathway to some outbuildings at the base of the hill where the main home sat. I looked back and marveled again at the gleaming red tiles, white stucco, and gray rocked beauty that was the Adams' family home. When we approached the buildings that stored the farm equipment, some motorcycles, four wheelers, and a couple of jeeps with oversized tires, I noticed Jack screwing a cap back on one of the bikes.

He looked up at the crunching sound of our approach. Walking into the sun, he squinted up at us and said, "Hey, Teren, Emma. I was just about to check out the cattle in the east pasture. You guys want to come along?"

Teren looked back at me, and I nodded eagerly. I'd lived in the city my entire life and had never seen a cow up close. Teren smiled and led me to one of the jeeps. His dad hopped on a bike and started it while we slipped into the open-topped vehicle. We started out after Jack, who was zipping along at a pretty decent pace. I supposed that if you live your whole life with someone who could cross a room faster than you could say vampire, you learned to be speedy where you could. We bounced along behind him on faint trails that I could just barely make out in the rolling hillside. Teren had a grin on his face and his blue eyes sparkled in the sunshine. Boys did love their toys.

We approached a long, white fence and slowed to park beside it. I could see a few cow heads poking up out of the amber grass and wondered if Teren could walk in there with them. Spike didn't seem to mind him, but surely a cow would have some innate sense of predacious danger and would run from him. But Teren followed his dad's lead and climbed the fence. He paused at the top and held his hand out to me. I gave him a wry look and scrambled up and over the fence by myself. He laughed once, then stood at the top of the suddenly narrow-looking fence and stepped off, landing the five feet to the ground as effortlessly as one steps off the front porch. Show off.

We walked among the cows. They didn't move much from munching on their meals, and certainly had no fear of Teren, who walked close by a few and even ran a hand along the back of one. I patted the head of another one. She looked up at me with huge, vacant brown eyes and I giggled. I'd never imagined a month ago, when I ran into Teren with my coffee, that the future would have me at a ranch petting cattle...with a vampire.

Jack inspected hooves or mouths or bellies of the beasts as we walked among them. I snuggled up to Teren's side as we strolled through the knee-high grass, watching for any fresh piles beneath us and listening for rattlers (I hate snakes). I looked around the pasture at the various brown and white cows, and then looked over to what I could see of the other pastures. I saw various bulks that must be more bovines, but nothing larger than that. I saw the building that must have been the ranch hand's house that Gran had mentioned, and beside it was an unmistakable building that could only be a massive barn.

"Are the horses in there?" I pointed over to the long building as Teren and I walked along.

Looking back at me, he shook his head. "No. We don't keep horses anymore."

I frowned. "That seems a little odd. Horses and ranches are kind of like peanut butter and jelly…they just go together."

He chuckled and kissed my head. "Are you hungry again?" I pinched his arm and he laughed again. "We had a hard time with them…falling ill, so we stopped bringing them in."

I eyed him suspiciously. "Falling ill?"

He kicked at a rock in the grass as we walked by it. His dad up ahead was busy digging something out of one of the cow's hooves. Teren sighed. "That's what the hired hands believed."

"And the truth would be…?"

He looked over at me. "Well, horses are more naturally spooked by us than the cows, so training them to overcome their fear was really more effort than it was worth, especially since we move faster than them anyway."

I nodded, thinking that was perfectly understandable, but then he continued, "And Great-Gran has a taste for them. We couldn't keep her away from the few we did manage to train. We just couldn't keep any alive for long…"

I stopped walking and stared at him, absorbing that. He stopped walking and shrugged. "After a few of those instances, we switched to bikes for the humans."

"Oh," was all I could think to say to that…so that's all I said.

His dad pointed out a couple cows that were expecting as we reached the edge of the herd. I ran my hand along the extended belly and smiled as the tiny creature inside moved slightly at my touch. I giggled again and stood up as Teren shook his head at my enjoyment. I pointed back to the pregnant cows as we started heading back towards the jeep.

"Do you ever name them?"

Jack laughed, a hearty booming sound, and Teren patted a cow's back as we walked by it. "Sure. This one's Tuesday," Teren said merrily.

I twisted my lips. "Nice."

Teren laughed with his dad. "We try not to personalize the food. It's not as enjoyable to eat, if it has a name."

"I'll keep that in mind," I muttered under my breath, and Teren grinned, so I knew he'd heard me.

Jack didn't and added, "Teren used to name them when he was a boy."

Teren sighed. "Dad."

Jack laughed and ignored him. "He named half Geraldine and half Bessie."

I laughed with Jack this time as Teren scowled at the both of us. I nudged him in the ribs. "Well, weren't you cute?"

Feeling more comfortable with Jack than say, Halina, I asked him, "What do you do with the cows the girls...eat?"

Very matter-of-factly he answered, "We butcher them and sell the meat, well, the meat that we don't use for ourselves or for the guys that help us out a few times a year. Adams Ranch is well known for high quality beef, and our cows are highly sought after." He smiled wide with pride. "We have the best steaks in three counties."

I smiled too. "Yes. Yes you do."

He gently patted me on the back as we reached the fence again. "I think you'll fit in just fine here, Emma."

After the tour, Jack cooked us some burgers and we ate on the back patio, enjoying the sunny day and the slight breeze. Alanna popped out with refreshing lemonades and stayed to sit in her husband's lap for a minute, making Teren roll his eyes in an adorable expression of embarrassment. Then she started shifting uncomfortably and excused herself, going back inside the house. I started wondering about this house of vampires, and what mythic rules applied to them, since they seemed to be ignoring all the rules I'd ever heard of. I thought about asking Teren, but he was enjoying a quiet conversation with his dad, so I figured I could ask him later.

Jack needed to fix one of the Jeeps, so Teren volunteered to help him, after making sure I'd be fine by myself for awhile. I assured him I would be, and gave him a lingering kiss before pushing him away to bond with his father. He seemed to really enjoy the guy time, and I wondered why he didn't visit more often. In the four weeks we'd been together he hadn't come out here once, and by the sound of Alanna's greeting yesterday, his last visit had been quite some time before that.

Back inside the house and wondering what I should do, I ran into Alanna at the stairs. "Alann…Mom, is there anything I can help you with today? Teren's fixing a Jeep…"

She smiled, and for just the slightest second, her pale eyes were almost sad. The look was gone before I could be sure, though. She wrapped her arm around mine and we started walking up the stairs. "No, dear. You're a guest here, and we get everything done that needs to be." She winked at me and grinned in a way that reminded me of her son. "Sometimes being really fast is very convenient."

I grinned too, as I thought about how much fun it would be to zip around on overdrive. She probably got more things done around the ranch before noon, all by herself, than a team of handymen could get done in a day. Girl power indeed.

"Why don't you spend some time relaxing by the pool? It's quiet out there—you could read a book from the library?"

That actually sounded quite pleasant, but I still felt a little guilty. "Would you like to join me?"

She patted my arm again as we reached the top step. "I'm going to visit with Mom for a while. I'll join you later." At the top of the stairs, she kissed my cheek with her cool lips and walked towards the heavy door at the opposite end of the hall from ours. Her long, loose hair swished across her back and her thick jeans rustled slightly, but that was the only noise she made.

I changed into my bathing suit. Teren had packed my two skimpiest bikinis and for a second, I considered revoking his pack-master status…until I noticed that he'd also packed my favorite book, one I'd read so many times, the binding was falling apart, *Where the Red Fern Grows*. I shook my head and again marveled at his odd skill. Grabbing my dark-tinted, pink-framed sunglasses, I slabbed on a layer of SPF. Snatching a plush towel from the bathroom, I made my way down to the pool.

My skimpy little black string bikini barely kept in all my curves, but the other one he'd chosen to bring was red, and for some reason, wearing that color made me feel a little like a walking all-you-can-eat buffet advertisement. I wasn't sure what he was thinking packing those to meet his family. Well, actually, I was pretty sure I knew exactly what he was thinking—I looked damn good in a bikini—but it wasn't the most appropriate thing to wear around potential in-laws.

The house was quiet, and I didn't run into anyone else as I slipped through the massive living room and out the back door to the patio. I found a comfortable looking chair with full sun exposure and laid out on my stomach, stretching my legs out. If I only had a Mai Tai and a chiseled man, fanning me with a palm frond, I'd have thought I was in some exclusive resort on a tropical island. I cracked open my book and prepared myself for some classic childhood adventure, hunting wily raccoons with lovable and unwaveringly loyal coonhound pups. I promised myself that this time I wouldn't cry, knowing all too well that, of course I would. I did every time. It was an odd book for a girl to like, or so I'd been told, but I did…I loved it.

I was halfway through the novel when I flipped over to my back. I started when I did.

"Thirsty?"

Alanna was standing at the foot of the chair, holding out a glass of lemonade. I hadn't even heard her approach. I took a deep breath and tried to calm my suddenly racing heart, all too aware that she could probably hear every wet, thumping pulse. I grabbed the glass and muttered a thank you before I took a long draw.

"You're welcome." She looked over my body and I tried not to blush at the oddity of what felt like an examination. She smiled with just one corner of her mouth and then looked up to the sky, where the sun was well below the halfway point, between high noon and horizon. "The boys should be done soon." She looked back to me and laughed—a tinkling sound like silver bells. "Those two do enjoy their free time. I think they may have given up on the Jeep and gone fishing." She pointed back towards a valley between two large hills. "They're over there."

Hmmm…that was another super power I wouldn't mind having. Knowing exactly where Teren was at all times. That could come in handy. Of course, it was a two way street, and that would be a little annoying if he always knew where I was too.

She shook her head, her black hair rippling. "Jack sure loves having him here. I think he gets a little overwhelmed sometimes, being around so many girls." She laughed again and sat in a chair beside me.

I laughed too. "I bet. How long has Teren been away?"

She sighed. "He's very good at calling us, but we haven't seen him in over four months."

Surprise washed through me. I couldn't imagine not seeing my mother and sister for that long. I got irritated at him for her, and it could clearly be heard in my voice. "Why has he been gone for so long? You don't live that far away."

She looked at me, and her pale eyes seemed to bore straight through me. I felt an uncontrollable shiver run down my spine and I held my breath. Breaking our intense eye contact, she looked at the river rock around her feet. "He has his reasons," she said quietly.

Before I could respond, she patted my knee and gave me a warm smile. "I'll let you get back to your book. That's a good one, I always cry at the end." She patted my knee one last time and stood. "Dinner's at dark," she said, as she turned to leave.

I wanted to protest that she didn't have to go, that she could stay and chat with me, but I could only watch as she silently slinked back into the house.

Teren and Jack came back just as the sun was hitting the highest hills. Jack was beaming at his son, who was holding a couple of large fish strung on a line. I wiped the inevitable tears from my cheeks as I closed my book and watched them finish walking up the path to the patio. Alanna flitted out from somewhere the second their feet hit the stones, and snatched the fish from Teren while giving him and then Jack a kiss on the cheek. She flitted away again and Jack laughed, watching her leave.

"Always in a rush, that one. The trout will probably be filleted and fried by the time we get in there." Amused, he shook his head at his wife.

Teren laughed at his dad's comment and then leaned over my chair and gave me a kiss. I smiled at him and then noticed that his jeans were wet from the knees down. "Did you catch the fish with your hands?" I asked sarcastically.

He grinned and winked at me, and my mouth dropped a little. Not answering me, he flicked his eyes down my body. "I like your suit."

I pursed my lips. "Yes. Interesting choice for your parents' house."

He leaned over and whispered in my ear, "Only showing off your...assets." He blurred away from me just as my hand was swinging around to clap him on the shoulder; I only caught air instead. I frowned and he held his palm out for me. Rolling my eyes, I let him stand me up. "Just kidding," he said, as he pulled me in for a tight embrace.

His mouth started distracting me as he brought his lips to mine. He was a fabulous kisser. I started getting swept away in the softness and stubble and wet warmth of it, when I felt his hand gently tug at one of the strings of my top.

"I will stake you where you stand if you pull that string out," I muttered against his lips. Remembering where I was, I looked around the pool area, but sometime when we'd been kissing, Jack must have gone inside. I felt a teensy bit embarrassed about that.

Teren chuckled. "I could sweep you upstairs, if you really aren't happy with that suit." His laugh turned a little husky and he started kissing me again, running his hand up my back to gently grasp my neck.

I started getting lost in him again, until I firmly remembered where I was, and what I had promised him at the beginning of this little journey. I playfully pushed him back from me. He was a little breathless, which made me grin. "Nope, you're cut off. Remember?"

He gaped at me and then tried to bring his hands back to my body. "You weren't serious about that, were you?"

I batted his hands away and giggled. I hadn't really been at the time, but with vampires around who could hear every delightful groan—I was serious now. "Yep. No treats for you, vamp boy." He frowned as I wrapped the plush bathroom towel around me. I grabbed his hand. "Let's go get ready for dinner. Your fish is probably nearly done." He pouted, but let me lead him to the glass doors to the living room.

"We could go somewhere really far away. I run really fast," he grumbled under his breath.

I shoved him through the door ahead of me. "Upstairs! Go change your wet clothes….and maybe take another shower." He grinned at me over his shoulder and we made our way to the stairs.

Gran was walking down one set of stairs as we were walking up the other. She glanced over at us, sighed and then looked away. She seemed really sad. I watched her glide down the stairs and wondered what vampires got depressed about. Teren wasn't watching her and didn't appear to be too concerned over it. Once we were at the top of the stairs and heading down the hallway, I asked him if she was all right.

Not looking at me, he said, "Yeah, she'll be fine."

"What's wrong with her?"

"You know, I am feeling a little grimy after the long day. I think I will take a shower." He kissed me on the cheek and then blurred into our room.

He left the bedroom door open for me, but I'd felt the proverbial door slam shut right in my face on the conversation I'd been trying to have with him. It stung as much as an actual door would have. Forcing calmness into my body, I decided that he just didn't want to openly talk about her problems here, with super ears everywhere, but surely he would tell me later. A voice in the back of my head screamed that that didn't excuse the rudeness, but I tried very hard to ignore that voice as I changed back into my jeans and shirt.

We came back down the stairs just as the final rays of sunlight were calling it quits for the evening. Teren led me to the kitchen, where all the women were talking around the table. They all stopped and looked over at us the second our feet entered the room.

Halina had an eerie smile on her face. "Good evening, Emma. Did you enjoy the sunshine today?"

I swallowed and made myself smile back at her. "Yes, very much." I turned my head to Alanna. "Your home is very beautiful."

Alanna smiled and took my hand from Teren's. Her much cooler hand led me to the chair I'd used last night. "Have a seat. Everything is ready." She pulled out the chair, plopped me into it, and effortlessly tucked me under the table. Teren sat beside me and rested his hand on my thigh. Jack entered from the kitchen, licking his fingers, and Alanna smacked him on the shoulder, making an affronted noise.

"Jacob Nathaniel Adams! You better not have been sampling that cake. That is dessert." She smacked him again on the shoulder as he grinned and kissed her cheek. I tried to make the mental image of a vampire baking a cake, but I just couldn't quite get there.

"I would never…" He gave her a wounded look and then grinned again, "…but if I had, it was wonderful, dear."

She shook her head with a soft smile on her lips and Teren chuckled beside me. Jack kissed her again on the cheek and she flitted into the kitchen. He took his place at the head of the table and Imogen and Halina sat in their respective seats across from me. Halina and Imogen talked in whispers while Imogen flicked glances at me. I couldn't hear what they were saying, but Teren was frowning and staring at the table in front of him…and I swear he was blushing. Curious, I tried to listen harder. Focusing more on trying to hear their quiet conversation than being courteous, I was blatantly staring at them. I stopped the moment Halina met my gaze. She looked very displeased. I thought I heard a low growl escape her throat…but maybe I was just hearing things.

Alanna broke the tension in the room as she flitted in with the fresh fish the boys had caught earlier. She brought in large bowls of a cold pasta dish and a veggie-filled green salad. Everything looked cool and refreshing and wonderful. She set a glass of red wine in front of Jack and me, and gave us glasses of water as well. She heaped up plates for the humans and then brought out the obligatory carafe of blood for the vampires in the room. I immediately dug into my food and ignored what Teren and the women were doing. In my head I kept repeating—"It's just wine, really thick, red wine." It was a little easier to stomach that way.

When Teren finished his "thick wine", I looked over at him. I watched him smile in satisfaction, retract his fangs and dig into his fish. And just like that, he was a normal, human guy, enjoying food he himself had caught, quite possibly with his own hands. I smiled at him and, noticing me watching, he smiled back and squeezed the hand still on my thigh.

His grandmother sighed and I looked over at her. Her fangs were out and her glass was still half-full, but she was looking at Teren and me so wistfully, that I didn't turn away from the sight of her. "The two of you remind me of my husband." She sighed again. "He was the sweetest man." I smiled at her recollection, until she continued. "And dumber than a box of rocks."

I sputtered a bit on the sip of wine I'd just taken and Imogen laughed at my reaction—a beautiful, rhythmic sound. "He never figured out what I was, and he never asked for an explanation. He thought I never showed my age because I had good genes, and I never ate because I watched my girlish figure." She sighed again, as her wistful look returned. "He never asked about the teeth. He never asked about the blood. Maybe he was smarter than I give him credit for. Maybe he just loved me for me, and it just never mattered to him."

"What happened to him?" I asked hesitantly.

Imogen smiled sadly and Halina, in a show of affection that I had yet to see, placed her hand around her daughter's shoulders. "He got real sick, not long before Teren was born. He didn't make it…"

Imogen dabbed at her eyes with a napkin and my heart squeezed for her. Suddenly, I wasn't seeing a vampire with a red tongue and sharp fangs. I was seeing a human woman still in mourning over the loss of the man she had loved deeply. It was a heartbreaking realization, that she would mourn him much longer than the average human would mourn their spouse...quite possibly forever, I wasn't sure.

"I'm so sorry, Imogen...Gran."

Collecting herself, she patted Alanna's knee. "Well, he gave me my daughter...before it was too late." She said the last part oddly, and gave Teren a look that definitely meant something. He shifted in his seat and it seemed like he was stifling a sigh.

"Teren..." she said in a pleading voice.

Teren's face got tense and he said something to her in a language I didn't recognize. Whatever he was saying sounded a little heated, and I could only stare at him in shock, both for his tone to the sweet woman across from us, and for the fact that he was clearly fluent in another language.

Imogen spoke back in the same language, her tone nearly matching his. Halina firmed her lips and nodded at whatever Imogen had said. Teren looked about to stand and shout at the two of them, when Alanna silenced the room.

"Enough!" Alanna looked at Imogen and Halina, and then over to Teren. Jack continued to eat his fish, ignoring what was most definitely an argument. "Emma is a guest and you are all being rude." She looked across the table at her husband. "Jack, how is the fish, dear?"

He smiled at his wife. "It's perfect as always, love."

They gazed at each other in adoration and, feeling the tension slipping from the room—and wanting to change whatever the subject of the fight had been, which, I had a feeling was me—I asked Jack, "How long have the two of you been married?"

He tilted his graying head and looked up at the ceiling. "Well, it's got to be over twenty-six years?" He looked back down at his wife with a clear question in his eyes.

She smiled. "Twenty-seven years, three months, twenty-two days and forty-two minutes."

He laughed and shook his head before turning to me. "As you can see, vampires retain things a bit better than us humans…especially as we age." He tapped his head and the entire table laughed, like this was really funny. I found myself laughing as well.

Still chuckling I asked, "So, no one questions the fact that she looks…" I didn't quite know how to finish that question.

Alanna did. "Half his age?" She giggled like a woman half his age. "We have a couple of other ranches across the country. We stay a decade or two in one, before moving to another, and although we try and keep to ourselves, when we came here, it was quite the scandal—the old man with his twenty-something wife and her sisters." She indicated herself, Imogen and Halina. "Being siblings is the easiest way to explain how we look. I think some may have thought he had multiple young wives though."

Again the entire table laughed and I shook my head at the thought. When Jack's laughs settled down he added, "It's pretty humorous since she is older than I am."

Alanna made an affronted noise. "Only by two years…that's not so much."

Wondering at the oddity of her smiling at him so lovingly, with her fangs clearly extended as she sipped on her glass of blood, I asked a question that I probably shouldn't have. "It hasn't been difficult for you to be married to a human? You've never bitten him?"

The entire room silenced, and I had the horrible feeling that I'd just asked something really, really inappropriate. Jack scratched his head and looked away, Teren fidgeted in his seat and Imogen grabbed her glass and took a long drink. Halina made no efforts to hide her glee—she openly laughed at me. Alanna shot her a look and she silenced.

"It's all right to ask. You're new to this. I'm assuming what you're really asking, is if it's difficult to not kill him?"

I felt heat rush into my face. "Yes. I was just wondering about the…thirst part of being a vampire."

Alanna smiled and laughed once. "Yes, we do seem to be portrayed as bloodthirsty savages who can barely control ourselves, don't we?" All the vampires laughed at that, and a shiver went down my spine. Alanna regarded me for a moment before answering. "Let me put this in human terms for you. If you're hungry and you go to a grocery store, would you lose all self-control and start shoveling food into your mouth?"

I grimaced at the image. "No."

She smiled. "It's the same for us." She looked over at him affectionately. "He may be astoundingly tasty, but I'm not about to end his life. I'd miss him too much." Jack gave her a warm smile. I focused on my plate, giving them some privacy for the clear love fest that was going on, while at the same time, suppressing another shudder that wanted to run down my body.

Imogen sighed, and I looked up to find her watching Alanna and Jack. Meeting my gaze, she said, very quietly, "Do you not find Teren attractive, dear?"

I blinked and my mouth surely hit the table. Do I *what?*

"Gran," Teren growled at her, and her youthful eyes regarded him before returning to mine.

"We know he's trying, young one, but you seem to be rejecting him. We don't mean to eavesdrop, but…he's such a good looking boy, surely you feel some desire for him?"

I could not even speak. Words could not fully describe the horror flashing through my body. I had no idea why my love life was being brought up at the dinner table, of all places, by Teren's grandmother, of all people. I didn't even know where to begin feeling offended. There was not one thing about the situation that seemed appropriate. Teren seemed to agree—he spat something wicked sounding to her in another language. Alanna looked upset, but I couldn't tell who she was upset with. Jack went back to studiously finishing his plate.

"If she is not willing to lie with him, she must be replaced," Halina said, rather coldly. I turned to gape at her, and suddenly knew exactly where to begin feeling offended.

"It's one weekend!" Teren switched back to English and sounded very exasperated as he glared at the both of them. "Back off!"

Halina narrowed her pale eyes at him; her wild hair seemed to bristle with her words. "One less weekend, Teren. One less, and you have wasted so much time already. Have you even been with her yet?"

I was ready to wake up from this absurd conversation. I was also ready to storm from the room in a huff. I think only sheer curiosity held me to my chair.

"What would you have me do?" Teren nearly yelled that at her and I flinched.

"Whatever it takes, boy!" she yelled back.

"No!" He yelled something else in the other language and she snapped something back.

I could barely keep my head from spinning right off my shoulders. Our enjoyable weekend at this dreamlike ranch with his, up until this point, pleasant family, was taking a turn for the worse. Everyone seemed to be angry that Teren and I weren't being intimate here, but that was just nuts. No family, not even a vampiric one, got angry because their son *wasn't* having sex under their roof. I must have been missing what the argument was really about. I wanted to defend my actions, I just wasn't quite sure what action I needed to defend. Maybe if they'd stop shouting in a language I didn't understand.

Picking my jaw off the table, I focused my frustrations at Teren, since he was the one I was the most comfortable with. "Stop yelling gibberish, and tell me what the hell is going on, since it's clearly about me!" I yelled, and instantly felt bad for both yelling and swearing at Alanna's table.

Everyone turned to stare at me, but Alanna was the one who responded. "They aren't speaking gibberish, dear, they are speaking Russian, and Teren is doing that, quite rudely, so you won't understand what he wants to keep from you."

My jaw dropped again as Teren turned his face to Alanna.

"Mother...please." His voice was quavering as he begged her. "You will ruin everything."

Halina scoffed. "Maybe, maybe not. Perhaps she will not be so reluctant if she knows."

"Knows what?" I whispered, feeling like a black hole of dread was opening up in my chest and was about to consume me whole.

Still staring pleadingly at his mother, Teren said in a quavering tone that tore my heart, "I wasn't going to tell her this yet. It's too soon."

"Too soon...? You're running out of time, Teren." His grandmother's face was a mixture of sympathy and panic. "Tell her..."

He sighed and ran a hand down his face.

Silence fell over the room. Teren sat slumped in his chair, looking for all the world, like he was sorry he'd ever brought me here. Jack had stopped eating and was looking at his son sympathetically and maybe even a bit sadly. Halina and Imogen were flicking glances between Teren and me, and I got the feeling that if Teren didn't tell me whatever was going on, they would. Alanna slowly stretched a hand out to her son and squeezed his arm affectionately.

Everyone in the room knew something. Everyone knew something that Teren didn't want me to know, something that he was speaking Russian, of all things, to keep from me. The dread in my stomach turned to fire as these facts settled in my head.

"Tell me what?" My tone was heated, but something was being discussed around the table that I didn't know anything about, and I didn't like that feeling one tiny little bit. "Teren...tell me."

He let out a sigh that was heavy with reluctance, and ran his hand through his hair. I was positive he wasn't going to tell me. I was sure he was going to say, "It's nothing," and sweep it under the rug, so to speak. So he surprised me when he muttered, "Fine...but you're not going to like it." He hung his head and I couldn't help but think that he looked utterly defeated, like somehow, he'd just lost everything. A chill went down my spine.

"That doesn't mean I shouldn't hear it. It's pretty obvious

your family thinks it's important…" I whispered, knowing they would almost all hear me.

Teren looked up at me then and there was nothing about his visage that looked like he was even remotely joking. Very flatly he said, "I will be dead within six months."

Chapter 5 – We Break Up

I think my heart stopped. It's one of those moments where you know your reaction is critical, and it's also one of those moments where you have absolutely no control over your reaction. If I'd had some semblance of control, I probably would not have reacted the way I did. No, I'm positive I would not have reacted the way I did. I would have been warm and caring and sympathetic. I would have held him and tearfully asked him what was happening to him. I would have encouraged him to sob in my arms and open up to me, and then his entire family and I would share a Norman Rockwell type group hug and we'd be a stronger unit for the revelation. That's how I should have responded.

This is how I did...

"That's not funny, Teren." I stood from the table, tossed down my silverware with an angry clink on the china, probably chipping it, and stormed from the room.

I trounced up the stairs, clomping angrily up each one. I wasn't sure why I was so angry. Was I angry at finding the greatest, most unique guy I'd ever met, just to have him be ripped away from me? Was I angry that he hadn't told me immediately—like, "Hello, my name is Teren and I'm dying," would have been a more suitable introduction than the one he'd given me? Or was I angry at the universe, for taking something that was too precious to leave?

Whatever the reason, I slammed our bedroom door shut so hard, that it rattled in the frame and a tiny sliver of wood fell to the carpet. I stared at the door and considered doing it again, when it suddenly opened.

Teren calmly entered the room that must have been ten degrees warmer due to my rage, and softly shut the door behind him. I knew that was a pointless gesture, they could all hear us. He may as well have left it open. Hell, we may as well of had this conversation in the dining room. I started pacing beside the bed and he watched me warily, like at any moment I might leap on him...which was a tempting thought.

I examined him as I paced. He looked fine. He looked tan

and strong and healthy—downright vibrant. He was fast. He was smart. He was virile. He was…alive. He looked anything but sick. We were supposed to have a chance. He was supposed to be my shot— my one shot at real companionship. I grabbed a decorative pillow, that sort-of looked like a giant Tootsie Roll, and chucked it at him.

"You're dying!"

He easily dodged the pillow, and the next one that I immediately threw at him. "Just my body…I'll be fine," he said, as he dodged a third one.

"You'll be fine!" I chucked a larger pillow at him, which also missed when he easily ducked. "Oh good! I was thrown off by the whole DYING part!" I yelled and tossed another pillow, which he avoided. "STOP DODGING!" I yelled as loud as I possibly could.

He sighed and stopped moving, and I pelted him with the last of the pillows—three square ones with elaborately twisted tassels. They hit his chest with a satisfying thud, and dropped to the floor at his feet. "Can we talk about this now?" he asked softly.

"No! Throw them back!"

He furrowed his brow and cocked his head. "What?"

I hopped on top of the bed and paced up there, my blood still boiling. "The pillows, throw them back up here as fast as your inhuman ass can."

I heard him loudly exhale but I could no longer see him, as he was just a streaking of movement. Pillows magically appeared around me and then he was standing still and waiting, with a frustrated expression on his attractive, doomed face.

I started chucking pillows again, and this time he let every single one hit him. "You son of a bitch!" A couple pillows hit his chest. "You couldn't have told me this before we came here?" A couple pillows smacked his thighs. "You couldn't have mentioned you had months to live?" A particularly good toss clipped his head and he slowly exhaled and gritted his teeth. "What happened to giving me a heads up?" The last pillow smacked him soundly in the chest. I sank onto the middle of the bed, my anger sapped with my last toss. I felt the tears starting and blinked several times.

He walked through the sea of gold and cream fabric, and crawled up to sit beside me. "I'm sorry. I wanted to tell you...it's just a hard thing to bring up in casual conversation."

I looked over at him as a stubborn tear dripped from my eye. "Hey, don't care for me, I'm dying, would have worked," I muttered sullenly.

"Come here." He grabbed my shoulder and pulled me tight to him. I swallowed several times to calm my emotions and my tears, and rested a hand over his perfectly thumping heart. "It's not as bad as you think, Emma," he whispered.

"Death is bad," I whispered back.

"I won't be dead-dead. Only the human side is dying. I'll still be vampire, just like Mom and Gran."

"What?" I looked up at him, thoroughly confused.

He rubbed my shoulder as he comforted me, and the realization that the dying man was comforting me and not vice-versa, wasn't lost on me. My guilt only added to my kaleidoscopically twisting emotions—anger, grief, confusion, betrayal. You name it, I was probably feeling it.

"We don't know why, but when we mixed breeds turn twenty-five, the human side of us kind of...gives out. For all intents and purposes we die, and the vampiric side takes over. That's what happened to Gran and Mom, and it's happening to me. I won't make it to twenty-six."

I searched his pale eyes and shook my head. "The human side dies...what does that mean? What will happen to you?"

With a soft smile on his lips, he gazed deep into my eyes and described his demise. "My heart will stop. I will no longer need to breathe. My skin will cool. I will no longer be able to eat regular food...and I'll live solely on blood."

"You'll be a true vampire," I whispered.

He shook his head. "No, I'll just be more of one than I am now. I'll be more like the others."

My face paled as I connected what he'd said, with the

memories I had of meeting his family—the youthful appearances, the cool skin, only drinking blood. "Oh…Gran and your mother. That's why they don't age…they're dead."

He nodded. "Technically, yes, although it's hard to think of them that way, isn't it?"

I scrunched my eyebrows together as I absorbed his fate. He'd be dead and yet alive. He'd be cold, and his chest would be silent, and he'd consist solely on blood, just like a creature straight out of a horror movie…and I'd be dating him. Or would I? This was a lot for a girl to take in. I'd overlooked the fangs and the occasional chicken-draining, mainly because he'd seemed so human. If everything that made him like me was suddenly lost…could I live with that? Could I fall in love with that? Was it too late?

"Your family says you're running out of time…to do what? What is it they want you to do before you die?"

He stood then, and started kicking pillows out of the way so he could pace beside the bed. Angry, he put his hands on his hips and shook his head. "Gran and Great-Gran just can't keep their big mouths shut. I did not want to have this conversation this weekend," he muttered as he walked. He glanced over at me on the bed, where I was watching him with my brow furrowed. I had the sudden feeling that whatever he was about to tell me, it was somehow going to be worse than the "I'm dying" speech. He stopped in front of me, his hands still on his hips. "Please understand that I wasn't going to mention this, because it doesn't matter to me."

My brow scrunched even more. "Okay," I said slowly.

He exhaled forcefully and ran a hand down his face. "They want a baby before I die," he whispered.

I shot up off the bed that suddenly felt like it was on fire. "They *what?*"

He held his hands out, as if to placate me. "They just want to keep the line alive, and we can't have children once the human side dies, so they're putting a lot of pressure on me to…to…"

"Knock me up!" I yelled, looking around for a pillow to chuck at him again. Unfortunately, he had kicked all of the ones near me to the other side of the room. "Are you kidding me? We've been together a month, Teren—a month!"

I started pacing beside the bed again, roughly brushing past where he was standing. He stepped back and tried to grab me as I walked by. "I know, Emma. That's why I wasn't going to mention it." I blocked his hands and kept pacing. "That's what they want, not me." He successfully grabbed my waist when I passed by him again, and pulled me into his side. "Why do you think I never come out here? It was bad enough when I didn't have a girlfriend, but since we've been together, God, they've been badgering me nonstop!"

I beat on his chest while he held me. "You may have mentioned this while you were spilling your fanged guts out to me! Did you not think your impending death, and your family wanting an heir, might be important enough to mention!" I smacked him good and then his hands grabbed my wrists. I jerked away from his grasp and started pacing again.

"You're really mad, aren't you?"

I stopped at the crest of my pacing track and glared back at him with my hands on my hips. "No. Why would I be mad? Your family only wants you to impregnate me with your vampire seed. Oh wait, no…that's not even right. They want you to impregnate *someone*, not necessarily me, if I'm not…how did Halina put it? Oh yeah— willing!" He looked down guiltily and I continued pacing…and ranting. "And the whole dying part! Yes, we can't forget that any day now, you'll be the walking dead, so we better get your little buddies doing their job before it's too late—no rush or anything, because you know, you'll be dead!"

He stepped in front of where I was surely wearing a line in the plush carpet and grabbed my shoulders. "I know. I'm sorry. I just didn't know how to tell you any of this."

I inhaled a calming breath and resisted the urge to slug him. "Continually stressing how human you were to me was probably not the best way."

He ran his hands up and down my arms and squatted to look me in the eye. "I am really sorry. It's a hard thing to say all at once. I thought segments would be best."

Very dryly, I said, "Anymore segments I should know about?" He hesitated, and I felt my stomach drop, but eventually he said no. "You might have mentioned all of this before I started falling for you," I said quietly.

He brought a hand to my cheek. "You're falling for me?" His voice was soft and soothing, but nothing else about the situation was, and I jerked away from his tender touch.

"I said *starting*. I'll just have to see now."

Slight amusement in his voice, he told me, "Take your time. I don't think I'm dying today."

It was not in mine. "Teren, I know you wanted to stay until tomorrow night, but…I want to go home now."

He sighed and looked at the floor. "Is this the deal breaker? Is this the part where I lose you? Where you finally run away screaming?"

I wrapped my arms around his waist and blinked back the sudden tears. "Well, I don't think I'll scream…but you not having a heartbeat is something to consider, and I can't do it here. I need my things, my bed—my comforts. I need to process this and I need to process it alone."

He wrapped his arms around my body and I could feel his heartbeat quicken as my head pressed against his chest. He sighed again and kissed my hair, and an overwhelming sadness drifted over me. Regardless of what we had been, and what I'd been willing to accept of his condition, things were different now. His condition was much more severe than he'd led me to believe, and maybe his family was right about an heir. If I wouldn't supply him with one—and I couldn't even think about that yet—maybe he should find another girl, before it was too late. The very thought made me clutch him tighter though, and try as I might to hold it back, a tear did escape my eye.

After another comforting moment of silence, Teren pulled away and kissed my head again. "I'll pack up our things."

He started blurring around the room, getting everything back together. Suddenly feeling exhausted, I sat on the edge of the bed and watched what little of his streaking form that I could see. The memory of his strong heartbeat echoed in my ear, and I tried to wrap my mind around never hearing that again. It was such a foreign concept to me that I couldn't even process it. I realized then, that Alanna and Imogen, and Halina too, I supposed, were all probably heartbeatless. That made my stomach a little nauseous. Teren stopped moving at the doorway and I noticed both bags full and heavy in his hands. He looked back at me and I had to blink back another tear at the forlorn expression on his face.

"I'll tell everyone we're leaving. I'll meet you in the car in a few minutes."

I nodded, knowing full well that he basically just told everyone we were leaving. Well, I was sure his family had some comments to make on this new development. I was probably being voted off the island at this very moment. I could just hear Halina— "She's weak, Teren, replace her and move on, before it's too late." I thought maybe Imogen would grudgingly agree with her; whatever steps were necessary for her great-grandchild. Alanna...well, I wasn't quite sure where she stood on the subject. Maybe she would defend me, maybe not. I was pretty sure Jack was just going to keep his head down and steer clear of the whole mess—smart man, that one.

Sighing, I stood and replaced the numerous decorative pillows on the bed, hoping to make the room as perfect as we'd found it, and understanding a little more why we were placed in what I had only just now realized, was indeed the most romantic room in the house. Once the room was more or less back in order, I shut the light off and closed the door behind me, shutting out the good memories as well as the bad.

I trudged down the elaborate staircase and once I was at the bottom, I stared at the naked woman statue for several seconds. I dabbed away another stubborn tear and considered heading out to the car and disappearing from this house without even a goodbye. Sighing again, I turned towards the hallway that led to the dining room. I just couldn't be so rude as to not say goodbye. They may all have had a secret agenda in being nice to me this weekend, but they had still been nice, and I could be the same.

I stopped midway down the hall when I heard voices coming

from the dining room. I crept a little closer, making sure that I couldn't be seen from the room. Once I was within earshot, I stopped and listened to what sounded like Teren having an argument with Imogen. I knew it was impolite to spy, but honestly, how often does a person get a chance to listen in on vampires discussing, well, anything?

"Teren, dear, I know you really like her but if she's not willing, maybe you should…"

"What if *I'm* not willing? What if *I* don't want this? Can't I just be with her, and have you guys happy that I'm happy?"

"Yes, of course we want your happiness but, you are the last of us. If you don't… We'll lose the line, Teren."

"Maybe that's a good thing, Gran. Maybe we shouldn't be continuing…this."

"Please, sweetheart…please?"

"Gran…" Teren sighed heavily.

I silenced my breath as I pressed against the wall. I felt figures shifting in the room, but no one spoke for a few seconds and I considered coming out of hiding. I was just about to make a move, when Teren's mother spoke up.

"Mom, I'd like to speak to my son…alone." Silence followed her statement and then she spoke again. "I think you should stay here with us, Teren."

"We've already been over this, Mom. I want to stay in San Francisco."

"You know the risk you are taking. You should be here, where it's safe."

Teren started speaking in Russian, which riled me a bit. I was really going to have to learn that complicated sounding language.

"You know I care more about you than a child…although, I would like to be a grandmother…"

Teren cut her off with the fast, fluent, foreign speech.

"She could stay here with you, Son. There's no need for you

to be apart from her, but *here* is where you'll be safe, both of you."

More Russian, a little heated now.

"I know that is what you believe, but what if you're wrong? The risk is too high."

More Russian…quite a bit more, he seemed to be ranting.

"Of course I know it's your life. I'm not trying to control you, dear. I'm trying to help. If we were of a different mindset, we'd just come collect you, and you know that. But we've let you stay away…for now." Alanna's tone was starting to get as heated as her son's. I wasn't sure what they were talking about, but I was sure it probably wasn't good.

More insolent sounding foreign tongue. Interesting how arguing with your mom turns you into a five year old, no matter what language you're speaking.

"Of course I know she's listening, but I will not speak that language. She should hear this, Teren. She should understand."

Teren switched back to English and my face heated. Of course they'd known I was here—super ears probably heard every thump of my impossible-to-quiet heart. "This is why I don't visit more often—none of you ever listen to me!" And with that, I could hear him turn towards the hall where I was guiltily eavesdropping.

He grabbed my hand as he walked by me in the hall. "Come on, we're leaving."

He jerked me after him and, looking at the dining room entryway for a second before he literally dragged me away, I saw Alanna's youthful face watch her son leave. Her eyes were so pained, and almost scared, that it shocked the inquisition about their argument straight from my head. As he ushered me from the house, I couldn't even remember the bits of their disagreement that I had understood, I only remembered Alanna's eyes.

Teren opened and closed the car door for me, like a perfect gentleman, but his mouth was tight and he looked stressed. Maybe coming up this weekend wasn't the best plan after all; it had certainly changed things for me.

"Are you all right?" I asked quietly, as he pulled away from the house and screeched down the bumpy drive.

"I'm fine, just an old disagreement, rearing its ugly head."

"One you didn't want me to hear…you were speaking Russian again."

He looked over at me and I could see the debate in his eyes. Turning back to the road, he finally said, "This one is between my mom and me. It has nothing to do with you or a baby…I promise." His tone was soft, but it was also firm. I knew I would get nothing from him if I pressed him about it. I'd also had my quota for the day on difficult conversations, so I let him drop it.

"Why do you speak Russian? Beautifully, I might add."

Maybe reassured that I wasn't going to press him, he smiled and finally relaxed a bit. "Great-Gran was born there, spent her first ten human years there, so she speaks it and taught each of us." He pulled onto the main road and I let go of my death grip on the door handle, since the never-ending jarring bumps were done with.

"Oh. Maybe you could teach me."

Teren looked over to me with wistful eyes and I remembered, once again, how things had changed. Here I was, asking him to teach me a complicated foreign language, when I wasn't even sure if we were still together. Silly me. It's sort of amazing how the brain can block out events, if they're bad enough. But as I watched his eyes drink me in, I remembered our fight, and I remembered why we probably wouldn't make it as a couple. He was a marked man. Death was stalking him and surely if I stayed to close to him, it would stalk me too.

"I would love to teach you someday, Emma."

His voice was quiet, like he understood the unlikeliness of that ever happening. His sad eyes turned back to the road and we made the rest of the sixty mile trip home in absolute silence.

When we got to my house, he wanted to walk me to my door, but I made him stay in the car. That was hard enough, having him at my door would be a near impossible temptation. Because a small part of me wanted to beg him to stay, to come inside and sweep me upstairs, and make me forget everything that was between us. The majority of me knew that was only a patch though, and wouldn't fix anything. It would only make it harder to separate, if that was what we were going to do.

Steeling myself as we sat in his car in the driveway, I looked squarely at him and stated as professionally as I could, "Please don't call or come over. I need time by myself."

He nodded, and his sad eyes glassed over. That nearly broke my resolve. His next sentence kind of did. "May I kiss you goodnight?" This time, I nodded.

That kiss, in the silence of his car, with the blue light from his dashboard splashed across our skin, would remain with me for the rest of my time on this earth. At the moment, it shattered my heart, but upon later reflection, it healed it as well. That one kiss made up my mind about him—it was that powerful. But not yet…that realization came a few lonely nights later.

As the tender warmth of his lips pulled away from me, I swear a piece of me was pulled away as well. I'd never been one to feel dependent on someone else for my own happiness, but gazing at his pale blue eyes, with the barely-there glow that only I could see because only I believed, I knew that I'd never fully be complete in this life without him. But I had so much to think about, and I needed him gone to do it.

I whispered goodbye and grabbed my bag from his trunk. He watched me the entire way, his hands gripping the steering wheel, like he was willing himself to stay in the car. It wasn't until I had my door closed behind me and I heard the electric hum of his car pulling away, that I realized that he never said goodbye to me.

I spent Sunday in bed. I spent Sunday in bed wallowing. I spent Sunday in bed sobbing uncontrollably into my pillow. I knew it was childish, and it wasn't solving any of my problems, but I was allowing myself a day to grieve. I grieved over our ending relationship, the could-be future that never would be, the black-haired, blue-eyed children that we would never raise, the growing old together that we would never do, the dinners we would never eat and the conversations we would never have. I cried over the spectacular sex that we'd never have again and of course, I replayed the last time we'd spent together over and over again, stupidly wishing that I had known it would be the last time, so I could have committed every detail to memory.

Mostly though, I cried for Teren. It's not every day that you hear that someone you care for only has months left to live. Granted, his death was not a permanent one, but it would drastically change things, as death has a tendency to do.

I was crying over the loss of his beautiful heartbeat, when I finally passed out from exhaustion. When I woke up, it was a dreary, rainy Monday morning, like the universe, in some small way, at least felt my pain.

Monday morning at work was like any other Monday morning at work. The people were tired and grumpy from their weekend being over. Clarice was particularly nasty to anyone who didn't seem one hundred and ten percent on their game. And over the thin walls, I could hear whispered conversations of sordid tales, some I'm sure were entirely made up. It was so much like every other Monday that it shocked me. So much had happened to my world that I had forgotten it had only been one weekend. It seemed like months should have passed, and everyone at work should be slightly different.

A grumpy Clarice leaving me with a stack of urgent papers that needed to be copied or faxed or both by noon, reminded me, yet again, how infinitesimal the time away had been. Tracey regaled me with details of her date with Hot Ben which, of course, had become a weekend with Hot Ben. Her blue eyes sparkled while she told me over and over that he was "The One" and they were made for each other; she could feel the lifelong connection already.

I'd heard this speech before. I'd heard this speech several times before, actually. I smiled in all the right places. I nodded, like I was really interested in all the right places. I laughed when she wanted me to and said "how sweet" when she wanted me to. I asked her about the sex, because I could tell she was dying to talk about it. I gave her the encouraging words for her "for certain this time" soul mate, in all the places she wanted to hear them.

Meanwhile, my head was calculating the possible flaws Hot Ben had that Tracey would find irreconcilable in the next three months. Maybe he snored. Maybe he left the toilet seat up. Maybe he spit uncontrollably when he was outside. Maybe he called his mom too much. Maybe he'd lose his magic in bed. Maybe his toes were too long. There was always something with Tracey, something that spoiled the blissfulness of first attraction, and had her dumping the man cold. I was fairly certain that whatever flaws Tracey found in Hot Ben…they paled in comparison to the dilemma I was facing. At least her boyfriend had a pulse.

Finally, her exuberant reminiscing ended and she seemed to notice my mood for the first time, even though I was trying very hard to be upbeat and normal. "You okay? How did the weekend with the In-laws-to-be go?" Her blue eyes narrowed in concern, and while they weren't the same shade as Teren's, they were close enough that my heart physically ached.

"We left Saturday," I stated meekly.

She cringed. "Oh, that bad huh? Were they real monsters or something?"

I inadvertently giggled, which in turn made me cry a little. I dabbed my eyes while she put a hand on my shoulder. "No, they were fine…I guess, but Teren and I kind of broke up."

She immediately hugged me and I swallowed, so no more tears would flow. Really, tear-apalooza all day yesterday was quite enough. "Oh, sweetie, I'm so sorry. I thought he was such a good one too. Well, there's always more in this town." She pulled back and got a wide grin over a thought that seemed to suddenly leap into her mind; if she were a cartoon character, a light bulb would have been suspended over her head. "Hey…Ben's got this cousin who's single. He's really not as attractive as Ben, but he's not bad. Want me to set up a double?"

I gave her a very pointed look. That was her fix to my heartache—a "not-bad" cousin?

"Too soon?" She backed off a bit and shook out her pale hair.

I patted the stack of papers on my desk. "I should get back to work." Tracey gave me another encouraging squeeze and then started to turn to leave, but I stopped her. "Trace?" I pointed to the calla lilies wilting on my desk. "Could you throw these out for me?"

"Sure, hun." She grabbed them and took them away with her and I swallowed about five times in a row to settle my emotions. I would not cry anymore today.

And technically I didn't cry anymore that "day." I did however, skip kickboxing. Tracey said Hot Ben was subbing again, and the last thing I needed to see was them all dewy-eyed at each other. I curled myself into a blubbering fetal position on the couch instead. Since it was after five, I was considering that "evening" and at least giving myself kudos for making it that long. Tomorrow was always another shot.

Tomorrow turned out to be my dwelling day. I woke up, put on my work pantsuit and a moderate blouse top—I didn't feel like being ogled by men...well, maybe by one man, but he wasn't currently an option—and dwelled. While I brushed out my hair and pinned half neatly up into a clip, I dwelled. When I ate my breakfast of cream cheese on a toasted blueberry bagel, I dwelled. As Clarice got after me for missing one tiny slip of paper in a finished report, Tracey gushed over her after-hours kickboxing session with Hot Ben, and the coffee pot in the break room leaked all over my conservative top, I dwelled.

I dwelled about the odds. What were the odds that I would run into a vampire-human mix? What were the odds that he'd ask me out and I'd accept a date with a perfect stranger? What were the odds that he'd expose himself to me and I'd sleep with him anyway? What were the odds that his family would adore me...as long as I bore an heir? What were the odds that my mostly human vampire, that I was falling head over heels for, would also be dying...? At least his body was dying anyway.

All of those odds seemed like one in a million to me. I seriously considered buying a lottery ticket on my way home, but honestly, with my luck, I had better odds of being hit by a stray meteorite.

Tuesdays were my dinner with Mom and Ash. I considered baling, but I missed them, and I didn't feel like repeating last night's fetal position anytime soon. I walked into the café with my head down. I walked over to their table with my head down. I walked just up to the corner of their table with my head down and then I lifted my chin up and put on my most award-winning smile. Faking it...that was my plan to get through dinner this week.

Unfortunately, I forgot that Ashley could see right through my mediocre acting skills. Her scarred face immediately frowned upon seeing mine. "What's wrong?"

"Nothing," I automatically spat out, as I sat down beside her.

Now, there is something that happens to most women when asked that very simple question. Our answer, regardless of our true feelings, is almost always the same—nothing—but our bodies' reactions are vastly different. If nothing is truly wrong, nothing happens. However, if something actually *is* wrong, the eyes betray the tongue and immediately start to water. My traitorous irises were now streaming like Niagara. At least I wasn't in a fetal position.

Ashley instantly put her arms around me and held me close. "What happened?"

As is usually the case when you've dwelled in sorrow for a while...I embellished. "Teren and I are through. We went to his parents' place over the weekend and had a horrid time and we fought constantly and it's just completely over." The story I just spat out actually took about five minutes through all the embarrassing blubbering.

My sister calmly patted my back as I told my slight fable. My mom got right to the point. "You met his parents over the weekend? Why didn't you mention you were doing that last week?"

I cried some more while Ashley interpreted my tears. "Mom, does that matter now? They've broken up."

"They only dated a month," my mom whispered.

I cried harder and sunk my head to the table. God, this was getting beyond ridiculous. My mother seemed to agree, but grudgingly tried soothing me the same as Ashley. Eventually my tears stopped and we resumed our weekly meal. They didn't ask me any personal questions for the rest of the night...thank God.

That evening, I apparently had no tears left, since I went straight to bed and straight to sleep.

Wednesday was bitch day…that was the nicest way I could frame it. I woke up mad. I put on the shortest skirt I owned and the reddest, clingiest top. I angrily ripped through my hair with a flat brush and tossed it all up into a high ponytail. I drove ten miles over the speed limit and mentally dared a cop to pull me over—Californians did love a good car chase and in the mood I was in, they'd get quite a show.

I yelled—actually yelled—at Clarice when she asked me to recopy a report because it wasn't lined up just right. I might have yelled something about where she could shove said report. Tracey ducked down behind her wall and avoided me…which was good. I couldn't deal with any Hot Ben stories today. I snapped at the men eyeing my purposely clingy shirt to "take a photo, it would last longer". I bit off the head of the poor barista, who didn't quite get my afternoon drink hot enough. And then I yelled at some jerk on the street that was walking in front of me, because he wasn't moving fast enough. See…bitch.

Sometime throughout the day, my sister must have called Tracey because that evening, they both showed up at my house and dragged me, nearly kicking and screaming, to a local bar. After threatening a couple patrons who were whispering about my sister, Tracey and Ashley started pouring vodka after vodka down my throat. I stopped snapping at people around four or five drinks and started loving on several of the burlier men in the room. By seven drinks, I was happily dancing with a few. By nine drinks I was praying to the porcelain God and cursing my friends and family.

Which brought me to Thursday…remorse day. With a throbbing head and a tilting stomach, I dressed in a long, shapeless skirt and a long, shapeless blouse. I pulled my hair up as much as I could and sullenly made my way out into the too bright, early morning sun. Wearing sunglasses to my chair, I apologized over and over to Clarice and offered to take in her dry-cleaning to make up for it. She seemed rather pleased with how I was dressed, and how genuinely sorry I seemed, and took me up on my offer.

Tracey smiled down on me from her side of the wall and I

cringed, remembering that at some point last night, Hot Ben had joined us and I may have…grinded on him on the dance floor. I threw her an apology and she laughed, loudly, and said she was just happy I had fun. I may have had fun last night, but in the dehydrated state I was in now, fun was the least of the adjectives I'd use to describe my day. After handling Clarice's dry-cleaning, and silently cursing at myself for doing it, I meandered home and made nice with a quart of Ben and Jerry's.

Friday arrived at long last and with it came…longing. I missed him. I missed his scent. I missed his smile. I missed his stubble. I missed his dress shirts and slacks, and the shoes that he always matched his belt to. I missed his espressos. I missed his dog. I missed the quiet conversations. I missed the walks in the park. I missed his touch. I missed his kiss. I missed…everything.

I don't remember the day. I'm not even sure if I went to work. All I remember was the gnawing ache of loneliness, ripping my insides apart. I couldn't inhale completely, it hurt. I couldn't exhale completely, that hurt too. This was when I realized what that last kiss had done to me. Somehow, that one magnificent kiss in his car had inextricably bound me to him. I had felt a connection in that moment that I'd never felt with another human being, and while his humanity was now in question, what with his human side dying and his vampire side taking over, one thing was not in question—I still felt connected to him, more than I'd ever felt before, more than I could imagine ever feeling again. It scared me…it thrilled me.

Halina had told me once that Teren had "claimed" me. At the time, I'd been a little offended, but now I understood. Now surprisingly, I felt the same. I felt a claim on him and I knew, with everything inside me, that I would see this through with him. Whatever was to come, we would face it united. That's the only way I could see my life unfolding now—wrapped protectively in his arms, whether they were warm and alive or cold as the grave.

I think I broke every traffic law there was getting to his house. I walked up his steps and lightly knocked on his door, wondering what to say to the man I'd avoided for days. Nervousness tickled my stomach as I waited the two seconds for the door to swing open, and then I saw him, and my nerves evaporated. He was stunning, better than I remembered—jet-black hair, shiny in the sunlight, strong, stubbly jaw, maybe a touch longer than he usually kept it, full lips dropped open in surprise at my arrival, and the loveliest shade of pale, but tired, blue eyes, that were regarding me with a mixed expression of hope and sadness.

It turned out that I hadn't needed to worry about what to say. It turned out that my body had fully intended on doing all the talking for me. I greeted him with my lips firmly latching on to his, one of my legs wrapping around his slacks and my hands running up his impressive chest. His answer to my body's question was lightning-quick as he pulled me inside, slammed shut the door, and streaked us both upstairs to his bed.

After that…he took his sweet time.

Chapter 6 – We Make Up

I woke up in a familiar bed with familiar, warm arms around me and a familiar, furry lump sleeping at my feet. I breathed in deep, now that I could again. I snuggled back into the warm, bare chest behind me. The arms holding me automatically tightened as he drew me in. It was the warmest, safest feeling that I'd ever had, and I couldn't quite believe that I'd put myself through nearly a week of misery by denying myself his presence. Of course I would stay with him through his transformation. What would my life be without him?

He nuzzled my hair as he inhaled deeply himself. "You smell so good," he murmured.

"Nearly edible?" I muttered back, as I turned in his embrace to gaze at him.

He raised his head to look at me, his eyes filled with a new emotion, a happy, peaceful one. He ran a finger down my cheek and then along the artery in my neck. "Delicious." He smiled softly.

I frowned. "Things are going to change."

He relaxed back on an elbow as he looked down on me. I scooted over to my back and stroked his arm lying across my stomach. "Yes," he said simply.

"When will you die?" I couldn't even say the word louder than a whisper, but he heard me just fine.

He shrugged. "I don't know. I suppose it could be any day."

I nodded and placed my hand on his chest, to feel the pulsating life beneath his skin. "I'll miss this."

He placed his hand over mine and we both felt his doomed heart beating. "I will too."

I looked up to his face as that registered with me. He was dying, and he didn't want to. I was so selfish—worrying all this time about how it would affect me that I hadn't even considered how he felt about it. Concern for him filled me. "Will it hurt?"

He stroked my fingers on his chest and looked down at the

pillow. He frowned. "No one will give me a clear answer on that. They just keep saying 'it's uncomfortable' or 'you'll be fine.'" He looked back to me and a trace of fear was in his eyes. "I'm assuming that's a yes, it's going to hurt like hell."

I reached up to stroke his face. "Are you scared?"

Teren closed his eyes briefly at my touch and then reopened them. "Yes," he whispered. He looked at the pillow again, and I ran my hand back down to his chest. My chest tightened in sympathy. "I know I shouldn't be. I know that I'll be fine." Returning his eyes to me, he searched my face. "But, I've only ever been human. This is what I know." He patted his chest, his heart, and then he sighed. "I will miss feeling my heart beat. I will miss coffee. I will really miss food. I will miss...feeling normal."

I pulled him to me for a tender kiss. "I'm so sorry, Teren."

We warmly kissed for a few moments and then he pulled back. Gazing at me in adoration, he brushed some hair off my forehead. "Don't be. I've known this was my legacy my whole life. I've had plenty of time to prepare myself."

"It will still be an adjustment for you." I cocked my head to the side as I studied him. "You're always going to look like this, aren't you?"

He smiled. "Yes."

I frowned. "How am I going to explain that to my family?" I looked down at his chest. "And we'll never be able to eat with them." I looked back up to his eyes. "Oh...we'll never be able to have dinner together."

"Sure we will. I'll still cook for you." He grinned and sat further back on his elbow. "I'll just have to start making you pork dishes. I think I'd starve, just living on chickens."

I had the odd thought of him draining a pig in the kitchen and couldn't stop the laugh. He laughed with me and then we kissed some more. Man, I'd missed that. After a moment, he pulled away again. "Things will change, Emma...but one thing, will not."

"What?"

"I'll still love you."

I could only stare in silence at the amazing, doomed man beside me. Warmth and emotion flooded my body and I blinked to keep back those darn tears. "I love you too." I ran my hand back through his dark hair and pulled his lips to mine again. I savored the heat of that kiss as our mouths moved together perfectly. "I'm going to miss your warmth," I muttered against the stubbly softness of him. "What else will change?"

He pulled back and thought for a moment. "Well, I'll be even stronger and faster. I won't age and I'll heal fast. My sense of smell will be even more acute. I'll be more aware of blood. I'll be..."

"Hungrier?" I asked hesitantly.

"Thirstier." He gave me a very pointed look as I absorbed that. I suppose if all he existed on was blood, he would need it more often and in larger quantities. I could see that being a problem, if he were ever really, really hungry—regardless of what Alanna told me about her and her husband.

"Will it be a difficult for you...being around me?"

"No, of course not. I wouldn't let this continue if I thought that. I'd never hurt you, Emma. I'm not going to turn into some crazed monster. I'll still be me." He hesitated and I could see a debate in his eyes.

"Just tell me. I don't like secrets."

He lay back on the pillows and gazed at the ceiling. I propped up on an elbow so I could see him better. He seemed to not be sure how to word what he was thinking about. I gave him another moment to reflect while I drew a circle on his bare chest.

Finally he spoke, although he still didn't look at me. "My mother may have downplayed the thirst." He looked over to meet my curious eyes. "She didn't want to scare you, they are still hoping for that grandchild, and my father really isn't in any danger from her, but the blood is more intoxicating than she led you to believe. And once I change, that desire will get worse. You'll be...tempting to me."

"I'll be food." He nodded solemnly. "Could you feed on me without killing me?" I surprised myself, both by asking him that and by being calm when I asked it.

He sat up on both elbows and gazed at me intensely. "Yes. I can sense how much is too much. I would never take more than your body could handle. I would never bring you harm."

I sat up a bit more as I regarded him with narrowed eyes. "How can you be sure of that? How do you know you can control yourself? You'll be more vampiric, maybe you just won't care?"

He shifted his body and brought a hand to my cheek. "My feelings won't change. I'll always care." His thumb tenderly stroked my cheek. "How do you know you can take one small bite of the sweetest dessert you've ever tasted and be satisfied?"

I thought about his analogy and tried to forget that in his scenario—I was dessert. "Well, I guess that would depend on how hungry I was. If I was starving, I probably wouldn't stop."

"I would never sample you if I were starving. I wouldn't come near you if I were anywhere close to starving." He completely sat up on the bed with me.

We were having a frank conversation, so I decided to just be frank. "You wouldn't just attack me and take it?"

He was shaking his head before I'd even finished my question. "I would never take it without permission. No…only if you wanted me to taste you." He looked down and his cheeks flushed with color. "I would actually love that. It's really quite…intimate. You may enjoy it too."

"I don't think so, Teren," I said very slowly. "Would you feed on anyone else, if I always told you no?" I found that I couldn't meet his eye when I asked, and I had to stare at my fingers tracing patterns in the silky sheets.

His hand came up and he gently grabbed my chin, making me look up at him. "No. I would never do that…ever. You're the only one I want to drink from."

That comment actually pleased me, which made me shake my head in bewilderment. "This conversation just got creepy."

He laughed and relaxed back down to the pillows. "Just? I

thought it was creepy ages ago, but I just kept going with it."

"Shut up." I smiled and laid down on him, putting my head on his shoulder and draping my arm over his chest. "Would my blood be sweet to you?"

He grinned as I looked up at him. "Like the finest wine."

"Hmmm...that's oddly flattering. Still pretty creepy, but flattering."

He laughed again and kissed my temple. "I do love you."

"I don't think I'll ever get tired of hearing you say that." I nestled deeper into his shoulder and let out a happy-with-life sigh.

"Well, you have as long as you like to listen."

Spike stirred from his resting place at our feet and stood up on the bed. He shook out his long coat and then lightly stepped in-between Teren and me and settled back down. We both laughed as we were forced apart from each other by his size. Spike licked my cheek and rested his head on my shoulder, almost protectively.

"Hey, boy, I missed you." I scratched him behind his ears. He thumped his tail and I could have sworn he smiled.

Teren sat up on the other side of him. "You missed the dog? Did you miss me?"

I shrugged my shoulders. "Maybe...a little."

He leaned over Spike to kiss me. "It seemed more than a little last night."

I grinned and pulled him down to me, making Spike scoot out of our way. "Okay...maybe a lot. Maybe I was miserable. Maybe I cried all the time. Maybe I told off my boss. And maybe I even got wasted and danced inappropriately with my friend's boyfriend. Maybe..."

Teren raised his eyebrows at me. "Wow, you were busy. I just sulked a lot." He cupped my face in his strong hands. "I'm so sorry I didn't tell you everything right away. I was so afraid you'd leave me."

I blinked back the darn tears again, although a couple may have made it past my defenses. "I'm not going anywhere. I missed you so much." I brought him to my lips and proceeded to show him, again, just how much I'd missed him.

Closer to lunchtime, I was lounging in the kitchen, wearing my boyfriend's just long enough dress shirt. Dressed only in gray lounge pants, Teren was making us a late breakfast of bacon and eggs.

I was very happy.

I came up behind him and slipped my arms around his trim waist. He smiled and turning towards me, popped half a piece of bacon in my mouth. He popped the other half, and I kissed his bare shoulder and hugged him tight, while he flipped my eggs. When he was done, he made up a plate for me (he must have picked that habit up from his mom), and set me at the table with a kiss on the head. He made us both cappuccinos and then joined me at his stylish kitchen table.

I held his hand while we ate, and periodically kissed his wrist as I gazed into his pale eyes. I couldn't help it. I almost felt like *I* was the vampire—I just wanted to devour him. And I definitely never wanted to let him go again. Which left one little situation we hadn't discussed yet. As he swept away our plates and made more coffee, I wondered how to bring it up to him.

This is what I came up with...

"Your parents will be thrilled that we're back together."

He set my coffee in front of me and sat back down. "Yeah, they'd be downright euphoric if they knew what we just did." He grinned. "Twice."

I laughed and shook my head. "That's just so wrong on so many levels."

He took a sip of coffee then shook his head. "Tell me about it. I never thought they'd go so far as to discuss my sex life over dinner, while meeting my girlfriend for the first time."

"I never imagined upsetting any parent because I wasn't...copulating like a bunny with their son."

He laughed at my turn-of-phrase. "God, I know." Closing his

eyes, he shook his head again. "They can be mortifying." He opened them and looked at me, a little embarrassed. "I'm so sorry about that. I think they're getting a little desperate."

I sipped my coffee and then grinned at him. "You think? They asked me if I was attracted to you. Like I'm not the one usually ripping your clothes off."

He let out a hearty laugh. "Yeah, well, I didn't feel the need to mention that to them."

"Thank you for that." I took a long draw of coffee while I watched him laugh. "So...they want an heir?"

He stopped laughing and set the coffee that he had just been about to sip, down on the table. His expression serious, he smoothly said, "Being with me doesn't mean that you have to get pregnant in the next six months."

"But if it's going to happen, it has to be before you die."

He averted his eyes. "That's what they believe, because that's how it worked for them. I don't think it works the same for me."

I blinked. "Why not?"

Teren blushed and glanced at me out of the corner of his eye. "Because...I'm a guy." He shrugged his shoulders, like that one statement answered everything.

I blinked again, not really understanding his argument. "So..."

He sighed. "Women have to be alive for a baby to grow inside them. Obviously, a dead body can't grow a life, can't provide the necessary nourishment." He looked down at his pants with an odd twist to his lips. "My...contribution just kind of hangs out and waits for the opportunity."

I couldn't help it—my happiness that we were in this mess together and the oddity of the situation, culminating in that last look at his pants—I started laughing. I started belly laughing. Tears were streaming down my face.

He looked at me, offended, like I was emasculating him. "It's not funny."

I managed to spit out around chuckles, "Your family is irked at you, because you haven't knocked up some poor girl yet. That's kind of funny."

He smiled then and finally laughed with me. "I suppose it is, in a way."

Eventually our laughter died down and I grabbed his hand. "Honey, I think your family is right."

"What?" he asked, curious.

"I think once your body is effectively dead, what swimmers you have will die, or at least they won't be viable for long. There's a lot going on in the male system. It takes quite a bit of hormones and nutrients to make and keep active baby-makers, and I don't know for sure, but I think you'll be shooting blanks afterwards."

"Anything else, Doctor?" he asked, keeping his features as blank as possible.

"It's just an opinion." I suppressed another laugh and shrugged my shoulders.

Shaking his head in amusement, he rolled his eyes. "I'm glad everyone is so interested in my reproductive system."

I spat up the last of the coffee that I had just swallowed and Teren softly chuckled into his cup. Collecting myself, I waited until he was taking a sip of his coffee before I responded. "Maybe you should just give them what they want?"

I was vastly rewarded. He spat up his coffee and stared at me open-mouthed. Still feeling on a high from just being back together with him, I stood up and straddled him in his chair. That made him smile, and he set down his coffee and rubbed his warm hands on my thighs. I gazed into his pale eyes and imagined for a second having a black-haired, blue-eyed, fanged child with him. It was an interesting thought, but it was all happening so fast…

"Why haven't you yet, since you know how important it is to them?" I asked in a quiet voice, not sure if I wanted an answer to that question.

He sighed and his hands stroked the outside of my bare

thighs. "Now you sound like them." He gave me an exasperated look as he asked, "Who exactly am I having this vampire child with?"

I raised an eyebrow at him as I laced my arms around his neck. "Surely, you've been with other girls before?"

Amused, he gave me a wry look. "I am twenty-five...yes."

"Well, one of those girls."

He was already shaking his head though. "I'm not bringing someone into this...situation unknowingly."

I blinked and pulled back to examine him. "I'm the only one you've ever told?"

He shook his head again as his hands slid up to my hips. "No. You're just the only one who hasn't run away...for long at least." He laughed and I smiled at his attractive, happy face. "There was even this one girl who tried to stake me—with a stiletto no less." He rubbed his bare chest. "That hurt a bit."

I laughed, then bent over to kiss his old injury. "How very *Single White Female* of her. What happened to these girls?" I tried to picture some woman trying to heel him to death, and the image made me obscenely happy.

"Great-Gran hunted them down—"

I cut him off by partially standing from his lap. "Oh my God! She ate them?" I had a momentary second of panic at the thought of that wild, black-haired beauty tracking me, if my reaction had been a little more extreme at his parents' place.

Teren pulled my hips back down onto his lap. "No, can I finish? She tranced them, made them forget...although, she probably did nibble a bit first." He furrowed his brow as he considered that possibility.

I ignored the nibbling part and focused on the more pertinent part of the sentence. "She what? She like...hypnotized them?"

He shrugged. "Sort of, yeah."

"Wow...can you do that?" I could see numerous instances where that little trick would come in handy—cutting in front of people in long grocery lines, dealing with the DMV, sneaking us into Hollywood movie premiers. He burst my bubble pretty quickly though.

"No, it's a full blown vampire thing. She's the only one of us that can do it."

"Oh, too bad…" No way was I going to ask her to hypno someone for me.

Teren laughed once. "Why, you want your mind erased? Something you want to forget?" He twisted his lips as he crossed his arms over his chest. "Maybe your dirty dancing with that guy…" His tone was a little disgruntled.

I bit my lip, wishing I hadn't mentioned that. "No…well, actually, yeah, I would like to forget that but no, I was thinking that'd be a handy trick." Excited, I leaned over his arms on his chest. "I mean for speeding tickets alone…"

Teren smiled as he slung his arms around my waist. "It's nice to see you'll only be using our powers for good."

Grinning, I rested my head against his. "Just being practical with my vampire boyfriend and his vampire family…especially if I'm going to have his vampire child."

He froze and stopped smiling. "You don't have to do that." His forehead moved against mine as he shook his head. "I'm not even sure if we should continue this…trait."

I pulled back to study his worried expression. "I don't know if I want to yet." I put my hands against his chest. "I guess I'm just telling you that I'll consider it. I'll consider it if you will."

He half-smiled. "Okay. We'll…consider it together then."

"Together…I like that idea. I love you." I gave him a warm kiss.

"I love you too," he whispered against my lips.

We spent most of the day lounging around his house in various stages of undress. We would have made his family proud— which both amused me and icked me out. We didn't bring up the baby topic again, or his impending demise, but both subjects swirled around my head. I was finally becoming okay about the latter event. Him not being as human as me would be a startling change, but really, I was in too deep with him to let that little hiccup ruin our relationship. And I looked at Alanna and Jack as my role models. They were happy. Deliriously happy I'd dare say, and we could have that, too. Plus, my boyfriend would be a hot twenty something for…well, quite possibly for eternity. I didn't overlook the bonus of that. Although at some point, I supposed that would make me a cougar.

The former event, getting pregnant within the year, that one was a little harder to wrap my head around. It wasn't that I'd never pictured having kids. I had even done the five second *what would our children look like* analysis on Teren's and my first date, but it was always a way off in the future event—right up there with teleporting and flying cars. It was definitely not something I thought I'd ever feel such enormous pressure to do right away. Most parents wanted their kids to wait until they were settled and ready—and preferably dating for longer than a month. But Teren's family didn't have the luxury of waiting. It really was now or never with them. That was a lot for a girl to consider.

Sunday, we decided to take Spike for a long walk along the beach. Happy as a pup could be, he yipped at birds, and dashed up to the edge of the water, before spinning and running back to a safe distance. I held Teren's warm hand in my own and marveled at the novelty of walking on a sunny California beach with a vampire.

"Why doesn't sunlight affect you?"

Teren laughed and looked over at me. "I have been waiting for that question ever since I first told you what I was. You held out much longer than I thought you would." I gave him a dour expression. Laughing again, he answered me, "Some of the vampire side effects seem to be diluting with each mixed generation." I looked up at him with a confused face, and he shrugged his shoulders and explained further. "Great-Gran is a full vampire, so she can't be in the sun at all…"

"Hence the being nocturnal," I stated and he nodded.

"Gran can be around sunlight, but she generally avoids it. She says it's like sticking your head in a hot oven."

I cringed as I remembered opening my mom's hot stove as a child and having that wave of heat blast me in the face. Being in that for only two seconds hadn't been enjoyable. "Oh, that doesn't sound pleasant at all."

"Yeah. Mom can be in the sun for short periods of time, but after a while, it does make her uncomfortable and if she stays too long, she burns—like an intense sunburn."

"Huh…and you?"

He held his palms up to the sunny sky. "I love the sun and it appears to love me right back. I suppose that could change when I fully cross over, but I don't think so. Mom and Gran said they were the same afterwards, in that regard."

"Interesting. What about silver and garlic and holy water?"

"Ah…are we having the myths conversation?" I squeezed his hand and nodded with enthusiasm. I wanted to know everything he could and couldn't do. Teren was amused by my reaction. "Well, they're much the same, although the water one is a complete myth, and garlic is more gross than dangerous."

"Oh…good to know."

He smirked at me. "Maybe I shouldn't be telling you all of our weaknesses."

I poked him in the stomach. "You don't seem to have any. You seem to have all of the benefits with none of the setbacks." He shrugged in agreement. "So…our kids would have that too?"

"Kids…now all of a sudden you want more than one?" I poked him again and he laughed. "Yes, our kids would be even more human." He said the last part quietly and looked over at the ocean, where Spike had finally gotten enough courage to dip his paws. His pale eyes were speculative, and I wondered what he was thinking about. Before I could ask though, he turned back to me with a bright smile. "I wouldn't mention anything about kids around my parents, unless you want them breathing down your neck…even more."

I laughed. "Don't worry. I had no intention of doing that." I sighed and watched a now semi-wet Spike bark at a seagull. "I suppose we should go back there soon. I should apologize for the way I left."

Teren swung our hands. "You have nothing to apologize for. They were out of line, and you had every right to ask to leave." He gave me a pointed look. "If I were human, I'd have done the same."

That was the first time he'd ever referenced himself as anything *but* human. It gave me a slight shudder, which I ignored, as I snuggled into his side while we walked.

"How exactly was Halina turned?"

"Standard vampire lore—she was drained of all her blood and it was replaced by a vampire's."

"Oh." I thought on that for a moment. He'd stressed earlier that he wouldn't be a monster, that he would still be himself when he changed, so, the vampire who changed her... I just couldn't see why anyone would turn a woman so obviously pregnant. "Why would someone do that to her, when she was with child?"

He looked down at our feet crunching along in the perfectly white sand. "Sometimes, people are just bad, Emma...whether human or vampire." I clenched his hand and laid my head on his shoulder as I thought about how true that was. The world was just a messed up place. He let out a weary exhale and I looked up at him. "Personally, I think he was just curious what would happen...to the baby, I mean." He shrugged his shoulders. "It's too late now. We can't ask him."

"Oh, did he run off and leave her alone?" For some reason, that sounded worse than him turning a pregnant woman. I'd think being a new vampire would be scary, especially all alone. Teren surprised me by laughing.

"No...not exactly." Curious, I searched his face for some hint of what he meant by that. He didn't leave me in the dark for long. "Great-Gran kind of staked him. She was a little...angry."

My mouth dropped wide open. "She staked him! A *little* angry..."

"Okay, maybe a lot."

"Remind me to never piss her off." A shudder passed

through me and if it were possible, I was now even more terrified of the teenage-looking vampire.

Teren nodded and smiled. "That would be best…" He obviously saw a side of Halina that I didn't, and he found part of her highly amusing.

"What happened to her husband? Imogen's father?"

"He died…around the same time." His smile left and his tone went flat.

Realizing that the vampire that turned her had probably killed him, which would explain the anger and the subsequent staking of her creator, I redirected the conversation. "So, you really can be staked?"

"Sure. We heal most everywhere else, but…the heart…destroy that, and with anything, not just wood, and you destroy us. We don't know why, but it's the one human thing we really seem to still need."

I squeezed his hand. "That's nice." Now he examined me for a hint of what I meant. "Something we'll still have in common," I explained.

We walked along the beach in silence while I held onto his arm. I discretely watched him as we shuffled along the sandy slope, edging down to the breaking waters of the Pacific—his tan skin underneath my slightly paler skin, his black hair shining in the sunlight, the slight rise and fall of his chest that was visible to me as the breeze compressed his shirt to him, his pale eyes watching his pup frisk back and forth from the surf to the dunes. He was so alive. It was hard to picture him any other way.

"Maybe the change won't happen with you. Maybe you're different…maybe you'll stay human?"

He looked down on me. His eyes were wistful for a moment, before he shook his head. "I can feel it, Emma. It's coming, I'm already changing." Stopping, he put his arms around my waist. "I'm sorry…but I will die."

I averted my eyes, willing them to not water; if he could handle this, then I could. I felt his hand on my chin and I looked up at him. The very edges of his lips curled into a smile and then he brought those wondrous lips to mine. For a moment, as the sea breeze tickled our skin and the heavenly scent of him, mixed with the faint residue of salt in the air, I forgot that things would change. That they already were changing. I took my one moment in the sun with my vampire, and forced out all the rest.

I spent Sunday night at Teren's again, so Monday, I had to wake up especially early so I could go home and change into work clothes. Teren worked earlier than I did, so he was almost ready to leave himself, when I finally got my slow body out the door. He handed me some coffee in a travel mug and gave me a soft goodbye kiss at my car, which hadn't moved from his driveway since Friday night.

I was all smiles and giggles as I drove home. I was all contented sighs as I got dressed and styled my hair into loose waves. I was all doe-eyed goofiness as I walked into work and spouted a merry good morning to Clarice, who grunted some sort of response. And I was reminded again just how much had changed in one weekend, when a familiar blonde cautiously peeked her head over my cubicle wall.

I shut the drawer where I was stuffing my extremely full purse when I saw the top of her blonde head. I smiled and laughed at her apprehension. "Hi, Tracey! Good morning." My voice was all happy and light, darn near rainbows and sunshine.

She poked her head up all the way. "Hey. You seem in a better mood." She narrowed her eyes. "You were really out of it Friday. I thought Clarice was going to random drug test you." She furrowed her brow, like maybe she thought Clarice should have.

I giggled in my happiness. "I'm not on drugs, Tracey. But I am happy." I stood up and leaned over the wall with her. "Teren and I got back together. Everything is…" I sighed like a lovesick dork, "wonderful."

She hesitantly smiled, maybe remembering my many mood swings last week. "That's great, Emma. If that's what you want…then I'm happy for you."

I frowned. "What do you mean, if that's what I want? Of course it's what I want."

She frowned too. "Well, you obviously broke up with him for a reason, and there are plenty of other fish out there. Just don't feel like you have to…settle."

I pulled back from the wall and made my way to my desk to turn on my computer. "I'm not. Nobody…settles for Teren Adams." I flicked the screen on and watched it come to life. "He's amazing, Trace…the best."

I looked over my shoulder and she made a movement liked she shrugged. "I'm just saying. I don't want to see you get hurt again." I smiled at her concern, and then she left that train of thought and hopped right on another. "Coming to kickboxing tonight? Lita's back teaching, but Ben's going to take the class with me…like my own personal trainer." She winked.

I giggled at my friend, my life, and my absurd circumstances. "Yeah, I'll be there."

Clarice's attitude never really changed with me. If I was happy, sad or peeved she was still snippy, curt and too picky to ever be truly happy. By the end of my work day, I was welcoming the stress-relieving side effects of heart thumping physical activity. The class was packed, as it usually was on a Monday night, and as I looked around at the thirty or so other participants in the mirror-lined room, I fed off the energy building and let myself get excited. Tracey and Hot Ben stood in the back and were mostly ignoring everyone else. He played with her ponytail while she felt his bicep. I couldn't help but notice that his blonde highlights exactly matched the shade of her hair. I stopped watching them after that.

Lita, dressed in skin-tight, black aerobic pants and a black workout bra, turned on the hard, fast music and skipped out to the front of the slightly springy, wooden floor. She led us through a series of warm ups, her brown ponytail bouncing behind her, as she went over her weekend mishap, a fiasco involving a sick dog and a box of missing chocolate-covered cherries.

Several people around me matched my laughs as we listened to her, but she had us sweating through the laughter in no time. Then we got down to business. By the end of class, I was drenched and sore and high with endorphins. I drove straight to Teren's house, all gross and sweaty. He didn't care. Before I'd even had a chance to knock, he opened the front door and pulled me in for a kiss. I showered and changed while he finished making dinner. Afterwards, we had a lovely meal on his patio and watched the sun begin to set.

And then I asked him...

"Will you meet my family tomorrow night?"

He glanced at me with a serious expression. "I don't know, Emma...that's a big step." He grinned as I glared at him. "Of course I will. Shall I pick you up after work?"

I leaned over the table and gave him a kiss. "Yes...you shall."

Patting his lap, Teren laughed at my comment, as I walked around the table to him. Plopping myself down, I snuggled into his warmth, and together we sat and watched the sun sink all the way from sight.

When I got home that evening, I called Ashley to let her know that Teren would be joining us for dinner tomorrow. I called her, for one, because she was my best friend and I told her everything, that I could, anyway, and secondly, because she was my go-between for Mom. I love my sister. She assured me that she would let Mom know that Teren and I had patched things up and were together and happy, and under no circumstances was Mom to badger him about the breakup. No, my daughter was a wreck, how could you do that? No, what are your intentions now? And definitely no, are you going to marry her and give me grandchildren?

I got enough of that on his side.

Chapter 7 – The Taylor Women

The streetlights flashed across Teren's face as his brows drew together in concern and his eyes softened with sympathy. Aside from the light jazz coming from the radio, the car was pin-droppingly quiet as he regarded me with compassion. My own face was a mixture of quiet acceptance and ancient grief. I bit my inner cheek to stop the emotion I could feel seeping into my body, seemingly absorbing into my skin from the stillness of the car and the solemnity on his face. Finally, his husky voice broke the calm.

"I'm so sorry about your father, Emma."

I'd told Teren about my family's situation, so he'd be prepared when he met them. It was a hard story for me to tell, even after all this time. I didn't cry anymore when I told people what my father had done for my sister, but the ache opened again. It took a few deep breaths and quite a few "let it go" mantras in my head to seal the wound shut again, but after a few moments of Teren's calming gaze, I did.

He'd been sweet and sympathetic while listening to my story, and now he was holding my hand as we drove to the charming café that had become almost a second home to my family. A trio of women that I had just invited a man into. This should be interesting. At least *they* wouldn't eye him like a meal, like I was pretty sure Halina had eyed me.

"Thank you." I replied quietly, my voice still a little thick. Clearing my throat, I added, "It was a long time ago, but Mom still doesn't like talking about it, so please don't bring it up." He gave me a look that clearly said *I'm not an idiot* and then he turned back to the road. "I should warn you about my sister." I really didn't like talking about the fire either, and mentioning Ashley's appearance was my least favorite part of it—her scars didn't define her—but a heads up was warranted.

Teren turned back to face me. "What about her?"

"She was injured really badly in the fire…she's quite scarred." I sighed.

"Oh." His voice oozed understanding and he squeezed my hand.

"She's all right now, although, she's had so many surgeries I can barely remember them all...but they've done all they can and she's still pretty..." My thoughts drifted off for a second.

He squeezed my hand again. "Don't worry. I'd never stare or make her self-conscious in any way."

I nodded and watched him drive for a moment. All of a sudden, I blurted out, "Can we tell her?"

He knew exactly what I meant. He glanced over at me with a furrowed brow. "It's not something I just go around telling people, Emma. It's...private."

This time I squeezed his hand. "I know that, Teren but..." I sighed. "She's my friend *and* my family. If I'm going to be a part of yours, I could really use her support."

Teren was silent, and just when I thought he was going to say no, he nodded and looked my way. "Are we telling your mother too, then?"

I grimaced. "God, no...she'd freak out."

Laughing, he shook his head and turned back to the road again.

We arrived at the café a little while later and Teren opened my door, just like the gentleman he was. I studied him as I stepped from his car: black, fitted shirt that matched his hair, worn un-tucked over perfectly faded jeans—he looked amazing. I adjusted my own short, black skirt and pink cashmere tank top and fluffed out my bouncy brown hair—I looked pretty amazing too. We made a cute couple. Teren smiled as I laced my arm through his and we strolled into the café locked together.

The hostess gave me a *Not bad* face as she eyed Teren, then she nodded to a table in the back corner. I smiled at her and pulled him in that direction. I started getting nervous as we made our way down the aisle. I peeked over at him to see if he had butterflies too, but he seemed calm and relaxed, like he was meeting my family for the umpteenth time instead of the first. It bothered me some, that he was so at ease, when I had been such a bundle of nerves before meeting his parents. But I decided that that was simply because his family could have ripped my throat out at any minute. My family was pretty…tame, in comparison.

We approached the booth in the back and stopped at the end of it. I noticed Teren's eyes widen just a little as he absorbed the sight of my sister, but his smile never wavered and his gaze was polite, not the unabashed staring that her disfigured head and body usually inspired. My mom and sister were a little more unabashed in their staring at him. They were both pretty curious about this attractive man who had me reduced to a quivering pile of sobs last week.

"Mom, Ash, this is Teren. Teren, my mom, Linda and my sister, Ashley."

Teren politely extended his hand to my mother. "Hello."

Her lips tugged up at the corner. "Hello, Teren. It's nice to finally meet you."

"And you." He extended his hand to Ashley without a second's hesitation. "Hello."

She smiled warmly, her eyes, the only part of her face not affected by her horrific, warped flesh, twinkled at the polite man before her. "Hello."

"May I?" Teren pointed to the seat on the bench next to Ashley, and she nodded. I took the seat next to my mother, who was smiling at him in approval. I ran my foot up the side of his jeans a bit as I smiled at him. He glanced over at me and grinned softly, his hand touching my knee under the table.

We made small talk, Teren asking every polite question there was regarding my mother and sister's lives, until the waitress, Debby, came to take our order. She didn't even look at the three of us women, knowing exactly what we would order. Instead, she eyed Teren, a little too enthusiastically, if you asked me, especially considering the fact that she was married. Teren ordered a really rare steak, which made me bite my cheek to stop the grin; my vamp liked it bloody. He noticed my gleeful reaction and winked at me. I coughed into my hand to not laugh out loud.

My mother kept up a steady stream of conversation about her and Ash, while we waited for our food. Once we were served and all digging into our plates, Mom moved onto Teren's family. "What do your parents do, Teren? Emma said she visited with them not too long ago."

I sputtered on the sip of soda I'd just taken, but Teren calmly answered her. "They run a ranch near Mount Diablo."

My mother seemed as taken aback by that as I had been, although, probably for completely different reasons. It's just not every day that you meet or hear about actual ranchers—human or otherwise.

"Oh…interesting. Maybe someday we could visit?" She smiled at the idea and my sister brightened as well. I sputtered again on the second sip of soda I'd tried taking. My mother shot me a look. "Are you okay, Emma?"

"Yep, just fine," I croaked.

Teren directed a low laugh towards me, then smoothly answered my mother. "Maybe someday that can be arranged. They're pretty busy right now. It's just the four of them. The help won't arrive for another few weeks."

My mom perked up, interested in his story. I was as well. I'd never heard him talk about his family to someone not in "the loop."

"Four of them? Who all helps out on the ranch?" Mom asked.

I cringed, wondering what he would say to that. He smiled and answered as effortlessly as if he were telling the truth. "My father, his wife and her two sisters." I blinked at him but tried to keep my expression even.

My mom shook her head. "Your father must have his hands full, with a house full of women." Teren grinned and I inadvertently giggled. Jack had quite a handful with those women. My mom ignored me; she was too interested in Teren's family dynamics. "So…I couldn't help but notice you said 'his wife' and not 'your mother'…"

Teren looked away and then back at her. His face looked

solemn. "My mother died a few years ago…cancer. My father remarried."

Mom stretched her hand out to touch his arm, while I tried not to gape at him. I'd never heard him lie about his family, but I suppose, if our families were ever going to meet, he would need an excuse for his mom's young age. I made a mental note to memorize his lie, in case I was ever asked about it. "I'm so sorry, dear." Mom patted his arm affectionately and by the look on her face, I knew that he had completely won her over.

Sure enough, for the rest of the evening she beamed at him, and the entire table talked and laughed in companionable comfort. Just like that, Teren fit right into my family, like he had always been there. And I loved him just a little more.

As we were getting ready to leave, I grabbed my mother's arm. "We'll take Ashley home, Mom. We were thinking about getting drinks after dinner and we'd love her to come." Ashley still lived with Mom while she attended school, and they often drove together; driving was a touch uncomfortable for Ash.

My mom gave me a critical look. "Emma…" Ashley was also only nineteen.

"I'll make sure hers are virgins, Mom." I discreetly winked at Ash, to let her know that I had no intention of doing anything of the sort. Ashley never got carded, people just kind of let her do what she wanted, which worked out well for us on occasion.

My mom sighed, "Okay…be careful."

I rolled my eyes at her. "We'll be fine." I didn't mention that I had my own personal pit-bull alongside me, although, I really didn't think of Teren as dangerous…unless you were poultry, of course.

We all stood, and were about to start walking up the aisle, when Teren offered his arm to Ashley. My mom had been about to do the same thing, and she grinned ear to ear when she noticed that Teren had beat her to it. "May I?" he said, with as charming a voice as I'd ever heard him use. My sister flushed and nodded. Ashley took his arm and they walked in front of Mom and me. I smiled at Teren's back as they walked ahead of us, heads bent in low conversation. Sometimes he seemed so much older than twenty-five, like he was from a different generation, a sweeter, more chivalrous one. I suppose his house being full of strong-willed vampire women, had something to do with that.

Once outside, Teren gave my mother a warm hug, all the while still lacing his arm with Ashley's. Mom looked downright giddy as she hugged me, and inwardly, I sighed. They loved him…the baby talk was going to follow soon. I'd be surrounded by it on both sides. Although, knowing my mom, the baby talk was going to be preempted by the "marriage" talk. My mom did love a good wedding.

We waved goodbye as Mom pulled away in her little compact, and then the three of us piled into Teren's car. He drove us to a local bar that was relatively clean and relatively quiet. The lights were dim, to create an atmosphere of "let's drink more" I guess, but some people still noticed us as we entered. They all instantly focused on Ashley. She straightened her shoulders, gripped Teren's arm tighter, and dealt with it, as she did every day of her life. My blood boiled at what she had to endure, and I shot some nasty glares at the looky-lous.

Teren quickly led us to a small, round table in a back corner, on the opposite side of the room from the pool table, so we could actually hear each other over the sound of the balls clanking together. Almost immediately, a short, rather dumpy waitress was at our side. Staring at Ash, and not even bothering to hide it, she asked, "What'cha want?"

Teren ordered a beer and we ordered rum and Cokes. The waitress scuttled off and Ashley relaxed her posture, just a bit. I put a hand on her thigh and she leaned her head against me.

"Thanks for inviting me out," she said politely, looking at both Teren and me.

"Well…we did have a hidden agenda," I said.

Ashley lifted her head from my shoulder and stared at me; curiosity was clear in her large eyes. I shrugged my shoulders and lowered my voice, "We wanted to talk to you about something without Mom around. Something you *cannot* tell her about."

Her back straightened and her curious expression shifted to excitement mixed with worry. "Oh my god, are you pregnant?" She looked back to the bar. "Not to be a prude, but you really shouldn't be drinking if you're pregnant."

Teren laughed pretty hard and I knew he was enjoying the fact that my family was just as interested in babies as his. Well, maybe not *just* as interested. I lightly smacked her on the arm and she frowned. "No! God, no! This is about Teren, not me. He's…a little different," I stated.

Ashley eyed him with quiet wonder, and he sighed a little, clearly not liking what was coming. "You are? How so?" she asked, her eyes sweeping over him, searching for something that made him as different as she was.

He looked about to speak, but just then our drinks arrived so he shut his mouth and waited. The frumpy woman set down his beer and our drinks, while flicking not discrete glances over Ashley's body the entire time. I felt like screaming at her, "Yes, she's scarred, we know that," but I knew Ashley wouldn't want the sort of attention that would bring to her. Ashley smiled softly at the woman through her half disfigured lips, and even thanked her when she was done.

The waitress mumbled something about enjoying our evening and then slunk off to the other side of the room. Ashley brushed off the encounter as she always did and turned to face Teren, since she was still waiting for his mysterious announcement.

I started to worry that Ashley wouldn't take it as well as I thought she would. What if she screamed? The bar wasn't packed, but there were a couple of beefy looking guys playing pool, and another guy at the bar who had gone way past beer-belly and was shooting for keg-belly. While they probably wouldn't physically be a problem for Teren—he was pretty strong and dang fast, after all—he wouldn't get out of the bar without causing quite a commotion. But I quickly pushed that thought aside. My sister's reaction would be quiet and contained. She wasn't one to bring unnecessary attention to herself. And if I was alive and well after so much intimate time with Teren, then he obviously wasn't *that* dangerous.

With Ashley intently watching Teren, he seemed unsure how to tell her. He looked over at me and shrugged in an inquiring way. I puckered my lips and thought about the best way to say it without sounding completely insane. There really wasn't one. "Just bluntly tell her?" I suggested.

He thought about that, then shook his head and smiled. "She'll just laugh." I grinned, remembering my initial reaction to the blunt way he'd told me. Ashley looked between us, confused. Teren sighed and leaned towards me. "I don't think she'll believe it unless she sees it."

I looked around the bar again. Aside from the waitress and the three large men, there were a handful of other customers, another waitress and the bartender. A few people were still staring at Ashley; those people quickly turned away when my gaze fell over them. I looked back to Teren. "Can you do that...here?" He had his back to the main part of the bar, but the bartender could still possibly see. He seemed busy pouring drinks and chatting with keg-belly man, though.

Teren took a quick glance around. "Yeah," he said when he faced us again.

My sister was finally tired of being in the dark, so to speak. "Do what? What are you guys talking about?"

Teren met her eyes and held her gaze; a very, very faint glow emanated from his eyes in the dim bar lights. His face was completely serious and I got those nervous butterflies again. "Ashley, I need to show you something. It will explain to you why I'm different...if you let yourself believe. I'm only going to do this once, so please pay close attention."

He slowly opened his mouth and her eyes automatically tracked the movement. What was left of her brows furrowed in confusion as she waited. Slowly, and with more control than I realized he possessed, he extended his fangs to her. The lengthening of his teeth to sharp and unnaturally long daggers was unmistakable. Watching him do it left no room for misinterpretation—he was vampire.

My sister's eyes widened to saucers. "Holy...crap..."

He immediately popped his fangs back up and closed his mouth. Cocking his head to the side, he studied her reaction. He looked as if he were waiting for her to toss her drink on him, or try to kill him. Ashley did neither.

Pointing at him, she turned back to me. "Seriously? Vampire?" I nodded and she broke into the widest grin her scars would allow. "That's so freakin' cool!"

She and I both started giggling as Teren shook his head at us. "What is it with you Taylor women?" he asked. We both laughed a little harder.

Ashley started in on the questions. She asked a lot of the same ones I did—how old are you, what can you do, do you live on blood? After she asked the blood question she blinked, and before he could answer, she said, "Wait…I watched you eat food?"

Now Teren and I glanced at each other and started laughing. In hushed tones, Teren proceeded to explain his condition to her. He left out exactly what he had left out the first time he'd told me his secret—that he was dying and that his family had certain…expectations before he died. Watching Ashley shake her head in disbelief while trying to absorb everything he was telling her, I understood better why he'd left that stuff out on the first go round with me. It was a lot to take in all at once. He was right, segments *were* better.

While Ashley was laughing over the fact that he had a dog named Spike, a couple of guys walked near our table and sat at the bar. They were the sort of guys who looked like they believed they were Pharaohs, and everyone should really be kneeling at their feet. They seemed in a perpetual bad mood that everyone wasn't. They took one look at my sister and one of them muttered "freak." I was just about to rip the gonads off that one, when from beside me I heard a low, animalistic growl. It was impossibly deep and absolutely terrifying. The hairs on the back of my neck stood straight out. I stared at Teren in shock—the noise had come from him.

He snapped his head around to the men. "Apologize," he seethed. I don't know if it was his faintly glowing eyes, the deadly intent in his voice, or the otherworldly growl emanating from his chest, but the guys immediately sputtered "sorry," and took off to the other side of the bar. Maybe, like most bullies, they were just completely chicken when confronted by a true threat. And from what I had seen and heard from Teren just now, he was definitely a true threat. Maybe I'd have to rethink my opinion of him not being dangerous.

Teren spun his head back around to us; he looked pale and unsure of himself. I was about to ask him if he was okay when Ashley touched his arm. He started, but Ash was too excited to notice. "That was the coolest thing I've ever seen! I wish you could have bared your teeth, that would have been just amazing, but I know you can't expose yourself like that." She patted his arm, like he was an obedient puppy that had just defended its master. "Thank you, Teren."

Ashley gave him a friendly smile. Finally seeming to be more like himself, Teren returned her smile and held her hand. "Don't mention it." From the faint tightness around his eyes, I kind of got the feeling he meant that literally.

We finished our drinks with no further provocations, although the men seemed to be gathering up their courage on the other side of the bar; they were eyeing Teren with a *We can take him* attitude. Not feeling the need to risk a confrontation, that would most certainly end with Teren displaying one of his many extra attributes, we paid our waitress and headed back to the car. I looked back at the creeps and noticed that they were bumping fists and laughing with each other, like they had just successfully evicted us from the bar. Idiots. They had no clue how lucky they were that Teren had no desire to actually fight them. They'd probably pee their pants if he did bare his teeth at them.

Once we were in the car and zooming to my Mom's house, Ashley examined Teren in the front seat. Looking over her shoulder to me in the back seat, she asked, "Is him being a vampire why you broke up?" She nodded her half bald head at Teren as she spoke.

I cringed, not sure how to answer that. I suppose, in the very simplest of terms, that had been the reason behind our temporary split. "Yeah…kind of."

Ashley shook her head at me, her expression disapproving. "That surprises me, Emma." She half-grinned. "Especially with your Brad Pitt as a vampire obsession."

I gaped at her and flicked her on the shoulder. "Shut up."

Teren started laughing. He eyed me in the rearview mirror, not even bothering to contain his chuckles. "Not into Anne Rice, huh?"

Frowning, I flicked him on the shoulder. "You shut up, too."

Teren and Ashley laughed and shared a companionable look. They talked with each other on the ride home, about Teren's work, about Ashley's schooling, and I smiled as I watched them. The few other guys I had introduced to my sister hadn't taken to her nearly as readily as Teren had. I supposed, just like Ash, he wasn't one to question someone else's differences. Lord knows he wasn't one hundred percent normal. And I'd definitely never had a boyfriend who had growled in her defense before. Seemed he was as protective of her as I was.

In Mom's driveway, Ash politely asked Teren, "Can I see them again?"

Teren shifted uncomfortably and looked down. I interceded on his behalf. "He really doesn't like doing it on command...it makes him self-conscious."

My sister completely understood feeling self-conscious and let it drop. She glanced at me, then back to him. "Thank you for inviting me out again."

She opened her door and I opened mine to take her spot. Teren looked like he wanted to walk her to her door, but I gave him a "just a minute" motion with my finger. He nodded and I stepped away from the car with Ashley. I grabbed her hand as I walked with her to the front porch. "Ash, you can't say anything to Mom...or anyone else. No one can know. We're trusting you with this."

She gave me a hug at the door. "I know, Emma. I knew how serious it was the moment he showed me. I wouldn't say anything. I won't...ever."

I gave her a kiss on the cheek. "Thank you. I knew you'd understand."

She nodded and then bit her lip. As I turned to leave, she grabbed my arm and pulled me close. With a flick at Teren, she said in a low voice, "Be careful, Emma. He might care for you, but he is still...dangerous."

I put my hand on her arm. "He's not dangerous to me. I'll be fine. I'll be safer with him than anyone else." I kissed her again and then turned back to the car as she went inside the house. Teren was smiling with his head down as I got back in the car. I realized that he'd just heard that entire conversation. "You need to work on that eavesdropping thing…you and your whole family."

He laughed. "Sorry…I'll work on that." He grinned over at me. "You're very sweet."

I laughed, too. "Just don't make me a liar."

"Deal." He restarted the car and drove me back home.

Sitting beside him, I watched his pale eyes study the road. I thought back to our time in the bar. I thought back to his reaction to those jerks. That was a side of Teren I'd never seen before. That was definitely a more vampiric side. I wondered if that side would be more prominent when he changed over. I silently watched him until he pulled up to my driveway and shut the car off. Then I turned to face him. "Did you really growl back there in the bar?"

Embarrassment washed over his face. "Yeah…I think I did." He stared at the steering wheel as he shook his head. "That was…unexpected."

I put a hand on his arm and he raised his eyes to my face. "You must really like my sister."

He smiled. "I do. I feel very…kindred to her. The instinct to protect her was very…intense."

I smiled too and ran a hand along his stubbly jaw. "Would you like to come inside? You can protect me?"

His eyes flicked down my body and then returned to mine, a touch unfocused. "I'd love to."

He woke way before me the next morning, leaving me a rose on my pillow with a note explaining that he'd had to run home to get ready for work. I wondered briefly where in the world he'd gotten a rose at this hour, but then decided that he probably could have run just about anywhere to pick one and been back in plenty of time. Definitely an ability I was jealous of. I wondered why he didn't just flick home, grab clothes and flick back, but maybe he'd just wanted to be romantic with the whole rose on the pillow and not a trace of the man thing. I inhaled the red petals and smiled—it worked, he had me.

Later during my day, an idea started forming in my brain while I was preparing a tax file for one of the firm's newest clients. The firm had several movie stars, recording artists, authors, internet startup millionaires, computer software entrepreneurs and foreign businessmen as clients. The firm was quickly working its way up to rival the "Big 6." Being Mr. Peterson's assistant gave you the opportunity to sit in on some of the meetings with these interesting people. Once again, being his assistant's assistant did not. The particular client that I was working on had developed a dating website that Google had purchased and planned on adding to their enterprise. The man was rolling in the dough now. I barely noticed the staggering numbers on his financial statements as this pesky little idea flicked into life.

I tried to push it back. It wasn't feasible. It wasn't appropriate, and on some levels it was downright scary, but the idea wouldn't leave me and the more I considered it, the more my heart started beating in excited expectation. I could at least talk to Teren about it. No harm in discussing an idea…crazy as that idea may be. I considered the pros and cons for the rest of my day. I considered the consequences as I punched my way through kickboxing, sans Tracey who skipped out to see a movie with Hot Ben. I rethought every tiny detail as I showered and took my time getting ready for my dinner date with Teren.

He met me at my car as I pulled into his drive. He had a half-smile on his lips and his hands shoved in his pockets, and I thought he looked like a very content, and incredibly handsome, normal man. That only firmed up the idea swimming in my head. He opened my door, as the never-ending gentleman he was, and extended his hand to help me out. I smiled and took it, letting him sweep me all the way up to his lips for a tender kiss.

"Hi," he muttered.

"Hi," I muttered back.

I pulled aside as he moved me out of the way and shut my

door. We walked to his front door hand in hand and I leaned my head on his shoulder as I plotted how to best bring up my admittedly crazy idea. I set my purse down on the table as we walked through the formal dining room, that now looked small and cozy in comparison to his parents' place. Entering his now quaint kitchen, I glanced at the oven, where something deliriously delicious was cooking away.

He dropped our hands and poured us each a glass of deep red wine. It made me smile that my vampire enjoyed the dark stuff. I tried to not think about the other glass of dark stuff he'd so thoroughly enjoyed at the ranch. To each his own. Who was I to admonish him for something I'd never even tried? I'd heard there were tribes in Africa that drank cow's blood for survival, so it wasn't purely a vampire thing. Maybe *I* was the one missing out on a scrumptious treat and I didn't even realize it. That thought made my stomach a little queasy, though. Baby steps.

He started to pull us towards the living room, maybe so we could enjoy our wine on his lovely shaded patio. The beginnings of my question slipped out of my mouth, just as I let his hand slip out of my fingers.

"Does being turned heal you of everything?"

Teren frowned at me for a second and then nodded as he understood my question. "Yes. When someone is changed into a vampire, all of their human injuries are healed, and they heal fast afterwards." Smiling, he leaned back against the counter. "I heard about this one newborn that ripped off her creator's arm after she discovered that her numerous piercings had closed. I guess he failed to mention that would happen." He laughed and took a sip of his wine while I absorbed that.

"What happened to him?"

He shrugged in a casual, nonchalant way. "Well, I guess if she didn't reattach the arm before the wound healed itself, then there's probably a one-armed vampire running around out there." He grinned. "Probably pretty pissed off, too." My expression must have been one of disbelief, because he chuckled and said, "It's just a story you hear, it's probably not even true."

Oh, cautionary vampire tales…nice to know they had those. "But the healing thing…that's true?"

He nodded and took another sip of his wine. "Yeah…why?"

I didn't answer him. Looking back on this moment, I probably should have answered him. But I was so sure of my hypothesis, and just so insanely curious, that I did something rather foolish to a soon to be irate vampire. In a casual manner, I set down my glass of wine. He charmingly tilted his head in curiosity. I picked up the slicing knife lying on the counter, the one that he had used to prepare our dinner, and before giving it a much needed second of thought, ran the blade over his knuckle.

His eyes widened as he too late realized what I was doing. He started to jerk his hand away which ended up making the cut much bigger than I'd intended. I had really just planned on a tiny, itty-bitty scratch…but what I got was a deep, welling cut across his finger. He dropped his wine glass, but lightning-quick grabbed it with his other hand before it hit the floor. He couldn't save all the wine however, and a large amount spilled over the edge of the glass and splashed ominously onto the kitchen tile. The blood on his finger oozed deep red and started dripping back towards his hand. He immediately put it in his mouth. Setting down his glass and sucking on his knuckle, his eyes burned holes into me as I froze, realizing what I had just stupidly done, to a potentially very dangerous person.

"What the hell was that!" he yelled at me, taking his finger out of his mouth for a moment. I could clearly see that it was still bleeding, and his fangs had extended at the taste of blood, even his own.

I immediately tossed the knife on the counter and backed up a step, wondering if I was quite possibly the dumbest person on the planet. "I'm so very, very sorry. Please don't be mad."

He shook his head and removed his finger again. "You're sorry? You sliced me open. Are you sure you're not nuts?" His tone had calmed and his expression shifted to concern, like I was now some threat that the big, bad vampire had to be scared of.

That look and the tone of his voice made me relax and step towards him. I let out a tiny laugh. "I'm sorry. I just wanted to see the super-healing thing."

I came up and put a hand on his arm, trying to pull his finger out of his mouth to look at it, but he stubbornly pulled away. His brow drew down to a point. "Emma..." He pulled his finger out and I could see fresh blood welling; guilt washed through me. I hadn't meant to hurt him. "I keep telling you, I'm mostly human right now. I won't heal like that, until I've changed over. Once I'm dead, you can slice me open all you like." He put his finger back in his mouth.

I bit my lip and put my head on his chest, genuinely feeling awful, but a little entertained by his comment and the annoyance on his face. Remorseful, I murmured, "I'm sorry, honey...I keep forgetting."

Teren sighed and put an arm around me. "I wish you'd remember. That really frickin' hurt."

The sulking tone to his voice was too much, and I burst into giggles. I looked up into his not-amused face and tried to kiss him, but he pulled away. Sighing and shaking his head, he started heading towards the living room.

"Where are you going?"

He turned and showed me the finger that was still oozing a little. "I'm going to get a Band-Aid, thank you very much." I bit my lip again and tried to stop laughing at the image of my fanged, vampire boyfriend needing to put a bandage on his boo-boo. It was too entertaining of a thought though, and I was still giggling as he left the room, shaking his head.

Once my laughter subsided, guilt overwhelmed me. Sighing, I grabbed a towel and bent down to clean up the blood-red splash of wine on the once pristine ground. It took some elbow grease, and some seltzer, but I eventually got the stain out and tossed the towel into the sink.

I followed where my sulking vampire had disappeared to, and heard him still rummaging around for an elusive bandage in the hall bathroom. I stopped in the door and watched him eventually find a box of them in the very back of the largest drawer. He was still sucking on his finger, a little more enthusiastically than a regular guy would, as he opened the box and pulled one out. He tried to unwrap it with one hand and chuckling, I walked over and took it from him. Pulling his finger out of his mouth, I prepared the special "H" bandage used solely for knuckle cuts and tenderly placed it on his skin. His fangs retracted as he silently watched me. Once he was all wrapped up, I gently kissed his finger, and his wounded look eventually turned into a loving one. Just as he was about to lean over and kiss me, I blurted out the real thought that had been bouncing around my head all day.

"Turn Ashley."

He froze, millimeters from my lips, and pulled back to stare at me. By the look on his face, you would think I had just asked him to stake himself. "What?"

I searched his eyes as I almost frantically repeated, "Turn her. Make her a vampire. She'd be healed, Teren...completely healed!"

He backed out of the bathroom with a sickened look on his face, like any minute he was going to lose his lunch right on his shoes. "No, Emma..."

I followed him with furrowed brows. "Why not?"

He shook his head as he backed into the living room. "You know how they're created. I'm not draining a human."

I grabbed his arm to stop him from moving away from me. He glanced down at my hand and seemed as if he wanted to smack me away. He didn't though. He just continued to stare at me, his body rigid with tension.

"Teren? You wouldn't be killing her. You'd be giving her a new life...a better one."

Now he did smack my hand away. He turned and strode over to the glass wall of windows. I watched the last rays of the sun flash on his skin as he rested his hands on his hips. I knew I'd messed up this talk on so many levels, but we were in the thick of it now. I timidly walked over to him, but didn't touch him again. Finally, he twisted his head to talk over his shoulder.

"You don't know what you're saying, Emma." He sighed. "I don't even know if it would work anyway," he finished quietly.

"Why wouldn't it...?"

His voice picked up heat as he turned his chest to me. "I keep telling you—I'm not a full vampire. I don't know if my blood is enough to change her."

At his tone, I stubbornly set my chin. "It's worth a try. What's the worst that could happen?"

He turned all the way around to face me. "She could die! My blood could do absolutely nothing and she would die, Emma. Permanently!"

I swallowed as I considered that possibility. It was one I hadn't thought of before. "Maybe Halina could—"

He cut me off. "No, she won't."

"But...she'd be normal. She'd be happy..."

Teren took a step towards me and placed his hands on my arms. Squatting down, he searched my eyes. "She *is* happy...don't you see that?"

I brushed him off and stubbornly shook my head as I crossed my arms over my chest. "She wouldn't be looked at like a monster."

He threw his hands up and laughed once; there was no humor in it. He started pacing the center of the room. "No, she would actually be one."

I stood in front of him to stop his movement. I placed my hands over his arms this time and looking down at me, he clenched his jaw. "You don't believe that. I know you don't," I stated. He shook his head and looked away from me. I thought again of the image of my sister healed and fresh and fast and strong. Tears stung my eyes at the thought of what her life could be, if she didn't have to put up with the whispering, teasing and constant staring. I squeezed his arms. "Please...think of what she'd be gaining."

He brought his eyes back to mine and his body relaxed when he noticed my tears. His voice relaxed as well. "Think of what she'd be losing, Em. She wouldn't be like me. She'd be one hundred percent vampire, like Great-Gran. She'd have to quit school and her dream of being a nurse. She'd have to hide during the day and she'd be…"

"She'd be free of the scars she's had since she was a little girl. Her constant reminder of what Dad sacrificed for her." There was a begging note to my voice and I tried to blink the tears back inside my body, but one escaped me.

He tenderly stroked it off my cheek with his thumb. "She's dealt with all of that for a long time, Emma."

"Because we didn't know of this option…"

"Vampirism isn't an option." His tone stated that as a fact and his voice hardened back up. A part of me got really ruffled. It was easy to say something wasn't an option, when you were swimming in that option. I was pretty certain that his views would be different if he had to look at things through Ashley's eyes—if he'd suffered the numerous painful surgeries, if he'd been brought to tears countless times throughout puberty, when boys and girls were at their meanest, and if he still had to endure life without the simple, loving companionship of a mate, something most couples took for granted every day.

"Yes…yes it is an option! She'd be healed." I dropped my hands from his arms.

Teren narrowed his eyes at me. I could see anger swirling in the paleness and I wasn't quite sure why this topic pushed his buttons so much. With a still heated voice he told me, "She wants to help people. You want to turn her into something that hunts people."

I had a little trouble spitting out my reply to that comment. "Your family doesn't. You could help her. She wouldn't…she would never hurt anyone. Just like you and the others."

"That's not true."

"What?"

Never removing his eyes from mine, he calmly stated, "Some of us have killed."

I felt all the blood drain from my face and watched his eyes take in my sudden paleness. I was instantly assaulted with images of my sweet, gentlemanly boyfriend draining whores in a back alley. I wasn't sure why I automatically pictured trashy women in that scenario, but whatever the woman, the picture was turning my stomach. I had to sit down. It wasn't a voluntary decision, I just sort of dropped down. Luckily, I was close to the couch and most of my body made it down there safely.

"What?" I breathed the word.

He sat down close to me, but didn't touch me, maybe sensing that I would bolt from the room if he did. His voice softened, but it was still laced with anger. That only increased my unease.

"The instinct is there...always. We all ignore it for the most part and for Mom and me, that's a pretty easy thing to do. It's pretty diluted in the both of us." I started breathing again, as I realized that he had just cleared himself as a killer. My stomach tightened as he continued on with who *had* killed in his family. "Gran has caved on occasion. She's not proud of it and she won't talk about it, but she has taken a life before...a couple times before. Great-Gran is not so hesitant or remorseful."

My pale face surely paled even more, as he confirmed that the one vampire who kind of scared the life out of me was the one vampire who would be the most inclined to take it. Teren watched me closely as he continued. "True, she lives mainly on animal blood, but she gets...bored. Every so often, she'll run into the city, find a lone human, usually a male but not always...and drain him dry. I have no idea what she does with the bodies, but she's very discreet."

"Why are you telling me this?" I felt tears rise again as I studied his steel face. He could have been telling me tomorrow's weather for all the emotion that resided in his features.

"Because I want you to understand that vampires and mixed breeds are different...and if I do what you ask, she will be different. She won't be like me. I want you to understand what you are really asking, because I don't think that you do."

Still, my stubborn streak continued. "You're different...your blood could be different. Maybe she'd be a mixed breed too..."

Teren shook his head. "Even if that were true...and I don't think it works that way, she'd be miraculously healed. How would you explain that to your mother, to everyone?" His lips turned down as he considered things I had not. Things I didn't want to think about because they were inconvenient to my end result.

"I don't know, I don't care—"

"And it will hurt...there is no way around that. She will panic. She will scream and thrash about, trying to get away from me, a man you've convinced her to trust. Are you going to hold her down while I suck the very life from her?"

I clasped my hands together and stared at the pinkness of the blood in my fingertips as I squeezed them together. "Seven seconds isn't so long...it would be quick."

Running a hand through his hair, Teren sighed with irritation. "I said I've heard it can be done that fast—by experienced vampires, who routinely kill." I looked up as his narrowed eyes searched my face. He brought his hands to his chest. "I've never done it. I've never even bitten someone. What if I don't get the exact right spot, in the exact right artery?" He shook his head and his face seemed to pale at the very thought. "It's a lot of blood. What if I can't get it out fast enough? It could take a few minutes. Do you really want to put her through that?"

With a quiet voice, I stubbornly persisted, "If we prepared her..."

He turned his face away from me and his voice went ice cold. "This conversation is pointless. I will not drain a human."

"Not even for me?" I knew I shouldn't have said that...guilt trips were generally not my thing. I realized I was sounding like his desperate grandmother, trying to beg him to get me pregnant. Hmmm, I guess, in a different way, I was a little desperate too. I was starting to understand the older woman better...although, now that I knew she had killed before, I found her a lot less grandmotherly.

"Not even for me," he said in his cold, even voice.

I wasn't sure what he meant by that, but I could hear the heavy iron door swinging closed on this conversation, and I knew once it closed, it could never be reopened. "Teren..."

His face snapped back to mine. "It is not your decision to make. It is mine and it is Ashley's. You cannot condemn her to a life you don't fully understand, simply because you *think* it will make her happy."

"But…"

"I will not kill a human. Do not ask again."

He stood up and strode from the room. His hands were clenched into fists as he turned the corner and I clearly heard each angry footstep as he went upstairs. A few seconds later his door slammed shut and I sat and stared at my hands. I never in a million years would have imagined that the first time Teren got really angry with *me* would be over him refusing to turn my sister into a creature of the night. How vastly different my life had become, in such a short period of time.

Chapter 8 – First Taste

Eventually he cooled off and came back downstairs. We ignored the fight. We ate our dinner and made small talk for the rest of the night and never again brought up the subject of changing my sister. It was still in the back of my head and I'm pretty sure, at least for that night, it was in the back of his, but he never again mentioned it. His answer had been pretty clear anyway.

Aside from that disagreement, our relationship went pretty smoothly. We went for long walks through the park or on the beach. Sometimes we brought Spike with us and he'd frolic and play while we held hands. Sometimes we went alone, and we'd find a secluded spot and kiss under the setting sun, my vampire was a touch on the romantic side. We ate dinner on his patio or out at a small bistro that we both liked. He started favoring bloodier and bloodier meat, and I tried not to think about the reason for that.

We went on a double date with Tracey and Hot Ben, who both enjoyed Teren's company. It didn't take long for it to turn a regular thing. We started going out to dinner or out to a movie once a week, and Teren and Ben would chat about typical "guy" things— some sports game that was on recently, the hot girl in the movie we'd just watched, or fishing, which apparently Ben was also into, although I didn't think he caught them quite like Teren did. Tracey and I would giggle as we watched our two completely normal—well, seemingly normal anyway—boyfriends bond. I hoped she took longer than average to find Hot Ben's flaws; hanging out as a foursome was very enjoyable.

Teren joined my family and I for our weekly dinners, which made my mom and Ashley joyously happy, as they kind of adored him. Especially Ashley, who usually sat beside him, chatting animatedly about school or a movie and even once about a cute boy she liked. Teren glanced up at me when she was talking about that boy and I had to clench my stomach. His face was sympathetic, like he understood what I meant about wanting to give her another life, one where she'd have a shot with the cute boy, but his weak smile and small sigh clearly told me that his answer was still no. He wouldn't change her. I tried to accept that.

We avoided his parents' place, but he often called them, and occasionally I was present for those phone calls. They were thrilled that we were back together and they were very sorry for pushing our relationship. They always asked us to come back to the ranch, so they could make up for their poor behavior. Teren always told them that now wasn't the best time. A long pause on Teren's end of the conversation indicated a lengthy response on his mother's side. Sometimes he'd fire off a sentence or two in Russian, which always made me frown. I decided it was time for him to teach me, but he seemed reluctant to do so. He kept telling me, "It takes a long time to learn. Maybe next week, when I have more time to commit to it." That "next week" never came, though, and I had the sneaking suspicion that he liked being able to keep me in the dark when he chatted with his family.

Everything was going swimmingly with my otherworldly boyfriend, and I made myself ignore the fact that every day, we were edging closer to "the change." Every day Death's ugly head loomed just a little nearer. I might have been forcing my mind not to think about it, but I still laid my head on his chest and listened whenever I could. I cherished every day that his heart was still beating.

On the one month anniversary of his "coming out" to me (which also happened to be the first time we slept together, although, I'm pretty sure that wasn't what we were celebrating), he sent me calla lilies at work again. Clarice left them on my desk this time and frowned in disapproval. She still believed that Teren was trying to lure me away to be his private, personal assistant. I suppose I was his assistant, in a way, as I did occasionally pick up his dry cleaning, bring him Starbucks, and remind him of his monthly editor's meeting. I just wasn't getting paid for it.

When he did it again on the second month anniversary of his fanging me (I loved that phrase and said it often to Ashley, who was the only human woman in the world that I could talk about all of my boyfriend's oddities with), Clarice finally started piecing together that maybe he wasn't wooing me for a job…maybe he was just wooing me.

"Emma."

I slapped on a bright, fake smile. "Yes, Clarice?"

She pointed to my new arrangement of calla lilies, merrily perched on the very corner of my desk, bringing a little cheer to my square, gray world. "Those are from that Adams man again at Gate magazine."

I tried to not sigh or falter in my smile. "Yes. Yes they are."

She tried to purse her lips, but the tightness of her bun seemed to make that a physical impossibility and she gave up the attempt. "Are you dating him?"

I did let the sigh I had contained out of me. It came out in a happy, contented, lovesick sort of way that made even me a little nauseous. "Yes…we're dating. We have been for a few months."

She nodded like she had secretly suspected that from the very beginning. The corners of my mouth turned up. "Well, I see. Are you going to go work for him?" she asked with an almost bored tone.

I blinked, not expecting that question. She still thought he wanted me to work there? "No…no, I think that would be weird…dating my boss." Not to mention a little inappropriate.

She shrugged, her shapeless blouse lifting a bit on her plump belly, revealing a basic black belt that I hadn't even known she was wearing. For the briefest odd minute, I imagined that her underwear was the most utilitarian and un-frilly stuff that she could find—and I was sure it was "goes with everything" beige. I thought of the black, lacy number I was wearing under my tight skirt and thought we could not be more unlike each other. Her next comment, though, made me change my mind some.

"It wouldn't be the first time. How do you think I got this job?" She winked and I blanched, and immediately stopped wondering about her underwear. I also forcefully pushed back the image of one day catching her and Mr. Peterson in flagrante on his oversized cherry desk. Ugh…some things a person just did *not* need to know.

"Oh…well, I'm not. I'm staying here." *Where I'll never be able to look Mr. Peterson in the eye again, thank you.*

She nodded and a smile actually broke out on her lips. It faded instantly. "Well, good. I'd hate to lose you. You're the only one around here that seems to know what they're doing."

My pride soared. A compliment from Clarice was like finding a cable car without a photo-snapping tourist—it just never happened! I was pretty happy right then that Teren hadn't nibbled on her for me. She knocked me down a peg after that with a "kind of" retort before she walked away. I shrugged off the backhandedness of the compliment and let my pride soar all afternoon. It wasn't every day that you got to feel like you were actually good at something and your work was appreciated, maybe even more appreciated than the others. It made my day.

By five o'clock, I was practically glowing with positive energy. The world was my oyster and I was going to shuck it. Every cloud had a silver lining and every rainbow ended in a pot of gold, just for me. I was the Queen of this little land called San Francisco and all would bow before my brilliance and beauty. I sauntered into the parking lot, thinking I rocked this job, I rocked this outfit and I rocked my lacy, black under things.

It was at this very high point in my day, when the universe decided my ego had soared quite high enough and I needed to be brought down a smidge…or completely flattened. I tripped over an invisible boulder near the back of my car. That's the only explanation—it was invisible. There was no way I simply stumbled and fell for no apparent reason. I managed to save my body from getting too banged up, but a piece of glass on the pavement sliced open my knee and it was bleeding to the point where I would almost call it gushing. I loudly cursed and looked around with heated cheeks, but thankfully, I was alone.

I brushed off my dirty, scraped hands and clamped one over my poor, oozing knee. With the other, I retrieved my purse; it had fallen close by, and an assortment of various belongings inside of it had tumbled out. I shoved my pink cell phone, red lipstick and a silver, metallic makeup kit, back in the bag and then dug around for my keys. All too typically, those had survived the tumble, and were still buried in the bottom of my purse-abyss. Finally finding them, I hobbled to the back of my car and opened up the bulbous trunk.

I let go of my knee to open the spare tire compartment, where I stored a first aid kit. Mom had insisted that I keep one handy, and right now I was heartily thanking her for her foresight. A rivulet of blood trickled down my leg as I opened the panel and brought out the blue kit with the international "help me" red plus sign. I found a wet towelette and opened it, along with an extra-large Band-Aid. I quickly wiped off my hands and gritting my teeth, wiped off my bloody leg and my bloody knee, making sure no stray glass was in the wound. When I was done, I slapped on the bandage. It was still bleeding, but I could get to Teren's and inspect it further over there. I wanted to stop feeling like an idiot out in the parking lot, where a co-worker could come across me at any minute. Replacing the kit, I closed the trunk and lickety-split, hightailed it to Teren's house.

I didn't knock at his house anymore—I just quietly walked right in. I didn't really want to explain my embarrassing fall, so I stealthily snuck in, hoping to at least rinse off in the hall bathroom before he heard me. But I wasn't two steps into the room before he was standing right in front of me. As I slowly closed the door behind me, I watched him close his eyes, tilt his head to the side and draw in a deep inhale. A shudder passed through him and a second later, it passed through me. I was bleeding. The vampire in front of me clearly knew I was bleeding. As he exhaled and let his mouth fall open with a pleased noise, I felt like I had just been mentally devoured. His eyes opened as I set my purse down beside the door. They were slightly unfocused as he gazed at me.

"You're hurt," he whispered.

I sighed and told my clumsy story to him. His gaze shifted to my knee, to the smidge of blood still visible on my shin and the red stain visible through the bandage, as the wound continued to bleed. I watched his mouth fall open again and his breath increase as he stared at my wound. Guilt flashed through me. This was something he obviously wanted and, here I was, just letting a plastic coated piece of gauze soak it all up.

"Teren." His eyes snapped back up to mine. "Do you want the blood?"

He blinked and his eyes refocused. "No." His voice was weak with no conviction behind it, like it was a conditioned answer, and not the one he really wanted to be giving me.

Feeling bad for denying him an opportunity that I never let him have—my blood—I reached down and pulled off the bandage. A fresh trickle of red warmth flowed like a tiny river down my shin and he groaned as he intently watched it. "It's okay, Teren. I never let you bite me, but I'm already bleeding, so you may as well…"

Like he was in a trance, he walked up to me and sank to his knees. He ran his hands up the back of my calf and ravenously eyed the droplet. Watching his desire, I began to wonder just how much he downplayed wanting me, wanting my blood. His eyes darted to mine. "Are you sure?" he asked. His voice had a twinge of *God, please don't change your mind* to it.

Was I making a mistake by giving him even a small taste? He seemed to want it so much…how in control was he? Seven seconds rang in my head for a moment before I dismissed it—he had already shown he wasn't interested in taking a life, not even when I asked him to.

"Yes." The word was barely a whisper past my lips, but he heard me.

He bent down and ran his tongue along the expanding red trail. He made a deep noise in his throat, and looked up at me once he reached my knee. His fangs had slid out as my blood had touched his tongue. He bared his teeth to me for just a moment, and then he set his lips along my knee. I could feel the edges of his fangs against my skin, but he didn't bite, he only used his tongue and lips to sweep away the fresh blood. I smiled as I watched his enjoyment. I knew it would have looked really odd if anyone had been here to see him licking my knee like a human ice cream cone, but he was so content, sucking away while he massaged my calf with his strong hands. A big cat, kneading the carpet while enjoying a fresh bowl of cream.

After a long moment, he pulled back and I could see that the wound had closed and no more blood was oozing, just a faint, red line remained. He took the bandage from my hand, replaced it along my knee and then gazed up at me; the look on his face was pure rapture. "Thank you. You…are amazing."

I felt like the most beautiful, bloody-kneed girl in the world. Renewed guilt flooded through me. He had enjoyed that…more than a little. Here I was, with a surplus of something that he obviously ached for. What was a little pain, if it gave him such pleasure?

"Do you want some more?"

He answered automatically, his eyes closing in bliss. "Yes." Shaking his head, he opened his eyes and seemed to come out of it. "No…no I'm fine, thank you."

He started to stand, but I stopped him by putting my foot on his thigh. This brought my bare thigh inches from his face. He stared at it and froze. "Take a bite, Teren. A small one," I quickly amended. He shook his head, but his eyes never left my body. "It's all right. I want you to." He finally tore his eyes away to look up at me. I reached out and stroked his cheek as his eyes searched mine. "You said it would be intimate and you'd enjoy it and I want to give that to you. I love you." He seemed to be debating whether or not he should do this. He seemed to really want it and not want it at the same time. I ran a hand through his hair. "I trust you."

He opened his mouth and I swear his fangs got longer. He turned back to my leg and the hands that had been on my calf, ran up my thigh, pushing my skirt higher. I suddenly realized this might do more for me than I'd expected. He started inching towards me and my leg started shaking in anticipation.

Nervous energy shot through me, both at the erotic body part I'd offered him, and the fear of what was to come…pain. A part of me was also fighting the natural instinct to bolt away from a predator, instead of willfully letting one approach. But I trusted him, and he would never take more than my body could handle. He would never hurt me. Well, aside from the puncturing of the skin part, but there was just no way around that. I was hoping it was going to hurt less than the throbbing cut on my knee had.

His stubbly face rubbed against my skin and he let out a husky exhale. I found that I did too. His tongue brushed against my upper, inner thigh and all fear left me. I needed him to do this…now. I inhaled a deep breath and released it slowly. My exhale turned into a sharp gasp when his teeth sank into my flesh. It hurt, but nowhere near what I'd been expecting. He hadn't bitten deeply, and the sensation was almost immediately replaced by the warmth of his tongue and his lips. He made a primal, satisfied noise deep in his chest, as his hands worked at my thigh. I waited to feel the warmth of blood seeping down my leg, like they showed in every vampire film I'd ever seen, but Teren didn't let one drop of my liquid gold escape his lips. He was ravishing me...he truly was devouring me. And the noises he made, combined with his hands on my leg and the warmth of his tongue on my bare skin did amazing things to my body. I grabbed his hair and, with a groan of my own, pulled him tighter to me. He obligingly bit deeper and I gasped again, but not with pain this time.

I heard him swallow a few times and wondered how much he was taking. I knew he'd stop though. I felt no fear, just curiosity. His hands started moving down my thigh and his lips pulled away until only his tongue remained, licking the twin holes until the bleeding stopped. I felt a little rubbed raw...and completely unsatisfied. Damn if I hadn't liked it as much as he'd predicted.

He looked up at me and his eyes were faintly glowing, even with the daylight streaming into the room. Looking completely satiated, he smiled in drunken satisfaction. I carefully sank down to my knees and pushed him back, so we were both lying on the floor of his entryway; we were both a little breathless. His fangs were still out and I could see my blood on his tongue. I couldn't have cared less. I thoroughly kissed him, and then made him satiate me.

At least an hour later, we were both lying in his bed, happy and satisfied. My thigh ached a little, and I was pretty sure I'd be bruised a bit around the circular wounds, but I didn't care about that either. His biting me had been the most intimate thing I'd ever experienced with a man—human or vampire. I sighed in contentment.

Snuggling tight to me, he kissed my head. "See...I told you, you might like it."

I looked up at him. "Yeah...well, that doesn't mean you get to just bite me all willy-nilly. I don't want to look like some junky, with track marks all up and down my body."

He chuckled and leaned over to kiss my ear. "I can be discreet," he whispered.

I sat up on my elbow and looked down on him. My brown

hair swept across my bare shoulder. He grabbed a strand and brushed it back behind my ear. "You enjoyed that a lot more than I expected," I said. Averting his eyes, he bit his lip. He almost looked worried. I brought his chin back around to face me. "It's okay. It's a part of who you are. It just surprised me, that's all."

Sighing, he looked over my face. "It surprised me too," he said quietly. He sat up in bed and I sat all the way up with him. He brought his knees up under the sheets and laced his arms over the top of them. Closing his magnificent eyes, he sighed again. "The desire is getting stronger in me. I'm starting to crave it…and…" He stopped talking and opened his eyes. He warily watched me, but didn't say anything. I could tell he didn't want to tell me whatever he was thinking about.

I put a hand on his arm. "What is it?"

He looked past me, at the far wall. "I'm starting to notice people, notice you."

"What do you mean?"

He returned his eyes to mine. He tried to smile, but failed and shook his head instead. "I notice your heartbeat, the pulse of your veins…the smell of blood on you." He looked down at his knees. "I was working in my office when you came in. I heard your car in the drive, but I wanted to finish the article I was doing…" He looked back up. "But when you opened the door and the smell of fresh blood hit me…I was downstairs before I even realized it. I couldn't stop myself, and I couldn't control rushing down…to be near it."

I swallowed. He had appeared almost instantly the moment I'd walked into the house. He had smelled me…from upstairs? I asked a question I didn't really want an answer to, but I needed to know the level of danger I was in being around him. "Did you want to attack me? Take it from me?"

He tried to look away again, but I grabbed his cheek and made him hold my gaze. There was clear guilt on his face and I knew the answer before he even opened his mouth. "Yes. For a fraction of a fraction of a second…I wanted to rip your throat out." I dropped my hand from his face as he admitted to the intensity with which he had wanted my blood. I had never anticipated those kinds of thoughts being in his head. Wanting a nibble was one thing, wanting to bathe in my blood as he destroyed my jugular, was quite another. His guilty look increased as he studied my stricken face. "Emma…I've never felt that before—ever. It scared me." He whispered that last part and looked at the sheets.

I composed myself, and tried to imagine the guilt and remorse he must be feeling at the horrific thought that had entered his brain. But it was only a split-second thought. He hadn't done anything that I hadn't willingly offered to him. I grabbed his chin again and gave him a light kiss. "You didn't, Teren. You didn't do anything wrong." I twisted my lips in amusement, as he watched me with sad eyes. "I practically had to gift wrap my thigh for you."

Shaking his head, he grabbed my hand and held it in his. "I still thought it. And I've never thought that way before. I've never seen people purely as…food." He looked down at our entwined fingers. "I'm worried that after the change… Maybe I'm wrong…maybe I'll be…"

I stopped his crazy train of thought. "No." He looked up at the conviction in my voice. "You won't, Teren. Not you. Today just took you by surprise, that's all. Once you get used to the new desires…you'll be fine. And you can taste me, if you really need it. Okay?"

He nodded briefly. His arms slid around me; one hand trailed down my body to my thigh. He brushed the red dots there with the back of his knuckle. "Did I hurt you very much?" His voice was soft and husky, as his eyes followed the motion of his finger under the sheets.

I grabbed his cheek and kissed him. "No…of course not. I barely felt it." After the initial prick anyway.

He tilted his head as he looked at me in adoration. "I love you."

I smiled as I wrapped my arms around him. "I love you, too. I must, I've never let anyone bite my thigh before." Chuckling, he pulled us both back down to the pillows.

He didn't bite me again for a while. I kind of thought it would get all tangled up with sex, and he'd take a draw every time we were intimate, but he didn't. He claimed I needed time to recuperate between feedings, but I got the feeling he just didn't want to get used to it, like I was some special treat that he only got on occasion. Call me crazy, but that made me feel kind of worshipped.

When he did bite me again, a couple weeks later, it was nearly euphoric. We'd been enjoying a bright afternoon, lying in the sun on the second story balcony. I was in my red "bite me" bikini and, needing a drink, I'd excused myself and slipped back into the house. As I was walking along the bookcase lined hallway that overlooked the living room, he had come up behind me with that blinding speed of his, and slipped his arms around me. He had me lying across the suddenly cleared off desk in his office in three seconds. Both of us breathing heavier, he ran his teeth along my outer hip all the way to the inside of my still-virgin thigh. I may have asked him to bite me. Frankly, I may have begged him to do it. He sank his teeth in and took a few long draws, while I marveled at the fact that I actually enjoyed it.

The holes weren't bad. It kind of looked like I'd tried a barbell piercing in my thigh, changed my mind, and took it out. By the time he'd taken the second bite, the first one had completely healed. Well, near completely. Two tiny specks remained that no one else would think twice about, not that many people were staring at my inner thigh. But the thrill of the memory gave me a rush whenever I peeked at them. With my aversion to pain, I'd never have suspected that biting would be a fetish of mine. Good thing I ended up with a vampire, I guess.

I confided my secret love to Ashley a few days later, when we met for lunch during my break at work. "Really…you let him bite you?" She seemed pretty taken aback by that, and I wasn't sure if the idea weirded her out, or if she knew me so well she was surprised I'd allow such a thing. Probably the latter.

"Yeah…I kinda like it." Okay, I really, really like it, but no need to creep her out, if she wasn't already.

Ashley shrugged. "Not something I'd peg you for, but all right." She took a sip of her soda and then eyed me critically. "You're being careful about it?" I scrunched my brows, confused. She sighed. "Emma...he's a..." She looked around at the semi-crowded diner, and at the couple of people staring at her, and she didn't finish her statement. Instead she said, "You're kind of playing with fire, if you know what I mean."

I cringed at her choice of words, but I did understand what she meant. She was worried about him losing control and killing me. Not something every sister has to worry about.

"He would never harm me, Ash. He wouldn't even do it at all, if I didn't ask him to, and he barely..." I looked around as well and lowered my already soft voice. "He barely takes any when he does it. No need to worry about me."

Ashley sighed but nodded as she took another sip of her drink. I thought again of my horrid conversation/fight with Teren about changing her. I wondered if I should tell Ash about it. Should I even bring up the idea, if Teren was so dead set against it, if it wasn't really an option? Should I give her that hope, if there was none? Although, Teren was not the only vampire-mix that I knew of... I stopped that thought right in its track. The surest way to end our relationship would be to have another member of his family turn Ashley behind his back. No, if it was going to happen...he had to be the one to do it, or at least okay it.

To get my mind off of what I really wanted to talk to her about, I mentioned the other thing that had been getting bigger and bigger in my head every day. "Teren's family wants us to have a baby...and I'm thinking about doing it."

She spat up her drink and started coughing. "Are you crazy, Emma?" She coughed some more and wiped her mouth. "You've been together what, three, four months now? Are you going to marry him? Can vamp...can he even have children?"

I waited until her coughing eased before I answered. I didn't know how to say this...she didn't know he was dying. Teren's blunt way was too harsh, too final sounding. I needed a gentler way. "Well, I don't know about the marriage part yet, but...because of what he is, he only has a few more months where he can make a child. After that, he'll be essentially sterile. We can't risk the exposure of going to a fertility clinic, so, if we're going to..." I shrugged.

Her patchwork face turned sympathetic. "Wow…so you really have to decide your whole future now, or you'll lose it forever, won't you?" She put a hand on my arm. "You could always adopt later, Emma."

Fanged, black-haired children danced in my brain while I thought about that. "It's not that simple…and the family really wants to keep the line alive." I gave her a pointed look. "Their lineage is special."

She nodded and sat back in her chair, her scarred hand rubbing her lip. "You're right…it's not that simple."

I smiled weakly and shrugged again. "What do I do? It may already be too late. It can take a while to get pregnant, and I've been on pills…we don't have the luxury of time."

Ashley dropped her hand to her lap as she thought. "I don't know. But if you do decide to get pregnant, it should be because the both of you want a child, not to please his family or keep his heritage alive."

I nodded and found myself dabbing sudden tears from the corner of my eyes. Interesting…was I crying over the idea of having his child, or the idea of *never* having his child? I found myself thinking about those tears all throughout my day. And you know how sometimes when you're dwelling on something, everything around you suddenly relates to the thing you're dwelling on? That was my day.

Everywhere I looked while I drove back to work, I saw mothers pushing strollers. Then Tracey told me about Hot Ben's sixteen-year-old cousin that just got knocked up; she was still claiming she was a virgin. Likely story that. Every other cubicle I passed as I left work had a baby picture prominently displayed in it. Some man in the lobby was congratulating another man, whose wife had just given birth to a healthy, happy eight-pound baby boy. I passed not one, not two, but three cars with those yellow "Baby on Board" signs. And lastly, on the drive back home, I saw a black-haired, pale-eyed little boy playing at the park. He so easily could have been Teren's, that I almost stopped the car to ask the mother who the father was. I think my biological clock started ticking on that drive home.

Teren picked me up a couple of hours later to go see a movie with Tracey and Ben. I considered what to say to him on the way to the theater. I settled for silence, because I still wasn't sure exactly what I was feeling. A pregnant woman in line behind us made me sigh in annoyance. Maybe thinking I was lonely, Teren grabbed my hand, and pulled me tight to him. I wasn't sure exactly what I was, but I was definitely something.

Tracey and Hot Ben sat in the row in front of us, holding hands and occasionally kissing each other. I sighed again, and not because my boyfriend wasn't equally attentive, he was, he was currently kissing my neck, but I think I sighed because of the endless amount of time Tracey had to consider her future with Ben. I felt my future tightening around me every minute.

We watched the movie with our hands clasped together, and during a birthing scene—of course—I searched Teren's face. His eyes were infinitesimally glowing in the dim light of the theater, but he was just casually watching the screen. If he was having any thoughts on what he was seeing, that he was maybe correlating to his own life, I wasn't seeing that debate in his features. Eventually, he noticed my attention, and he turned to smile at me. I smiled back, gave him a light kiss, and laid my head on his shoulder, determined to make it through the damn movie without that clock vibrating my entire body.

I tried to change the direction of my thoughts on the way home, by talking about my day. "I had lunch with Ashley today."

Teren glanced over at me with the corner of his eye, and I was clearly getting the *Don't bring up changing her* vibe, as he softly said, "Oh...yeah."

I bit back the frustration; that heavy, barred, steel-bolted, locked door was never going to be reopened. He just wouldn't even discuss turning Ashley again, and I knew better than to bring it up. Well, I knew better than to directly bring it up. "I'm not trying to start anything...but...why wouldn't Halina change Ashley? Not that I'd ask her to," I quickly tossed out, when I noticed his glance had turned into a full on glare. "I would just like to understand."

His expression softened as he gazed at me a moment, then he turned his attention back to the road. "Great-Gran never asked for this life. It changed everything for her. Her husband, a normal existence for her daughter…never being able to see the sun again. She misses that…everyday." He returned his eyes to me; they were full of compassion. "She won't bring another person into her torment. She just…won't."

We passed the street before mine, and I noticed a pair of new parents, beaming as they opened the front door of their house—a car seat was carefully cradled between their arms. *Well, wasn't that peachy?* I just couldn't seem to get away from this today. "Then why do they want a child? Isn't that bringing another person into the life?"

He shook his head and gazed back to the road. "Being mixed is different than being full." He flicked a glance at me and shrugged. "Look at me. I enjoy nearly everything a human does—sun, silver, a regular job and a regular life." *Yeah, just a regular Joe…only with no more heartbeat in a few more months.*

Teren bit his lip and was very quiet as he pulled down my street, and into my drive. I could see that he was thinking of something he wanted to tell me, but either he didn't know how to say it, or he didn't know how I'd react to it.

"What?" I asked.

Turning the car off, he twisted in his seat to face me. "The day I told you…the day you saw my teeth, you made a comment that was…" he smiled warmly at me, "right on the money."

I scrunched my brows, trying to remember that conversation; a lot had been said and done that night. He explained when he saw my confusion. "You said that I should marry a full vampire and have a child with her, if I didn't want to dilute the line. Having a child with an undead vampire isn't actually possible, but…your theory is what my family is hoping for."

I tried to grasp what he was saying but I couldn't quite get there. Teren filled in the blanks for me. "They are hoping that one day, if we keep having children with humans…the vampirism will genetically fade out, and they'll be…"

"Human," I breathed, suddenly understanding.

He nodded, his expression serious. "Yes. They want our line

to be human again."

I stared at him with a blank expression that must have looked like confusion to him, but I suddenly knew exactly what I wanted. "I'll do it," I said calmly, no trace of indecision in my voice. Now he scrunched his face, confused. "I'll have your baby," I explained. "We'll try…anyway."

Teren immediately shook his head. "That's not why I told you. You don't have to…"

I grabbed his hand and held it with both of mine. "That's not why I want to. Well, it's not the only reason." A bright smile stretched across my face as I squeezed his hand. "I'm yours, forever, and I want this with you. I want a family with you." I searched his eyes, as I felt mine welling up. "I want to carry on your line, and I want to do it before it's too late."

His gaze softened as stared at me. "Have you been thinking about this a lot?"

"Yes…in the back of my mind." Remembering my day, I shook my head. "But today…I kept seeing signs everywhere and I don't know—it just feels like I'm supposed to do this, like *we're* supposed to do this."

His eyes narrowed as he studied my resolved expression. "Are you sure?"

"Yes," I firmly stated. He was still solemn and I frowned. "Don't you want to have a baby with me?"

He stared into my eyes for a long time without responding. I felt the entire world slip away as our gazes locked. Time stood still and for the moment, the only thing that mattered was this perfectly starry night, and my vampire and me beneath it, safe and secluded in his quiet car. And of course…his answer, which he finally gave me.

"Yes."

The next day I was giddy to tell someone about Teren's and my crazy plan to jumpstart our family. I was all smiles as I sat in my teeny cubicle and listened to Clarice boss me around. I wanted to shout at her, "Guess what? I just tossed out my birth control pills this morning!" I didn't, though.

I poked my head over the wall at Tracey once Clarice left, but Tracey looked glum so I didn't mention my pregnancy plan. She explained that last night, after the movie, she and Ben had gone out for drinks and he had told her that he loved her. Now, for most girls, hearing a really cute, sweet boy say those words, would be cause for celebration, but for Tracey…well, I could almost hear the funeral march on poor Hot Ben and his misguided heart.

I encouraged her that that was a good thing, and they would surely work out and have a great life together. Wasn't I peppy, optimism girl today? She nodded, said "sure," and then went back to staring at her computer, brooding. I knew that before the end of the day, she would have a list of reasons why he just wasn't right for her. They wouldn't make it to the weekend.

I exhaled a sad sigh as I sat back down. I had really enjoyed our little foursome. I suppose having a baby with my soon-to-be dead boyfriend, would have irrevocably changed the relationship anyway.

I held in my giddy excitement until after work when I cancelled dinner plans with Teren to go to Ashley's and tell her all about my future baby while Mom was out with some girlfriends. I suppose my choice was counterproductive to the actual making of a baby, but I was too excited to share my decision with someone and she, aside from being my best friend, was the only person in the world I could share the news with.

We sat on the living room floor with a half-gallon of peppermint ice cream and giggled over the idea of me being hugely pregnant with a vampire baby. Ash had kind of expected my decision after our lunch yesterday, so she wasn't too surprised at my announcement. And because she loved me, she kept whatever fear and doubt she must have had to herself, and she only showed me unconditional support. I loved my sister.

Mom eventually came back home from her evening with the girls and, laughing at the sight of us hunched over a container of ice cream, she grabbed a spoon of her own and sat in-between us. We switched to topics suitable for a parent in the room, and the three of us chatted, bonded and devoured *our* version of a tasty snack.

After leaving Mom and Ashley's, I drove straight to Teren's

place. I didn't even think about it, I just instinctually did it. Really, I was thinking about Ashley's reaction to my news and what I'd tell Mom in a few months when I did, hopefully, get pregnant. I had a feeling she'd take it pretty well, too. There was something about being a grandmother that brought out the acceptance in parents. Plus, she liked Teren, loved him, even. I still wasn't sure how to explain him to her…but I supposed I had years before she noticed that he never looked any older. With his camouflaging stubble and rugged good looks, he could pull off looking twenty-five for another decade, so I had plenty of time to think of an appropriate excuse.

Teren's lights were on as I pulled into his semi-circle drive. He greeted me at my car door, and his smile was loose and casual, like he didn't care at all that I'd cancelled our plans and then shown up afterwards anyway. He only looked happy that I was with him. He pulled me into his arms as I stepped out of the car and I dragged my wrist across his lips. "I've already had dessert…but do you want dessert?"

He crooked a smile at me in a way that was so incredibly attractive on him, and then he kissed my proffered body part and shook his head. "No, I'm fine, thank you."

I laced that wrist around his neck. "Shall we get right to the baby making then?"

Laughing, Teren scooped his arm under my knees and lifted me up. He swept me through his open front door, like a bride being ushered across the threshold by her new husband. Once inside, he closed the door with his foot and walked us upstairs to his room at an achingly slow, human pace.

With deliberate slowness, he laid me on the bed. My breath caught as he hovered over me. He was so handsome. A dim lamp in the corner of the room dulled the glow of his eyes, but not the love in them. He adored me, heart and soul, and I saw it every time he looked at me, felt it every time he touched me. I was his, and he was mine.

With practiced ease, he undressed me and I undressed him. When we were both bare, his eyes drifted over my body, like he was memorizing me. His fingers quickly followed his gaze, and every section of skin that he touched tingled with excitement. I wanted him. His hand rested on my stomach, where our future child would hopefully be growing soon. His expression was peaceful and hopeful, like he was wishing the same thing. Then his grin turned devilish, and his fingers traveled south. That did me in. I was more than ready, and I needed him now.

I grabbed his shoulders and pulled him over the top of me. As soon as he was lined up, he pushed into me. A satisfied groan escaped us once we were one; there was nothing in the world quite like the moment we joined together. Teren started to move, and I clawed at his back, his hips. I wanted more, but I also never wanted this feeling to end. Inevitably, it did end though. Breathless, hearts racing, we finished at the same time. The connection and closeness I felt when we cried out in unison was indescribable. He slumped against me to catch his breath, then rolled onto his back. I snuggled into the crook of his arm, happy, satisfied and deeply in love.

We hadn't been finished nearly five minutes, before I started giggling. I was pretty sure I knew the answer to my question, but in my excitement, I asked it anyway. "Do you think I'm pregnant now?" I let out a content sigh and laid my cheek on his heart-heavy chest.

He laughed deep within his body and ran a hand through my hair. "Patience…it will happen when it's supposed to."

Black-haired children filled my mind and I sighed again, a little less contentedly. "Time is the one thing we don't have a lot of, Teren." I pressed my ear to his chest and relished each steady thump. I was constantly surprised by how much I wanted his child. Maybe it was the fact that we only had a little over three months left, assuming that he didn't die before his birthday, of course, that had my desire for it kicked into overdrive.

Teren sighed with a sound that matched my own, and I wondered if he now wanted this as badly as I did, if my acceptance of it had kicked in his desire. If that were the case, I might be spending the next three months flat on my back in his bed. I smiled into his chest. I could think of worse ways to pass the time.

"I know, Emma," he whispered as he stroked my hair.

Thinking about time, brought my mind around to the inevitableness of mine ending. I wasn't sure about Teren, but I was sure about me. My life was finite. I wasn't sure if I wanted to know the question rolling around in my head, but curiosity drove it out of me. "Would our child be...immortal?" I looked up at his face, to see if he was going to laugh at me, but his pale eyes only regarded me with love.

He shrugged. "I don't know. We're not sure how long any of us mixed vampires will live."

I raised myself up to his elbows on his chest. "Oh...what about Halina?"

Then he did laugh. "I think Great-Gran will be around until someone stakes the old bat." He continued laughing, then shrugged. "As for the rest of us...there just aren't any others like us, so we have no idea." He showed me a one-sided smile. "We're all watching Gran very closely."

He winked and I laughed at him. "You're very odd."

"So I've been told." Smiling, he ran his hand back through my hair.

I swallowed at the look of immense love on his face. "Will you miss me when I've passed on?"

Without missing a beat, he shook his head. "No."

I smacked his shoulder and he laughed. "Thanks."

Still laughing, he grabbed hold of my hand before I could smack him again. "Okay, yes..." He grabbed both of my wrists and pulled me up on top of him. "I will wear black every day, incoherently muttering your name, as I shuffle through the meaningless existence of my bleak eternity."

I twisted my wrists to hold his hands, placing our laced fingers on either side of his head as I hovered above him. "Well, that's better."

He chuckled, then looked at me more seriously. "I don't think I'll have to suffer without you for long."

"Oh, why not?"

Using his super speed, he instantly rolled us over, so that I was beneath him and he was hovering above me. He grinned as he looked down on me. "I think I'll simply die of boredom without you around."

Pursing my lips, I pushed him off me. He lay on his side, propped up on his elbow, gazing down at me. "Well, assuming you make it through the boredom of my absence...would you live for hundreds, maybe thousands of years?"

He shrugged again, his muscles flexing with the movement. "It's possible...if we end up to be more like vampires in that sense then, yeah, we'll live until we can't stand another second of the monotony and we stake ourselves."

I frowned. "That's not something you should have to decide." He cocked his head and scrunched his brow, not following me. "Your death," I explained. "No one should have to choose when to die. It shouldn't be up to you."

He relaxed his features and gave me a wry smile. "It may not be. Vampires aren't universally loved. Some people have certain...prejudices. If we were ever discovered..." He shrugged again. "I could be staked tomorrow."

I sat up on my elbows. "What? You really think you'd be attacked by villagers with pitchforks?" He grinned, and I continued, "I don't think the culture is like that anymore." I shifted to my side and sat up on an elbow, so we were facing each other. "I think you'd be a rock star. You'd be the most famous person in the world. You'd have photographers tracking your every move, people lined up for miles to catch a glimpse of you, and girls everywhere, throwing themselves at you, begging to be bitten." I raised an eyebrow at that particular thought.

He raised his eyebrows right back at me. "That doesn't sound like much of a life. Well, the girls part wouldn't be so bad." I shoved his shoulder back and he leaned in to kiss me. "It wouldn't be quite so glamorous. Not everyone's a fan."

I shook my head and ran a hand down his jaw. "Well, either way, I'm sure you'll outlive me." I smirked and rested my hand on his heart. "I'll be a pile of dust before you know it."

He smirked back. "Thanks...I'm really trying to not think

about that."

I gazed at him for long, silent seconds, my heart swelling with love and sadness. "Protect our child and our child's child and that child's child. Live as long as you can," I seriously told him.

He cocked his head at me, his expression equally full of joy and pain. "Sometimes, I wish there was a way to make you just like me…"

I smiled and blinked back the tears. "But there isn't…and I don't want to be a full vampire, not that you'd change me any more than you'd change Ash." I kissed him and a tear escaped the very corner of my eye. "We'll just take each day as we're given it…okay?"

He nodded, and one small tear rolled down his cheek. I had to swallow several times to stop the urge to sob at seeing the love of my life so emotional over the thought of outliving me, grotesquely outliving me. I didn't know if I'd have the strength, if our roles were reversed. But, he'd have his family for support and hopefully, he'd have our child as well. I kissed him again, deeper than before, and he wrapped me in his arms, almost as if, by holding me tight, he could stop my all-too-soon finale.

Chapter 9 – Let's Try This Again

The Internet became my free time addiction. When Teren and I weren't actively trying to make a baby, I was doing research on how to conceive. We had the basics down, lots and lots of sex—check and check—but I searched out every tip and legend on how to improve my odds. I paid particularly close attention to the old wives' tales, since my boyfriend was sort of a walking folktale. I looked up dozens of medical sites, conception sites, pregnancy calendars, baby names (getting a little ahead of myself), and even various sites on fertility gods—we even sacrificed a chicken to one. Okay, Teren was just making us dinner and took his pre-meal libation, but I swiped a drop of blood from his mouth and made a swirly design on my stomach. Teren immediately licked it off, which led to a playful, baby-making romp on the kitchen floor, so really, I felt like it was successful.

We tried every tip there was. We tried the best recommended positions, and there were about five, since no one could seem to agree on it. We tried it first thing in the morning, the middle of the afternoon, and right before bed. For a while, we even tried the not moving afterwards for twenty minutes thing. Well, okay, there was no *we* involved with that one…just me. No, he got to go downstairs for a midnight snack, while I hung out, looking like an idiot with my legs up against the wall. Yeah, it was as lame as it sounds. I quickly gave up on that one.

I tried eating certain foods and avoiding others. I gave up my sweet, yummy afternoon coffee treats. I triple checked his underwear, making sure his clothes were…loose enough. Giggling like idiots, we even tried getting completely wasted and having sex in his car, in the driveway, of course. It worked for teenage girls everywhere, so I figured I'd give it a shot.

We were only slightly over two weeks into it and already Teren was having a great time. He told me on numerous occasions that we should have been trying to have a baby months ago. I rolled my eyes at that, but his comment did bring up some bad feelings. We'd never gone back to his parents' place since "The Weekend." We'd left so abruptly, and I still felt a bit guilty. There were plenty of back-and-forth conversations with his family though, and I apologized to his mother every chance I got. She always assured me that apologies weren't necessary, and that they were the ones who had been rude, but now that we actually *were* trying and we had every intention of giving them the heir they craved, I felt like it was the perfect time to go back.

Teren didn't seem quite so sure. Occasionally on the phone, I'd hear some foreign words being spouted, none too politely, and I'd place a flag in my brain to ask him what he was still arguing about with his mom. If they were bugging him about a baby, then he should just tell them that we were trying. I'd never heard him mention it, but it didn't have to be a secret, on his side of the family at least, so he could certainly tell them. In fact, he probably should, although, I liked the idea of telling them in person.

When he hung up the phone, and my question was on the very tip of my tongue, he would distract me with that darn capable mouth of his, and I would completely forget about both asking what they were discussing, and demanding that he teach me his secret language. But if I mentioned visiting again, he'd sigh and say, "It went so badly last time. Let's just wait until you're pregnant." I didn't mention that there was a large possibility that I'd never get pregnant. I wasn't entertaining negative thoughts—that was one of my conception tips. I wasn't sure how positive thinking correlated to my uterus, but I was trying to keep an open mind.

At work, I'd sneak onto websites when Clarice was busy with Mr. Peterson in his office. Thanks to her revelation on the nature of their relationship, I did *not* want to think about what they were doing in there. I was researching "Signs that you might be pregnant" (wishful thinking on my part) when Tracey popped her head up. I immediately snapped over to an Excel spreadsheet, but her eyes widened a bit—she'd seen.

"Oh my God! Are you...?" She pointed to my stomach.

I flushed all over and crossed my legs, resting my arms protectively over my stomach. "No, no, of course not. Have you heard from Ben?"

Her face fell immediately. After Hot Ben had made the mistake of professing his love for her, she had indeed come up with a list of reasons why the honeymoon was over. She broke his heart, dumping him cold. I hadn't seen or heard from him since. Tracey never talked about him, but in a move that I had never, ever seen from her before, she didn't talk about anyone else either. If I didn't know any better, I'd say she was mourning the loss of him.

My bringing him up evaporated the embarrassingly obvious website from her mind. With life draining from her face, she ruefully pouted, "No...he hasn't called or tried to come over. He didn't even send me flowers." Tracey was used to a little bit of "take me back" wooing after her guy-dumps. I think the fact that Ben had just seemed to disappear was unnerving her more than she'd anticipated.

"Well you did dump him, Trace."

"I know...but he said he loved me. Shouldn't he try? Shouldn't he fight for me?" She tilted her head and I could see tears—actual tears—forming. This was new.

"Tracey...do you love him?" Tracey usually never dwelled on dumped beaus, and she definitely never cried.

She instantly shook her head. "Of course not. Don't be silly." She dropped back down to her side of the wall and I thought I heard light crying over the rustle and bustle of office noises. Hmmm...very new. Maybe if Hot Ben did show up again, there was hope for them yet.

Since our weekly habit of going out with Tracey and Ben was now over, Teren and I had been going out with Ashley instead. She loved hanging out with us, and she always had a new vamp-related question for Teren. He answered every question patiently, and nothing was ever off-limits for my sister to ask. She never asked him about turning someone, like, maybe her, which I'll admit, saddened me some. A part of me was hoping that if she asked him directly, with no prompting from me, he wouldn't be able to resist her. I had no desire to become a dark-dwelling creature, but for Ashley...

That evening, we were getting ready for another fun filled outing with my sister. Teren was standing in front of the massive wall of windows in his living room, laughing on his cell phone with a co-worker who had given him four tickets to a Giants game tonight. Good baseball tickets in San Francisco were hard to come by, the stadium frequently sold out, and these seats were really, really good.

From what I could overhear of the conversation, his friend was leaving the tickets at will-call. Once he was off the phone, we were going to go pick up Ashley. Since we had an extra ticket, and Mom loved a good game, and a good stadium dog, she was coming with us. We were going to spend this beautiful summer evening watching an all-American game with an all-American vampire.

Teren was focused on his conversation with Mike, whose name I'd also overheard, when his home phone rang. Looking at the handset resting in its charger on the table beside me, I noticed it was his mom calling and I automatically picked it up. Teren glanced over at me as I whispered, "Your mom." He nodded as I pressed the talk button.

"Hello."

"Oh, hi, Emma. Is Teren there?" Alanna's warm voice filled my head, and I pictured her leaning against a counter in her massive kitchen, a button-up work shirt tucked into dark blue jeans, her long hair brushing her shoulders, and a huge smile on her beautiful, youthful face.

I smiled at the image. "Yeah, he's on the phone. Do you want me to let him know you called?"

She paused. "Actually…maybe I could talk to you." The image in my head changed to a shifty smile, as I heard a slight plotting note in her tone.

"Sure…what's up?"

"I keep asking Teren to come back out here. Jack misses him so much. We all miss him…and you too, of course, dear." I could hear the warm smile returning in her voice and my mental picture shifted as well. "Anyway, we'd like both of you to come out this weekend. There is something very important that we need to talk to Teren about."

I blinked at the intenseness in her voice now. "Of course…of course we can do that." We actually had important news to tell them as well. I wondered what they needed to talk to Teren about though.

Her voice got hurried and rushed, like she was really late, for a really important meeting. "Okay, great. We'll see you this weekend.

Have a good evening, dear." And then she hung up the phone.

I barely had a chance to say "bye" into the now dead line, before Teren was ripping the handset out of my limp fingers. His cell phone was clenched in his other hand and he was staring at me with his mouth open in disbelief. "What did you just do?"

I looked up at his face, confused. "I…have no idea. What did I just do?"

He sat down beside me on the couch and ran a hand through his hair. "You just agreed to go to my parents' place this weekend."

I stared at him as I repeated the conversation in my head. I couldn't be positive, but I was pretty sure those words had never crossed *my* lips, which meant he had heard his mother talking through the phone, while standing over by the windows, while chatting to Mike. His hearing was astounding…as was his lack of privacy. I frowned at him.

"I was having a private conversation." I crossed my arms over my chest. He needed to grasp the concept of boundaries, regardless of his super abilities.

He brushed aside my irritation with a sweep of his hand. "You were talking to *my* mom." He looked at me with an intent expression as he sat with his elbows on his knees. "We should have talked about this, before you just agreed to it."

I matched his intent look. "They want to talk to you. It sounded important."

He shook his head. "I know what they're going to say, and it's not important."

I raised an eyebrow and waited for him to fill me in…he didn't. I sighed. "Well, we have news for them." Smiling, I grabbed one of his hands; he was still clutching the home phone with it, like somehow he could undo what I had just done, by squeezing the life out of the handset. "We can tell them we're trying, Teren. Think of how happy that will make them."

Sighing, he shook his head. "We're only trying. There's no guarantee…"

"They won't care, Teren. Just trying will give them hope…think of it." The sullen look on his face didn't change and I frowned. "I want to go over there…okay?"

Teren closed his eyes and I could see the resignation in them when they reopened. He exhaled a dramatic breath. "Now you *want* to go into a vampire nest?"

I grinned and, removing the tightly held phone from his hand, slipped his arm around me. "Yes. This time…yes, I do want to go."

He shook his head again. "It's your funeral," he said even more dramatically.

I kissed him, lingering a bit on his softly smiling lips. "They won't hurt me…not since you've claimed me," I murmured between kisses.

Pulling back, he cocked an eyebrow at me. "I've claimed you?"

I nodded and bit my lip as I examined this beautiful man beside me, casual and perfect in his just-tight-enough Giants shirt and khaki shorts. I ran my hand down his chest, feeling the life beneath my fingertips as his shirt rose and fell, perhaps, just a touch faster than before. My eyes watched my fingers, of their own accord, trail down his body to rest on the edge of his shorts. They went under his shirt and curled over the inside of his waistband. The skin of his trim waist pulled away from the backs of my fingers as his stomach clenched. Taking the fabric of his shorts with me, my fingers pushed back to find that skin. They trailed back and forth along his warm stomach and his waistband, while my eyes watched them, fascinated.

"We don't have time to make a baby right now."

My eyes snapped back up to his at the sound of his clearly strained voice. His eyes were unfocused, staring at my lips, and his chest was most definitely rising and falling faster. Enjoying his obvious reaction to my touch, I smiled demurely. "I know."

He dropped his cell phone and slapped his palm over my hand that was still caressing his stomach. Flattening my fingers against his waist, he said, "Then you really need to stop doing that."

I smiled a touch wider, removed my hand from under his, and ran it back up his chest. I brought it up to his cheek and pressed my body along the length of his. "You're so easy."

Smiling, he kissed me. The kiss deepened and his hand around my shoulder ran up my neck. A wide variety of erotic options flipped through my head—every place on my body that I suddenly wanted him to touch me, sliding my leg over his and straddling him, hearing every delightful noise that action would elicit from him, running my hands back through his hair and pulling him even tighter, into a scorching kiss. But the image of Mom and Ashley sitting on their couch, waiting for us to make an appearance that would never happen, if what we were doing kept progressing, doused my body with cold water. I couldn't do that to them. They were looking forward to tonight, and Teren and I would have plenty of time, on another occasion, to lose ourselves in each other.

I broke off from our intense kiss, and was surprised to see that we'd both gotten more carried away than I'd realized; we were both nearly panting. I almost reconsidered with the look on his face…but I pushed him back when his lips went for mine again. "We do need to get going…"

He tried for my lips once more, obviously not caring. "Teren…Ash is waiting…"

He pulled back, then sighed. "Fine. Aren't I supposed to be mad at you anyway?"

I grinned, stood, and held out my hand to help him up. "You know you can never stay mad at me for long." I tilted my head and gave him my best innocent look.

Shaking his head, Teren let me help him up. "Let's go get your mom and Ashley and watch a little baseball, so I can stop thinking about your bare legs wrapped all the way around my waist, while I bite you in a spot that only your skimpiest bikini will hide." His voice was low and silky smooth.

I gaped at him with my mouth wide open while he grabbed his phone and his wallet. Trying to remember why we had to leave, I stood there like that for several achingly long seconds. Eventually, it took Teren laughing, grabbing my hand, and pulling me out the door with him to remember. That's right…baseball. It had never sounded more boring in all my life, and I loved baseball.

Teren eyed me pensively throughout the game, and I had the feeling that he was dwelling on this upcoming weekend with his parents. Really, he seemed more nervous about seeing them now than I had been about meeting them for the first time. I wasn't sure why that was. Surely now that we were trying for a child, he had less to worry about from his family?

Our seats for the game were right along first base in the front row. I could practically see the beads of sweat on the back of the first-basemen's neck, and I had a super close-up view of those incredible pants baseball players wore—truly, those pants were the real reason why a large portion of women even bothered to watch the game. My sister and I were sharing a plate of nachos, while Teren and my mom each had a hot dog. Teren and I sipped our ridiculously expensive beers as the sun sank below the stadium, casting a pinkish glow over the sky. The air was cool, but not cold. The whoosh of the ball met with a resounding crack of the bat, and the cheesy let's-get-the-crowd-riled-up music, blasted out of the speakers spaced around the park. It was the perfect night for baseball.

Teren was still eyeing me speculatively, when an Arizona Diamondback at the plate, ripped a low-lying foul ball. I had two seconds to realize that no one was going to be able to catch it, and it was coming straight for us. My mom and Ashley noticed as well, and I heard them gasp and shift away in their seats. Teren was still staring at me though, and unfortunately, he was the one that was sitting on the edge of our row, right where the ball was zipping along at what felt like the speed of light. He either noticed my eyes widening or heard the collective gasp of the crowd, or quite possibly, his super accurate hearing heard the crack and calculated the destination of the ball without ever looking, but his head snapped around at the same time that his hand snapped up. But not in front of his face—in front of mine. His fingers curled around the ball, just as I realized that my poor vision hadn't seen its trajectory clearly enough. He had never been the one in danger; my fragile head had been about to be the recipient all along.

We stared at each other in absolute shock. Warm gratitude

flooded my body, but it was instantly drenched with ice-cold panic. My boyfriend had just reached up and snatched a baseball—traveling quite possibly over a hundred miles an hour—out of the air, with one quick glance, barehanded, like it was no more of an effort than plucking a falling maple leaf. To me, it was a neon sign flashing above his head that he wasn't entirely human. I wanted to glance around the stadium and search for stake wielding lunatics, but my eyes were glued on his.

Eventually, and in actuality it had only been maybe five seconds at most, he doubled over in his chair and clutched his hand, letting the ball roll onto his lap. I sympathetically laid an arm over his shoulder and took a chance at looking over the crowd. Several people around us were eyeing him with either an awed face or a *Man that must have hurt* face, but no one was giving us the *He's a vampire, circle and stake him* look.

I rubbed his back and whispered in his ear, "Are you okay?"

Groaning and rubbing out his hand, he mumbled, "Yeah, I'm fine." He kept up his exaggerated pained noises for a couple more seconds, and then straightened and held his hand up to the crowd. There was some applause near us and then everyone relaxed again, seeing that he was okay. My mom and Ashley gushed at what an incredible sight that had been, and my mom remarked that she'd never seen someone move that fast. Ashley winked at her comment and reached over me to squeeze his knee. Teren nodded and smiled at the both of them, and then looked at me and let out a soft sigh.

"That was too close," he whispered, as he kissed me.

"You shouldn't have done that." I said it no more than a faint breeze over my lips, knowing he would hear it.

He leaned in to whisper in my ear, since I didn't have his perceptibility. "I couldn't just let it hit you."

I looked over at him and sternly said, "Don't expose yourself for me."

He frowned and leaned into my ear again. "I would stake myself to protect you, and there is nothing you can say to make that truth go away, so will you please stop being all noble and self-sacrificing and just thank me already."

I blinked and pulled away to see him grinning a crooked smile at me. I laughed and then leaned in to kiss the hand that had saved me from a world of pain. "Thank you. Did that hurt?"

He shook his hand out a little and flexed it. "It didn't feel good. Nothing is broken, but I'm going to have a pretty decent bruise tomorrow." He showed me the edge of his palm, where it was redder than the rest. I wondered for a second if he could smell the blood pooling under his skin. I kissed his injured palm, then leaned back into his shoulder. Still smiling, he twirled his hard-won ball over and over in his other hand.

"I'll thank you properly later," I murmured. I felt him chuckle and kiss my head and we watched the rest of the game, from our almost too-close seats, in relative peace and quiet.

We ducked out after the game. A few people did stop him to pat him on the back and tell him what an amazing catch that was. Thankfully, the cameras hadn't been fast enough to record him casually reaching up to snag a ball from in front of my face, or we would have been enduring replay after replay of the event on ESPN. As it was, all they had was a shot of him clutching his hand and then showing it to the crowd. They only played the clip twice and, although it was pretty impressive that someone had caught a ball barehanded like that, he looked completely normal and human in the clip, so we watched it with easy grins on our faces. Well, his grin was easy…mine was a little lusty. My vampire looked damn good onscreen. After watching his victorious television debut, we picked up where we left off before leaving for the game, and I thoroughly thanked him for his superhuman abilities.

Teren seemed in a more upbeat mood when he picked me up the next night to head over to his parents' place. I supposed he'd had a great afternoon, telling his co-workers about his impressive catch. Mike especially, since he would have been the one sitting in that seat last night if he had gone to the game. I wondered how Teren had modified the story to make it seem more human. Turned the straight-line fowl into a lofty pop fly maybe? I'd have to ask him in case anyone asked me. Interesting, how dating a vampire had taught me to corroborate stories.

He walked through my front door and kissed me, then reached down to pick up my full bags. I had debated having him pack again, since he was so good at it, but after deciding that I could be self-sufficient, I had packed it myself. I was a little surprised that he wanted to head up on a Friday night. With all his hemming and hawing, I thought for sure he'd at least postpone it until Saturday afternoon. But he had an exciting story to tell, and he was looking forward to getting up there now. On the drive over, he started talking about the game, and how eager he was to tell his dad about the catch and show him the deepening bruise on his palm. He'd even brought the ball to give to him. I smiled at the very human response of wanting to make your parent proud of your abilities, even if you were genetically enhanced.

We bounced down their super-long driveway and I inhaled a deep breath as the mansion that was the Adams Ranch came into view. It was spectacular. My human mind had dulled the memory of it, and now my brain was being scorched by its perfect beauty. The late rays of the sun cast a red glow on the already red tiles, making them gleam like bright red drops of blood. The stark whiteness of the stucco walls further emphasized the crimson roof, and I almost expected that roof to start dripping like a fresh wound. I couldn't help but think how fitting the style of the home was for a group of vampires, what with the bone white and blood red coloring. I swallowed as I remembered that this group of vampires weren't entirely innocent, and weren't entirely giant kitty cats, like Jack had assured me they were. I placed a hand on my stomach. They would never hurt me. I had something they wanted—a willing uterus. And I had something even more important than that to assure my safety…Teren's heart. That was most definitely sacred to them.

Teren put the car in park beside the zippy looking sports car, which had to be Halina's. I could easily picture her in a skintight dress, flying down a pitch-black highway with her wild black hair streaming behind her. Of course, I then had to picture her speeding into the city, to pick up a cute boy or two… Not relevant, I reminded myself. I wasn't going to think about that right now.

My eyes shifted to the meticulously inlaid rocks that formed a perfect line, just below midpoint, all the way along the home. As Teren walked around to my door, I marveled at how perfectly each rock had been chosen and twisted into place, so that it seamlessly created a natural looking wall. I laughed to myself. A wall of stone to protect the vampires sleeping inside…just like a real medieval castle. I was smiling at that thought as Teren pulled me from my seat. His eyes were softly glowing in the darkness of the parking area, in the cleanness of the non-light polluted country air, but I didn't feel the pull that I had felt the last time we were here. I kissed his cheek and clutched his hand, turning away from those engaging eyes. I was willing to follow him anywhere…no creepy, hypnotic light needed.

We walked under the massive overhang in front of the solid looking front doors, and I grinned at the merrily twinkling lights strung up under the eaves of the huge timbers. That was a feminine touch. Alanna's hand probably; she had exquisite taste. We reached the doors just as they swung open. Alanna embraced her son at human speed, her arms wrapping around him and her head resting on his shoulder. Teren was not surprised in the slightest at her perfect timing, and he wouldn't be, what with that quaint blood connection that they shared. He would have known exactly where in the house she'd been waiting, where all of them were waiting.

I watched mother and son with a soft smile on my lips that eventually shifted into shock. Alanna's face was turned towards me and her pale eyes were shut, as she enjoyed having her son near her again. But what had me startled, was the small river of blood escaping the corner of her inner eye. It wasn't like the blood that had run down my leg when my knee had been sliced open. It was thinner, pinker, like it was diluted with water or some other substance. It didn't look like she was injured. It looked like she was crying—tears of blood. I supposed that worked with the whole vampire thing, but it was still pretty shocking to see. Teren didn't cry a whole lot, but I wondered if that would happen to him, once he changed.

Alanna pulled back to gaze at him. "We've missed you, son."

Teren sighed and ran a thumb over her tear, wiping it away. "Don't cry, Mom. Everything's fine."

Alanna nodded and detached from him. Straightening herself, she brushed away the bloody tears and turned to face me. With a beaming smile, she embraced me just as tightly as she had Teren. "Thank you for getting him here," she whispered. I knew Teren had heard her comment, but the whispering clearly conveyed her emotion, and I warmly returned her squeeze.

Jack was behind Alanna and greeted us congenially after she stepped away. He clapped Teren on the back as they went over to get our bags from the car. While the boys grabbed our things, I could hear Teren going into the excitement of the game with his father. Here was the only male he could really boast with, without changing one single thing about the story. By the look on his face, and the tone of his voice, I could tell it was a relief for him to talk about it without having to hold anything back. I again wondered why we didn't visit more often.

Alanna herded me into the house. As we walked past the sun portrait that had so moved me the last time I'd been here, I pointed it out to her. "That sunrise painting sure is beautiful."

Alanna paused and looked at it, almost as if my saying something had reminded her that it was there. She took her fingers and lightly trailed them down the canvas. A heavy sigh escaped her. "It's a sunset." Her voice was low and soft and filled with sympathy. "Halina painted this. It was the last sunset she ever saw. The last beautiful thing she ever saw…right before she was changed."

I stared at it again, in awe. The meticulous brush strokes, the layer upon layer of color, the perfect recapturing of the glorious beauty of light. It could have been painted by any of the Renaissance masters, but it was painted by a forever nineteen vampire. A vampire, who as Teren once told me, longed for the sun daily. I tried to imagine what she had been like as a young, pregnant human wife, watching her final sunset, committing it to memory, not even realizing at the time that it would be the last one she ever saw. The picture was so vastly different from the sultry, laughing hunter that I'd met before, that I almost couldn't envision it. But that human woman was in Halina somewhere, and it had painted this masterpiece, and the longing in it tore my heart.

"It's all right, dear." Alanna placed a cool arm around my shoulder and stroked it. I realized I'd started to cry and, embarrassed, brushed aside the few tears. Alanna only smiled at me and led me into the kitchen, where she said her mom was just finishing up dinner, so she hoped I was hungry. I smiled—she'd said almost the exact same thing the last time I'd been here.

Imogen greeted me the moment my feet touched the stone tiles of the kitchen floor. She swept me into a cool embrace and I forcefully blocked the knowledge that I now had of her past hunting experience from my head. She was still the sweet, grandmotherly figure that I remembered from my first encounter, and I just couldn't see her any other way. She pulled back from her embrace to look at me and regret marked her youthful features.

"I'm so sorry about the last time you were here, dear. That was so unconscionably rude of me. I should never have meddled in your private affairs." Her pale eyes flicked over to Alanna's and I wondered if she'd been coached on what to say to me.

I genuinely smiled back at her, knowing it didn't matter anymore. Teren and I were trying to give them what they, and me, wanted, and soon, they would all know that. "Thank you, Imogen."

"Gran, dear…we are all still family, hopefully."

I hugged her again. "Of course." She stepped back and ran her cool hands up and down my arms before squeezing them.

"Quite the love fest going on up here."

I startled from Imogen's embrace as Halina soundlessly breezed into the room; it suddenly felt half its size. The sun must have completely set while I'd been reuniting with Alanna and her mother. Halina cocked her youthful head at me, her thick, black hair following her movement. I couldn't stop flicking my eyes over her body; she was wearing a skintight, blood red dress with black thigh-high boots. She looked vastly out of place at a ranch, more like she should be dancing atop some table at a London hotspot. She was so different in style from Imogen's skirts and loosely swept up hair, and Alanna's jeans and button-up work shirts that I began wondering if her being one hundred percent vampire had altered her behavior, or if she had just been a repressed wild child in her human youth. It was still so hard to believe that this creature before me had painted that great beauty behind me.

"I see the human came back." She leaned back against the counter, grinning at me with a crooked smile. She looked over at me with such a calm look of self-assurance that a chill went through me.

I might be off-limits to Halina, but she apparently was not on an all-animal diet and that sickened me a bit. I would need to double-check with Teren that my friends and family were also taken off of Halina's menu. In fact, if she could leave all of San Francisco alone, I would sleep much better at night.

"Good evening, Halina," I said, as respectfully as I could. Halina was the only one who never tried to alter what I called her. I don't think the words "Great-Gran" could have escaped my lips in her presence anyway.

Suddenly, all of the women smiled and turned as one to the doorway. I frowned, wondering what they were doing, until a second later, when Teren entered the kitchen with his father. He warmly gave his grandmother and great-grandmother a hug while Jack, twirling the baseball in his fingers and grinning broadly at his son, relayed the story to his wife. Alanna slung her arms around her husband and listened, engrossed in his story, along with the other women in the room. I watched the multiple sets of pale eyes as Jack was talking, and wondered if they had heard Teren telling this story to him outside, and they were listening purely out of respect. I wasn't quite sure how incredible their hearing was, but from all I had seen so far, it was very impressive.

Jack finished his story and they all turned to Teren with soft eyes and light chuckles. All except Halina, who still had her arms slung around his waist. She looked up at Teren with clear disapproval on her face. "You could have been exposed." Her frown deepened as she glanced at me. "Nothing is worth you being shown to the world." She looked back at his face and, for the first time, I saw true fear in her eyes. It startled me and a tiny flow of compassion for her trickled into me. Halina searched his face as she continued in a near whisper, "Think of what they'd do to you."

Teren smiled down at her and kissed her head. "I'm okay…everything is fine." He rested his head on hers, while she closed her eyes and clutched him tight, looking for all the world like she was scared that those villagers with pitchforks would burst through the front doors at any moment. Teren laid his eyes on mine and smiled widely. "Everything is just fine."

After a few more moments of catching up, Alanna ushered

everyone into the massive area that they quaintly called a dining room, and we all took our respective seats. Jack took his traditional place at the head of the table with Teren and me on one side and Halina and Imogen on the other. Again, Halina sat directly across from me and eyed me with that half-grin that was so disconcerting. The foot of the table was left open for Alanna, who was busy flitting back and forth between the kitchen and the table, bringing in trays of food.

I struggled with wanting to help her, but I knew she viewed me as a guest and would only forcefully push me back under the table if I even tried to stand. She was very strong…I wasn't even going to bother trying.

She brought out steaks and my mouth watered at the smell. I noticed that one of the larger steaks was extremely rare and very bloody. I almost expected it to moo at any moment. I smiled at how well Alanna and Imogen understood Teren. I hadn't heard him tell either woman, but they had known that he now liked his steaks much rarer than he had the last time we were here. I supposed that made sense, since they had both already gone through exactly what Teren was going through now. I grabbed his hand under the table as he hungrily eyed that bloody steak.

Alanna swished out the rest of the food: roasted red potatoes, sautéed mushrooms and freshly baked dinner rolls, still steaming with just-from-the-oven goodness. She brought out wine and water and loaded up plates for all the humans. Then the carafe came out, and I felt Teren drop my hand. I looked over at him and watched his fangs extend before he had even tasted a drop of the blood we both knew was in there. His mouth opened a touch wider, and with the steak virtually forgotten, his eyes followed the carafe, like suddenly he was a man dying of thirst and that container held his salvation.

Without a word or a look at him, Alanna poured his goblet first and immediately gave it to him, once again knowing her son's needs. He took it from her hand and drank half of it before stopping. Once he had some in his system, he seemed to come back to who he was and where he was, and turned to look at me. I grabbed his hand under the table again and smiled. He needed this. It was just a part of who he was now, and I could deal with that. He grinned at me with his fangs still extended and finished the rest of his drink. His mother poured him another one before setting the carafe in front of Halina. I could see that Alanna had poured glasses for everyone else while I had been busy watching Teren. Grabbing the one she had poured for herself, she sat at the foot of the table.

After Teren's second glass, he seemed to relax into his chair. Slowly, he began to dig into his food. It didn't seem to hold the appeal to him that the blood had, and I noted that for future reflection. Imogen asked Teren about work. Alanna asked me about my job. Halina seemed to agree with me that Teren should…well, her words were "remove" my boss, but I felt like we were sort of on the same wave length. Jack asked about my family, which led to a lengthy conversation involving my childhood tragedy. I studied Halina's eyes while I relayed the seriousness of my sister's wounds to the room. Much to my dismay, Halina, while engrossed in the story, didn't seem touched enough to offer any vampiric help. The thought didn't even seem to cross her mind as I discreetly watched her. Maybe Teren was right about her refusal to change someone, deserving or not.

I wrapped up my tale just as dinner was finishing up. Everyone looked full and happy as Alanna flitted to the kitchen to bring out a chocolate cake, for the three of us still on solids. It shocked me a little bit to realize that I hadn't even noticed the women drinking their bloody cocktails. It hadn't unnerved me at all this time. I was getting immune to it already. I tried to see the positive in that thought.

We dug into the decadent dessert before us and I was pretty sure I was going to gain ten pounds this time. I was also sure that now was as good a time as any to break our news. And honestly, I couldn't contain it any longer. I'd been dying to tell someone for so long and, here I was, seated in a room full of people who would actually be thrilled over the fact that I was trying to have a baby, out of wedlock, with a man I'd only known for four months.

I cleared my throat and every vampire turned to look at me. Jack noticed that I had their attention and brought his head up from his cake to watch me too. "Um…" Teren grabbed my hand under the table and squeezed it, signaling that he knew what I was going to say and that he'd let me tell it first. Okay, he could have been thinking that he was ready to head upstairs to that luxurious bed awaiting us, but I preferred to think he was throwing supportive thoughts my way. "Teren and I are…" I glanced over at him and he smiled warmly and nodded—yeah, definitely being supportive. I smiled back then giggled. "Well, we're trying to have a baby."

I felt so weird telling the room that we were basically having lots and lots of sex. I felt even weirder when pin-dropping silence followed my statement. Noting the odd absence of sound, I started to swivel my head to take in their faces. I didn't even make it a fraction of an inch to look at Alanna, before I was covered with black hair and cool arms. Three women were hugging me, kissing my head and rubbing my stomach, which was a little odd, since I was pretty sure nothing was in there yet. Halina and Imogen were the most ecstatic with my news. Alanna was happy, but more reserved. I was more than a little uncomfortable with their lavish felicitations, but I didn't try and stop it. I understood what this meant to them, and I let them have their moment.

Teren laughed at their reaction, causing the whole maelstrom to shift his direction. His mother slung her arms around his neck, while the other two each took a side of his chest. He tried to pat them all at the same time, but it was a near impossibility.

After a moment, they started shifting between the two of us, offering words of advice, encouragement and congratulations, which, still feeling odd about my personal revelation, made me wonder if they were congratulating me on having tons of sex. The bizarre thought made me laugh and Teren, who could sometimes pick up on my odd observances, laughed with me.

A calm voice broke through the excited chaos, "Would you three back off now. You'll never get grandkids that way." Giggling, the women sat back down in their chairs and I looked over at Jack; he was smiling at his son with pride. "Congratulations you two…I know you'll have time." He nodded with encouragement and I could feel tears sting my eyes.

I'd nearly forgotten that cursed word in my exuberance. *Time.* The one thing we battled daily. The other women in the room seemed to remember that dreaded word as well, and a layer of sadness laced with tension, filled the room. If we were too late… If

Teren changed before I could get pregnant…

Nope, no pressure on my uterus at all.

Alanna broke the sudden unease in the air by clearing her throat and placing a hand on Teren's arm. Sighing, he studied his plate before looking over at her. Her eyes dreadfully sad, she seemed about to speak, but Teren shook his head and set his lips in a hard line. She removed her hand and said nothing.

Just when I was about to ask what was going on, Alanna stood and started sweeping away our empty dessert plates. I turned to Teren, going to ask him anyway, but he had engaged himself in a conversation with Halina. He asked her to tell me about the painting in the hall. I realized then, that he had heard me ask Alanna about it and he had heard me cry. Darn those vampire ears.

Halina raised her lips into a soft, sad smile, and instantly she was transformed into a lost, innocent teenager. I began to see what Teren saw when he looked at her—a child, scared, pregnant and unsure of the world. Halina began describing her memories of the very last time she saw the sun, and I openly wept listening to her. The ache in her voice was palpable.

"My husband and I married at what would now be considered a young age, eighteen, but back then it was common. One of our favorite things to do every evening was watch the sun set. To us, it signaled the end of a long day on our farm." Her eyes were distant as she lost herself to the memory. "One of our greatest hopes was to fill that farm with a handful of boisterous children." She glanced at Teren with soft eyes. Returning her gaze to me, she continued. "We would hold hands as we watched the gold, reds, oranges and pinks fill the sky, and we'd talk about our dreams and goals. And as I listened to my husband on that porch, I pictured scores of our children, grandchildren and great-grandchildren watching the setting sun with us. It was all I ever wanted."

Halina dabbed at her tears with a napkin. Thick, pureblood tears, not the watered-down pink version of Alanna's. She didn't talk of what happened after the sunset. She didn't talk of her beloved husband's death or, in a way, her own. She didn't speak of giving birth while her body changed over and she didn't speak of ending the life of the vampire who had created her. She only spoke of the sun, and how she ached for it, and all that it represented. I was grateful that she didn't speak of the horrors…listening to her describe that one perfect sunset, was hard enough.

Teren put his arms around me as I sobbed for her loss. Maybe he was right about my sister.

Moments later, I made the mistake of yawning, and Alanna insisted that I go upstairs and retire. She'd prepared the same room that we'd used the last time we were here. I tried to tell her I was fine, and I'd like to stay up and talk with them, but my body betrayed me and yawned again. Laughing, she led me to the hallway and gently pushed me down it. I waved goodnight to the room and looked back at Teren, still seated at the table.

"I'll be up in a minute. You go on ahead." He smiled and flicked a glance up at his mother and then over to Halina, who was sadly staring at the table. I thought maybe he felt bad for having her bring up a painful subject. Maybe he was going to sit and comfort her a while.

I smiled at his sweetness and nodded back at him. Alanna kissed me goodnight on the cheek and then turned to stand at the edge of the table beside her husband. No one said anything, and I got the impression that they were all waiting for my heartbeat to be upstairs, and out of earshot. That thought made me want to stay and eavesdrop again, but I already knew that was pointless; they could hear every wet thump, from probably every room in the house. They could probably even smell me.

I walked down the hall to the foyer and then up one side of the dual staircase. I wondered what was so secretive. Maybe they were just going to discuss some aspects of Halina's life that I'd find…unsavory. I really didn't want to hear about her killing anyone. Honestly, I was having a hard time just processing that fact. She had seemed so sweet and innocent while telling her story, but I knew for a fact that she wasn't. She killed. She killed without remorse. I knew it was survival for her, and she certainly was not the only person who had killed before, but I liked to think that most people felt bad about it. It was off-putting to think otherwise.

Shoving the thought from my head, I opened the massive double doors that led to our honeymoon suite—that was what it

184

looked like, so that was how I thought of it. The massive satin-on-satin bed sparkled in the reflected glow of the lit fireplace. Warm candlelight was wavering from pillars, spaced in groups of three, on nearly every flat surface of the room. I listened for the mood music but didn't hear any.

I chuckled at his family's never-ending, subtle attempt to get their son lucky. I laughed a little harder at the fact that it never seemed to occur to his family that I'd be on protection from day one, to prevent the very thing that they'd been hoping so badly for. Even if Teren and I had done what they'd wanted us to do the last time we were here, I wouldn't have gotten pregnant. I guess birth control was not something vampires took into consideration. And Teren would certainly have never wanted to tell them about it. They bugged him enough as it was.

I shook my head at the oddity of it all and shucked off my clothes. There was something in this suite that I had really wanted to try last time, but never got the chance to. I was tired, but I wasn't missing another golden opportunity. Walking into the upscale bathroom, I turned on the jetted tub. I smiled as the warm water flowed through my fingertips. Heaven awaited me. Rummaging through the cupboards, I found a bottle of bubble bath and squeezed out a couple of gloppy drops. Instantly, the water started foaming and sudsing with filmy half circles that refracted the bathroom lights.

Finding a hair scrunchy, I pulled my long, brown mane into a high ponytail and slipped into the silky smooth water. Shutting off the faucet, I relaxed back into the contoured tub. I sighed and closed my eyes, listening to the water sloshing with my slight movements, the bubbles bursting with tiny pops. The scent of fresh lilacs filled my nose, and the heated water left a slight dampness to my face and hair. It was the most relaxing thing I had ever experienced.

I was just beginning to be pulled into a satisfying slumber, when a light touch along my cheek brought me around. My water was cooler, although still plenty warm, and a good chunk of the bubbles were gone. I guessed I'd already fallen asleep. I looked up at Teren, sitting on the edge of the tub, cupping my cheek in his strong hand.

"Hey, sleepy," he whispered.

I made a satisfied noise and stretched my limbs in response. His eyes tracked the movement of my muscles under the nearly transparent water, and I smiled. "Come join me…the water is still warm." I sloshed my hand through the bath, purposely revealing even more of my body to him.

Just one edge of his lip curled up and I swear my heart rate increased—I loved that look. He slipped his shirt off and started working on his jeans and my heart *definitely* sped up—I really loved that. I scooted over in the tub as he slid in beside me. He shifted me, so I was mostly on top of him, and then he relaxed back into the warm bubbles, well, what was left of the bubbles anyway. Twisting, I laced my arms around his neck and kissed his cheek. Then I rested my head on his shoulder and snuggled into his warm skin, warmer than the water even. One of his hands rubbed my back, while the other stroked my leg, making tiny waves splash across our skin. I was wrong before—*this* was the most relaxing thing I'd ever experienced.

We stayed snuggling in the massive tub, until the water cooled too much for me and I shivered. He noticed immediately and held me tighter. "Ready to get out?" he asked.

"No…" I held up my wrinkled fingers. "But I guess I'd better."

Smiling, he shifted me over, so he could stand. I fully appreciated my view while he stepped out of the tub and grabbed us towels. Wrapping one around his waist, he held the other open for me. I stood, shivering a little more in the now comparatively chilly air, and then I stepped into his warm, fluffy towel embrace. I laughed and kissed him as he wrapped the fabric around me.

He started walking me backwards, through the bathroom door to the bedroom. His kiss deepened with every step and every thought but this warm, half naked man before me, fled my brain. He backed me right up to the bed and, without ever pausing his magnificently talented mouth, he bent down and picked me up.

With only the slightest break to toss the multiple decorative pillows out of the way, he laid me on the covers and sank down on top of me. His kiss picked up intensity. His tongue flashing along mine did wonderful, tingly things to my insides. His hands began unwrapping the lush towel from around my body, and my legs twined around his. My hands ran up his bare back to clutch at his hair as a particularly good moan escaped me. Hearing myself made me instantly remember where I was. I gently pushed him back. Breathing heavier, he looked down at me in confusion. "What's wrong?"

I glanced around the seemingly private room as I struggled to calm my breathing. "I still can't do this here."

He understood what I meant. Smiling, he moved in to kiss my neck. "Emma..." he murmured against my skin. "They'll be respectful. They like you."

I pushed him back again, more forcefully this time. "When I came upstairs...what could you hear?"

Sighing, Teren slumped over to my side. "Well, obviously I heard you run the tub..." I raised my eyebrows, knowing that even his dad had probably heard the water surging through the pipes. He exhaled again. "I heard you sigh contently as you sank into the water...I heard the bubbles popping."

My mouth dropped wide open. His hearing was even better than I thought. "Oh my God! That's why, Teren."

He shook his head. "But I was really listening for you. They'll tune us out. Lord knows I've had to..."

I ignored that comment; I did not want to think about what he'd had to endure. I shook my head. "I can't, I'm sorry...it's just too weird. It's like they're all in the room with me." I shrugged my shoulders, hoping he understood. "It's not like I can just ask them to all take a long walk, so I can have sex with their son."

He cocked his head as he listened to something I couldn't hear, and then he started laughing. I was confused for half-a-second, until I understood exactly what I had just done...what I had just said. I covered my face with both hands, completely embarrassed. "Oh God...did I just...?"

Still laughing, he uncovered my face. "Yeah...you just cleared the house. I wouldn't have been quite so blunt, but that worked pretty well."

I closed my eyes, mortified. "That super hearing is really annoying."

He cringed. "You're telling me. Great-Gran is very…friendly with some of her guests. You have no idea what I have had to make myself *not* listen to."

I giggled at the look on his face and then, for the first time here, I completely relaxed into his arms. He finished un-wrapping my towel and then shucked off his own. I watched the glow of candlelight dance across his skin and stared into his pale eyes; they were just faintly glowing.

"Are you still hungry?" I asked, almost timidly.

He pulled back and looked at me with burning, passionate eyes. "No, I'm fine."

I found that I wasn't. I surprised both him and myself, by what I said next. "Will you bite me anyway?"

He exhaled and his fangs slid out with his breath. His eyes roamed up and down my body, perhaps looking for the best spot. I didn't care where he did it, just so long as he did. It still surprised me how much I got from the experience. I guess you've never felt real intimacy, until your partner has ingested you.

Teren seemed unsure where to take the blood from. I brushed the hair off my neck, exposing the vein to him. He held his breath and locked eyes with me. He'd never taken blood from such an exposed spot before. His eyes clearly asked *Are you sure?* And I was. I wanted that depth. I wanted that intimacy. I wanted his teeth in me. I also started to wonder if something was quite possibly wrong with me.

"Go ahead…I love you."

His eyes were overflowing with love and tenderness as he gazed at me. "I love you too."

Then he bit me.

Chapter 10 – The Plan

I woke up to a strange warmth on my neck. Strange…but pleasant. Then the familiar stubbly sensation of Teren's jaw brushed my sensitive skin, and I realized the warmth I was feeling was his mouth. I opened my eyes and shifted to look at the black head nibbling on me. He pulled back and smiled at me and for the briefest moment, I wondered if he'd been feeding on me while I slept. I didn't like that thought, so I pushed it out of my head. He wouldn't do that. His teeth weren't out anyway, so he had probably just been reminiscing. Last night had been pretty darn incredible—even for us.

"Sorry if I woke you."

A languid smile graced my lips. "It's all right. I think I prefer that to my alarm clock."

I felt the small wounds in my skin and flushed, realizing how incredibly visible those were going to be to the entire world. Worse than a hickey even. He had been extremely gentle, as gentle as one can be, piercing through flesh, and the wounds were very small; they'd probably be nearly healed by Monday. I'd only have to make it through the weekend with the neon flashing sign upon my neck that screamed—*yes, your son bit me…and I enjoyed every darn minute of it*. I flushed again, thinking about how I'd unintentionally cleared the house last night.

Teren noticed my changing skin tone. Maybe he even smelled it. He ran a finger over the puncture marks, sweeping my fingers away in the process. "You don't have to be embarrassed." He kissed my neck again, right over the wounds. "You're beautiful…these are beautiful."

I smiled and rolled my eyes. "They pretty much brand me as yours, don't they?"

He brought his fingers to my cheek. "I love how much you trust me. I love you so much, Emma. I'd never hurt you."

I narrowed my eyes at the sudden seriousness in his voice, the sudden glistening in his eyes. I gently cupped his cheek. "I know that, Teren. I love you too."

After a few soft kisses, we peeled ourselves away from the enormous bed—it was bigger than two of my kitchen tables pushed together—and got dressed for the day. I didn't have any clothes that even came close to approaching my neck, so I didn't even bother trying to hide it. I threw on a v-neck shirt, jeans and boots, and brushed out my hair, which I decided to leave down. I might not be able to hide it, but no need to flaunt it. Teren came up behind me after dressing in jeans and a long-sleeve shirt, and brushed aside the hair from my neck to kiss me again. He was sure enjoying the memory. I added that to my growing list of things to reflect on.

Eventually, I was groomed well enough to face his family, and we left the little sanctuary we'd discovered last night. A moment's embarrassment flashed through me a second before my foot stepped into the dining room, but it left me the second my foot actually did enter the dining room. I finally felt at peace here, and I wasn't about to let a little modesty ruin that for me. Besides, the women weren't going to tease me about what had happened last night. They had all given birth to children and were all well aware how one was created. Well, most of them wouldn't tease me…I wasn't entirely sure about Halina. She would probably get a kick out of making me squirm, but I didn't have to worry about her. She was secreted underground, hiding out the sunlight for the next several hours.

Alanna and Jack gave us a cursory glance when we entered the room. "Good morning, you two. Hungry?" Alanna smiled as she asked us about breakfast. Jack nodded a greeting and then went back to his coffee. Nope…not a big deal at all.

We sat at the table while Alanna brought out ham, eggs, toast and coffee. Teren, Jack and I, filled up our plates and ate while Alanna sat beside her husband. They talked with each other for a few minutes, voices low and loving, and then they brought Teren and me into their conversation, asking me more about my mother and sister. Teren had almost as much to say about my sister as I did, and just like me, he didn't mention her scars again. We both viewed it as irrelevant to her personality, and I loved that he felt the same way about her.

Halfway through breakfast, Alanna started fidgeting in her

chair. After another minute, she politely excused herself and flitted away. I wondered what life would be like if the sun made you uncomfortable. She had been sitting with her back to a bright patch of sunlight, but even light being filtered through the window had eventually been unpleasant enough that she'd had to leave the room. Teren had his face directly in the sun, and seemed as oblivious of its rays as I usually was. I put a hand on my stomach, grateful that any child we had would be more like Teren and I in that respect. They'd still have a mostly normal life.

As we finished our last piece of toast and took our last sip of coffee, Jack Palance walked into the room. I swear that's who it was. The dead actor had just stridden into the room. Same height, same build, same leathery face, same don't mess with me look, and same *I was born a cowboy, and I'll die a cowboy* demeanor. If he hadn't been standing in a bright shaft of sunlight, I'd have assumed some vampire had turned the famous man, and his death had been faked for the media.

Teren's Dad stood up and shook the man's hand. Alanna walked normally into the room—one of the few times I'd seen her walk into a room at regular speed—and gave the man a brief hug, friendly, but professional. I realized that this man must work for them, right before they introduced him.

"Teren, you remember Peter?" His dad indicated the man beside him.

Teren stood and nodding, walked over to shake the man's hand. "Yes. Good to see you again."

Teren stretched his arm back to where I had stood up from the table, and was starting to approach them. "Peter, this is my girlfriend Emma. Emma, this is Peter Alton. He runs the crew that helps my dad out a few times a year."

I nodded, said hello, and stretched my hand up to the intimidating man; he was a good half-foot taller than Teren and half again as wide. I inwardly smiled, remembering that Teren was still probably stronger than this man. Heck, tiny little Halina was probably stronger than this man.

"Hello, Miss, nice to meet you." His voice had the rough,

raspy quality of a lifelong smoker and his hands were the rough, calloused hands of a man who worked hard for his living. All he needed was a stallion to sit upon, and he'd be the Marlboro Man.

Jack clapped the rough-looking cowboy on the back. "Peter and I have to head into town this morning. Some of the cows have gotten foot rot, and their medicine finally came in." He looked over at his son. "Come with us, Teren."

Teren glanced over at me and frowned as he met Jack's eye again. "Dad...Emma."

Jack brushed off his concern with his hand. "She'll be fine with Alanna and the girls. Come with us."

As Teren looked back at me again, I noticed Jack and Alanna giving each other conspiratorial glances, and I suddenly wondered if Jack stayed out of vampire affairs as much as I thought he did. Teren was still frowning at me, so I squeezed his hand and smiled. "I'll be fine. Go spend time with your dad."

Whatever was going on, better to just get it over with.

Teren sighed, perhaps thinking the same thought. "All right." He tossed a sharp look at his mother, before focusing on his dad and Peter. "Let's make this quick though."

He kissed me goodbye and then followed his dad down the hall. I could hear Peter's deep, gravelly voice as he started relaying the cows' condition to Teren. A lot of technical words were spoken that I didn't understand, and I could faintly hear Teren ask interested questions in response, before the distance between us finally became too great and I could no longer hear him. I had no need to hear him leave, to know when he did however. I knew the very second that Teren Adams had driven off the property. Alanna made that quite apparent.

Thinking I could help clean up in some small way, I was picking up Teren's and my dishes when she materialized by my side in the dining room. At first, I thought she had just zoomed out to collect the plates. I was sure she was going to tell me that I was a guest and I shouldn't be doing any work, like somehow, helping out would break some huge etiquette rule. Or maybe she was just afraid that my arms would fall off, being just a fragile human and all. But while she did take the plates away from me and start walking to the kitchen with them, her tone and her voice were quiet and serious, and her comment had nothing to do with me cleaning.

"We need to talk, Emma." She spoke quickly, like she was afraid Teren would be back at any second. My heart spiked a little.

"Okay…what is it?"

She set the plates down in the deep, basin sink built into the center island. Leaning against the counter, she collected her thoughts for a second. Then she looked up at me with an intensity in her eyes that rivaled Halina's. "I need you to convince Teren to stay here."

I blinked, not expecting that at all. "Here…me…why?"

She stepped back from the counter and wrung her hands, just like a woman in a silent movie, who was deeply distressed about something. "He needs to be here where it's safe. You need to make him see that."

"Safe?" I shook my head. "He wants to stay in San Francisco." I wasn't sure what exactly he was in danger from, but I had heard him tell her that before.

Shaking her head, she stepped towards me. "You must convince him that he is better off here. You must, Emma…he won't listen to me."

I crossed my arms over my chest. "What's going on? I thought I knew everything. Is he hiding more from me?"

Clearly torn, Alanna looked down. She obviously didn't want to be the one to have to tell me this secret, but she knew it was important for me to know—the old rock and the hard place. Finally, she sighed. "You do know everything…at the very basic level. What he doesn't want to tell you… What we keep fighting about…" She looked up at me and her eyes were brimming with pink, unshed tears. "Is the seriousness of his conversion."

My heart stopped at the look of panic, fear and sorrow on her face. Whatever made a mother look like that…had to be bad. "What do you mean?"

She came over and rested a hand on my arm; a slight shiver

went up my skin, and not entirely from her cool touch. "When his body dies, the vampire in him will take over."

I knew this much...my body tensed, waiting for the horrid punch line.

She stroked my arm with her thumb as she continued. "When he awakes...he will be hungry." I relaxed. That didn't sound so bad. Of course he'd be hungry. I'd be hungry, too, after dying. "He'll be *deathly* hungry," she quietly finished.

"Deathly?" I didn't like the sound of that.

She nodded, her face sad and solemn. "If he doesn't eat right away...he'll die. The vampire side will die...right along with the human side. We all felt it during the changeover. It's basic and primal and the most urgent thing your body has ever felt. He will never again be as hungry as he is in *that* moment. It's his body's instinct, screaming at him to eat or perish. And he will. He'll do what he has to...to survive." She whispered that last part.

I thought about her words for a moment, then my entire body went cold with the realization. He was going to die and reawaken monstrously hungry...in the middle of the city. In his office...or his car...or...in my bed. My eyes snapped up to Alanna's cool, pale ones, the pink tears now dripping down her cheeks.

"He'll attack someone? He'll attack...me?"

Alanna nodded. "And he won't stop. He will need so much blood...or he won't survive the change. More than you can safely give him, more than anyone can safely give him. Probably a few cows worth." She shrugged her shoulders as more pink tears dropped. "Where is he going to find that in the city? At work? In his backyard? In yours? He should be here..."

I ran my hands through my hair, trying to absorb all of this. He'd never mentioned thirst like that. He'd never mentioned that he'd be near death and starving so much that he'd lash out at anything with a pulse...even me. I couldn't comprehend it. "No...Teren wouldn't...no."

Alanna sighed. "Halina did..."

I froze and felt pieces of my heart cracking. "What?"

Alanna sighed again. She was about to answer when Imogen swept into the room. We both turned to face her. It startled me some that she was downstairs when the house was warm and cheery with sunshine. She cringed back to a dark corner, but she still looked to be in physical discomfort, if not outright pain. Alanna began lightning-quick closing curtains. When the room was as dark as she could get it, she turned to face her mom.

"Mother, you should be upstairs, where you'll be more comfortable."

Imogen repeatedly blinked her faintly glowing eyes. It was pretty dark in here, but streams of sunlight still showed through the curtains. "No, dear…I should be here for this." She sighed and looked away from her daughter's eyes. "Oh, Alanna…can you ever forgive me?" I blinked, wondering what she meant.

Alanna went to her mother's side. "There's nothing to forgive."

Imogen looked back up at her. "I was so concerned about keeping the line, that I nearly forgot what he'd soon be facing…and his stubbornness." Imogen turned to face me. "My daughter is right…you need to convince him to be here, where he won't hurt anyone, where he won't expose himself."

What they were talking about was certainly important, but my mind was on other things. "What do you mean…what Halina did?"

They both sighed as one and looked at a spot on the floor, where I assumed Halina was sleeping. Finally Imogen spoke, "She really had no choice…and it destroys her still…the memory…"

"The memory of what?" The words barely croaked out of me.

Alanna met my gaze. "The conversion is much the same for new vampires, as it is for us. She was so hungry when she woke…she attacked her husband. She didn't even realize what she was doing, until he was gone."

Alanna grabbed Imogen's hand while they spoke of her father's death, at her mother's hand…or teeth. The cracks in my heart shattered, and fear surged straight through me, followed immediately by anger. "He didn't feel the need to mention this to me? That he might kill me, before he even realizes it! That wasn't worth mentioning?" My tone was getting louder and more heated with each sentence. Alanna released her mother and walked over to me.

"That's why we wanted to tell you. I would have told you ages ago, but he made me promise. He's going to be very upset with me..."

"Not nearly as upset as I am! How could he not tell me? How can he play with my life like that—with everyone's in San Francisco! You may all be fine with Halina chomping on people, but—"

I immediately stopped talking as soon as I realized what I'd inadvertently spouted. Imogen and Alanna both stared at me, stunned. Apparently they didn't think Teren would mention that to me. Sometimes I was surprised he had as well. Imogen looked down, and red, thin tears dropped to her cheeks. It was then that I remembered that Halina wasn't the only one who had slipped up.

"Imogen...I'm sorry..."

She nodded and fled back up to her room. I sighed and slumped against the counter, dropping my head into my hands. Me and my big mouth. Alanna came up and put her hands on my shoulders.

"We're not perfect, Emma...but we try." She rubbed my back comfortingly as she spoke. "Please, try and convince Teren." I nodded and she kissed my cheek. As she made to leave, she looked back over her shoulder. "I'm going to go talk with Mother. Don't feel bad about this. It's her burden to bear, and she does...daily. She has only taken two lives and it was when she was a very new vampire. As for Halina..." She looked down at where the eldest vampire slept, then back up to me. "You should ask Teren again about Halina. I think he may have over-simplified things for you. There are always shades of gray in this world...try and remember that."

Speechless, I watched her leave to go comfort her mother.

I spent several minutes in the kitchen, collecting my thoughts. Just when I thought Teren was being completely honest with me, something new would sideswipe me, and I'd feel dazed, confused and angry. Why did he never willingly confess these secrets to me? Did he still think I was going to bolt on him? He should know better by now. If I was going to have his child, then I was obviously in it for the long haul. Someday, the big jerk was going to have to trust me.

When staring at the dirty dishes that Alanna had surprisingly left alone in the sink, did nothing to calm my body, I headed outside to the sunshine. It was mid-August and the morning sky was a cloudless, perfect, azure blue. Back home, near the bay, the morning fog that rolled in almost like clockwork during the summer mornings, would just be beginning to burn off. Here, farther inland, the temperature was a bit warmer than home, and no trace of the thick, misting comfort laced the hillsides.

I took off my shoes and socks and rolled my pant legs up to my knees, then sat at the edge of the pool, dipping my calves in. The water was cool and refreshing; I considered splashing my face with it, anything to snap reality back to me. I felt like a rubber band that had been stretched too far, and had finally broken apart, one half flutteringly uselessly behind the rest. Would life with Teren ever have any semblance of normalcy?

I bounced my legs along the back wall of the pool and watched the ripples expanding away from me. Near my body, the ripples were huge, splashing up to wet my jeans, but the further away from me they got, the calmer they became, stretching longer and staying lower to the surface of the sparkling water. I felt some metaphoric significance in that.

I don't know how long I sat with my legs in the water, mesmerized by the rhythmic motion, but eventually I felt a body standing beside me; its shadow partially blocked the reflected sunshine on the tiny waves around my shins.

I looked over my shoulder at Teren. He was smiling at me, apparently oblivious to my mood. He wouldn't be for much longer. He held out his hand and stiffly, I let him pull me up to standing. He slipped his arms around my waist and I let him, but I did nothing to return any of the warmness in the gesture. He still didn't seem to notice.

"Miss me? We got the cows taken care of." He nodded his head to the direction of the barn. "Dad, Peter and the guys are seeing to them now. I should probably lend a hand. Cleaning the feet and giving them medicine, it's a lot of work." Sighing, he shook his head. "Life on a ranch…" He grinned and I frowned. That seemed to clue him in that things weren't as hunky-dory as he thought.

"Are you okay?"

I grabbed his arms and pushed them off my waist. "Halina killed her husband." I hadn't planned on what to say…and that's the kind of stuff I say when I don't think it through.

Teren blinked and glanced back at the house. "Wow…I didn't think they'd tell you about that." When his eyes returned to mine, they were definitely tight, he was definitely nervous. That irritated me even more. Grabbing my hands, he tried to lace our fingers as he gave me a wide, fake smile. "Want to go watch Dad with the cows? It's actually pretty interesting, and I could show you the ranch hand's house. There's a half dozen people staying there now and they've got this—"

He was starting to pull me away from the pool, away from the conversation that he could probably feel coming. I knew I felt it. The anticipation of it was making the hairs stick up on the back of my neck. How could he not have told me…?

I jerked my hands away from him and held my ground. I cut off his pointless, distracting chatter by shoving my finger in his chest. "Halina killed her husband, because she was so hungry after the change, she couldn't stop herself. A change that you're about to go through. A hunger that you're about to face. A hunger that your family thinks will end in my death."

He closed his eyes and for a second, I thought steam might come out of his ears. When he reopened them, he turned his body to the wall of windows that led back into the house. "I cannot believe you. After I specifically told you last night *not* to tell her, you go and tell her anyway?" He was speaking to his mother, his mother tucked away in the house somewhere, quite possibly still on the second story with Imogen. He was speaking to her with the exact same volume that he'd used when he'd spoken to me, right beside him. She apparently heard and responded, because after a brief pause, he added, "We'll discuss this later."

He turned back to me and his face seemed to age by years. My face was tight with irritation...if not pure anger. His eyes took in my stance—hands on hips, feet braced for a fight—not a picture of pleasantness at all. He sighed. "That won't happen, Emma. I promise." He looked back at the house again and sullenly muttered, "Unbelievable. They never listen to me."

He promises? That was his heartfelt assurance that he wouldn't rip out my throat and swim in the pleasure that was my blood...a promise? Well, I felt better already. As long as there was a "promise" in place, then I was practically drenched in a silver suit of impenetrability. But, oh yeah, silver didn't affect him, and promises meant nothing when put up against raw, animal instinct.

"Teren."

Still staring back at the house, he ignored me. "It's like talking to a wall...three pious, we-know-what's-best-for-you walls." He shrugged his shoulders. "It's like I'm invisible."

"Teren..." My tone clearly indicated that I wanted his attention, but now *I* was invisible—he was completely ignoring me in his little pity party.

"It's like I don't even—"

He wasn't able to finish whatever sulking thought he'd been absorbed in. Wanting his attention, I pushed him, fully clothed, into the massive swimming pool. I half expected him to bounce off the water and start walking on top of it. He didn't. Shocked, he sputtered and flailed around in the water, until he realized we were near the shallow end and he could stand. He stood in the waist-deep water, and beads of it ran down his hair and face. He gaped at me with his mouth wide open.

"What the hell?"

He was rather adorable, angry and soaking wet, staring at me like I'd just slapped him for no apparent reason, but the cuteness of it instantly dissolved in the heat of my own anger. "Is there ever going to be a time when I hear these monumental events from *you* first, and *not* your family? Don't you trust me?"

He walked to the edge of the pool. His shirt clung to his

chest and water droplets flew from his lips as he spoke. "Of course I trust you...more than anyone." He shook his wet head and furrowed his brow. "I don't want to scare you with things that aren't important."

Now I gaped at him. I sort of wished we were upstairs and I had some decorative pillows to chuck at him. I didn't, so I clenched my fists instead. "Aren't important? That you may kill me isn't important? Seriously?"

He raised his sopping hands. "I won't. I have a plan..."

I cut him off before he could break out his, I'm sure, brilliant plan. "Tell me things first! Important or not! Let *me* decide what I should or shouldn't be worried about! Stop keeping me in the dark!"

Still looking to be in absolute shock, he stared at me in silence. Then, slowly, he nodded. "All right. Yes, my mother is right. I'll be thirsty, extremely thirsty...but I'd never hurt you." He shook his head, like he could simply shake away my concern. "There will be time anyway...time to get me here."

I relaxed my stance. "What do you mean?"

He hopped up on the edge of the pool, his jeans clinging to him as much as his shirt. I cringed at the soggy boots I could see below the water; they were probably ruined. I carefully sat beside him, dipping my legs back into the coolness. Teren placed his hands over the sides of the pool and looked at me. "It's not instantaneous. I'll know it's happening. I'll tell you it's happening. Instead of driving the man having a heart attack to a hospital..." he shrugged, "you'll drive me here. Then I'll be out of the city and around lots of food...and everything will be fine."

I absorbed that for a second, and then I smacked him across the chest, making him grunt. "That's your plan? Good Lord, Teren. Were you ever going to fill me in on this little scenario of yours? One that I play a rather huge part in!"

He cringed back when I smacked him again. "Yes...eventually, when I felt it getting closer."

I dramatically sighed and shoved him back into the water. He was more prepared this time and at the last moment, he grabbed my leg and pulled me in with him. I screamed as I was suddenly surrounded by frigid water. I clutched at his warmth, momentarily forgetting that *he* was the one I was angry with. I remembered my irritation, the moment he started laughing.

"Halina loved her husband and killed him anyway!" I snapped. Then, as the realization of what that statement truly meant for us hit me, I softly said, "What if there isn't time? What if you...?"

Teren shook his head as he held us close together under the water. His knees rested on the floor of the pool and my legs wrapped around his body. I clung to him tighter as his pale eyes searched my face. "There will be time...and I won't. I'd rather die than hurt you."

I rested my head against his and words failed me. I couldn't speak what was flying through my mind. I couldn't put vocals to the thoughts, like saying it out loud would make it so horrifyingly real, that the simple act of speaking the words would somehow damage us both. Pulling back, I stared into his eyes and felt the same haunted restraint from him. He wouldn't say the words either. Even if we didn't speak them...they were all I heard as we tightly clutched each other in that pool.

If it came down to that scenario and he didn't kill me...he really would die.

We stayed in that pool, holding each other, for a peaceful eternity. Eventually he grabbed the back of my head and gently brought me to his shoulder. "I really should help my dad," he whispered.

I nodded against the cold, wet fabric of his shirt, and we both stood, dripping and freezing, and exited the pool. At the edge, he faced the windows and simply said, "Mom." Instantly, Alanna was there with towels for us. Teren thanked her but didn't look at her. I watched Alanna eye him with the guilt-filled, tired eyes of someone who had betrayed someone else's trust for their own good.

I sighed, hating the tension between these two people who obviously loved each other. "This is ridiculous," I muttered, as I scrubbed my hair dry. Both vampires turned their downcast heads to me. Teren stopped squeezing the water out of his jeans as I continued. "You both love each other. You both want the best for each other." Alanna looked at him hopefully; Teren eyed her uneasily. I smacked his shoulder. "Get over it and give your mom a hug." He looked back at me, surprised at my tone, and then chuckled. Alanna's musical laugh joined his, and she flung her arms around his wet body.

"Okay, Mom…" He hugged her warmly and then pushed his wetness away from her. He looked at her with a serious expression. "I will do what's best for me. Please respect that…and please, stop telling my girlfriend things that I should be telling her." He smiled lamely at the end.

Alanna ran her fingers back through his wet hair. "You know I love you, Teren. I'm sorry I worry so much. I just remember what it was like…it's harder than you think it is. I eventually had to send Jack away to protect him from me, just in case…" She let out a sad sigh. "It was the longest separation of our marriage."

"I know, Mom…" he said softly.

She sighed again. "All right…" She grabbed his chin and looked him over. "We're always here for you." She seemed about to cry again, but instead, she quickly kissed his cheek and fled back to the house.

I smiled at him as we both finished toweling off. He smiled back and shook his head. "You're better at this than you realize, Emma."

"Better at what?" I indicated the water behind me. "Better at dumping you in the pool?"

He shook his head and pulled my damp body into his damp body. "At being a part of my world. You don't know how rare you are." He kissed me and whispered, "I won't keep anything else from you…I promise."

I kissed him back. "That's all I ask…thank you."

When we were dry enough that we were at least not dripping too badly, Teren scooped me up into his arms and sped me upstairs. Once we were in our room, we both changed into clean, dry clothes. Teren frowned as he stared at his sopping work boots, the only shoes he had with him for this trip. I looked away and got really busy putting my completely dry shoes back on.

While I went to freshen up in the bathroom, a still scowling and shoeless Teren excused himself to go find a pair of boots to wear. Even though I shouldn't have found it entertaining, I smiled the entire time I dried and styled my hair, thinking of him plodding around the house in only his socks. Served the secretive vampire right.

When I was finished with my loose, bouncy hair, I redid my makeup essentials. My mascara had run down my cheeks so badly that I'd had to wash my face and start all over. I'd have to remember to pack the waterproof kind, the next time my vampire decided to drag me into the pool. Afterwards, I exited the bedroom to go find Teren. I didn't have to search too hard. He was stepping off the final stair, just as I approached them.

I smiled and peeked at his feet. He was wearing black, men's work boots that had seen much better days. One of the toes had a worn spot that was going to eventually be a large hole, and a seam along the side of the other one had come apart; the shoe made a flopping noise whenever he walked. I bit my lip to not laugh. He frowned as he followed my gaze to his feet.

"One of the hands was my size. These are his backup boots." He sounded about as pleased with the situation as he looked.

I did chuckle then at his sullen explanation. Walking over to him, I laced my arms around his neck. He ran his hands around my waist but didn't stop frowning at me. I lightly kissed him. He still frowned. I kissed him longer. He kissed back, but as we pulled apart, his frown returned. Determined, I grabbed his face and kissed him hard and deep. I felt it throughout my entire body—felt the closeness and intimacy, felt the rush of desire. As I pulled away, just slightly breathless, it pleased me to see that he was breathing faster as well…then the damn frown came back. Stubborn indeed.

Not one to give up quite so easily, I remembered this morning and his clear infatuation. I moved the hair away from my neck, exposing the still pink wounds. Then I grabbed him and pulled his mouth down to the area. That worked. My vamp's tongue started running over the spot where he'd bitten me last night. A deep noise rumbled in his chest and his hands pulled me into his body. His breath became even heavier, as the pressure of his mouth against my skin increased. Not wanting to be any more obvious than we were already being, I suppressed a groan and clutched his head even closer to me.

Great, now I was going to have puncture marks and a hickey. I couldn't quite find it in my body to care enough to stop him though. Then something I hadn't expected happened. I felt it happen. I felt his body stiffen in response to it happening. I think it surprised him, as much as it surprised me.

His fangs slid out as he sucked on my neck. I felt the sudden pressure of them grazing along my skin. I felt him make another noise, deep in his chest. I heard him exhale, and then I felt him adjust his mouth...to bite down.

That was when both of us stiffened in surprise. That was when he seemed to realize what he was doing. A trickle of fear, mixed with excitement, flashed through me as he pulled away from my neck, and timidly met my gaze. His eyes were wide and surprised and his fangs were still out as we stared at each other.

"I'm sorry," he whispered, as he worked on slowing his breath.

I worked on mine as well. "It's okay...you didn't do anything." He looked about to argue with me and I grabbed his face and pulled him close. "I love that...you love that. Give me a day or two to strengthen back up, and I'll be begging you to do it again."

He shook his head. "I almost did it anyway...and I know I shouldn't take anymore after last night. I shouldn't weaken you like that..." He spoke quietly, but I knew he wasn't being quiet enough. I made myself ignore who all was listening to this though.

"New desires, Teren...remember? We'll figure this out together, okay?" He finally nodded, but he still wasn't smiling. I playfully added, "I'll just keep in mind not to tease you, if it's a no-biting day."

He finally gave me a small smile and a soft chuckle. Shaking his head as his fangs retracted, he muttered, "Thanks. Let's go help Dad." We turned and made our way down the staircase, hand in hand.

Wanting to shift the focus away from what had just happened in the hallway, which I was pretty sure he was still beating himself up about, I asked, "Why does your family bring in help? I would think your dad and three vampires could handle everything around here just fine." While I really was curious about that, my question was mainly a distraction for the both of us. I didn't want to think about his repeated assurances that he'd never hurt me, especially since it was becoming quite clear that his desire for blood had already started increasing lately.

Teren took a long moment before responding. Definitely dwelling then. "Huh…oh, that's mainly for show." He shrugged his shoulders. "It would just be weird if a ranch this size didn't have extra men year round, or didn't bring in a crew during peak times."

I nodded as I thought about that…quite the constant charade that they lived in.

We made our way down to the building that stored the Jeeps and, grabbing one, we zipped over to the barn near the ranch hand's house to help out with the cows. Well, Teren helped out with the cows. I mainly stood a safe distance away, so I didn't inconvenience the busy men as they cleaned between swollen toes with lines of twine, and injected medicine above the cows' shoulders. There were a couple of cowboy-looking guys helping Teren, Peter and Jack, and they got through the twenty or so cattle, just as the sun was starting to fade.

I was a little surprised that I watched the whole darn thing. Eventually, I felt comfortable enough around the beasts that Teren handed me some twine and lifted up a massive foot, so I could scrape off some of the dead tissue between the stretched out toes. It was as gross as it sounds. But I did it, and I felt pretty empowered when Teren said I did a good job. Maybe I'd give up my pantsuits for denims and work shirts. As a cow pooped on my boot and Teren laughed at me, I thought, maybe not.

The long, low barn had several dry, clean stalls waiting for the scraped and medicated cows to recuperate in. They usually stayed in the fields, but Teren said they'd need a few days to heal…just like me. I smiled as I watched Teren and his father deftly maneuver a couple of surly cows into a nearby stall. Teren had a huge smile on his face the entire time. When one of the smaller cows, aimlessly started to wander away from the group, Teren ran around and stopped her. I wondered then why Teren didn't bring Spike out here. Surely wrangling cattle would over joy his pup?

He seemed so happy and at ease with this life that he'd grown up in. I wasn't sure why he'd ever left it in the first place. He was a great writer and seemed to enjoy his life in the city, but here...it was like watching his true nature emerge. It was beautiful.

I was grinning like an idiot when he walked back to me. I may have even had embarrassing tears in my eyes. "You all right? Bored to tears?" he smirked.

I shook my head. "I'm fine. I could watch you do this all day."

He laughed. "You may think differently about that, after we're done cleaning the barn." He indicated the holding corral, where we'd kept the cattle waiting to be medicated and cleaned. There was poop and other unpleasant things everywhere in the straw. I frowned and tried to casually walk away but laughing, he grabbed my arm and handed me a shovel. "Everyone who helps—cleans."

Sighing, I helped him and the guys clean up. He was right. By the end, I'd changed my mind about wanting to watch him do anything else at this ranch.

Chapter 11 – Finally Comfortable…Almost

After finishing with the cows, Teren showed me the ranch hand's house that had been empty the last time I'd been here. It was roughly the size of Teren's place in the city, but it seemed tiny in comparison to the family home on the hill. It reminded me of a large, log cabin, straight out of Little House on the Prairie. I could easily picture Halina standing on the front steps in a long, old-fashioned dress, watching the sun fade with her husband. As I walked through the doors, I wondered how long the Adams had owned this property.

There was a stone fireplace, dormant in the still warm air of summer, in the center of the large living room. Two long couches sat along either side of a long coffee table, stacked high with "guy-type" magazines: Sports Illustrated, TIME, Sport Fishing, Farm and Ranch…no Good Housekeeping anywhere.

Teren indicated a hallway to our right, which led to a kitchen and dining area for the crew, and a hallway on our left, which led to bedrooms. Stairs on either side of the living room led up to more guest rooms, which looked out over the vaulted living room. Those rooms had a close up view of the heavy timber beams that made up the backbone of the house. I counted the upstairs bedroom doors that I could see over the balcony railing. There were four on either side of the living room. Add those to however many were downstairs, and the cabin had a decent amount of rooms. I briefly wondered why they used a separate home for guests, when the main house had two extra buildings, jam-packed full of empty rooms. But then I looked over at Teren, remembered our near fanging this afternoon, and decided the vampires just liked their privacy.

Thinking about my neck wound, I carefully adjusted my hair over my shoulder as the burly workmen shuffled into their house. No need to tip them off. Teren went over to a tall blond and a shorter, graying man. I was about to follow him over there, when I noticed a man around my age with green eyes and a messy head of brown hair winking at me. It caught me off guard. It wasn't that men never flirted with me, I just wasn't expecting it from people who worked for Teren's dad.

I walked over to Teren and laced my hand with his. He

introduced me to the two men he was speaking to, and the green-eyed man immediately turned and left for the hallway to the kitchen. Apparently he hadn't realized who I was, and flirting with the boss's son's girlfriend, was a no-no. I smiled to myself as I shook Jackson's and Christopher's hands.

I was just finishing meeting the rest of the men, and wondering how long green-eyes was going to avoid meeting me, when Halina suddenly appeared in the living room. It must have fully darkened while we'd been talking. I was pretty surprised to see her out here, mingling with the humans. I was even more surprised that the humans didn't seem to notice how un-human she was. The men didn't seem to catch the oddness of her skin or the wisdom in her eyes. I was pretty sure they weren't getting past the fabulousness of her body, stuffed into a tight, black skirt, with a blouse that clung to every curve and almost, but not quite, covered all of her toned stomach.

She casually walked up to Teren and me. Her eyes flicked over my neck, like she could see the wounds through my hair. "Enjoy your evening last night?" Her lips curled into a crooked smile that made me flush everywhere. I knew she wouldn't resist mentioning it.

I put on my big girl panties and dealt with it. "Yes, Halina…we did. Thank you."

She chuckled at my response and then proceeded to sling her arms around the green-eyed man, who had come out of hiding at hearing her voice. I guess flirting with the boss's sister-in-law, which is how Halina's youth was explained to the outside world, was all right.

Teren averted his eyes from the sight of his Great-Grandmother licking the man's neck. "That's our cue." Grimacing, he nodded at the door. We waved goodbye to the crowd that didn't care about us at all anymore, and made our way back to the main house.

As we were bouncing along in the Jeep, I remembered my earlier thought about his pup. "Why don't you bring Spike here? Wouldn't he love barking at cows?"

Teren chuckled. "Yeah…he would." He threw a look back

over his shoulder at the guest house. "Great-Gran…she kind of…"

I filled in the blanks that he was being so tentative with. "She eats dogs, doesn't she?"

He shrugged. "She's really not too picky. I don't think she'd hurt *my* dog…but no need to tempt her."

Right.

Irritation flashed through me. "Why does your family condone her behavior?"

He looked over at me, and I could tell from the set of his jaw that he knew I wasn't talking about dogs anymore. "Emma…"

"No, don't Emma me. Your mom said I should ask you about her, and you promised to not keep me in the dark anymore, so spill it."

He sighed. "Well, for starters…have you ever tried to stop a full vampire from doing something they *want* to do?"

No…I could barely get my partial vampire to do what I wanted him to do. We drove up to the garage type building and he shut the Jeep off. He hopped out, jumped over his door, and walked around to my side to open mine; always the gentleman. I let him, and he continued his train of thought while we walked up to the house.

"I've talked with Great-Gran about it before…but she enjoys it. She's a predator, a hunter. She loves the thrill of the chase, and the excitement of that first bite." I clenched my stomach with my hand and tried very hard to stop the images that were flooding into my brain. Teren grabbed my hand and stroked it with his thumb. "I may have let you believe the worst about what she does." I looked up at him, confused, and maybe a touch hopeful.

"She's not a killer?"

He frowned. "No, she kills." I frowned, too. Ignoring my expression, he finished his thought. "But not always. Most of the time, she only takes a small draw, and then she makes them forget it ever even happened. Most of the time, the people live."

Well, that didn't sound so bad. I started to feel a little better about her…until he continued. "Occasionally though, she'll run into a person that she believes has served their purpose." We reached the poolside and Teren stopped and looked out over the water; it was now moonlight sparkling in the tiny waves. "The first man she purposely killed...after accidentally taking her husband's life, was molesting a little girl at the time. She spared the girl and drained the man dry. Every life she takes...offends her in some way. It's usually because they've hurt a child."

He looked back at me with eyes that were softly glowing in the darkness. I swallowed. "She's what...some vampire vigilante?"

He frowned. "Except she's not handing them over to the police...she's executing them."

I nodded and we both silently watched each other. Shades of gray indeed. I wasn't sure how to feel about this. Another thing to reflect on later, I guess. As we walked into the house, I at least began to finally feel like Halina wasn't going to eat me or my family any more. One small positive, I suppose.

Halina rejoined us while we were finishing up dessert. She swept into the room and poured herself a glass of still steaming blood from the carafe. No one asked her where she'd been. No one gave her much more than a cursory glance. She'd been licking her lips when she'd entered the room. I was dying to ask her if green-eyes was still alive, but after Teren's comments by the pool, I felt pretty good about his chances of survival. And if she *had* killed him...well, he'd probably deserved it. I still wasn't sure what to feel about that— except grateful that I'd never be on her hit list.

Halina sat next to Imogen and calmly sipped her glass of blood. She noticed me trying to discreetly watch her and she grinned. "Do you need us to go for another walk tonight, Emma?"

I forced myself to not react to her clear goading. Alanna and Imogen respectfully looked away from me and Jack...just looked confused. Teren shot her a nasty look, but said nothing. I guess I was on my own. I swallowed and mentally replaced Halina with my boss. I could talk to my boss.

In my most respectful tone—she was my elder after all—I answered, "No, Halina...Teren and I are going to watch a movie with the family and then go to sleep. We won't be trying for a baby tonight."

I couldn't believe I'd just said that…out loud…to his family. Halina looked equally shocked that I'd admit such a personal detail to the room. She stared at me, her bloody fangs visible in her open mouth, then she started laughing. Shifting her pale eyes to Teren, who was also staring at me and looking a little shocked, she said, "I like her, Teren."

Teren turned to her and started laughing. Eventually the other vampires started chuckling, and even Jack laughed once and shook his head. I forced down the blush and laughed with them. Teren grabbed my hand and kissed the back of it. I felt a layer of tension and unease lifting from the room as laughter filled it, and I began to feel as comfortable with this family as I was with my own.

We finished our meal with pleasant, and appropriate, conversations, and then we retired to the living room to watch a movie together. Teren and I snuggled on one end of the massive couch while Jack pulled a large projector screen down from the wall. He pressed a button on a remote and from behind us, a machine built into the wall started projecting *Legends of the Fall*—classic Brad Pitt ranch movie.

As Halina crossed in front of where Teren and I were entwined on the couch, my legs over his lap, his arms over my legs, she leaned down to whisper in my ear, "You really should try tonight. You *are* running out of time." She gave me a pointed look as she pulled away and I could only lamely nod at those intense eyes.

Teren sighed underneath me. "Thanks for the advice."

Halina smiled and rumpled his hair, before walking over to sit next to Imogen. She snuggled with her daughter, and suddenly she looked more like a teenage girl at a slumber party than a vampire vixen. Finished with prepping the movie, Jack went over to sit with his youthful wife, who slung her legs over his lap in a similar fashion to mine. She kissed his neck and let out a happy sigh as he laced his arms around her. Jack didn't seem to care in the slightest that her body was cold and her chest was silent. They were definitely my vampire/human relationship role models.

I only partially watched the movie—during the scene where

Brad Pitt's character bends his hat in greeting and water droplets jump off of it, I wondered again if Teren had a cowboy hat somewhere. I partially watched the content vampires in the room—Halina and Imogen were whispering and giggling over something on the screen, and I got the impression Halina was eyeing the horses more than Brad. I partially scanned the impressive room—my eyes frequently drifted back to the flame-encrusted fireplace. Such an amazing piece of work. What I mainly did though, was feel the life and vitality of the man beneath me.

His hands stroked my thigh as he watched the movie, and my hand rubbed his stomach. I laid my head on his shoulder and occasionally pressed my lips to his neck, feeling the heat of life beneath my skin. I didn't want to think about him changing. I didn't want to think about the day he was destined to die. I didn't want to think about the responsibility of getting him to the ranch safely, so when he awakened to his new life, he wouldn't do something we both regretted. I didn't want to think any of those thoughts right now as I snuggled with him. And of course, since I didn't want to think about them, they were forefront in my mind.

I blinked at the screen when credits were rolling across it. Somehow during my brooding, I must have fallen asleep. Teren was holding me close, one hand on my hip and the other gently stroking my hair. I looked around with my eyes, but we appeared to be alone in the room.

I infinitesimally stretched and he kissed my head. "You missed half the movie," he said.

Fully stretching, I looked up at him. "Sorry…I guess ranch life wears me out."

He grinned and ran a hand down my cheek. The room went pitch black as the movie flickered out and his eyes glowed bright in the darkness. I let the feeling of peace and serenity wash over me. I'd do anything he asked anyway, but the serenity his eyes gave me swept away my fears for our future.

"Teren?"

"Yes," he whispered, his hypnotic eyes never leaving mine.

"Take me somewhere…anywhere."

In the pale glow he was casting, I could see his lips turn up into a smile. "How about I show you my favorite place here?"

I returned his smile. "I'd love that."

He stood, and even though he was lifting my weight as well as his own, the move was effortless. Gripping me gently, but firmly, he walked us outside to the back patio. Then a breeze was blowing through my hair as he ran us away from the house. I didn't care where we were going. I didn't care how fast we were moving; we would just be a blurring streak to the casual observer. I laid my head on his shoulder and enjoyed the sensation of moving fast without feeling like I was moving at all.

We stopped at the edge of a deep, slow moving creek. I really was only aware of stopping because the wind was no longer brushing past my face; it was that smooth. I marveled at the moonlit water before me as Teren set me down. It was idyllic. Long, tufted grasses lined the banks and the occasional ripple broke the tension of the lazy water, as some creature below it popped up to kiss the sky. Toads and owls filled the air with a quiet symphony, and I could easily picture a young vampire lying in the grass, listening to the sounds of nature around him.

I smiled as I looked over at Teren. My grin grew wider when I saw that he was shirtless and working on his jeans. "What are you doing?"

"I thought I'd go for a swim, want to join me?" he asked. I laughed and was about to answer, when he focused those glowing eyes deep into mine. "I could always make you…"

I pushed him away from me and tore off my shirt. "I am immune to your hypnotic ways…but I will join you." He laughed and we both finished removing our clothes.

I watched his flawless form enter the water and then dive under the deep surface. I crept up to the edge and dunked in a toe— it was freezing. Teren's head popped up near the middle of the easy flowing stream, and he casually held himself in place with a light back and forth motion of his hands.

"Come on. Just jump right in." He flashed me a gorgeous smile, and I suddenly wanted to be in his arms more than I cared about the cold. I gritted my teeth and ran into the water, my toes sticking a bit on the mud at the very edge. Gracefully, I dove under the frigid liquid and swam until I felt his body. I popped up right in front of him, gluing my legs around his waist, my arms around his neck. His hands worked a little harder to keep us both afloat and he laughed.

"Not so bad, right?"

My teeth rattled a little with the cold, but I nodded. Eventually his warmth alleviated my chill and my body acclimated to the water surrounding it. I relaxed the death grip my thighs had on him and lightly treaded water with my hands. Seeing me more at ease, Teren grinned and leaned over to gently kiss me.

"It's beautiful here, Teren," I whispered in between our kisses.

Never taking his eyes off mine, he nodded. "Yes, I know...beautiful." His gaze tracked down my body and I knew he wasn't talking about this perfect place he had taken me too. I felt flushed and tingly all over.

He replaced my arms around his neck, and swam us closer to the edge until his feet could touch the bottom. When he could stand, he wrapped his long arms around me and pulled me in for a searing kiss.

"Teren...tell me everything is going to be okay," I said, during a brief break in our kiss.

He pulled back to look at me; his face showed none of the doubt and fear that I would have felt if I were him. "Everything is going to be fine, Emma." His voice was low and soothing, full of assurance. He truly sounded like he believed that, like somehow, he knew it would all work out. I wished I felt his certainty. If things went wrong...they could go really wrong.

"Do you promise?" I knew the words were empty and pointless, but I sort of needed to hear them anyway.

His hand came up to cup my face. "I promise." His eyes searched mine, and the soft glow mellowed my momentary flood of panic. "I promise," he repeated, before bending down to kiss me.

Our kiss picked up intensity and urgency, and just when I was sure our heat would evaporate this idyllic brook, he picked me up and walked me to a soft spot of grass along the bank. Water rolled down our bodies and dripped off our hair, but I felt none of its chill as Teren laid himself over me, giving me his warmth, giving me everything he had. And in return, I gave every part of myself over to this remarkable man, who completely had my heart. Very quickly, his favorite place soon became my favorite place.

I awoke the next morning feeling satisfied, content, and in love with this wonderful ranch. I also woke up alone in our humungous bed—*that*, I didn't love. I looked around the empty suite. The fireplace was cold, the candles snuffed out, the curtains drawn tight, so that no light would touch my face to wake me up. I wondered if Teren had thought of that little detail before slipping away. We'd considered sleeping out under the stars last night, in that long grass near the creek, but the slight breeze along our damp skin had us redressing and hightailing it back to our plush, warm room in no time. I would never forget that stream, though.

I stood and stretched my arms high into the air, wondering where my vampire had taken off to, and why he hadn't awoken me. A small surge of *God, what else is he hiding?* panic filled me, but I pushed it back. He'd said he wouldn't do that anymore. If he was going to trust me, then at some point, I would need to trust him. I'd work on that.

I shuffled off to the bathroom, hoping maybe he was in there, but that room was also empty. I examined my I-had-sex-in-the-grass-last-night hair, and sighed at the straggly mess before me. After picking out a few long strands of dry blades, that had somehow managed to stay with me for the past several hours, I brushed the rest out into some semblance of order. I examined the pale, red wounds on my neck. They were now surrounded by a light, bluish bruising. Thank you for that, Teren. They were better than yesterday, but were still a huge announcement of my boyfriend's newest fetish, so I left my hair loose around my shoulders. I might have to wear a fifties-looking scarf tomorrow at work. Clarice would love that.

I finished primping myself in the bathroom and headed back to the bedroom to change clothes. I found my last pair of jeans and my last fitted button-up shirt. A last day of vacation feeling washed through me, and I smiled at how different this trip was from the last time. I liked it here. I liked being here. I liked watching Teren be here.

Thinking of Teren, I decided to test his impressive hearing. I sat on the edge of the bed and looked down. In a voice so low that the fabric of the bed swallowed it, and I was sure there weren't enough sound waves left to travel to wherever he was, I whispered, "Teren, I need to see you right now. Please come here."

I began to count in my head. I got to five and then the door was swinging inward. His concerned eyes swept the room before focusing on me in the bed. He was wearing a pair of black jeans that nicely set off the gray button-up shirt he had loose over the top of them. It was a yummy sight to see first thing in the morning. His blue eyes sparkled with concern. "Are you okay? What is it?"

I half-smiled as he closed the door and sat beside me on the bed, his face still looking worried. Very seriously, I said, "I missed you. You don't get to just leave me alone in a cold bed anymore without saying goodbye first." I twisted my lips at him. "Especially if there are no roses being left on my pillow."

His face was blank for a minute, then he relaxed into a laugh. Running his hand through his black hair, he shook his head. "I did try and say goodbye." He laughed a little harder. "You grunted at me and told me to go away..." he shrugged his shoulders, "so I did."

I pursed my lips at him. "I did no such thing."

He smiled in a knowing way. "Go ask my mom if you don't believe me. She was laughing about it when I went downstairs to see her this morning."

I clasped a hand over my mouth, embarrassed. Damn those vampire ears. And just when I was feeling so comfortable, too... I straightened my shoulders. It was fine. It wasn't like I'd asked them to take a walk again.

"Your family needs to work on boundaries." I blushed a little, knowing that I'd basically just said that directly to his family...but it was true.

He nodded. "I know. Believe me, I know."

We spent the morning with Jack and Alanna, eating breakfast and having breezy conversations, like no tension had ever filled this little family. It warmed me that whatever awkwardness there had been between mother and son seemed to have faded. Teren seemed to have forgiven her. She did cast concerned glances at the both of us throughout the morning, and I knew that she was desperately hoping Teren would stay near, that we would both stay near, but I also knew that Teren had no intention of doing so, and there was nothing I could say to make him change his mind. For some reason, he wanted to be on his own, and he wanted to stay in San Francisco.

Later, we went upstairs to Imogen's room and I apologized profusely for the subject I had brought up yesterday, when I'd crassly mentioned Halina's eating habits and chastised her for it, therefore also chastising Imogen, who wasn't entirely an innocent grandmother. Imogen shook her head as I said I was sorry for the hundredth time. "Dear, my burdens are my own. I'm not asking you to share them with me."

"I know...I just feel really bad for even bringing it up. I'm sure it was hard for you..." I paused, not sure where I was going with that. Teren grabbed my hand and squeezed it, while Imogen looked over at us from a picture of a blonde-haired, smiling man, who I could only assume was her late husband.

"The act itself was actually very easy," she said softly, and Teren looked up at her with surprise in his eyes. Imogen didn't talk about this, and after that statement, I wasn't sure if I wanted her to. She tilted her head at me and her eyes aged as she reminisced. "It was more like letting go of a wall around me. Letting go of struggling to maintain being decent and normal and...caving into the pure passion and aggression of insatiable hunger."

Teren's eyes danced as he listened to her describe her level of thirst back then. I watched his face with curiosity. Would it be like that for him too? Imogen's eyes flicked to his and then back to mine. "It's the watching them die part that haunts me...that forever stops me from caving again." She closed her eyes and shook her head as a red tear dripped down her cheek. "I can't do it. I can't live with the guilt of it." She opened her red eyes to sadly smile at me. "I can't live with any additional guilt, I guess I should say."

Standing, I crossed the room to embrace her. She returned my hug lightly at first, and then with more pressure. I felt her crying, and I rubbed her back. How odd to be comforting a vampire. How odd to be comforting someone who had lustfully killed on more than one occasion. How nice to know that, even after decades, someone can still feel so badly for taking a life that they never would again. It reaffirmed my decision that I never wanted to be a full vampire. I never wanted the temptation to take a life. I never wanted their level of guilt.

We talked with her a while longer on more pleasant subjects and discovered it was close to dusk when we were through. Teren looked at me as we walked down the stairs. "We should probably leave soon...I've got an early meeting tomorrow."

I sighed as I clutched his hand. "Yeah...okay." It was so wonderful here I almost hated to leave it. Of course, it would be nice to get back to closed doors that actually meant something. Maybe I should work on inventing vampire-strength earplugs.

Teren cocked his head and look distracted for a second. I stopped on the step and watched his face. He seemed to be listening to something. I strained my inferior human ears, but heard absolutely nothing. Finally, he looked over at me.

"Great-Gran wants us to come down to her rooms." He indicated the windows by the massive front doors. "It won't be completely dark for another hour and she wants to say goodbye."

He must have noticed the startled look on my face, even though I had been trying very hard to keep it even. "She really won't hurt you, Emma." He smiled at me reassuringly as he pulled my hand down the stairs.

"I know that," I sullenly muttered. I knew she wouldn't attack me, but I still wasn't relishing walking into her domain. Teren led me through the living room and over to a door that I'd just assumed was a closet next to some built-in shelving. He opened the door and we entered into...a closet. I looked around, confused, as Teren closed the door behind us. It was a walk-in closet with shelves along two of the walls. The shelves were full of women's shoes, jackets and other outerwear. A few of the shelves held mundane home essentials like lamps, matches, blankets, umbrellas, flashlights. There was also a couple of board games, and resting on the very top shelf—a rifle. I swallowed as I looked at that, but then decided that, in this house, that was probably the least harmful thing in the building.

As Teren fully closed the door, darkness engulfed us. His bright eyes glowed in the dark and I had a sudden "Seven Minutes in Heaven" flashback. Amused, I threw my arms around his neck and giggled as I kissed him a few times.

"And what are we doing in here, Teren?" I asked between laughs and kisses.

He returned both my lips and my humor. "Visiting Great-Gran," he casually replied. Then he reached out to the blank wall opposite the closet door and gave it a sturdy push. Something clicked and the wall gave way. I gaped as it swung open to reveal steep wooden stairs.

Evenly spaced lights lined the stone wall that seemed to descend into the middle of the Earth. Bracing myself, I took a deep, steadying breath. Teren laced my fingers in his and gently pulled me down the stairs. The staircase wasn't as long as I'd feared, and at the bottom it turned a corner into a stone hallway.

Now, I'd pictured Halina's lair a million times in my head, and a couple times in my nightmares. I always pictured rough stone walls, with manacles holding barely conscious men, with dripping, bloody wounds. I pictured a dirt strewn stone floor with large, dark stains that no amount of cleaning would wash away. Centered in the room on an obsidian dais, I pictured a massive, black coffin, lined in blood-red velvet. I pictured squeaking rats skittering around the floor, scurrying away to the darkest portions of the near-dungeon. I pictured snow white candles and wrought iron candelabras, straight out of Phantom of the Opera. I imagined a dank, musty odor that reeked of death. What I had never, ever pictured…was what the room actually looked like.

We walked around the corner of the hallway, and entered what I could only describe as a queen's bed chamber. The windowless stone walls were light gray and smooth to the touch.

Heavy, beaded tapestries hung around the room, all of them depicting glorious sunsets. The most beautiful, elaborate gold lamps hung between each of the tapestries, providing plenty of light for the room. The floor was a smooth, white marble with thick, padded, burgundy area rugs spaced evenly throughout. Further ruining my dark imagination, Halina slept in a regular bed. It was a beautiful four-poster canopy bed with sage and burgundy satin bedding and romantic, gauzy white curtains along the sides that were tied to the poles in an open position.

The room was well lit from the lamps, but she also had clusters of tall and short pillar candles on her mahogany dresser, vanity and the matching coffee table at the base of her bed. The burning candles made the room smell sweet and spicy, like cinnamon rolls. A couple plush chairs rested on the other side of the coffee table and three doors opposite the wall of the bed led to other rooms that she used. I was pretty sure that at least one of those rooms was a massive closet, holding her wide variety of skintight dresses.

The place was beautiful and majestic and a little heartbreaking, with the multiple reminders of daylight around the room. Aside from the tapestries, there were photos of the sun on her nightstand and dresser, and spectacular canvas paintings that she had created were drying near an easel set up in one corner of the room. Next to that was a tall bookcase, with just about every color of oil paint in the world inside of it.

Taking a final sweep of the room, I noticed a black and white photo on her vanity of an old-fashioned couple standing in front of a house, a house that looked suspiciously like the ranch hand's house. The woman was healthy, happy and obviously pregnant, wearing a long, flowing dress with her hair elaborately twisted on top of her head. The man had his arm around her and was the spitting image of Teren…only years younger. I realized I was looking at a picture of Halina and her husband…when she was human. The photo was a startling contradiction to the vampire, who was coming out of one of the three doors I'd glanced over earlier.

"Thank you for coming down," she purred at Teren as he walked over to give her a hug.

My eyes again flicked to the photo of Halina's husband and I marveled at the resemblance. I'd originally thought Teren looked like the women of his family, but I was wrong. He resembled his great-grandfather. I watched Halina eye him with fondness as they pulled apart from each other, and I clearly saw what Halina saw every time she looked at him—the man she'd inadvertently killed. I instantly ached with sympathy for her.

"Good evening, Halina," I said warmly.

"Almost, give it another fifty two minutes." She smiled over at me with a small half-grin. "Good evening, Emma."

I sort of had an odd desire to hug her. She seemed to sense that and her half-grin twisted to a wry one. I didn't really feel like touching her after that. Sympathy only goes so far after all. She indicated the plush chairs before the coffee table and Teren and I each took a seat. I glanced at Teren and wondered how long he planned on staying down here; I'd been expecting a quick hi/goodbye.

Halina brushed between us and crawled up on the coffee table, to sit next to the candles perched there. I watched her adjust her short, tight, black dress as she swung her legs behind her, to sit on her hip. I again stared at the picture of her as a modest human woman and marveled at the difference. She seemed to notice my gaze this time.

"Attractive, wasn't he?" Her voice was layered with sadness as she glanced at Teren out of the corner of her eyes.

I had been studying Halina in the photo, but looked back at her husband upon her words. "Yes…very." I peeked over at Teren as well, before my eyes rested on Halina's. She noticed my examination of Teren and her husband, and knew I had spotted the resemblance. She smiled warmly at me, for quite possibly the first time ever.

"His name was Nicolis. His family was Russian as well." She spoke a long flowery sentence in the odd sounding language. I cocked my head and waited for an explanation of the words. She didn't give them. Teren hung his head, and a sense of sadness swept through the stone room, making me shiver. The silence lasted for a solid thirty seconds before Halina spoke again.

"I'm glad you came back, Emma." She raised an eyebrow at

me. "Although, I *was* looking forward to tracking you down, if you didn't accept Teren's condition." My mouth fell open with an audible sound, as I realized that she really would have hunted me down and "wiped my memory" if I hadn't come back. She smiled at the look on my face. "I do so enjoy the hunt…"

The shiver came back up my spine at her words. Teren coughed into his hand. "Well, she did, Great-Gran, and I didn't need your help this time."

That made me look at Teren oddly. Exactly how many times had he spilled his heart to unwilling women? How many girls had dated Teren that no longer remembered it? Halina seemed to understand my strange expression and laughed. Teren glanced over at me and coughed again.

"Well…we should probably get going…long drive." He tore his eyes away from my narrowed ones and looked back to Halina; she was fluidly rising from the coffee table. Teren stood and embraced her. "We won't stay away so long," he said reassuringly, as he picked the tiny woman up.

She giggled like a teenager until he set her down. "Good…we do miss you." After I stood from the chair, Halina faced me and placed a hand on my stomach. The sudden move shocked me into stillness. Her expression took on a longing wistfulness, and I remembered her story from the other night…about wanting to fill a farm with children. I wondered if her mournful gaze was for hoping I got pregnant soon, or for wishing she was still able to. Either way it softened me, and I placed my hand over her chilly one.

She jerked her eyes up to mine, seemingly surprised that I would willingly touch her. Honestly, I was a little shocked as well. Her face relaxed as we stared at each other. "The baby will be strong and healthy," she said as she gently patted my stomach. Tears unexpectedly stung my eyes, as I suddenly hoped she had an unnatural ability to sense these things. She dashed that hope by adding, in a near pleading voice, "I believe there will be time."

I nodded and finally embraced her. She was hesitant at first to return my hug, but eventually she warmly clasped me back. Teren was smiling when we pulled apart. "We should say goodbye to the others," he said, before he briefly hugged her again. "Goodnight,

Great-Gran."

"Goodnight, Teren…Emma."

We left her absently staring at the photo of her long dead husband, and then we made our way to the hallway leading back to the stairs, and out of Halina's throne room. Once back in the closet, Teren pulled a piece of string attached to the inner door frame that I hadn't noticed before, and yanked the false door closed with a small click. As he opened the other side, I thought over the meeting with Halina. I still wasn't pleased that she killed, and I really wasn't sure how often she did that. Teren made it sound like she merely…hunted, and that most humans made it out from under her teeth safely, but the knowledge that she *would* take a life was a disturbing thought to have when you were around her. Sometimes she could seem so fragile and innocent though…like when she spoke of the sun, or her husband.

"What did Halina say?" I asked as we walked back into the living room.

He understood what I was referencing—the Russian that they all spoke and I didn't. He gave a sad glance back to the door before answering me. "She said that he was the ray of light that lit her world, and the moment she ended that light, hers died as well…" He looked back to where my eyes were tearing up again. "She said she paints every sun as a memorial to him…"

That was just too much to bear, and the tears dripped down my cheeks. Teren smiled and rubbed them away before giving me a tender kiss. I savored his warmth and his strength and fortified my stomach. Darn emotional vampires.

While not completely dark yet, the sun was low enough, that Imogen was in the kitchen with Alanna and Jack. Knowing they were both in there, Teren headed straight to the kitchen from the living room. I wondered what that felt like to him, this odd blood connection that instinctively told him exactly where his family was. Did he feel it in his skin or was it a nagging sense in his head, like a GPS navigator that he couldn't turn off…"turn right at the next corner." It'd be interesting to feel what being an Adams vampire felt like…for maybe a day. After that, I'd be tired of hearing every bump and whisper for a half mile, having people intuitively know where I was all the time, and of course, the craving blood thing. That still did not sound appetizing at all.

We exchanged hugs and niceties, and said goodbye to his family. They politely asked if we wanted to stay for dinner and although Teren did eye the empty carafe waiting on the counter, he said we had to get going; he had an early day tomorrow.

Both women rubbed my stomach, just like Halina had, and I suddenly felt like a good luck Buddha statue. I knew they were all imparting well wishes and hopeful thoughts, but it just made me feel really weird. I dealt with it though. This was important to them and, who knew, maybe their vampire mojo would work on me? I *was* keeping an open mind on those urban legends. As Imogen rubbed her hand over my stomach a second time while Teren peacefully chatted with his father, I wondered with a slight bit of irritation if *he* was going to be rubbed. It was a two person project after all.

After a ten minute goodbye session and more promises to return soon, Teren zipped to pack our stuff and load up the car. Three minutes after that, we were bouncing down their long driveway. I turned in my seat to watch the last of the sun wash over the house of vampires.

"You had a good time, didn't you?" Teren asked, watching me.

I nodded and sighed in happiness as I faced back to the front. We passed under the Adams sign and I chuckled again at the odd thought I'd had on my first arrival here. They were still a little spooky, but now they were a lot less creepy. I was starting to love this little Adams Family. And I did already love their son. I rested my head on his shoulder and laced the fingers of his free hand in mine as we hit the asphalt of the highway.

"I had a great time, Teren."

He kissed my head and we began our sixty mile drive back home.

Chapter 12 – A Camping We Will Go

Monday morning came with me rising alone in my bed. Of course, I'd also gone to sleep alone in my bed. I found I didn't like that nearly as much as I liked falling asleep in Teren's warm arms, his heart thumping against my back. But Teren hadn't been lying about his early morning meeting. He had dropped me off, insisted on helping me with my bag, which I really could have handled by myself, gave me a long, lingering kiss goodbye and then headed home.

I'd had the momentary, *Hmmmm...I should drive over there, slip into his house and crawl into his bed while he's sleeping* thought, but I had decided that sounded too Fatal Attraction-ish, and stayed put in my cold, lonely bed. Then I'd wondered if Teren and I should just move in together already. The thought made me laugh out loud. Here we were, actively trying to get me pregnant, and I had to wonder if we should live together? Our relationship was so backwards...but I kind of loved that it was.

I thought about my weekend while I brushed my hair for work, and took a minute to examine my neck. It was healed enough that I could pass it off as a rousing make-out session, if anyone asked—and really, who besides Tracey would ask me that at work? I did make sure my hair covered it though. I thought about the fight Teren and I'd had, and the argument he'd had with his mother.

He'd asked her pointblank to not tell me the details of his conversion and she'd done it anyway. I'd be upset at my mom, too, if she'd done that to me. But we weren't talking about letting some embarrassing childhood memory slip out in conversation, we were talking about the possibility of him killing me or killing someone else. *That* was worth her betraying his trust. That was something I needed to be aware of.

As I got dressed, I wondered what I was going to do with that information now. I slipped on my slacks and a lacy camisole and replayed his thirst during the couple of dinners that I had witnessed. Teren had stared at the blood on the table like he wanted to stick his head in the pot and drink it dry. I'd never seen him look quite so foreign, and it had been a little shocking, and possibly even a little frightening. But I had to believe that it was just his body preparing him for the conversion. That he'd calm down about it, once he switched over. I mean, the girls hadn't seemed that affected by the blood on the table. Imogen even sipped hers, like it was a twenty-year-old Scotch. The intenseness of his desire had to be because it was new. It just had to be.

Because if it wasn't...

I didn't finish that thought. He was in an adjustment period. We would be fine. He assured me of that constantly. I already wasn't thrilled about his "brilliant" plan though. I was supposed to somehow get a dying man to my car, and to the ranch, before he woke up ravenously hungry in the middle of the city. Really? Was I superwoman now? What if it happened at work, and by the time I got there, he'd passed out? Well, okay, technically he'd be dead, but I was thinking of it as him being passed out so I didn't lose my marbles. Was I supposed to secretly drag his limp ass to my car with no one seeing us? And what if someone else found him first? Did I break into the morgue and pop him out of cold storage? There were so many ways his plan could go wrong that my mind was starting to spin. I had to forcefully switch to another train of thought. Hell, I needed to pull into a different *station* of thought.

Emptying my brain of conception-reducing worries, I slipped on my jacket. Feeling the wounds on my neck, I fluffed my hair around my shoulders to cover them with the long strands. Teren had sure enjoyed doing that. Personally, I thought the thigh would be more appealing, being a little sexier body part and all, but he'd sure gotten excited over just the memory of biting my neck. I wondered if that was because the artery was so close to the skin. He'd be able to feel it with his lips before he bit down. And being so close, he barely had to bite before he got a nice little stream. I laughed as I grabbed my bag and unburied my keys from inside it. Maybe, like a lot of men, my vampire was just a little lazy, and didn't want to have to work very hard for his meal.

I was still chuckling over that thought as I walked to my cubicle. A couple of men eyed me on the way to my desk and I rechecked that my hair covered my injuries. The men seemed more focused lower on my body however, and I silently thanked my cleavage-enhancing lacy camisole for distracting their attention. I plodded over to my cozy chair and stuffed my still-full purse in the drawer. Even though, a few weeks ago, I had spent a solid twenty minutes cleaning out the junk that had collected in my favorite large bag, some garbage must have crawled back in already.

I was considering downsizing to a smaller bag that left me no option for pack-rattery, when Tracey bounded to my cubicle and leaned against a wall. "You are not going to believe the weekend I had," she sighed.

I shoved my drawer closed and took in the elated expression on her face. The glow in her eyes and the softness of her smile meant only one thing—Tracey had found another love interest. Poor Hot Ben probably had zip of a chance after all. I played my suspicions off with cluelessness though.

"What happened?" I asked in my most interested voice, while I silently felt bad for her dumped beau.

She sighed and placed a hand on her heart. "Ben finally called me."

I blinked at that. He did?

"He did?" I immediately asked after the thought.

She bit her lip. "Yeah. He said he was miserable and missed me and wanted to come over." She sighed again and gazed at me dreamily. "He was so sweet, Em, and sounded so lost...I just couldn't say no."

I held back a smirk. Of course. *He* was the one in misery and she was simply doing him a favor by letting him near her. Couldn't be that she was missing him just as badly. Oh no. I wondered if Tracey would ever take a little closer look at her own feelings.

Before I could find an appropriate comment to her situation, she continued. "He came over and we talked and had dinner and..." Her eyes lost focus for a while, as she reminisced on the remainder of their evening. I was fairly certain it had involved a lot fewer clothes than the evening had started with. She came back to herself and her blue eyes locked onto mine; a serious glint was in them. "I never knew it could be like that with him. It was sort of...magical." She gave me a hopelessly goofy grin and I knew my poor, clueless-about-her-heart friend, had finally felt the first twinge of love for a boy. And it had only taken her twenty-six years and over twice that many boys to do it. Some people just fight against feeling content.

"I'm so happy for you, Trace. I think you two are really great together." I matched her lovesick look with one of my own. I was a girl hopelessly in love with a vampire after all. "Teren will be so happy to continue our double dates. He really likes Ben."

Tracey started nodding while I was still speaking. "Oh, I know. Ben likes him too. Although…"

A slight panic shot through me…had he noticed something? Tracey didn't seem to catch my look and she finished her thought, "Ben swears he saw his eyes glow once." Shaking her head, she started laughing. "Sometimes, that boy has the strangest imagination." She glanced at her boss's door and then started walking away, muttering something about glowing eyes and ridiculousness.

Right…imagination. Hmmm. I hoped Hot Ben's imagination never became a problem.

Ben subbed our kickboxing class that night and, since I hadn't actually seen him in a while, I took a moment to take in his features—black shorts, tight, black shirt that nicely emphasized his chest, bleach blond highlights in his light brown hair, and a chiseled face that was causing quite a stir with a couple of teenage girls in the corner of the room. He looked like same old Hot Ben, but was he different? Had he pieced together anything? It seemed impossible that he had; suspecting that someone you know is a vampire just doesn't happen in real life. I'd need to watch him extra close now, to be sure.

He got us sweating pretty good in our workout and my mind eventually stopped worrying about it. When class was over he came up to me and I tensed a little, wondering what I'd say if he asked me anything. I planned on laughing and giving him my best *Are you mental?* face, but when he came up to me, it was only to tell me that I did a good job in class and that he was looking forward to hanging out with Teren and me again. I smiled and relaxed. There was no way he suspected anything even remotely close to the truth about my boyfriend. And I liked Ben. He was good for Tracey. I smiled as I watched them leave the group fitness room hand in hand. They were warmly smiling at each other, even though they were both dripping with sweat.

I met Teren for dinner afterwards, and he was just as thrilled as me that we'd have dates with Tracey and Ben again. I smiled that my vampire liked my friends. Aside from me, he really didn't seem to hang out with anyone. Occasionally, he'd meet with a coworker for a beer. I'm assuming that was with Mike, since they were close enough for Mike to give him those amazing baseball seats. And occasionally, he'd be on the phone with other friends, talking about a sports game, fishing stories, or an article for work, but he never really went out regularly with other people. Just me.

It made me a little sad to think that because of his impending doom, he was purposely distancing himself from being close to another person. A really close friend would probably notice his changes afterwards. And the rest of his family did pretty much keep to themselves on their "little" ranch. I suppose it's easier to hide what you are if no one is looking too closely. That made me glad that Teren had me. He'd be so lonely during this scary time if he didn't. And finding a girlfriend after the change would have been a lot more difficult. Maybe. He was darn attractive after all.

Time sped up in the way that time can when you're happy and content. Teren and I continued our baby making efforts with a near zealotry. Halina was right, we were running out of time. We met with my family and talked over the myriad events that happened to a person over the course of seven days, the things that we could mention at least. My neck wounds had faded away by the time we got together, but I didn't speak of them to my family. Not even to Ashley. That might have stretched even her tolerance level. We went to work every day, we took his pup for long walks at the park, and Teren often made me dinner, usually enjoying his chicken-draining more than the actual meal.

It was a few weeks after our wonderful weekend at his parents' ranch that Teren and I went on our first double date with Tracey and Hot Ben, since their reconnection. I suggested we go to a nice restaurant that Teren and I had gone to before, down by the wharf. Tracey thought that was a great idea and set it up with Ben. I chose going out to eat, because it was the one activity that we'd no longer be able to do as a group in a few months. Teren's birthday was in November…we were already in the first half of September. His days of being able to digest were quickly dwindling. I tried not to think about what else was dwindling. Despite our best efforts, as of last week, in the most obvious way my body could tell me, I still wasn't pregnant.

We all sat at a white, linen-covered table with a spectacular view of the bay, sipping our wines—two reds, two whites. Ben held Tracey's hand and eventually leaned over to give her a soft kiss. She stroked his hand with her thumb and leaned her head on his shoulder. It made me smile that they'd finally crossed over to the next level of intimacy.

I grabbed my own man's hand while we chatted about things to go do together: a movie Tracey wanted to go see, a baseball game Ben wanted Teren to get tickets to, a new dance club that was opening up in a couple weeks—standard dating stuff. Then Ben threw out an idea that filled my belly with apprehension.

He causally tossed it out there as the waiter was walking away with our food orders: Lobster Thermidor for Trace, Salmon and King Crab Roulade for Ben, Duck a l'Orange for me, and for Teren…the bloodiest prime rib they could legally serve him, of course.

"So, you guys want to go camping this weekend?"

I sputtered on my wine and couldn't answer. While I recovered, Teren chipperly said, "Sure. I love camping. Where do you want to go?"

I turned my head to discreetly stare at Teren. He'd said once that he liked camping, but, he'd also mentioned that it was hard to disguise his eyes and Ben had already thought he'd seen them once…

"I reserved a spot at Yosemite months ago, and Trace and I are going. There's some really great country over there, once you get away from the city."

I cringed at Ben's words, but Teren seemed perfectly relaxed. "Sounds great. I love Yosemite Valley. We could hike up to the Falls." Then Teren seemed to remember that I existed. He turned his head to me and twisted his lips in question. "Is that okay with you?

Do you want to go?"

That took me back. Was he going to go whether I did or not? Maybe I was wrong about his tendency to only hang out with me. Maybe he just hadn't found the right "bromance." I forced my features to maturity. "Of course I'll come too. That sounds…interesting." I raised my eyebrow on the end of that and Teren grinned before returning to his wine.

Tracey perked up from beside Ben. "Oh good. Someone to do girlie things with me while the boys fish."

I smiled at her and tried to picture the upcoming weekend. I just couldn't quite get there though. My vampire and I were going camping. My glowing-eyed vampire was going to be one with nature, with his possibly suspecting guy friend and a woman who would scream so loud if she ever found out what he really was, that she'd alert everyone as far south as San Diego to the situation. Interesting indeed.

I couldn't dwell any longer on it, or secretly whisper to Teren that he was nuts and he shouldn't agree to go, because our appetizers arrived. Oyster shooters. I gave Teren a secretive smile as I took one. Like we needed an aphrodisiac. Like there was any chance he wasn't going to get lucky tonight. Teren noticed my private smile and gave me one right back; he knew full well where our night was headed.

Not too long after our appetizer arrived, our main courses were brought out. Everyone's meal was topnotch, but I did notice Teren's lack of enthusiasm over his food. The last time we'd come here, he'd devoured his meal, but tonight, he was kind of picking at it. I squeezed his knee under the table in encouragement and he looked over at me with a tiny, unsatisfied smile.

That was when he started staring.

It started with just a simple glance at my neck while he lazily ate his prime rib. Then he looked back for a few seconds longer while he took another bite. About two thirds through his meat, he openly stared at the arch of my neck while he chewed. With three or four bites left on his plate, he gave up the pretense of eating and his eyes bored holes into the vein of my neck. If he were Spike, and I was a bacon-flavored rawhide bone, there would have been drool from

Teren's mouth to the floor.

Tracey and Hot Ben were too busy feeding each other from their respective meals to notice Teren's absolute interest in my body. I smacked his thigh, but he wouldn't stop staring. Knowing that he should be able to hear me, I whispered at him to stop it. He was either too preoccupied to listen, or he didn't care. His mouth dropped open and his eyes ran up and down the length of skin from my ear to my shoulder. I suddenly remembered his fangs dropping down at just seeing the carafe at his parents' place, and I got really scared that Teren was going to lose himself to this craving, and expose himself to my easily freak-outable friend.

I wanted to snap my fingers in front of his face, but that felt too obvious of a maneuver with Tracey and Ben sitting so close. They were still engaged in complimenting each other's meal choices, but really, if one turned our way and saw the look on Teren's face, a look that clearly was saying to me *God, I want that so bad*, they'd be pretty weirded out.

I grabbed Teren's hand and gave him a rough yank. That didn't work like I'd planned. He opened his mouth wider and hissed under his breath, bringing his head closer to me. We had already been sitting near each other, both on the same side of the table, chairs touching, but now he was leaning into my shoulder, staring down at my neck…and he was starting to breathe heavier.

Tracey laughed at something Ben had said and started to turn her head to me. With my hand, I covered my neck, as casually as I could, hoping that would break Teren's focus. "Emma…did you hear that?" Tracey turned all the way to look at us and scrunched her brow when she saw Teren. "Is he all right?"

My heart was thudding so hard I thought it might jump out of my chest. I risked a glance over at Teren; he'd snapped out of it a bit and was focusing on his plate as he tried to breathe steadier. His face was pale, and he almost looked confused.

I grabbed his hand, making him look up at me. His brow furrowed and he frowned. "Actually, he's feeling a little sick." I said, looking over at Tracey. "We're gonna go outside for a minute…get some fresh air."

Tracey's face oozed sympathy as she watched me grab my clutch purse and stand him up. Ben's concerned eyes matched hers. "Hope you feel better, man."

Teren lamely nodded while I started walking him through the sea of linen-covered tables. I wondered if he had even heard any of that conversation…or anything during dinner. I walked us through the elaborate double doors out of the restaurant, and then looked around for a secluded spot. Across the parking lot I saw an elegantly fenced in area for the garbage receptacle. The gate on the wooden fence was partially open, so I knew it wasn't locked. Looking around for witnesses and not seeing any, I pulled Teren in that direction.

He hesitated at first, not seeming to understand what we were doing or why, but then he relaxed and let me pull him. He'd either stopped wondering or stopped caring. The glum look on his face didn't leave him, though. I pulled us through the gate and shut it behind us. It was dark with the gate closed and Teren's eyes glowed at me. I used the peace from his gaze to calm my wildly beating heart. He had almost fanged me in front of Tracey and Ben…I was pretty sure of that.

For even more privacy, I moved him to the far side of the dumpster and then I began to hitch up my flowy, knee-length dress. That seemed to break through his melancholy.

"What are you doing?" he asked, in a thoroughly confused voice.

I gathered the light, breezy fabric just above my thigh, bunching the material against my purse as I held my leg up to him. "Drink." My tone implied an order.

He blinked and started to back away. I grabbed his dress shirt and pulled him closer. "Drink, Teren," I firmly repeated.

This time, he shook his head and looked around the dark, enclosed area with the large, green container overflowing with rotten seafood and plastic bags of filth. "No, Emma…not like this."

I grabbed his face and made him look at me. "You are going to attack me in the middle of that restaurant, if you don't get some blood in you. Will you please just drink me now, so we can go back and have dessert without massively freaking out our friends?"

With a guilty face, he nodded and exhaled a slow breath. I shoved his shoulder down as he bent to one knee. He placed my leg on his shoulder, so he'd have a better angle, and I leaned back against the fence to support my weight. He made a low noise in his throat; the vibrations affected me more than the slight coolness of the approaching fall air. Goose bumps danced across my flesh as I felt the stubble of his jaw brush across my thigh. I ran a hand back through his hair, allowing myself to breath heavier. It was private out here…no one would know what we were doing. And if anyone suspected by the noises, even though we were both being pretty quiet, well, I was pretty sure they would expect to see something other than a man dipping into my femoral artery.

"I shouldn't want this so bad…" I heard him mutter, his breath hot against my tender skin.

I was about to tell him I felt the same way, when his teeth grazed my leg and I felt them extend to fangs. He sank them in without a second's pause and we both groaned a bit. He worked his hands up both legs while I held my dress for him. He took long, deep draws and made groaning, satisfied noises, like he was finally getting what he really wanted. A part of me delighted that I could give him something that pleased him in a way nothing else could. A part of me was worried about how deeply this seemed to please him.

He took another couple deep draws, and just when I started to feel the tiniest bit faint, he tilted his head and his eyes flashed to mine. I held my breath at the fire I saw burning in the glowing orbs. Bedroom eyes had nothing on sucking-on-your-thigh eyes. I stopped caring about Teren's needs as I stared into those eyes. I stopped caring about Tracey and Hot Ben wondering if he was okay. I stopped caring about a busboy coming out here with a bag of garbage. I stopped caring about anything outside of those blazing, blue eyes, and I started caring about my own needs.

Dropping my purse with a dull thud to the concrete, I grabbed Teren's face and yanked him off my thigh. He came freely, blood dripping off his chin, a warm trickle of it running down my leg. He usually licked the wounds closed, but I hadn't exactly left him the option. I pulled his face up to mine, not caring about the blood on his tongue, his fangs in my mouth…only needing him.

His hands scrunched my flimsy dress up to my waist and then ripped down my underwear. My hands made short work of his belt and slacks. We were both panting as we took our passion for each other to a whole new level.

Pushing me up against the fence, Teren held my bloody thigh at an angle and moved into me. I clamped my mouth shut to contain the moan I wanted to make, while Teren let out a satisfied noise that I hoped no one heard.

Squeezing my thigh with one hand, my dress being held against my hip with the other, Teren thrust into me over and over. The openness of our location, the strain of not letting myself cry out, the cool air against my skin, all made me reach my peak faster than I would have thought possible.

I held my breath as euphoria washed through me. My eyes fluttered closed and my head hit the fence behind me. I shuddered and clutched his back as the overwhelming intensity rippled through my body. Teren adjusted his position inside of me, as he drove into me with abandon. A few wild thrusts later had him slowing, stiffening, and then relaxing against me with a deep groan.

Having sex with a vampire beside a waste bin overflowing with smells that churned my stomach, after letting said vampire drain my leg to near shaking, was definitely right up on the top of my *Things I never imagined myself doing* list. Teren had opened my world in ways I'd never anticipated.

After our intense moment, we both clutched each other and tried to calm our breaths. He pulled away from me and licked a smidge of blood from my chin. I closed my eyes and smiled. Then I remembered the trickle down my thigh that I'd felt earlier.

I exhaled in a grunt. "Great...I'm bleeding."

Teren fixed his clothes, wiped the blood from his chin and gave me a cocky smile. "Not a problem."

He returned to his knee and cleaned the red trail with his tongue, staying on the circular wounds until the bleeding ebbed. I tried to not enjoy it too much. Really, once by this reeking dumpster was enough, and we did have curious friends waiting. But damn if it didn't turn me back on a little bit.

Teren seemed to understand the look on my face when he was done. "Later, Emma. We do have people waiting." He handed me my purse, then my silky underwear. Flushing, I slipped them back on. In the faint light that he emitted, I checked my clothes for bloodstains. I appeared to be all clean though. I looked over Teren's clothes as his fangs retracted; his seemed to be clean as well, thank goodness.

His face was happy and relaxed, and held no trace of the confusion or turmoil he'd shown earlier. I carefully watched him as he took my hand and led me out of that darkened area that we'd just christened. A light smile was on his lips and his eyes had the slightly unfocused look of someone a little tipsy. He walked straight and confidently though; it was just an odd, satisfied look on his face. A look I realized would be painfully obvious to Tracey, when we sat back down with them.

I stopped him as we started walking back through the parking lot. He turned to look at me, all happy and content like. I frowned. "Can you try and look like you've just been sick…not like you've just had sex?" I straightened out his clothes again and rechecked us both for bloodstains in the brighter lights of the lot.

"I'll work on it," he chuckled, the look not leaving his face at all. "I'm just so…relaxed."

I scrunched my brows as I examined his features. "You should give me a heads-up, the next time your urges get that bad."

He half-grinned and started pulling me towards the restaurant. "I'll work on that, too."

Once inside, I slipped away to the bathroom to see to my leg while Teren went to sit back down. I didn't think it would bleed again; Teren was generally pretty good about making sure my wounds weren't flowing before he left me alone. I liked to think that was out of concern for me, but honestly, it could have been because he didn't want to miss a drop of his liquid diet. Feeling that "better safe than sorry" was a more prudent approach to dating a vampire, I'd started packing Band-Aids in my purse.

After making sure I was one hundred percent alone, I lifted up my dress and examined the wounds in the gilded mirror. The bite marks were larger than he'd ever made them before. I thought back to the moment and realized that it had hurt more than usual; he hadn't been as gentle as he typically was with me. I'd just been too turned on to care. I sort of cared now, as I ran a finger over the red marks.

Digging through my purse, I found a bandage and pulled it out. It was just large enough to cover the area. As I was patting it into place the bathroom door opened. I immediately dropped my dress and crumpled the bandage wrapping in my hand.

Tracey walked through the door, sweeping the room until her eyes met mine. "There you are. Are you okay?"

I stuck on my fakest smile as I discreetly dropped the bandage wrapper into a nearby garbage. If she had come in just a few moments earlier and seen the fresh wounds..."I'm great, Trace...just freshening up."

She nodded, understanding that feminine need. Taking a second to glance over her own appearance in the mirror, she fluffed out her blonde hair and checked her eyes for stray makeup in the corners. "Okay...well, the guys ordered us a Bombe Alaska to share, and they just dropped it off." She glanced over at me. "You missed the fire show." A Bombe Alaska was the same as a Baked Alaska, except a ladle of lit brandy was poured over the meringue top of the dessert at the table. It made for a fun little presentation before the flames died out.

I frowned, genuinely disappointed. "Oh...that's my favorite part." She finished prepping and I asked her, as casually as I could, "How's Teren? He thought he was feeling better, once we got outside."

Tracey smiled as she grabbed the door handle. "Oh yeah...he seems great. Near elated, I'd say." She raised an eyebrow at me as she opened the door. "What exactly were you guys doing out there?"

With the look in her eye, the smirk on her lips and the suggestive tone in her voice, I knew that she knew exactly what we'd been "doing" out there. Well, the tail end of it anyway. I looked away with a soft, embarrassed smile, and she laughed at me as we left the room.

I thought over our garbage receptacle escapade on the drive home. I thought about the moment before that, at his eagerness while feeding on me. I rewound a bit before that, to him muttering that he shouldn't want it so bad, and then I rewound a little more, to him mentally draining me at the table.

I cleared my throat. It was loud in the relative quietness of the car. "Um…Teren…"

"Yeah," he replied, his voice slightly husky.

The alluring sound made my pulse quicken, but I forced my head back to my troubling thoughts. "What was that at the restaurant?"

With a serious expression Teren met and held my eyes. "Well…" he looked back to the road, "sometimes, when a man and a woman really love each other, there is just no other way to express it but physically. And sometimes, the overwhelming desire to be together, takes a person over in the oddest places, and you simply cease to care where you are or who's around." He looked back at me with a wry grin on his lips. "Sometimes urges just need to be filled." His voice when he said that almost made me grab the wheel and make him pull over…but we weren't on the same page.

"I'm not talking about the sex…jackass." I rolled my eyes while he chuckled, clearly enjoying teasing me. "I'm talking about dinner, when you were staring at me like I was a lamb chop…remember?"

He grinned and looked over to me again. "Oh…don't sell yourself short." His eyes roamed up and down my body, making me feel hot all over. "You're filet mignon, at the very least," he whispered.

Again, I ignored his attempt to deter me with his evocative talk. "Will you be serious for a moment and answer me?"

He sighed, and with genuine sincerity on his face, he looked over and whispered, "I don't know, Emma." His eyes went back to the road. "Food has been…" he grimaced, "…losing its appeal to me." He shook his head. "I was eating that steak and thinking about how, if we were at my parents' place, I could have a glass of blood with it." Just his eyes flicked over to mine. "Then I heard your heartbeat and I saw the vein in your neck quiver." His eyes went down to that vein in my neck, as he continued in a husky voice. "I started imagining that sweet warmth filling my mouth, rolling over my tongue, coursing down my throat. I pictured my lips on your skin, the groan you would make in my ear." His eyes raised to meet mine. "I just couldn't care about the steak after that."

Well, holy hell. *I* didn't care about the steak after that little description. I leaned over and started sucking on his earlobe. His mouth fell open in a heavy exhale. "Take me home, Teren...quickly," I whispered. His foot slammed down on the accelerator.

***

"Teren, I'm not so sure about this..."

Teren paused in picking up our tent, leaving it on his half circle drive for the moment. "It's just camping, Emma. It will be fine, really." He effortlessly lifted the tent up with one hand and shoved the heavy bag into his trunk, like it weighed no more than a pillow.

I scowled at the display. "You can't do stuff like that around them."

He rolled his eyes. "I know that, Emma. I have been doing this for twenty-five years, you know." He indicated the bags and coolers around our feet. "I just don't want to be late, and we've got a lot to pack."

"Teren..." My tone indicated that I wasn't done disagreeing with him yet. He frowned at me as he picked up a full cooler and breezily put it in the car. "He suspects. How are you going to hide your eyes?" I asked.

Teren gave me a blank look, then laughed. "Is that what you're worried about? My eyes?" He continued laughing while I scowled again. It really wasn't that funny...or preposterous. Ben had seen them glow before, and if he saw them this weekend on our little camping excursion, well, who knows what he'd think?

Still laughing, Teren said, "Trust me, Emma, he's already written that off to a weird angle, or a flash of stray light...or a brain aneurism." He looked over at me with a wide grin. "He's not suspecting what you think he is. It's not like I was staring deep into his eyes, trying to seduce him or anything," he quipped.

I twisted my lips at that comment. "Well, even if it was for just a second, he still saw it, and you said it was hard to hide in the countryside—"

He cut me off by walking over and squatting to look me in the eye. "I was playing with you, Emma. Okay? It will be fine."

He kissed me on the cheek as I bit my lip. "But…how are you going to hide it?"

He sighed. "During the day, it obviously won't be a problem." I already knew that, so I waited for him to continue with an impatient expression. "I will be in front of the fire before it gets dark. I will stay within the firelight until you and I retire for the evening." He playfully grabbed me and pulled me tight to his body. "And then, I'll glow all night long for you in our tent. Perfectly alone and perfectly safe…okay?"

I tried to find the flaw in that to argue with, but his lips were on mine then, and my argument drifted off my tongue when his brushed against mine. Darn capable kisser.

Finally, he pulled away from me. "Stop stressing, okay." He continued packing our car while I kept on stressing…in my head.

I imagined all the ways this weekend could go wrong. I imagined the innocent, from Ben seeing him lift our impossibly heavy bag one-handed, to the not-so-innocent: Ben walking in on Teren caving to one of his new, primal urges, and sucking my other leg dry. Both seemed equally possible and equally horrific. But I was still coming. I wasn't about to let my vampire go off to possibly expose himself without me.

Teren finished loading up his Prius, while I watched and worried. Spike, maybe sensing my unease, or maybe just being excited for a road trip, was bounding between Teren and me, circling my legs and licking Teren's arms. After Teren was done loading up our stuff, his fishing pole shoved in last, he bent down and rumpled the fur around his pup's ears.

"Sorry, pal…you can't come this time." I cocked my head and wondered why, while Teren gave his dog kisses on the nose.

Looking over, Teren seemed to understand my curious face. "The park only has certain areas you can take dogs, and we'll all probably go fishing so…" he shrugged and stood up, "he'll have to stay home this trip." He ruffled Spike's head one last time, before grabbing his collar. "I don't think Tracey was too thrilled about a dog coming, anyway. I think she's scared of dogs." He threw me one last lopsided grin before walking his Collie around his house, to the large indoor/outdoor kennel that he'd built in the backyard for his beloved pooch.

I chuckled internally at that comment. Tracey was scared of Spike? Teren was ten times more dangerous than that mellow canine. Of course, Tracey didn't realize that, thank God. Teren came back a few moments later without Spike, and I pictured his furry dog finding the fresh rawhide that Teren had left for him, circling a few times on his cozy doggie bed, and burrowing deep into the plush blankets for a long day of bone gnawing—doggie Heaven.

Teren gave me a peck on the cheek, and then we hopped into his car and started the near four hour drive to Yosemite National Park. Teren called Ben on the way over, to let them know we were headed out. It was early Saturday morning and our hope was to be there before noon. I sipped the espresso Teren had made for us while he calmly chatted with Ben for a few more minutes.

My stomach was an anxious mess as I thought over Teren's firelight plan. I started at the feeling of his hand dropping to my knee. "You're worrying."

I looked over to see his lips curved in an amused smile. "One of us should be, Teren. Sometimes, I think you're too casual with your secret."

He frowned. "What would you have me do? Never leave my house? Stay hidden away from the world, so that I never experience any of it?" His eyes drifted back to the road, while his hand went back to the steering wheel. "You're starting to sound like my parents." He shook his head, a little irritated. "I don't want to be scared of what I am…of who might find out. I don't want to spend every day, locked up on a ranch with people just like me." His eyes shifted back to mine. "I want to live, Emma. I want to experience everything this life has to offer. I don't want to hide." His hand reached out and he stroked my cheek. "How else would I have met a fascinating, beautiful woman who irritates and enriches me?"

I grinned and rolled my eyes. I supposed he did have a point. You couldn't really live, if you were always being super cautious. Sometimes risks were warranted. I just wasn't entirely convinced that "camping" was a necessary risk. I forced it to the back of my head. It was Teren's secret. If he was comfortable with this level of exposure, then I guess I would have to be, too. Because really, the last thing I ever wanted to hear him utter again was that I was sounding like his parents.

I sank back into the seat and enjoyed the beauty of the California countryside as it flew by me. Teren squeezed my knee again, turned up the radio, and relaxed back into his seat as well. This weekend would be fine. This weekend would be fun...even if I had to choose to believe that.

We chatted about his work on the way. His newest assignment of, "The Best Bike Trails in the City, That You Don't Know About", was turning into one of his favorite pieces. We chatted about my work and how Clarice had me prep a tax file for Jon Voight, and I briefly got to see the actor in the hall before he disappeared into Mr. Peterson's office. I told Teren that I'd practically met Brad Pitt, and he looked at me with a peculiar expression. Smiling with enthusiasm, I explained that since he was Angelina Jolie's father and she was with Brad Pitt, then I'd just successfully placed myself in "Six Degrees of Separation" with Brad. Yeah, he rolled his eyes at that too.

We were talking about what kinds of fish Teren was hoping to catch on the trip, and he assured me that he'd only use his pole to catch them, when we turned a corner through the scenic sequoias and the focal point of Yosemite Valley came into view. Half Dome peak was one of the most recognizable peaks in the world. It could be seen from nearly everywhere in the valley. It looked like Paul Bunyan had walked right up to the mountain and swung his axe, cleaving the top of it in two. Then Mr. Bunyan had strode off with half the tip and left behind a perfect, well, half dome. It was a breathtaking sight.

A little surprised at how quickly we'd made the long drive,

and wondering how fast Teren had pushed his little Prius, I looked around at the thick, green blanket of trees lapping up to the majestic gray peaks that were formed into unique shapes and sizes through eons of erosion and glacial carving. The passage of time deep within the layers of those rocks, made this twenty-five-year-old human girl feel very mortal and insignificant. The entire valley imbued a sense of permanence that was difficult to grasp. Being in this place made you believe that we were all pebbles in a much bigger pond. A pond with infinite edges that we would never fully see or understand...nor were we meant to.

Entering the valley, we drove past what looked like a perfect rectangle of granite, reaching as high as it could towards the Heavens. This particular formation was known as El Capitan, and it was a stopping point for rock climbers from around the world. As we drove miles below it, I imagined I could see tiny humans dangling from seemingly too-thin ropes as they scurried over the dusty surface.

Teren glanced up with me. "Rock climbing might be fun one day," he casually said.

I looked back at him with an *Are you serious?* face. "After you're all super-healy, you can go up there, but you couldn't pay me to go with you. I'd rather not break every bone in my body...thanks."

He laughed at my comment as we continued driving through the sea of sequoias. Eventually, we pulled into the campground. The trees encroached on our car as we drove under a canopy of the majestic, red-barked monoliths. I could see ragged scratches along some of the trunks, reminding me that we humans, and one vampire, weren't the only inhabitants of the forest.

We drove over the pine strewn road to a lot in the back, where Ben must have told Teren our reserved space was. Pulling up next to Ben's gray Honda Pilot, we parked and stepped out of the car. The sunlight hazily filtered through the massive limbs high in the air above us, and the distinctive smell of the pine trees, interspersed among the redwoods, hit my nose and made me smile. I glanced over the top of the car at Teren, who had a smile similar to mine plastered on his face. Nature could be so beautiful.

We walked a few feet into our camp and I smiled at Tracey,

who was helping Ben set up their tent. And by helping, I mean she was idly holding a pole in her hand while he figured out which way the X pattern was supposed to line up. Spotting me, she waved, giggled, and dropped the pole. Ben frowned at her while every piece of the tent fell apart. Teren laughed and went over to help him while Tracey came over to me.

"Cute pants," she exclaimed, as she flicked a pocket flap on my side. I laughed as I looked down at her cargo pants; they were the exact same as mine, only khaki, not sage. Apparently, we had both shopped the same fifty percent off rack at Macy's last week.

"You too."

She adjusted her t-shirt and ran a hand back through her loose hair. "Thanks. Shall we make lunch while the boys work?" She nodded her head back to where the guys were struggling with the tent. I grinned as Ben lost a pole somewhere in the fabric, and the entire half that they'd managed to erect fell down. Ben ran a hand through his highlighted hair and sighed, while Teren laughed at his misfortune.

"Yeah...good idea."

We rummaged through the coolers in the cars and made up some sandwiches for everyone. We found a bag of chips and some sodas, and then packed the coolers into the provided bear-proof food lockers. There was nothing about having our food locked away in a 33x45 inch metal locker that made me feel any better. Just the fact that bears roaming around the campground was so commonplace that they'd felt the need to install these lockers gave me pause. That was a little closer to nature than I wanted to be.

Coming up behind me, Teren laced his arms around my waist and whispered in my ear, "Don't worry...I think I can take a bear." I looked at him over my shoulder as he opened his mouth and flicked his tongue over his canines. I laughed at the implied gesture, and felt a little better about the situation. No matter what, my pit bull would protect me.

Turning in his arms, I slung mine around his waist. "I'm sure you could," I whispered. "And what a treat that would be for you— better than a chicken."

He laughed at my comment, and I hugged him. Over his shoulder, I could see the successfully raised tent. My eyes slid over to where Teren had also set up our smaller, and more easily put together tent. It was a few feet from Ben and Tracey's and back a bit from the fire ring. Breaking apart from Teren, I searched his eyes. The campground was well shaded with the towering trees around us, and while there was still plenty of light, it wasn't the same as being directly under the sun. I was attuned to Teren's glow, so I clearly saw it in the whites of his eyes, but no one else would notice…until nightfall.

I sighed and he smiled. "It's fine, Emma…don't worry."

Ben came up behind us and clapped Teren's back. "Worry about what?"

Teren smiled and casually said, "Bears."

I blinked my eyes at him in surprise. It was so easy for him to lie. Although, it wasn't really a lie. I was a little concerned over that, too.

Hot Ben gave us a glorious smile as Tracey came up and wrapped a hand around his toned stomach. "Don't worry, I've been coming here for years and I've never seen one. It will be fine." He patted Tracey's hand while he spoke, and I wondered if she'd had the same concerns that I'd had. Knowing Tracey, I was sure she had.

We contently ate our little lunch. Well, everyone except Teren was content. He eyed his sandwich a little grumpily, and I wondered if maybe we should have found a way to sneak in some blood to keep him satisfied. Oh well, he'd have to deal with it until bedtime…then he could get a nibble off me. After our meal, we debated what to do, while we removed all traces of food and put away the rest of our stuff.

Since it was only just after one in the afternoon, we decided to hike the Upper Yosemite Falls trail to Columbia Rock; it didn't go to the top of the falls, but it was a much less strenuous climb, although still a pretty good workout. We all got into our hiking shoes, shoved some water, trail mix and a digital camera into Ben's backpack, and drove to the trailhead to park our car for the couple hour hike.

The first thing I noticed was that there weren't a lot of people on the trail. Most of the visitors also seemed to be doing the lower trail; there were plenty of couples with young children and older grandmas and grandpas shuffling along those paths, taking pictures of the vista around them. Ben explained that it was because the famous falls were dry for another month or so, until the winter snows fed them again. He said he liked coming here this time of year, because it was quieter, less touristy.

I agreed as we neared our destination of Columbia Rock and no one seemed to be around us. Tracey and Hot Ben were on the edge of the rock, snapping photos of the trickling falls, the granite mountains surrounding them, and the valley of green trees nestled between them, when I heard a sound behind me that made me forget every worry I'd ever had about Teren's eyes. In a flash, I was reminded of the real fear I should have been worrying about all along.

Teren and I had been standing quite a ways back from the edge, away from Tracey and Ben, as we caught our breaths from the hike and looked at the majesty before us. The noise I'd heard, was him dropping to his knees, clutching his chest, and groaning in pain. Tracey and Ben hadn't noticed yet, and I immediately dropped to his side.

"Teren…what's wrong?" I frantically whispered.

He looked up at me, his face contorted in agony as he clutched his hand over his heart, like an old man having a heart attack. That was when it hit me. He *was* having a heart attack. He was about to die at the top of an hour long hike up a mountainside, and at least a four hour drive from the ranch. He was about to die in a place that I couldn't possibly even begin to remove his limp body from on my own. He was about to die, and reawaken, in a place where currently only me, Tracey and Ben were present. He was about to wake monstrously hungry and one, if not *all* of us, were about to die, too. And then, a still hungry vampire would be loose among the crowds of men, women and children that we'd passed on the way up to this slope.

I immediately realized how foolish this trip was. Now was not the time to be in the middle of nowhere, and hours away from the safety and solitude of the ranch. My earlier concern of exposure was near silly now. That had never been the real issue. *This* was the real issue. And it was happening now…

His eyes tightened in pain as his hand reached out for me. I had no idea what to do, no idea how to help him. Should we start down to the car now, while he was still conscious? Do we clue in Ben and Tracey, or just quietly leave while they were snapping scenic photos. I wanted to scream at him to give me answers. I wanted to comfort him as he was dying. I wanted to cry. I was too scared to do anything though. I just watched his hand slowly snake up to my neck.

Then that hand grasped my neck and jerked me forward, until my lips crashed into his. His mouth found mine and hungrily pressed against me. Confused, I started to push him away. He laughed and pulled me closer, parting my lips to sneak his tongue inside. That was when my second startling revelation hit me. He was *faking*.

I jerked away from him and smacked him soundly across the head. He frowned and rubbed his ear. "Ow, Emma," he pouted…the jerk actually pouted.

In a harsh whisper, I screeched, "Don't you ever joke about that again, Teren! I was scared shitless!" I smacked him again on the head. "I had no idea what to do!" I tried to smack him again, but he grabbed my hand and pulled me into his lap. "I'm supposed to take care of you, and I had no idea what to do!" He brought his hands to my cheeks, his eyes showing genuine remorse for his stupid joke. I could feel frustrated tears forming, and I tried to blink them back. "I had no idea what to do…"

I couldn't hold back the sob and he quickly pulled me into his shoulder and scooted us to the far side of a large boulder, where Tracey and Ben wouldn't be able to see us. Rocking me back and forth on his lap, he rubbed a hand up and down my back.

"I'm sorry, Emma. I'm so sorry. That was a stupid joke. I'm sorry." He kept repeating it over and over, as he rubbed my skin under my light jacket.

Eventually, my fear subsided and my tears dwindled. Feeling a little stupid over my reaction, I pulled back to glare at him. "That. Was. Not. Funny." He sheepishly held my eyes as I stated, "Do not ever tease about that again."

Cringing, he solemnly nodded. He helped me fix my face, and then we stood up and joined a still oblivious Tracey and Ben in viewing the glorious beauty before us. It felt a little less majestic to me with a small river of fear still flowing through my system. Yes, he had been stupidly messing around with me, but that didn't change the fact that we shouldn't be here right now. If that had been real...

I couldn't even finish that thought.

Chapter 13 – The New Plan

"We shouldn't be here, Teren," I whispered. The breath needed to make speech barely passed my lips, but he heard me. His lips compressed into a tight line and his jaw clenched with the restraint to not answer me.

This was the fourth time I'd uttered that since our descent down the mountainside back to the car. Each time Teren had ignored my near imperceptible speech, but I knew his abilities, I knew his stubborn, vampire ass could hear me. We were driving back to the campsite, with Tracey and Ben chatting away in the back seat about all the miraculous things we'd seen—eagles, deer, rabbits, claw marks from bears on trees, what Ben swore was a mountain lion paw print and of course, the stunning view. Teren and I nodded and smiled every once in a while, but neither one of us were really listening. We were having a near silent argument. One I was determined to win.

"Tell them you are feeling ill and we have to go home." I spoke so low, *I* couldn't even hear me.

His eyes not leaving the road, his jaw not unclenching, he slowly shook his head no.

I suppressed a sigh. "You're being stupid. We shouldn't be way out in the middle of nowhere. We should be closer to home."

He closed his eyes for a second, and then reopened them and looked in the rearview mirror. "Hey, Ben," he said casually, like he wasn't as irritated as I was. "Want to do a little fishing when we get back?"

I turned in my seat to give him an icy glare. *Really*. Was he just going to run off and ignore how irritated I was?

Hot Ben glanced at Tracey, who dreamily nodded at her bleach-blond highlighted fisherman. His chiseled face returned to Teren's in the mirror. "Sure, man…sounds great! We'll catch us some dinner."

"Perfect," Teren said happily. He gave me a pointed look. "That's the most perfect plan I've heard in a while."

I snapped my head away from him and resisted the urge to smack that smug look off his face. Jerk. Big vampiric jerk.

When the car stopped at our campsite, I immediately got out and huffed over to our tent. Noisily pulling the zipper, I ducked inside. I re-zipped it on the inside and silently cursed that I didn't have a heavy door to slam...that would have been much more satisfying.

"You are such a freaking asshole! Your vampire ass better stay far away from me," I sullenly muttered, knowing full well he could hear me. Sure enough, a heavy sigh answered me from the other side of the tent.

I paced the inside, while I listened to Hot Ben and Teren gathering their supplies. Tracey giggled at something that Ben was doing to her. I suddenly hated how easy their relationship was, especially since Teren and I were smack-dab in the middle of a secret fight. I could see Teren's body blocking the light, just on the other side of the fabric separating us, and I had a sudden moment of sadness sweep over me. That thin barrier between us suddenly felt metaphoric in the worst possible way. In that instant, I wanted him in here with me, more than I wanted to continue the fight...but he'd injured my pride. I couldn't cave that easily.

I watched his shadow bend down to pick up his fishing pole near the tent, then straighten back up. His shadow paused, and for a moment we stared at each other, without really seeing each other. I knew he knew exactly where I was in the small tent though; he'd be able to hear my heartbeat, even all the way outside.

"Ready, Teren?" I heard Ben calling, from over by the vehicles.

His shadow never moving, Teren softly said, "Yeah...I'm ready."

His shadow narrowed to a thinner sliver as he turned away from me. I couldn't handle that. "Wait," I whispered. His shadow immediately hesitated and the shape of his head turned towards me. "Please come back before dark. Please be careful."

It was as close to "I'm sorry and I'm hopelessly in love with you, so please don't let anything happen to you" that I could say, without conceding defeat.

I watched his head drop as he absorbed my plea. He nodded, and I felt that he truly understood everything I was silently saying to him. Stepping closer to the tent, he raised a hand up to the fabric. I raised my hand as well and our fingers touched through the thin material. I had to hold in the tears at that insignificant, but so powerful connection.

I swallowed and his shadow fully turned away from me. Then I heard his car hum to life and crunch over the small twigs along the road as they slowly drove away. I curled into a ball on our sleeping bags and desperately tried to stop the sudden panic that flew into my throat. What if something happened while he was gone?

I was in that fetal position when I heard our tent being unzipped. I looked up to the door, right as Tracey poked her blonde head in. "What'cha doing in here?" She looked around the small space before returning to my eyes. I prayed they weren't glistening. Apparently they weren't, for she cheerily stepped inside, re-zipped the tent, and plopped down on the bag beside me. Lying back with her arms above her head, her long hair fanning out around her, she sighed, "Isn't Ben dreamy...?"

She then began a fifteen minute soliloquy on the perfection that was Hot Ben, while I tried to force down the fears and insecurities I had about my relationship with Teren. I tried to be the good friend that listened, encouraged, asked the right questions, and probed for all the right secrets. The secrets that she acted like she didn't want to talk about, but really, she did, she just wanted to be asked.

I tried...it was difficult at first. I still felt like sobbing, and even though Tracey was oblivious to my bad mood, I was sure waterworks would clue her in. And I couldn't talk about it with her. I couldn't tell her that my soon-to-be-dead boyfriend had just jokingly faked his death, and it had made me realize how terrifying that day was actually going to be for me. I couldn't ask her what I should do about it. I couldn't ask for opinions on how to change the stubborn man's mind. I couldn't tell her that the stress was giving me an ulcer. I couldn't talk with her about any of that...because she couldn't know his secret. Unlike my sister, Tracey would not handle it well.

But eventually, talking with Tracey about her mundane relationship eased my mind, and as we were laughing over Hot Ben's toe-sucking fetish, my heart finally started to lift. I silently thanked Tracey, for the unknowing support that she was giving me.

After a while we emerged from the cave-tent I'd been hiding in, and we attempted to do something adventurous while the men were gone—we tried to make a fire. We walked back to where you could buy bundles of firewood and picked up a couple each. Feeling like quite the do-it-yourselfers, we giggled all the way back to our campsite. We got an offer of help from a friendly, older man, playing with his two grandkids a couple of spots away, but we politely refused his offer, since we were feeling pretty good about ourselves.

We felt less good about ourselves when we struggled with the actual making a fire part. Neither one of us had ever done it before. It didn't seem like it should be rocket science though. We made a little tepee with wood, shoved some newspapers that we'd found inside Ben's car underneath it, and then lit those papers with a match I'd found among Teren's things. The paper lit immediately, curled, blackened and then drifted away on the wind, leaving just barely scorched wood above it. We lowered the tepee and tried again. After the third attempt, we finally had a nice little blaze going and we did a little girl-power jig, right there by the fire pit.

That was when the boys showed back up. The headlights flashed along our gyrating bodies and laughing, we both looked over as the car shut off. Tracey squealed and ran to Hot Ben's side, throwing herself into his arms and showering him with kisses. My reaction was much more restrained…Teren and I weren't exactly on the best terms right now, after all.

Teren slowly opened his door and got out; his eyes never left mine. My heartbeat suddenly shifted into triple time, and I focused on maintaining an even breath. He cocked his head to the side, like he was listening to my reaction, and then biting his lip, he walked over to where I was standing beside the fire.

"I'm back," he said softly.

I nodded, tears filling my eyes. "I can see that." My arms slipped around his neck and my head buried into the crook of his warm skin. I inhaled the scent of pine, water and pure man that came off him, and squeezed him tight as he lifted me a good foot into the air.

He exhaled a long breath and nearly squeezed the life from me as he held me in that position. It wasn't exactly an end to our argument, but it was an acknowledgement that we were still in this together. We were still hopelessly in love.

I brushed a couple of tears off my cheeks as he finally set me down. His pale eyes locked on my tears, concerned, and he seemed about ready to speak, when Ben and Tracey came up to us. "Did you tell her about the rainbow?"

Ben clapped Teren's shoulder, while Teren muttered, "No, I hadn't gotten to that yet."

Ben looked at me, his expression animated as he held his hands out, indicating a size. "Yeah, we caught this rainbow trout that was at least this big. Right, Teren?" Teren glanced over at the distance between Ben's palms and feebly nodded. Ben swished his hands. "We had to release it, 'cause you can't keep rainbows…but it was cool." He pointed over to a bucket beside Tracey. "We got a couple of browns for you guys to cook up." He gave Tracey a loving look. "Nice fire, babe." She giggled, and they proceeded to make out for a couple minutes.

I sighed and met eyes with Teren again. He sighed, too, then pointed to the fire. "It is very nice." His eyes flicked around the forest that would be darkening within a half hour. "I think I'll have a seat." I nodded and sighed again as he went to sit down. We may have acknowledged the love between us, but we needed to have some words, too, and we couldn't do that with Tracey and Ben right beside us.

Tracey and I went about figuring out how to fillet and prepare fish for frying. Ben had to come over to help us at one point, which led to more inappropriately graphic displays of affection, but eventually we started cooking them, and our campsite filled with the smell of oil, fish and spices. We dished up our meals with the food the boys had caught, and then we all sat around the campfire and ate the fish with some rolls, a green salad and a bottle of wine.

The sky darkened as we ate, and the absence of light made

me even more aware of sound. I heard the snap-crackle of the fire, the light laughter of our neighbors in the campground, the skittering of small animals in the underbrush, and the larger creatures, rustling among the trees. I hoped none of the noises were bears. As we cleaned up all evidence of dinner, Tracey seemed to feel the same.

"You don't think any bears are around, do you?" she nervously asked Ben.

He gave her an award-winning smile, making her flush, but Teren answered before Ben could, "There aren't any bears in the area tonight."

They both stopped flirting with each other to look over at him, and I shut my eyes for a moment. I knew he knew that because of his extra abilities; he could probably distinguish an animal's heartbeat from a human one, and a bear would have a pretty big heartbeat. Perhaps he could even smell if any bears were nearby. But Tracey and Ben wouldn't know why Teren seemed to know that with such certainty.

With everyone looking at him, Teren shrugged his shoulders. "I talked to a ranger while we were fishing. He said there hadn't been any bears around the campsites for a while, they're all higher up the mountains." He nodded his head over his other shoulder, indicating where the bears supposedly were.

I narrowed my eyes, wondering if any of that was the truth or not. Ben nodded. "Is that who you were talking to?"

Teren met my eyes and nodded. "Yeah."

I held his gaze for a long time but I couldn't read him. I didn't know if he was being honest or not. I hated that I didn't know for sure. I hated how good he was at lying and yet, at the same time, I understood why he was. I searched his eyes while he searched mine, and I decided to just let this one go. We had enough issues between us tonight. Before I looked away, I noted that he was right about his eyes; there was a distinct enhancement that I could easily see, but a normal human would write it off as an odd play of light from the fire. His eyes were fine. His eyes were no longer the problem.

After cleaning up, Tracey sat in Hot Ben's lap, and before long, their fun flirting turned much more serious. Giggling, they hastily said goodnight and darted off to their massive tent. They never even looked twice at Teren's eyes—they only had eyes for each other.

Teren and I sat on opposite sides of the fire, staring at each other. His eyes bored into mine, reflecting the firelight back to me—orange irises in a sea of startling white. Our stare down was interrupted by a ranger walking down the road.

"Ten o'clock, fires out." He told us, politely, but firmly, as he walked by.

Knowing that all Californians took fire safety pretty seriously, we stood and immediately doused the flames. Teren's eyes obviously glowed as the last of the orange flames died out.

"I'll be in the tent," he muttered.

"I'll be there in a minute," I replied.

I watched his form in the darkness, his glowing eyes turning to regard me once before ducking into the safety of the tent and disappearing. I sighed and grabbed a flashlight, making my way to the bathrooms before bed—I had no desire to pee outside.

When I got back, I slipped into the tent and changed into thermal pajamas. It got pretty cold at night here. I thought for sure Teren was already asleep, until the glow of his eyes ignited into life and turned to watch me.

I slipped into the two sleeping bags that we had zipped together to make one large bag, and Teren's hand hesitantly reached out for me. I shifted towards him and he placed his hand on my stomach; his face was blank in the dim light he emitted.

"You're still mad at me," he whispered, shifting to his side to face me.

I sighed and brought a hand up to cup his cheek. His eyes closed for a fraction of a second, momentarily slipping us into darkness, before reopening. "Yes," I said simply.

He sighed and rested his head against mine. "I'm sorry, Emma. How do I make this go away?"

I pushed him back a little. "You don't make this go away,

Teren. We have to talk about this, really talk about it."

Rolling over to his back, he removed his hand from my body; the glow of his eyes splashed along the ceiling of the tent. "There isn't much to talk about, Emma. I was joking around…it was inappropriate and I'm sorry." His eyes flashed back to mine. "How long are you going to keep punishing me?"

I sat up on my elbow, my eyes narrowing. "Punishing you? Teren…this isn't about your stupid joke."

Now he sat up on an elbow. "Then what are you so mad about?"

I let out a disbelieving sound. Did he really not grasp this? "We shouldn't be way out here in the middle of nowhere, Teren." He rolled his eyes, which pissed me off even more. "Your parents are right. It's not safe," I whispered.

Leaning in close, his eyes flared with anger. "God, you sound exactly like them now. Have you switched to their side?"

I shoved his shoulder away from me. "There are no sides, Teren. There is safe and there is not safe." I indicated the looming forest around us full of innocent people. "This is *not* safe."

He ran a hand down his face, plunging us into darkness again. "It was a joke, Emma. I'm not dying this weekend. I could feel it if I were, and I'm not—I'm fine!" His voice was low, but harsh. I listened in the darkness for anyone who could have overheard that, but all I heard was the escalating sounds of Tracey and Hot Ben's flirting. I stopped listening, and focused on Teren's dark shape.

I grabbed his cheek, and he reopened his eyes as he moved his hand away from his face. Able to see him again, I took in the thin, hard line of his lips, felt the rigid tension in his jaw. My own muscles felt tight as liquid fire flashed through me. "You could feel it? Are you a freaking psychic now?" His mouth dropped open and the glow of his eyes narrowed. He started to answer me, but I beat him to it. "How do you know what it's going to feel like? How many times have you died, Teren?" I snapped in a low voice.

His face came right up to mine again, only inches away, and a flash of something else mixed with my anger. I pushed the minute desire back and focused on my anger. "I know my body, Emma."

I scoffed at that. "Really? That's why you nearly took a bite out of me at dinner a few nights ago? 'Cause you know your body so well?"

He backed away, the glow shifting down as he studied the floor. If I could see more of him, I was sure I'd see that he was blushing. "It's not happening right now," he sullenly muttered.

I flopped to my back, annoyed. Neither one of us was going to budge on this tonight. Teren flipped onto his back, and we both stared at the seam in the ceiling that his glowing eyes illuminated. Clear sounds of passion were drifting over to us from the tent next door, and Teren's hand under the sleeping bag scooted over to brush against my leg. The slight movement made a different kind of heat pulse through my body, but I forced it back as well. No way the jerk was getting lucky now, not after the afternoon we'd had.

Not sensing my mood, his hand grasped me more firmly and started traveling up my thigh. I still didn't move, not encouraging, but not discouraging either. Teren rolled to his side and brought his other hand to my stomach.

His warm lips found my neck. "Emma…," he breathed against my skin, "let's not fight…" The ache in his voice just about killed me, but I pushed him back.

Surprised, he blinked his glowing eyes as he studied me. I ignored the hypnotic, trancelike feeling of that gaze and looked away. It was a rare event when I turned Teren down, and it had never happened since we'd decided to try for a baby.

"Emma?" he asked softly.

I turned back to the glow of him. "No, Teren…not tonight."

"Aren't we trying for a baby?" he scoffed.

My eyes narrowed. Well, that just made this a heck of a lot simpler. I poked a finger in his chest. "I said, not tonight." I circled the finger in the air over my body. "This is a restricted area. And you no longer have clearance."

Irritated, he shifted his glowing orbs away from me.

"Goodnight, Emma."

I rolled away from him and moved to the edge of the bag, so we weren't touching. "Whatever, Teren."

I awoke the next morning in a cold, empty sleeping bag. I looked around the small tent, but Teren had slipped out and wasn't with me. Sighing, I stretched and massaged a lump in my back, where I'd apparently slept on a boulder. Getting some fresh clothes for today, I unzipped my bag and scrounged through my stuff. I dressed as quickly as I could in the still-chilly morning air, slipping on my hiking shoes last.

Sliding out of the tent, I immediately spotted Teren. He was sitting alone by the fire, poking the ashes with a stick. He looked sullen and unhappy, and I hated that we were fighting. He didn't look up when I approached. I sat beside him, resisting the urge to touch him. I hated it though, and with a heavy sigh, I stopped resisting and let my hand fall to his knee.

He looked over with soft, pale eyes. "I'm sorry," he quietly said. "I hate fighting with you. I was..." He looked around the campsite, like he was suddenly unsure of what to say.

"An ass..." I supplied, with a slight curl of my lip.

He let out a small laugh as his eyes returned to mine. The mound of tension between us seemed to dissolve in that laugh. We relaxed in the camp chairs, his arm draped over mine on his leg, our shoulders touching. "Yes...an ass. I'm sorry, it's just..." He searched my face while he searched for words. "My entire life, I've had people telling me what I should do, where I should go, when I should marry, when to have children..." He shrugged his shoulders. "I got so sick of it. I just wanted to be my own person, with my own goals, and my own dreams." He pointed at the ground in front of him. "I wanted my own life."

He looked out over the forest as he spoke in a whisper, "I fought hard to live in San Francisco...away from them. I think they only finally let me to appease me, like eventually they'd snatch me back." He shook his head. "I guess when people start trying to force their way on me, that old resentment rears up, and I just get really...defensive."

Looking over at me, he meekly smiled. "I'm sorry. I don't want to be that person with you." He cocked his head to the side in an adorable way. "Forgive me?"

I swallowed as I studied his beautiful face. He was so amazing, how could I not forgive him? Smiling, I leaned in to kiss him. I pulled him in deeper, until our kiss was intense and passionate. When Teren started to breathe heavier, I pulled away and whispered, "I'll think about it."

We both laughed and sat back in our seats, resting our heads together and enjoying the stillness of the morning. Finally, he broke the quiet. "I'm really sorry I screwed up this weekend. That was really stupid. I didn't mean to scare you." I nodded against his head and closed my eyes, to hold in the sudden tears. "I love you, Emma," he whispered.

"I love you too, Teren," I whispered back.

We let the fight between us die as we tightly held each other's hands. There would be time. We could discuss it more, later. For a long, peaceful moment, we watched the leaves dance in the light breeze and listened to the morning birds calling to their mates, then a zipping noise signaled the arrival of our site-mates.

I watched Tracey as she stepped out of her tent. She wore fresh clothes as well, and had her long blonde hair pulled up into a ponytail that mirrored my dark mane. She zipped back up the tent, leaving Hot Ben behind. Maybe he was still sleeping. Their night had been a rather long one.

Yawning and rubbing a kink in her back, she walked over to where Teren and I were cuddling by the dead fire. She sighed as she sat down opposite us. "I don't know if I can do tent-sex again," she muttered, right in front of Teren. He lightly coughed and I could feel him smile as he kissed my hair. Tracey continued, like she was only talking to me. "I swear I have a rock permanently embedded in my ass." She rolled her eyes and tried to rub out her bottom. "Next time he can get the rock in his butt, I'm taking the top."

Teren stood at that point. Running a hand through his hair, he looked back at me. "I'm gonna…get some…firewood…or something." He leaned down to kiss me and then walked away from

Tracey, lightly shaking his head.

I smiled as I watched him leave, then turned back to Tracey, who didn't seem to catch that he left because of her sharing. Tracey and I chatted about more specifics of her evening, details that Teren definitely would not want have wanted to be privy to, until eventually Ben peeked his frosted tips out of the tent. Tracey grinned at the sight of the rugged I-haven't-shaved-in-twenty-four-hours-and-my-camping-hair-is-a-rumpled-mess hotness that was Ben. He grinned back at her as she rose to meet him with an adorably sweet kiss. I was pretty sure that Tracey would put up with a lot more rocks in her ass to be with Ben.

A few minutes later, Teren came back with a couple loads of firewood. Looking a little relieved that the "girl talk" was over, he nodded at Ben. After Ben greeted him, the boys went about making us a warm, filling breakfast. I briefly kissed Teren when he handed me my plate of bacon and eggs. He grabbed my cheek and stared at me intently, like he was trying to silently convey just how horrid the last several hours had been for him. I nodded while my eyes moistened. I understood; I'd felt it, too. He acknowledged my nod with a soft kiss.

"I love you, Teren…but we still need to talk about this…later," I whispered under my breath as he sat down beside me with a plate of his own. He held my gaze for a few long moments, then he nearly imperceptibly nodded.

Relief filled my body. He was going to at least talk with me about it—hopefully without getting all defensive and pissy. I understood where he was coming from but I didn't think he understood where *I* was coming from. Without asking me, he'd heaped a lot of responsibility on me in this "plan" of his and I was scared. No, scared didn't cover it…I was terrified.

After breakfast, the guys wanted to do a little more fishing and Tracey and I decided to join them. We spent the remainder of that lazy Sunday along the banks of the Merced River. We drove a few minutes to a parking area and walked along the rocky edges of the picturesque stream. Ben would say, "This looks like a good spot," and Teren would throw me a sly glance and respond with, "No, I think the fish are further upstream." I bit back a smile, knowing my vamp was sensing things that poor Hot Ben would never be able to.

Everyone listened to Teren's suggestions and we ended up stopping at a spot that looked like an artist had painted it. Thick, majestic Douglas firs and sequoias lined the banks of the broad, slowly churning river. Huge boulders created perfect spots for Tracey and me to sit and dip our fingers into the icy waters. Teren and Ben moved a few feet away from us and cast their lines into the clean, crystal-clear stream that was home to huge trout. Even I could see some occasionally swimming by. Eagles were perched high on some nearby tree branches, watching for meals of their own, and Half Dome peak provided a magnificent backdrop that was almost too perfect to believe was real. It was a stunning location.

The boys chatted back and forth about fishing lures and other places around California that they'd been. I noticed that Teren never mentioned his parents' ranch and the fishing hole he and his dad frequented, and wondered if that was because Ben would naturally ask to see it and that was just something Teren wasn't willing to let happen yet. That thought reminded me that my mom had wanted to see the ranch. Hmmm…maybe she'd forget if I never brought it up again. Yeah…right.

Tracey and I found a nice spot on some large, flat boulders to lie down on, and we enjoyed the warmth of the sun on our faces while we chatted about work, Ashley, and our fishing boys. We had flipped onto our stomachs and were sort of ignoring the men, as we chatted about the latest celebrity gossip. I was sharing my "I practically know Brad Pitt" story, which Tracey appreciated a lot more than Teren had, when an icy blast of cold water hit my previously warm lower back. I screamed. Tracey matched my startlement as her own skin was suddenly exposed to the frigid river water.

I flipped over and glared up at a laughing Teren. He was standing above me, wiping his wet hands on his jeans. He and Ben had thought it funny to cup a handful of icy water and dump in on our backs. Why does that sort of thing amuse men so much? I jumped up and smacked his shoulder while he laughed and backed away from me. I heard Hot Ben spouting something behind me and knew Tracey was probably smacking the crap out of him too.

Teren suddenly picked me up and scooted me back into the forest a little ways. I could hear Ben and Tracey giggling, but I could no longer see them. Teren backed me into a tree and pressed his body along the length of me. I suddenly didn't care about the fight we'd had. I suddenly didn't care that he'd just doused me with water. I suddenly didn't care that our friends were ten feet away.

I ran my hands up his back and pulled him tight against me. His lips hungrily met mine and he made a deep noise in his chest as his hands ran over my body. I threaded my fingers through his hair as my tongue sought his. I moaned in his mouth when we brushed together.

His mouth scooted over to my ear and sucked on the lobe. "I want you," he growled. I gasped, amazed at how much that feeling was reciprocated, how much I wanted him. His mouth trailed down my neck as his hard body pressed into mine.

"How do you want me?" I murmured.

His blazing eyes pulled back to look at me and my breath increased at the passion in them. His fiery eyes flicked back to the bank, where Tracey and Ben were still laughing. When they flicked back to me, his fangs were extended. "Every way," he husked.

Well, damn…

I struggled to remember that our friends were a short distance away, and I couldn't entertain this little vampire fantasy right now. I ran my finger along an extended tooth and he quivered. I pressed the pad up against the point until it poked through the flesh. I cringed at the momentary pain but stopped when his warm mouth closed around my finger and started sucking.

Oh, hell…

"Hey, guys?"

Ben's voice shouting to us from the riverbank startled me from the hotness of the moment. Teren stopped sucking on my appendage and lightly shook his head; his fangs retracted as he did. Taking a deep breath, he forced himself away from me and smiled with just the corner of his mouth. I struggled to put myself back together as he answered Ben.

2

"We're coming," he shouted towards the bank.

I heard Tracey laugh and mutter, "I bet they are." My face heated at her comment and Teren chuckled and looked at the ground. When we were both more collected, he extended his hand to me, and I happily took it. We emerged from the forest a few minutes later. Hot Ben and Tracey looked at us with knowing smiles before laughing and cuddling into each other's arms again.

"Ready for lunch?" I muttered, walking over to Teren's backpack to get the picnic we'd tucked in there. Only light laughter answered me and my face flushed even more.

A few hours later we were on the highway, driving through the sea of green trees, heading back home to Fog City. We were zipping along a few paces behind Ben's SUV, and I could see his and Tracey's heads leaning together in a sweet kiss. I thought about how tender and romantic their weekend had been, and how different an experience mine had been. Not that Teren and I hadn't had our moments—that last by the river was still burning through my body—but for the most part, our weekend had been an enlightening one.

As Teren had been helping Ben take down the tents and load up the vehicles, and Tracey had been regaling me with tales of more camping trips she wanted our foursome to take, my mind had been spinning with the ineptitude of Teren's plan.

It wasn't going to work. I needed him to see that. I needed him to at least consider that possibility, without ripping my head off. I looked over at his softly smiling face as we followed Ben's vehicle away from the park. I hoped that smile would stay on his face after this little conversation...we needed to have it though.

"Teren..."

The edges of his lips curled down as he instantly knew what we were going to talk about. So much for the smile. He looked over at me out of the corner of his eyes. "You want to do this now?" he asked.

"I just want you to listen to my side...that's all."

His eyes relaxed and his mouth softly curled into a smile again. "I can listen. I am capable of that."

I exhaled in a long, calming breath as his eyes went back to the road. Seeing the smile still on his lips, I quietly began, "I'm terrified, Teren." He turned to look at me with furrowed brows, and I continued before he could interrupt. "Your little stunt yesterday has clearly shown me that I can't do what you're asking of me. I just can't, Teren."

He returned his eyes to the road with his forehead still scrunched. I couldn't tell if the expression was anger, confusion or worry. Finally, he shook his head and said, "I'm only asking for a car ride, Emma. It's not as big a deal as you—"

He wasn't understanding my dilemma. I cut him off. "Assuming, by some miracle, you call me in time and I get to your heart-attacking body before everyone else, assuming I manage to get you into my car before a single person around figures out what's going on, assuming all of that, how long will the actual conversion take Teren? How long do I really have to get you to the ranch?"

He blinked and let his train of thought end without a fight. He stared at the road, thinking about it, and I could tell from his expression that this was the first time he'd considered that part of it. I realized that, just like I hadn't looked at every angle when I'd asked him to change Ashley, he hadn't looked at every angle in his quest to stay in San Francisco. Sometimes we only see what we want to see.

When he finally spoke, he answered me quietly, and a little humbly, "Great-Gran said Gran's conversion took half of an entire day." I considered that, as his face fell with his next realization. He continued in a near whisper, "Gran said Mom's took four hours."

Icy shock made the hairs on the back of my neck stand up. I blinked and gaped at him. "Four hours? From Twelve? Teren, in one generation it condensed that much? Who knows how long it could take for you?"

He looked over at me, and I could see real fear behind his eyes as he came to a startling conclusion. "It could take under an hour for me," he stated, returning his eyes to the road.

Panic filled me, as I realized what that meant. "Your parents live an hour away. Even if I got to you right away, even if you were still conscious in the car when we started the trip…if we got held up in traffic or the tiniest thing went wrong, or if it was even quicker than an hour…"

Teren swallowed and spoke my greatest fear, "I would wake up in the car…alone with you." He immediately added, "I wouldn't hurt you, Emma. I swear."

"Teren…what are you willing to risk on that? Are you willing to risk my life on a death-inducing thirst? Are you willing to risk yours?" He twisted to stare at me, his mouth dropping open. He hadn't known that I knew how severe his thirst would be, that I knew how severe the ramifications of his *not* drinking would be. He didn't know that I knew he would die, if he didn't kill me. He realized it now.

He briefly closed his eyes before returning his vision to the road. We had lagged behind Tracey and Ben while we'd talked, and that happy couple was no longer within sight of us. That seemed a little appropriate, considering the conversation we were now having.

"What do you want me to do, Emma?" he asked, heavy reluctance in his voice.

I laid my hand over his knee. "I want you to go to the ranch. I don't want this burden. I don't want this risk." He glanced over at me with sad eyes. "I want you to be safe, Teren."

He looked back to the road and was silent for so long, that I was positive he'd begin fighting with me again when he did speak. But, with a heavy sigh, he finally conceded the fight. "Okay. I'll go."

He didn't speak again for the rest of the exceedingly long drive home, and I felt every mile go by in the oppressive silence. I found I couldn't speak either. I found that I had no words. I didn't feel like gloating that I'd won the fight, that he'd finally be safe. If anything, I felt guilty that I'd coerced him into doing something he didn't want to do, even if it was the smarter choice.

We pulled up to my house hours later and he sweetly helped me carry my things to my room. But sadness marked his features, like the reality of his situation had finally tightened around him, and he was having trouble accepting it. He'd lived for so long in a sort of stubborn "I'll do this my way" denial, that he'd overlooked some truths about his situation. Those truths were eating him up inside now; I could see it in his countenance. He looked on the verge of a breakdown.

After the last of my stuff was plopped onto a wicker chair in the corner of my small bedroom, Teren murmured goodbye and turned to leave. I grabbed his arm, stopping him. He looked at me with heartbreaking eyes that were quickly filling with tears. One finally dropped to his cheek and I felt my own eyes watering.

"I'm so scared, Emma." His voice quavered, and another tear fell down his cheek, following the same path as the first.

I immediately pulled him into me and kissed him. He returned the kiss with ferocity and instantly started stripping clothes off of me. It was the only comfort I could give him. It was the only comfort he could give me. Things were changing…rapidly, and fearing that change, we clung to this one moment of physical bliss in my small Victorian bedroom.

Chapter 14 – Decisions

Teren's moment of panic quickly subsided with our passionate lovemaking, and he fell asleep in my arms, happy and content and with probably a full pint of my blood in his system. Before I followed him into slumber, his terrified face filled my mind and his quavering words filled my heart—"I'm so scared, Emma." I knew he was scared to die. I knew he was scared he'd hurt me. His fear was only solidifying mine. But I'd do this for him. I'd be strong for him.

Early Monday morning, he rolled over in my bed and woke me with soft kisses on my shoulder, neck and cheek. With clear reluctance in his voice, he whispered, "I have to go get ready for work," in my ear. I smiled that he'd remembered to wake me before he left. I sleepily watched him find his clothes in the gray-on-gray, pre-dawn light of the room. Once dressed, he leaned over and gave me a final goodbye kiss. If he'd had the time, I would have pulled those clothes right off of him again. He didn't though, so with a small sigh, I ended our warm touch and whispered goodbye. He paused at my doorway and gave me a heart-stopping crooked grin.

God, I loved that man.

I couldn't fall back asleep after he left, so I got up early and clunked around my tiny, peaches and cream bedroom. This house had been my grandmother's house and this bedroom had been my mother's. Out of respect for my long dead grandma, I slept in what was technically the second bedroom, although they were both the same size.

Mom had had no desire to move back here after Grandma had passed. She really enjoyed sharing a two bedroom, single story home with Ashley, near the campus. But she hadn't had the heart to sell the home she'd grown up in. It was fully paid for anyway and a good investment. When I'd finished college, Mom had offered me a pretty spectacular rate on rent, since there was no way I'd just live here for free, mooching off of her, and I'd eagerly accepted the cute little home. I supposed if I ever finally moved in with Teren, Ashley would come live here, although the steep staircase was a challenge for her.

I left my simple, yet elegant, little room and walked across the hall to the main bathroom. My grandma had had a thing for lighthouses and the bathroom was done in a clearly nautical motif. We'd all found it much too cute to change, so we left it as a little homage to her. I turned on the water for my shower and when it was warm enough, I pushed aside the curtain depicting a cliff side with raging waters below it and a lone, stoic lighthouse atop it, and stepped inside. I sort of felt like that lighthouse, alone, and trying to be brave while torturous waves crashed below me, with only my one brightly shining lamp to light the darkness.

Okay, maybe the metaphor was a little dramatic, but I was feeling a little dramatic after our weekend. Teren had really scared the piss out of me, and fighting with him like that was something I never wished to do again. But I'd won…and now he was leaving. And even though I understood the necessity of it, I hated the reality. There was nothing I wanted more than for him to stay here in San Francisco with me, for us to move in together, and for him to get me all barefoot and pregnant. That was what I really wanted. Not him an hour away, with me visiting for booty calls…ugh.

I shampooed, rinsed and repeated my hair, and stepped from the shower clean, if not refreshed. I supposed Teren and I still needed to talk about when he would leave and when I could visit. His being so far away, would be a challenge in the whole baby making department. We'd talked before about ways to prolong creating a baby—freeze some of his stuff or something, but we'd decided that having his vampiric DNA around curious doctors, with labs running numerous sorts of tests, was just too great a risk of exposure, even for something this important. No, our way was the old-fashioned way, so "visits" were an inevitability. But I'd do it. I wasn't about to give up on our dream, because of a little problem like geography. It was only an hour anyway. I would drive an hour every night to be with him, baby or no baby.

I plugged my hairdryer into the socket below a lighthouse nightlight, and dried my tresses while my mind tumbled. Being alone was the hardest part. There was just no one to talk over my problems with. I suppose Alanna would listen to every word I had to say, with an open, silent heart and comforting, cool arms. But conversing with Alanna probably meant conversing with Halina, and while things between us weren't quite as strained, she wasn't exactly someone I wanted to confess fears with.

Tracey was definitely out. She'd never want to be in my line of sight again if she knew the truth about Teren. She'd probably never want to be in California again. She'd snatch up Hot Ben, and they'd go to Arizona or something. Somewhere far more sunny and vamp-deterrent, than here.

Churning over my options, I threw on a pencil skirt and a long-sleeved blouse; Teren's latest nibble had been on the crook of my arm, while said arm was wrapped around my back. Yeah, don't ask. I debated talking with Ashley. True, she did know Teren's secret...sort of. She knew he was a human-vampire mix. She knew he had fangs and occasionally liked to puncture my skin. She did *not* know he was dying.

Sitting on the edge of my bed, I slipped on my shoes and considered her reaction. She would probably take it better than I had. I was still a touch embarrassed over my emotional blowup the night Teren had reluctantly told me he had months to live. As I was wondering how to tell my sister, I realized just how difficult that must have been for him. I didn't know how Ashley would react, but I knew she'd love me no matter what. Our relationship had been so new back then that Teren would have had no clue if I was going to walk away or not. And I almost had. I could see now that he had been right in trying to shield me from the truth of his condition. As much as I hated to admit it...if he'd told me any earlier, I would have bolted. I had to love the man first, before I could accept the truths that came along with loving that man.

Finished dressing, I walked into the hallway and tossed a quick glance at the main bedroom that was now set up as a guest room. The bed still had Grandma's lacy quilt on top of it and the room still lightly smelled of roses, a smell that had seemed to permeate Grandma. Sometimes Ashley slept there, when she stayed over on nights she was too tired to go back to her place with Mom, but mostly the room was empty, the door closed. Heading downstairs, I carefully watched my high heels traverse the narrow steps, and wondered if my rose-smelling, lighthouse-loving grandma, would have accepted my situation. I smiled at the thought. She probably would have. Mom was constantly telling me that I was just like her.

Another Monday morning found me facing the exact same crowd of dreary worker bees who'd rather be redoing Sunday—going to a barbecue, drinking beers on a boat in the bay, and as one guy I passed in the halls was saying, enjoying an "afternoon delight." Everyone wanted to be gone, except for Clarice. She was waiting for me at my little square office, with a stack of papers in her hand. Her bun looked exceptionally tight this morning and her face looked exceptionally displeased. I discretely checked my watch, but I wasn't late. I had two minutes to spare.

"Here," she muttered, handing me the stack before I could even set my purse down. "I need all of these copied within the hour."

I looked at the six-inch stack in my hands and mentally sighed. Sometimes I thought I was crazy working here. I could be on a ranch, wiping cow poop off my boot. Right now, that sounded like so much more fun. "No problem, Clarice."

I didn't ask about her weekend and she didn't ask about mine. We both knew that neither one of us really cared. Just straight to work—all professionalism here.

That professionalism faded the minute Clarice waddled back to her desk and Tracey poked her head up at me. Her face was all romantic bliss, like she'd gone to sleep being lullabyed by the London Philharmonic Orchestra, and awoken in a sea of rose petals. It occurred to me, that I really had no idea how romantic Hot Ben was, and that might have indeed been her night. Although, I doubt he'd be able to get the actual London Philharmonic Orchestra. San Francisco High, maybe.

"Hey, Em, did you and Teren have a good time?" Before I could answer, she added, "God, that was great. I love camping." Her smile got even wider and she bit her lip. "I can't wait to go again."

I inwardly laughed at her delighted face. I knew exactly what part she was thinking about. I knew she'd get over that rock thing. Not entirely enjoying my memories of the past few days, I smiled my best, fake smile. "Yeah, we had a great time, Trace. We're in next time, for sure."

She giggled, then ducked back down to her office. I'm pretty sure she'd be drawing hearts around Ben's name today. For someone who'd resisted falling, once she had, she fell hard. A sudden wave of sadness hit me, as I thought that that might have been our last camping trip with Ben and Tracey. It was getting late in the season to go, and Teren's birthday was in a couple of months. By next spring, he'd be a bloodsucking corpse. How exactly would we explain him not eating for days at a time? And what would he eat? Well, at least Tracey and I wouldn't have to worry about bears anymore...

The rest of my work day trudged by with a slowness that matched my moody heart. By a quarter to five, I decided that I needed to speak to another human being about this, or the stress was going to eat a hole through my stomach. I rang my sister and asked her to come over to my place...without Mom. She understood that that meant I wanted to talk about Teren and his "condition". Solemnly, she said she would.

Tracey pouted at me when I told her I wouldn't be in kickboxing tonight, and Teren asked me if everything was okay when I told him I wasn't coming over later. I assured him I was just meeting with my sister. With a sad, I'll miss you sigh, he told me to tell her hello and that he'd see her tomorrow night at dinner with my family. After telling him I loved him, I hopped into my yellow bug and drove home to wait for Ashley to come over. I still wasn't entirely sure what to say, or entirely sure how she'd take it.

About an hour later, I heard a light knock on the door and let Ashley in. She smiled at me through her disfigured lips and I hugged her. She had curled the long, brown locks on the side of her head that still had hair, and it attractively framed her face. I touched a springy strand. "You're beautiful," I told her.

"Thank you." She smiled politely as she glanced over my full head of wavy hair.

As it sometimes did when I was around her, a tidal wave of guilt assaulted me. It wasn't as if I could have done anything for her the night of the fire, it had started in her room and Dad had barely gotten her out, but I'd played the "what if" game in my head until my cheeks were drenched in tears. I tried to fight back that feeling, as I led her to the living room. Ashley didn't like pity, and she chose to live without regrets. I struggled daily to be the woman my sister was.

We sat on my two-person sofa, and I stared at the green walls of my living room. I'd painted the room last year in a tranquil shade of sage green that I'd picked out. It was only when the room was firmly coated in three layers of that relaxing green, that I'd noticed that the color on the walls didn't quite match the version in my head. It was more of an "I'm about to be sick" green. I hated painting though, and had refused to redo it, so I'd brought in cream curtains and a really beautiful antique coffee table, to try and distract from the walls. That queasy green color was sort of matching my insides right now, and I was a little irritated with my painting laziness.

"Are you okay, Emma? You look a little ill?" My sister put a hand on my leg and I looked back at her and tried to smile. I wasn't sure if I succeeded. Her next comment made me think I hadn't. "Did you and Teren break up again?" Her eyes looked really disappointed at that prospect, which made me believe that she might handle this better than I thought.

I shook my head. "No, we're fine. He says hi, and he's looking forward to seeing you and Mom tomorrow."

Ashley relaxed back into the sofa and smiled. She really did like him…maybe she'd be okay with liking a dead man? "What did you need to talk about, then? It sounded pretty urgent."

I sat back in the sofa as well, regarding her for a moment. Her half brows were scrunched together as she went through a list of options in her head, as to what might be going on. I was pretty sure she wasn't anywhere near the truth. Finally, I spoke softly to her, "Do you remember when I told you that Teren only had so long to have children?"

Her face scrunched as far as the scars allowed, as she thought about that. "You said he'd be sterile soon." Her face brightened momentarily. "Are you pregnant?"

I reflexively put a hand over my stomach and swallowed back the sudden tears. "No…not yet." She shook her head, still looking confused. Taking a deep breath, I continued. "Teren is…" I racked my brain for another way to say it…a less harsh way. I didn't come up with one and spilled it to her, the same way he spilled it to me.

"He's dying."

Her hand flew to her mouth and her eyes instantly watered. I cringed that she was having the same "permanent dead" thoughts that I'd had. As she started to respond to me, I quickly added, "Just the human side of him. He'll still be a vampire. He'll still be walking around, and talking and joining us for meals. He just won't be breathing or have a heartbeat or...actually be eating with us."

Her eyes widened as far as they could and her hand dropped to her lap. "You're gonna date a vampire."

I grinned at her. "I am dating a vampire, Ash."

She shook her head. "Not really...I mean, he drinks cappuccinos."

I started laughing uncontrollably as my fear mixed with my remembered amusement. I'd said that exact same thing to him once. Confused but entertained by me, Ashley started laughing as well. I was wiping tears from my eyes before I finally came down from my mini-high. She'd stopped laughing first and was giving me a very serious look.

"So...he can't have children, because he'll be dead?" I nodded and she sighed and hugged me. I melted into that embrace and savored someone finally comforting me for what dating a vampire had thrust onto my life. I knew the changes were happening to *him*...but sometimes, I just needed someone to hug me, and say that everything was going to be okay.

Ashley patted my back and did just that. Tears of sadness started to form, as the next thing I had to tell her took me over. They spilled down my cheeks as Ashley pulled away from me. She wiped off a few drops as I brokenly told her, "He's leaving, Ash."

Her eyes watered as she whispered, "What?"

I shook my head, irritated at my own dramatics, and explained. "It's not safe for him to be around people when he changes, so he's going to go live at his parents' ranch for a month or so." More tears slid down my cheeks, as more dramatics slid from my mouth, "I'm going to miss him so much."

She ran a hand down my shoulder. "But a baby..."

She let her thought trail off and, annoyed at the way I was explaining this, I angrily brushed away my tears. "I'm just being an overly dramatic girl," I muttered. Her face twisted into confusion again. I let out a slow, even breath, trying to rein in my emotions before I continued. "I'm going to visit him at the ranch every night. I'll still see him and we're still going to try." I rolled my eyes. "I'm just being emotional."

She put her arm around my shoulder and pulled me tight. "You have a lot on your plate. You're allowed." I relaxed into her side and relished the comfort of her closeness. She continued in a whisper, "What do you mean, it's not safe for him to be here?"

I cringed and closed my eyes before responding to her. She probably wasn't going to like this. "He would most likely kill someone, if he was too close to a human after the change."

Her hand dropped off my shoulder and she scooted away to look at me. "What?" Her tone had dropped a full octave, as what I'd said flooded her thoughts. I knew she liked Teren but, well, even I had difficulty with this part of it.

I reached for her arm to try and mollify her. "It's okay. He won't hurt anyone. It's just a greater risk if he stays."

Her eyes were huge with panic now. "Emma…you shouldn't be around him." Her gaze crisscrossed over my body, and I was really grateful that she couldn't see his latest feeding frenzy. "You shouldn't let him bite you."

She backed away from me and I scooted closer to her. "He won't hurt me, Ash, I'm safe." Wow, in trying to reassure my sister, I was suddenly starting to sound exactly like Teren. Maybe if we both repeated that phrase often enough, it might actually start sounding true.

Ashley stood up and put her hands on her hips. The brown hair that beautifully framed her face, was now framing an irritated face. My sister normally kept her cool, but we *were* sisters, and at times her temper could be a match for mine. It must be genetic. "Let me try and understand what you're saying." She put a hand to her forehead like she suddenly had a headache. "He is about to die…" She looked at me intently. "Like what? Have a heart attack or something?" I nodded at her correct guess.

She started to walk back and forth in front of the couch. Pacing must also be genetic. "Okay, so he's going to have a heart attack and he isn't going to make it. His heart will give out and what makes him like us will die." She looked over at me for confirmation and I nodded again, wisely keeping my mouth shut while she processed her thoughts. "Then, when he's all cold and heartbeatless and...dead..." She stopped walking and stared at me blankly. "He's going to rise from the grave and start ripping the throats out of innocent San Franciscans?"

I frowned at her harsh portrait. "No..." I looked away as I considered what about that wasn't true. Unfortunately, there was really only one part. "He wouldn't make it to a grave. We think he'll change over within an hour." I returned my eyes to her re-startled face. "Maybe less."

She fell back down onto the sofa with me. "Oh my God, Emma...oh my God."

I patted her knee in reassurance, both hers and mine. "We've fixed this. I've finally convinced him that I can't get him to the ranch in time, and so he's going to spend the last couple months of his life there...around lots and lots of yummy cattle."

Her expression shifted from shock to irritation. "He wanted you to take him there?"

Oops. Perhaps I shouldn't have mentioned his crazy plan, since we had a new one in place. I swallowed and answered slowly, "Yes...but..."

She cut me off as her voice heated. "He wanted you to drive him there? He wanted you to be alone in the car with him, when he woke up all crazed and starving?" Her face was definitely red now. She abruptly stood and made for the door.

"Where are you going?" I asked, confused.

With her hand on the knob, she looked back at me and indicated through the door to the outside. "I'm going over to his house...so I can stake him."

I twisted my lips at her. Yeah, definitely shouldn't have

mentioned that part. Her anger was practically swirling in the air now. "Would you stop it, and come here and sit back down." She huffed for a minute and I really thought she was going to leave. I patted the seat beside me and, very grudgingly, she removed her hand from the door and returned to my side. Crossing her scarred arms over her chest, she let out a heavy sigh. I patted her knee again. "He thought he had more time, Ash. He thought he'd be out of it for hours, and I could get him there and get away, with plenty of time to spare."

I looked back at the front door and pictured my vampire, all alone at his house, possibly wondering if we were still okay. My lips curled into a smile as I realized that we *were* okay. Everything was going to be fine. "We thought he had more time." I looked back at her, the smile still on my lips. "But we see now, that he doesn't have that kind of time so we're fixing the problem. Everything will be fine, Ashley."

I ran a hand down her hair and she relaxed as she looked at me. I could see in her face that her momentary anger had dwindled back down to the calm and reasoned Ashley. "Would he really be able to resist eating you after the change? Can you still date him, that way?"

I smiled and nodded. "It will only be bad when he first wakes up…then he'll be fine. Then he'll be my Teren again." My voice was calm and soft and free of any trouble, like my body suddenly felt.

Ashley was still unsure. "Why when he wakes up? Shouldn't he be less inclined to…to…eat people, after such an ordeal?"

I smiled and told her my biggest fear, aside from him killing me, of course. "His body will be starving…beyond starving, I'd say." I put a hand on her knee and rubbed it a little; the scarring on her knee cap was apparent, even through the fabric of her khaki slacks. "If he doesn't eat right away…he will die…permanently."

Ashley stared at me with a stunned expression. I looked over her face and smiled at my own remembered expression. Shocked into speechlessness was probably a better way to handle the news than yelling at the potential in-laws. Finally, tears filled her eyes and spilled down her cheeks. She gave me a fierce hug. "I'm sorry, Emma…I didn't know."

I hugged her back, no longer needing the comfort, but greatly appreciating the sentiment. "I know, Ash. Nobody knows."

She pulled back and another tear followed the first. She put a hand to my dry cheek. "You must be so lonely…dealing with all this by yourself."

I swallowed and shook my head. "Well, I'm not anymore. I have you."

She let out a small laugh and held me again. I closed my eyes and breathed out a long exhale. Fear was so much easier to digest, when you didn't have to do it alone. It felt so good to share.

We conversed about more mundane topics for the rest of the evening. Before leaving for the night, she gave me a swift hug at the door and told me I could call her anytime if I needed to talk about it…and to tell her when it did happen. With moist eyes, I told her I would, and that I'd see her tomorrow for dinner with Mom.

As I watched her stumble a bit on the steps down to my driveway, I thought again about Teren changing her…and dismissed it. He was right, she was happy. Maybe someday she would bring the topic up to Teren, if it occurred to her, but it wasn't my decision to make for her. I wasn't the one that had to live her life. And she *was* living it, she was doing just fine.

Tuesday morning, I awoke from a dream about Teren changing in the middle of dinner tonight. In the dream, the change had been nearly instantaneous and he'd popped his fangs out after slumping at the table for a mere three seconds. Then he'd viciously smiled at my mom and ripped her neck wide open. Blood had spurted everywhere, just like in some gory Tarantino film. He'd been moving on to my sister, his face streaked with Mom's blood, when I'd woken up, screaming. I was pretty sure that wasn't going to happen tonight, but the dream had been terrifying, and it only reaffirmed our decision of him spending the last part of his humanity away from other humans…away from me.

With a heavy sigh, I got ready for my day. Later at work, seeing Tracey's happy, love-crazy face only deepened my sigh. I shouldn't be jealous of her. She had taken much longer than most to get to this stage. But I was only human, and her carefree relationship was a little grating at the moment. I was actually happy when Clarice gave me an assignment that kept me down in the records room for most of the afternoon.

By quarter to six, I was in Teren's car, being driven to the café where my horrid dream had played out. I considered telling Teren about my dream, but when I glanced over at him and saw the tightness of his jaw, I reconsidered. Teren wasn't looking forward to any of this, and he was probably having some bad dreams of his own. No need to add mine into the mix.

I placed my hand on his knee and gave him a reassuring smile. He looked over and gave me the softest, barest hint of a smile in return as he laid his fingers over mine. I laced them together and his eyes drifted back to the road.

"I told Ashley you'd be leaving soon, so it could come up tonight if she told Mom anything." I paused for a moment and then filled him in on the rest of that conversation. "I told her everything about you...about what you're about to go through."

He looked back at me with wider eyes. "Oh," he whispered.

I felt him loosen our hands and I clutched him tighter. "We should talk about when you are leaving, Teren." He said nothing, just stared at the road as we sped towards my family. "Will it be this weekend?" My voice shook a little when I asked. Even though he needed to go, I wasn't ready for him to leave.

Noticing my tone, Teren glanced at me and stroked my finger with his thumb. "No, Emma."

Not liking that response, I stared at him as he pulled into the parking lot. "Why not, Teren? Wouldn't sooner be better than later?"

He pulled into an empty space and shut the car off. With a deep, calming breath, he turned to face me and I suddenly had the awful sensation that he was going to tell me he'd changed his mind, that he was staying in San Francisco.

His eyes searching my face, he quietly said, "I have to finish up work, Emma. I can't just disappear for a couple months." He looked down at the console between us and stroked my fingers again. "I'll give them two weeks and then I'll take a sabbatical. I should be able to finish up a couple articles by then," he muttered.

Not being able to take the sadness etched on his face, I unlaced our hands and cupped his cheek. His expression turned morose. "Come with me, Emma," he whispered into the stillness of the car.

I blinked and my brows drew down in confusion. "I am going to come with you, Teren. I'll help you get settled and visit—"

He cupped my cheek now, cutting me off. "No, stay out there with me...stay with me."

There was such a deep longing in his voice that I closed my eyes for a second. I opened them when I felt his lips brush against mine. He pulled back from our brief kiss with pale eyes full of need. "Please," he whispered.

"But...my job..." That really wasn't my argument. I just couldn't speak the real one yet.

"You never take your vacation time...you've got a lot saved up. Take that." He shrugged. "Or just quit. You hate that job anyway." I pursed my lips. I didn't hate the job...certain aspects and dumpy bosses maybe, but the job, no. "I don't know, Teren..."

His hand on my cheek started caressing my face, as his eyes roamed over my features. "I need you there, Emma. I'm...I'm so..." His voice trailed off, as his anxiety choked off his speech.

I put my hand over his and leaned into his touch. "I know, Teren. I know, baby," I whispered.

"Then stay?"

I paused for a long time. I knew Mom and Ashley were already waiting for us, we'd parked right beside Mom's car, and I knew that Teren was anxious about my answer, his eyes were flitting all over me, trying to gauge what I was feeling, but I didn't really want to speak my true fear out loud. I knew I had to though.

"What if you kill me at the ranch?" I barely spoke the words and they warbled as they came out.

Immediately his other hand cupped my cheek and he held my face close to his. His eyes glistened, as he answered me in a passionate voice, "I'm incapable of hurting you, Emma." A tear dripped down his cheek. "I will not do it." He shook his head and then leaned in to kiss me. He pressed against me fiercely, like he was willing my lips to believe him. I wanted to, but instinct was a powerful thing to fight against. Especially live or die instinct.

"Teren..." I tried again, when he pulled away and rested our heads together.

He cut me off with a sad sigh. "I'll send you away, Emma."

I blinked again and moved away from his face to look at him. His eyes were still brimming. "What?"

"After I die, I'll have Dad drive you far away from me." He sadly shook his head. "You may not have time to get me there safely, but I will have time to get you *away* safely."

"But your mom made it sound like... She sent your father away before..." I let my voice trail off, as I remembered his mother's concerned voice when she'd told me about her conversion.

He let out a soft sigh. "My mother is a bit overprotective. Haven't you noticed that?" I smiled as I considered that she was. Teren didn't smile with me. He continued in a voice heavy with emotion, "I need you there, Emma. I need to be with you every second before...this happens." Another tear dropped down his cheek and I brushed it away with my finger. "I need you to be there when I die."

My voice caught in my throat as I gazed at him. I could feel my eyes getting thick with tears of my own, and Teren's face started to get hazier as the moisture filled and obscured my vision. In a hoarse voice, he finished his death bed wish, "I need your face to be the last thing my human eyes see."

My tears spilled over and I began to sob as he clutched me to his shoulder.

Ashley didn't mention anything at dinner, when we were finally both put together enough to enter that damn café, but she eyed Teren throughout the meal with a mixed expression of sadness and wariness on her face. I thought maybe I shouldn't mention our new, new plan, until it was time to act on it. No point in worrying her needlessly. There was no way I was staying away from the ranch now though.

There is just no possible way to turn down your boyfriend when he asks to stare into your eyes as the lights fade from his. I really didn't want to see it, I was sure the image would haunt me my entire life...but I couldn't deny him. At this point, I didn't think there was much I could deny him.

Mom didn't seem to notice the melancholy at the table, and stoked our conversation with witty tales of her girlfriends and her neighbor's yappy dogs. I watched her features as she spoke and laughed, wishing for just a moment that I could clue her in on my real situation.

Then I looked over at Ashley and saw the faint tightness around her eyes and the forced angle of her smile, and thought better of it. Sharing my stress with another family member would just be selfish. Mom would gain nothing at all for knowing it. She would only be terrified for her daughter's safety, if she did know. Maybe someday, when all of this was over, I'd tell the warm, slightly pudgy woman across from me about the otherworldliness of my boyfriend. But not today.

We wrapped up dinner with ice cream and discussions about Ashley's new schedule for another year at school. Her eyes lit up when she talked about her classes, and a genuine smile spread on her face when she talked about visiting the hospital where she hoped to work. She had her own life planned, her own future mapped out and, much like Teren, she was determined to see it through on her own terms. I loved them both just a little more for their fierce independent streaks.

We kissed Mom and Ashley goodbye. Teren pulled Ashley aside and whispered something in her ear. She glanced over at me while they talked and then she closed her eyes and nodded, hugging him tight. They held each other a few moments longer than standard protocol, and I distracted my mom with small talk, so she wouldn't notice and ask what was going on.

As Mom and Ashley got in Mom's car and pulled away, I asked Teren what he'd said to her. He looked at me, the glow of the parking lot lights highlighting the tiredness of his eyes, and softly said, "I told her that I'd never hurt you. That I'd do anything to protect you, and she didn't need to worry."

He gave me a soft smile and I grabbed his hand. "Come home with me." He nodded and we went over to his car, to start our short journey to my home…before our long one, to his family's.

Chapter 15 – The Journey

Wednesday morning found me waking in bed with a much calmer feeling in my stomach. I would be with my vampire to the very end. I would hold his hand and tell him that he meant everything to me, as the life in his eyes flickered out. I was still horrified at the prospect of watching him die…but I was resolved to do it. He wanted this. He needed this. And I would be there for him, in the only way I could be.

Kissing my cheek and whispering that he loved me and he'd see me after work, Teren left me a couple hours before I had to leave myself. I stretched in bed and with a deep, relaxing breath in and out, I mentally prepared myself to have a conversation with Clarice about taking some much needed time off of work.

Hoping to score some points with her, I dressed in the way that she preferred—a long, heavy skirt and a frilly, long-sleeved conservative top. I piled my thick hair on top of my head and grabbed a fitted jacket before heading out the door to make a request that my boss was either going to approve…or she'd lose me.

She happened to be at my desk with a stack of papers when I approached her. My heart started quickening at the anticipation of the conversation. Her plump face took in my near carbon copy recreation of her own outfit, and a slight tugging at the corners of her lips indicated a smile.

She handed me the stack when I was within arm's length. "I need these copied and faxed by lunch," she said brusquely.

"Good morning, Clarice." I said, grabbing the papers and slapping a forced smile on my face. "I wanted to give you a heads-up, but I'll be giving you a written notice as well…" I took a deep breath and spoke with my exhale, "I'm taking all of the vacation and sick time that I've accrued in my time here, two weeks from Friday."

Her jaw dropped as she gaped at me. I'd worked here since graduating college. I'd never used any of my paid time off. Up until yesterday, I just hadn't had any pressing desire to go anywhere or do anything that couldn't be done in a weekend, or the week the office shut down after tax season—time off that didn't dip into our vacation time. They considered that our yearly bonus, I considered it perfect. The company allowed you to rollover any unused time, and didn't have a cap on how much you could roll over. You could even give away your vacation time to someone else, as a group once did for a woman going through chemotherapy a few years ago, before I'd started working here. As it was, I had a decent amount stored up.

Clarice looked surprisingly at a loss for words. Finally, she sputtered, "Oh...well...of course." She looked around the office as she did calculations in her head of how long I would be gone. "I guess I'll get the temp agency to get someone out here to replace you..." Her eyes came back to my face and her brows knitted in concern. "You are coming back...right?"

I smiled, genuinely happy that I was wanted here in my odd little family. "Of course. I just have a...a family situation that needs my attention."

She smiled widely for the first time I'd ever seen; it faded immediately. "Well, I'll need to see that in writing, as you said, and the dates will need to be clearly specified for your departure and return."

I smiled inwardly at the return of "professional" Clarice. "Sure...no problem." Well, the leaving date would be easy—two weeks from Friday was what Teren was giving his work, but the coming back date? I'd just have to pick a date as far out as I could and hope for the best.

Clarice compressed her lips as she regarded me. "You could have given us longer than two weeks to prepare."

I cringed an appropriate amount. "Sorry...it was sort of an emergency that popped up at the last minute. Thank you for understanding," I threw in, as she looked about to protest.

She swallowed her complaint. Flicking my stack of papers with her finger, she pointedly said, "By noon. I don't want you slacking off because you're leaving soon."

I stifled a sigh. "No problem, Clarice."

She waddled across the aisle to her spacious desk in front of Mr. Peterson's office, and I turned to set down my stack of urgent papers and my starting-to-get-heavy purse.

I'd barely shoved the purse in my drawer before Tracey's blonde head popped up over the wall. "You're leaving?" Her eyes scrunched in a mixture of annoyance and concern.

A soft sigh escaped me as I looked over my sad-faced friend. When I got back, things would probably be different in our friendship. Not that she and I wouldn't still talk nearly every day, have lunch every so often, take kickboxing together, and maybe even occasionally take Ashley out for a drink…but the double dating aspect of our relationship would change.

What we could all do together as a foursome would change, and how close Tracey and Ben could get to Teren would change. To lessen the risk of exposure for Teren, there would just be a lot more…carefulness when we were all together again. The breezy casualness of our group outings would be gone. I'd miss that.

Smiling sadly, I answered her question, "Teren's Dad is sick, and Teren needs to take some time off, to work at the ranch, until he gets better. I'm going as well…to help out." Teren and I had talked about what to tell people last night. This was what he was telling his boss and coworkers…it would work for mine as well.

Tracey's face fell in sympathy. "Oh…is he going to be okay?"

I knew she meant Teren's Dad, but Teren's jet-black hair, pale blue eyes and lightly stubbled face leapt into my head, and I had to swallow to force back the sudden tears. "He'll be fine, Trace."

She nodded and, accepting my lie, reached out over her wall to pat my shoulder. I tapped her arm in thanks, and she ducked her head back down to continue on with her day. I got to work on my papers, forcing my mind to completely shut off.

I spent every waking moment that I could with Teren as we prepared to leave. There were several more conversations that we had to have. The first, and easiest, perhaps, was calling his parents. He waited until Friday evening to do it. At his reluctance to pick up the receiver, I wondered if his stubborn pride would even let him make this phone call. As he blankly stared at the thing, I considered punching in the numbers for him.

Looking at me, and perhaps noticing my expression, he sighed and finally dialed his family home.

"Hi, Dad," he said when the line picked up. He leaned back against the kitchen counter, tucking a hand into his pocket. Walking over to him, I untucked his hand and slung his arm around my waist. Teren smiled and kissed my head as he listened to his dad talk to him for a few long seconds.

During a break in the conversation he muttered, "Will you tell Mom that I'm coming home...to stay." He said it very quietly, and I wondered if his dad's normal human ear even registered the sound.

Teren straightened a bit and his eyes unfocused as he listened to a voice on the other end. Rolling his eyes, he shook his head. "Mom...put Dad back on." As he closed his eyes, I smiled at his mom's enthusiasm. "Please stop crying. I'm fine...Emma's fine...you win." He opened his eyes and sighed. "I know, Mom. I know it was never a contest."

Smiling softly, he started rubbing circles into my back. I ran a hand up his chest and our eyes locked as he spoke with his mother. "She's coming too. I want her there." His tone was final. It clearly said *There will be no debate on this.* I smiled and kissed his jaw.

His mom apparently gave no argument, for the next thing he said was, "Wagyu...really? Well...thank you." His lips lifted to a genuine smile and I wondered what they were talking about.

His fingers ran through my hair as he smiled down on me, still listening to his mother talk in his ear. For a moment, I wished I had his uncanny hearing, so I could be privy to their conversation. "I'll be coming up in two weeks." He frowned into the phone and stopped stroking my hair. "It was the best I could do, Mom." He paused as he listened. "I have a job...a life that needed some loose ends tied up..."

He scowled. "Mom..." His tone was getting irritated and I cleared my throat in warning to the both of them. Teren paused, smiled and then laughed. "Yes...she does do that." He grinned with a crooked smile, and again, I wondered what they were talking about.

"Okay…I love you too, Mom. Give my best to Dad and the others. Bye." He hung up the phone and slung both arms around my waist. I waited for an explanation on the many pauses, but all I got was a warm set of lips on my neck.

"So…" I began, struggling to remember the bits and pieces I'd heard, while Teren's soft lips traveled up my skin.

"So…" he huskily repeated in my ear.

I resisted the urge to press my body against his and run my hands through his hair. When I pulled back to look at him, his eyes danced with playfulness. "What did they say?"

His hands lowered to firmly cup my backside and he pulled me tight against him. "Do you really want to talk about this now?"

I ignored how incredibly nice that felt, and pushed back on his chest to separate us. "Wa…gyu?" I said, stumbling a bit over the odd word.

He laughed and relaxed his hold on me. "A couple months ago, they ordered me some cows, just in case I changed my mind about the ranch." He ran a finger through the hair by my ear as he shook his head. "Kind of an incentive. They're arriving next week." Shrugging, he finished with, "It's actually pretty nice of my parents. Wagyu cattle are the best around."

My face scrunched in confusion. Was I missing something obvious? He laughed as he looked at my bewilderment. Ignoring his amusement, I asked, "Are they raising these Wagyu now? Do they expect you to stay and work there?"

He tilted his head as he broke into a wide smile and a laugh. "They're congratulations cows." I shook my head, still not getting it. "Emma…" He brought his two fore fingers to his mouth and held them in front of his lips like fangs. "Congratulations. Here's your cow…cheers."

I shut my eyes and shook my head. Oh…duh, right. I reopened my eyes and raised an eyebrow as I regarded him. "You and the girls aren't going to go hunting or something, for your first day as a dead vampire?"

He grimaced. "I hate hunting. Fishing I like, but hunting…"

he shook his head, "no thanks."

I smiled at my very unvampire-like vampire. "You are such a disappointment," I muttered, kissing him.

Laughing, he grabbed me tight. I tried not to gasp, but it came out anyway. "I bet I could change your mind," he growled.

I bet he could. Not giving in to his very clear desire just yet, I pulled back. "Why don't you like hunting? Isn't that some instinctual part of being a vampire?"

He cocked an eyebrow at me, as he smiled. "Why don't you like shoe shopping? Isn't that an instinctual part of being a woman?"

I pursed my lips. He was right…about the hating it part. There was nothing that irritated me more, than trying on pair after pair of they-just-look-funny-on-me shoes. Chuckling at the look on my face, he said, "Why would I want to run through the countryside like an idiot, when Bessie will just stand there and let me drain her dry?"

I rolled my eyes as I gazed up at him. "You're just…you're a metro-vampire."

His face contorted into an odd expression. "I'm what?"

I put on my matter-of-fact face. "You're a metro-vampire. You drink espresso and drive a hybrid and work for a lifestyle magazine and dress better than any other man I know." I playfully dug my finger into his chest. "You just don't want to get your nails dirty, running through the woods after your dinner."

He gaped at me in mock shock, then he cocked his head to the side. "Wait…why are my nails getting dirty in your little scenario? Am I falling down a lot after the change?"

I started to glare at him and was thinking about smacking his smartass, when his lips were suddenly on mine again. When his tongue slid into my mouth, I stopped my pointless, flirty banter. When his hands firmly found my ass again, I stopped stifling the groans I'd wanted to make, and when he zipped me to his bedroom, he proved that his manliness, vampiric or otherwise, was never in question.

After a long couple days of phone calls—shutting off services, holding mail, paying bills in advance, all the mundane stuff you have to do before a long trip, we were back at our Tuesday night dinner with my family, and we had to break the news to them. It wasn't as if I were going all that far away, but there really was no telling when Teren's change was going to happen, so I wouldn't be leaving the ranch for any reason. And it wouldn't be safe for them to visit…not until after.

Teren and I sat down across from my mom and Ashley, and right away I knew Ashley knew something was up. Her brown eyes— eyes that were the exact same light shade as mine—burned with questions that she wanted to ask, but couldn't in front of Mom. I'd pull her aside later, but for now, she'd have to buy the lie that we were about to spill to my mom.

Mom seemed to notice the tension in the air as well. She tucked some of her chin length hair behind her ears and eyed the two of us speculatively. I looked at Teren, hoping for a way to be honest with my mom, without having to tell her the truth. That just wasn't possible though.

Mom broke the silence with, "God, you're pregnant, aren't you?"

My eyes snapped to hers, and Teren started laughing nervously beside me. I wanted to laugh with him, brush off her concerns, but I wasn't pregnant yet and I really wished I was, so my eyes started to tear up. Teren stopped laughing when he noticed my eyes. Squeezing my hand, he leaned down and casually kissed my cheek. After he did, he quickly whispered, "There will be time."

I gave him a brief nod and forced the *Don't be silly* grin onto my face for my mother's benefit. "No, Mom," I exaggerated.

She sighed with relief, then her jovial face sparkled with playfulness. "Are you getting married? Do I finally get to plan a big wedding?" Her eyes, the same shade of brown as Ashley's and mine, glowed with the thought of planning the big day for her daughter. I swallowed and forced back the tears. I wasn't even sure if that day could happen, not that Teren had asked me yet. But he wouldn't exactly be the champagne swilling, cake eating groom. How would I explain that to her?

Teren leaned down and kissed my cheek again. He didn't whisper anything that time and I slumped a little at him not taking that opportunity to ask me. Was he getting cold feet? The thought that my vampire, who actively tried to knock me up daily, would in a few months actually *have* cold feet, made me giggle with barely contained hysterics. My mom watched my odd reaction and then started laughing herself. Teren and Ashley joined in and we all had a moment of levity, for no apparent reason.

When the laughs died down, I muttered, "No...not yet, Mom." Teren squeezed my hand on the word "yet", and looking over at him, I noticed him winking at me. Hmmm...maybe he did want that future for us?

Teren filled in the blanks on our big announcement, while I continued gazing at him. "My father has fallen ill and I need to be with him...to help out on the ranch for a couple of months, until he's better." My mother's expression turned sympathetic. As she looked about to reply, Teren cut her off with, "Emma is going to come out with me...to help my step-mother."

Mom's face softened into a small smile as she gazed at me in approval. My sister, however, gasped and tears sprang to her eyes. She looked shocked and horrified, and about to loudly protest...right in front of Mom.

"But...Emma...?"

My mother looked over to her with thin lips. Teren looked about to say something, but I quickly beat him to it. "Ash...I need to go to the restroom, will you come with me?"

Her mouth in a hard line, she nodded her half-haired head and stiffly stood from the table. I rose from the edge and, locking my elbow with hers, quietly walked away.

Ash wasn't so quiet. "Emma...that's nuts. You can't be around him while he changes. That's...that's near suicide!" She was whispering, but I shushed her anyway. I looked back at Teren; he was flushing slightly as he tried to assure my mom that nothing was wrong. He'd clearly heard my sister say that and I'm sure he wasn't crazy about the comment.

Ashley didn't say anything else and we shuffled into the bathroom in a sullen silence. I checked under all the stall doors. When I was positive we were alone, I turned back to her.

"Emma...please," she started immediately.

I put my hands on her arms. "He asked me to be there when he died, Ashley. How could I possibly say no to that?"

Examining my face, she opened and shut her mouth several times. "But...Emma...?"

I ran a hand down her scarred face as her tears spilled over. "Please don't worry about me, Ash. His family will keep me safe." She closed her eyes and started to cry in earnest. I held her close and rubbed her back. "It will be okay, I promise." I didn't mentally overlook the fact that the only assurance I could give her was a promise, and I knew from experience just how empty those promises can sound.

She held me back and cried a moment longer on my shoulder before pulling back to look at me. I wiped some tears off her cheeks as she sniffled. "You'll be careful?" she asked hesitantly, like she didn't want to sound too approving of my plan, but she knew she had no choice—my mind was made up.

I held her face in both hands. "I will be the most careful human around a hungry vampire, that anyone has ever seen...okay?"

Pursing her lips, she shook her head, but then she nodded. To ease her mind even more, I added, "I won't be there for the actual change. Once his heart stops, his father will drive us safely away, until Teren has had his fill of cattle."

She looked at me blankly, and then smacked my shoulder. "You couldn't have led with that! Geeze, Emma...I was picturing them tying you down next to him like some virgin sacrifice."

Rubbing my shoulder, I rolled my eyes and we both started to giggle. "I'm hardly a virgin, Ashley."

She laughed harder and gave me a huge hug. All was forgiven. "I love you, sis."

I held her back just as tight. "I love you too. I'll be fine...okay?"

"You better be," she muttered and I thought I heard her add, "I'll stake his ass, if you're not."

Cleaning up our sodden faces, we hugged one last time before exiting the bathroom to rejoin dinner. Teren and my mom were laughing over something as we calmly approached the table. Teren eyed me with a clear question in the slight arch of his brow. Too low for the others to hear, I muttered, "She's fine...we're fine." He nodded once and flicked his eyes to Ashley as she sat down.

Meeting his gaze, Ashley muttered something under her breath. I didn't hear what she said, but Teren's eyes saddened as he flicked a quick glance to me. He nodded briefly to Ashley, before picking up his fork and resuming his meal, which had arrived while we'd been in the bathroom, since the waitress, Debby, knew perfectly well what we'd order.

I glanced up at Ashley across from me as she picked up her fork. She gave me a small grin before shifting her focus to her meal. My mother seemed oblivious to the silent conversations going on around her, but after wiping her mouth with a napkin, she did ask me if I was all right. "Yes, I'm great. Everything is great," I assured her.

She gave me an odd look for half a second, and then asked Teren, "What will you have to do on the ranch?"

I wondered if Mom suspected something was going on, but was choosing to ignore it. My mom would fight for me like a mother bear if the situation called for it, but Teren and I were happy, and relatively healthy, so whatever was going on, obviously wasn't dangerous in her eyes. Sometimes, living in ignorance is the easiest way to get through life...especially when it comes to your loved ones.

After the meal, we hugged goodbye in the parking lot. Teren muttered something in Ashley's ear again, before helping her into the car. Once we were back in his vehicle, I asked, yet again, what he and my sister were chatting about. With a half-smile, he told me, "At the table, she threatened to kill me if anything happened to you. I just told her that I would let her stake me, if anything happened to you."

I shook my head in disbelief at these people who loved me so fiercely.

The following week and a half were a blur. I'm sure the days happened. They must have. I was pretty sure time travel wasn't possible. Of course, just a few months ago I'd felt the same way about vampires. But somewhere in the goodbye meals with my family, a final double date with Tracey and Hot Ben, who was anxious for Teren to return for more "guy time", and arranging for Spike to live with my mom and sister while we were gone, so we didn't tempt Halina, days flew by.

Tracey threw me a going away party on my last day, much to Clarice's dismay. She brought me a bouquet of wild flowers and enough chocolate cupcakes for the entire staff, which I think finally made Clarice okay with the whole distraction. After handing me a cupcake with a lit sparkler on the top, Tracey and I hugged for several long seconds. We both had tears in our eyes as we pulled apart, and I already missed my vivacious friend.

After the mini bon voyage, I went home. Teren was already there in my drive, waiting for me so we could prepare for our trip. I packed multiple bags of clothes and supplies for our "vacation that wasn't a vacation" and then we added my stuff to Teren's few bags. My addition loaded up his Prius to near bursting. Teren wryly commented that his parents did own a washing machine, so I didn't need to pack half my closet. I gave him a sour face for that. Over packing was a woman's prerogative. I'd even refused his offer to do it for me again. As good as he was at it, the selecting and folding of clothing calmed my mind and my nerves. Honestly, I think that's why I seriously over packed. Stopping had caused my mind to drift to unpleasant things, so I'd purposely avoided doing it.

And so, on a cloudless, blue, autumn Saturday morning, after a peaceful night of holding each other until we fell into a deep sleep, my vampire and I headed out to his parents' ranch, where he was slated to die within six weeks. I cast a final glance back at my house as we pulled out of the driveway. The early morning sunlight sparkled in the windows and the house almost looked like it was winking goodbye to me. I smiled at the blue beauty with the old-fashioned white shutters and flower boxes, and a bright red door. My grandmother's house, that looked like a half-gallon carton of milk smashed in-between other half-gallon cartons of milk, each holding the other up for support. I was going to miss it. I silently wished the house well in my absence, and turned back to the road.

We were quiet as we drove along, passing by people walking their pets and older couples, holding hands as they went about their morning. I watched a particularly cute, wrinkled couple and let out a soft sigh. That would never be Teren and I, but we would still have a great life together. Once we got through his death, of course.

Hearing me sigh, Teren stretched out his warm hand and placed it over mine on my knee. I turned my palm and laced our fingers together. He exhaled in a long, steady breath, like he was struggling with a nervous stomach. He glanced over at me and tried to smile, but it quickly fell off his face.

Feeling a jittery tension in the air, I tried to lighten the mood. "You know, you never did teach me any Russian."

He looked over at me with a genuine smile on his lips. *Mission accomplished.* "I guess I didn't, did I?"

I raised an eyebrow and patiently waited for him to start. He laughed, once he realized I wanted my first lesson right now. With a smile still on his lips, he flicked a glance back to the empty stretch of road, leading to a main artery out of the city. Returning his eyes to me, he warmly said, "Ya tebya lyublyu."

I scrunched my brow and tried to repeat the odd sounding phrase. "Ya tebya…"

"Lyublyu," he said again, with a warm glow in his eyes that matched the one on his lips.

I tried again, saying the words as close as I could to English, so the strange pronunciation made sense to me. "Ya teb-ya lou-blue." He nodded, his smile proud. Feeling more confident, I spouted it out again, trying to match his authentic cadence. He laughed a little and nodded again.

When his eyes turned back to the road as we hit the highway, leading us away from our homes, I wondered what I'd said. "What did I say?" I scanned his face as I asked him. His eyes twinkled in the morning rays, but he didn't answer me. That wasn't a good sign. I frowned. "Teren…what did you have me say?"

He started chuckling at my tone, but he still refused to answer me. I exhaled a dramatic breath, "Oh God. You made me say something dirty, didn't you?"

Laughing in earnest, he looked over at me with adoration clear in his features. Shaking his head, he softly said, "It means 'I love you'."

I felt my cheeks heat as I started laughing with him. Squeezing our laced-together hands, I looked out the window at San Francisco streaming by me. Darn romantic vampire. As more and more of the city fell behind me, and romantic Russian syllables danced in my head, I asked Teren something that I'd randomly thought one day, back when he'd first told me what he was.

"Do you ever walk down the street and have a woman pass you and think—hmmm…I'd like a bite of that girl?" I twisted my head to grin in his direction.

Teren laughed at my odd question. "Of course…who doesn't?" He shrugged and continued laughing, all worry momentarily gone from his features, as I kept the mood in the car light.

I frowned playfully. "I'm serious, Teren."

He bit his lip to rein in his chuckles and looked back over the road. "Well, if I see a pretty girl, who smells appealing, I may wonder for a second if her blood is a particularly good…vintage." He shrugged again. "But that's about it."

I smiled as I thought about my next question. "Did you think that about me?"

He looked over at me with an open, loving, honest face and then responded suggestively with, "Why do you think I called you?"

My body felt red-hot all over. His eyes lingered down my skin before turning back to the road. His smile was that alluring half-grin that was so darn sexy. My hand clutching his suddenly wanted to be running through his hair and across his strong shoulders. I may have gotten carried away with my mood relaxing questions.

For a long time, I stared at him with open interest in my eyes, while he watched the road; his grin never left him. Just as I was about to tell him to pull over somewhere, before we reached his parents' place of super-hearing mood killers, he pulled the car over.

Confused, and slightly alarmed that he maybe could read minds now, I looked around at where he'd stopped. We were quite a ways from the city now, away from the main highway and on a slower, less traveled road. In fact, there weren't any cars coming or going on this dusty stretch of blacktop for as far as I could see. But before I could get too excited over that prospect, the reason Teren had pulled over became glaringly obvious.

On the side of the road was a small camper, the kind that looked like a fifth wheel trailer and a pickup truck had given birth to a truck/trailer hybrid. This poor creation was suffering from some sort of vehicular malaise. The engine hood was propped open, and someone was underneath it, examining the underbelly. All we could see were a pair of denims dangerously protruding out onto the road. If this street were busier, he'd probably have gotten his ankles run over by now.

Teren separated our hands and made to open his door. "What are you going to do?" I asked.

He gave me a quick peck. "I'm going to see if I can help. I know a little bit about cars, working on my dad's jeeps." He shrugged. "And if all else fails, I can at least call him a tow truck."

I glanced at his cell phone sitting in the console, and then back up to him. I raised an eyebrow in question. "Are you just trying to delay us?"

Teren rolled his eyes. "No...I'm trying to help someone." He cracked his door and nodded his head in the direction of the incapacitated vehicle. "Come with. You can time me." Grinning, he opened his door and got out.

Shaking my head at his clear attempt to set us back a few hours, and, honestly, I had come up with much better ways to delay us than him sweating all over a rusty engine block, I opened my door and stepped out into the cool breeze of this fine California morning.

Crunching through the dirt along the side of the road, I

joined Teren at the front of his car and clasped hands with him. Together, we walked over to where the man was still buried underneath his vehicle. We walked right up to the man's shins and Teren bent down a little to talk to him. "Excuse me, sir? Can I help you in any way?" Teren politely asked the set of legs that still hadn't moved. When no one responded, he again asked, "Sir?"

Teren cocked his head and started to look up, like he'd heard something. That was when my feeble human ears heard something. It was a faint metallic "pop", like something under great pressure had been released. That was the last thing that made sense to me, for a very long while.

A loud, scraping metal noise immediately followed the pop, like a crowbar being dragged behind a car flying down the freeway. Before I could even ascertain where the noise was coming from though, I was being lifted into the air by Teren's strong arms. Confused by the sudden movement, I clung to him with both hands. Just as I was about to ask him what he was doing, a sickening wet thud filled my ears, and we both started to fall over. I landed heavily on his stomach, Teren screamed in pain.

"Teren…baby…?"

Hopelessly confused, I searched his agonized face while my hands ran over his chest. Scooting off to the side of him, my hands and eyes drifted over his body. I began to worry that I'd really hurt him when I'd fallen on top of him. I also wondered why my never clumsy boyfriend, had seemingly fallen over for no apparent reason.

That was when my hand got to his legs…to what used to be strong, healthy, intact legs. My fingers felt the wetness of his jeans and startled, I pulled those fingers to my face. They were red—the deep, dark red of freshly exposed blood; his jeans below his knees were quickly becoming saturated with it. He jerked in pain when I accidentally touched his injuries, and he cried out in agony.

I wiped a shaking hand on my jeans and sat back so I didn't cause him anymore pain. Looking up at the vehicle, I saw a steel rod bar protruding out from under the frame of the camper. It was close to the rear tire, at a ninety degree angle to the vehicle. I could see a thick suspension coil attached to it and looking closer at the front tire, I saw the clip where the rod had once been secured to the vehicle. That was when my brain started making connections.

The pop I'd heard, was something or someone releasing the bolt that was holding back the rod. With that clip released, the rod had flown back towards the rear tire, kinetic energy giving it strength and speed that no human would be fast enough to get away from. But Teren wasn't entirely human. He'd heard the pop and calculated what it was. He'd had just enough time to scoop me above where the bar was sweeping around, but he hadn't had time to scoop and run; the bar had hit his legs full force, midway between his knees and his ankles, smashing his shins into a bloody, fractured mess.

It was in this daze of *What the hell just happened?* that I noticed that the pair of legs we'd approached earlier were gone. A hole dug under the vehicle would have provided a person more than enough room to hide and wait—wait in their trap. A trap we'd inadvertently sprung. Then a shadow blocked out the morning sun on one side of my face and I instinctively turned to look at it.

A grizzly man, wearing a green army jacket with a knife clipped to his belt, faced me. "Morning, sweetheart," he calmly said, right before he brought his fist around to my temple and knocked me out cold.

Chapter 16 – Abomination

I never again in this life want to wake up the way I did after being socked in the head…not that I ever wanted to be socked in the head again. I didn't. It hurt. A lot. But waking up with a throbbing ache in my skull and a tender bruise on the very edge of my eye socket, hurt worse than the actual hit. Irritation swept through me, but it was immediately replaced by ice cold fear. I was no longer outside. I was lying on my back, on the floor of a dirt strewn camper that was gently rocking back and forth in the unmistakable sway of road movement.

As these facts entered my brain, stubborn irritation cropped back up. *Seriously? I've been kidnapped? Seriously? Teren and I have been kidnapped? Teren…oh God…*

I shifted my head and saw the blood first; a trail of it along the floor led me to the slumped form of my honey. He was resting against a faded brown chair with ripped cushions that had been hastily sewn back together in a ragged, zigzag pattern. His legs were a red, sodden mess stretched out in front of him. His head was lying back on the chair and every jarring bump of the vehicle elicited a groan from him.

I said a silent prayer of thanks that he was still alive and, ignoring my aching head, which seemed so trivial now in comparison to Teren's injuries, I carefully crawled over to him. Avoiding all contact with his lower body, I placed a hand on his cheek. He groaned and his eyes fluttered. I looked around the small cabin, but nothing in here was going to help us get out, not with Teren's legs in the mess they were.

I held his face close to me as I took in the small, white kitchen table, that looked about ready to collapse, the stove and small sink, forming the rest of the kitchen, and a room near the back, that probably contained a nearly impossible to use toilet. On the other side of us was the front of the vehicle, mainly consisting of the driver's area. Space over the truck cabin held a thin mattress that was trying to call itself a bed.

Luckily, or maybe unluckily, the driving portion of the camper was enclosed, and I could neither get to it, nor could our captor get to me. I tried to think of a way to block the main door by the bathroom, so that he couldn't get back here when the vehicle stopped, but really, that wouldn't solve anything. Teren would bleed to death and I'd starve to death and the captor would win anyway. Assuming our death was his primary goal…and I was going to go ahead and assume that, since the way we'd been taken wasn't exactly welcoming.

A pothole in the road banged the back of the camper down and Teren woke with a cry of pain. His eyes, unfocused and full of stress, flicked to mine. His face relaxed infinitesimally. "Emma…you're okay." His voice was strained with contained tension. I could tell he really wanted to scream again, but he didn't want to freak me out. He might as well have. I was already freaked out.

I kissed his forehead, after wiping off some of the perspiration. "I'm fine, baby. Shhh…rest, Teren. Please."

He weakly lifted his head to look around at where we were. His eyes rested on his bloody jeans and his face paled even more. "Oh God…I remember," he muttered, then he flinched as a jar in the road bounced him.

"Do you know what's going on?" I whispered, not sure why I was whispering, but feeling the need for quiet at the look of restraint on his face.

He gritted his teeth and shook his head. "No…" I looked down at his legs while he searched my face. They were bad. I didn't know if any bones shards were poking through his skin and I really didn't want to know. Just looking at the blood was horrifying enough.

"Emma…" His weak voice brought my gaze back to his eyes, so beautiful and so filled with agony. "Please…run if you can." I was already shaking my head and his crystal blue eyes brimmed with moisture. "Don't…don't you dare stay because of me." His voice picked up heat. "You run."

I stared at him with a blank expression, knowing for all the world, that I was incapable of honoring his request…and then I nodded. He closed his eyes and laid his head back on the chair in relief. I kissed his forehead again and held in the tears. "Thank you for saving me," I whispered against his clammy skin.

He muttered something that sounded loving and his eyes fluttered, but they didn't open, and he didn't speak again. He didn't move again either, just sat there with his head back on the chair, either resting as I'd asked him to…or passed out from the pain. Needing to do something, I carefully undid his belt, and then undid mine. Thankfully, we'd both gone for the rancher, belt buckle look. We'd even joked to each other about it before this little fiasco. I wrapped the belt around his thigh, above his knee, and gritting my teeth, cinched it tight. He cried out, but didn't wake up. I did the other one. He no longer cried out.

I laid my head on his chest and felt tears that I hadn't been aware of, roll off my nose to splash on his shirt. "I'm sorry, baby. Please hold on…" I whispered, and only the occasional creak of the old camper answered me.

We drove in that near silence for what felt like days. It couldn't have been days, since the sunlight coming through the smudged window over the table never left us, but it felt like days. I worried over Teren's legs, and wondered if my hastily construed tourniquets were actually doing anything. I worried over how I was going to get a man who couldn't walk away from the predator in the cabin. I stressed over where he was taking us. I stroked Teren's cheek, soothing him with reassuring words, that I didn't really feel, whenever a big enough movement brought him out of his pain-induced stupor. And I wished for the first time ever that Halina was with us. Even though it was daytime outside and that wasn't possible, I wanted her to come rip the man's bloody throat out.

Finally, the camper pulled off the main road to a bumpy dirt road. I think my heart went into overdrive. The camper, although frightening in its own way, had been my home for hours, and I was in a comfortable zone of terror with it. I knew every fault line in the rickety table. I'd counted every water stain in the ceiling and I'd even named the resident spiders living in the kitchen window—Fred and Daphne. Whatever new hell we were being led to, was all the more nerve-racking simply for its newness.

The bouncy road jolted Teren to alertness and he cried out in continual pain. When the bumps became a rhythm that wasn't stopping, he clamped his mouth shut and grabbed my hand. He squeezed so tight I thought he might break me. I'd have let him. I brushed back his hair from his now slick forehead and whispered what encouragement I could. Struggling to remain conscious, he closed his eyes and nodded.

Eventually the jarring stopped. Eventually the sound of the tires crunching along a dirt path stopped. Eventually the camper stopped. I'm pretty sure that's when my heart stopped, too. Teren opened his eyes and let out a sharp exhale of relief. Well, as much relief as he could possibly feel right now. With glazed eyes he turned to look at me and, needing comfort as well as wanting to give it, I kissed him. With tight lips, he returned my kiss.

Abruptly the camper door swung open and surprised, we broke apart. A large man, taller and wider than Teren, with coarse, graying stubble that looked as hard and unwelcoming as the man's personality must be, entered the vehicle that now felt tiny. "Well, isn't that nice. Kissing your soon-to-be dead lover goodbye, huh? Sweet." His voice had a gravely edge to it that was as unpleasant as everything else about him. A scar across his lower lip buckled the skin as he smiled. "It'd be even sweeter, if he weren't a spawn of pure evil."

He stepped into the small kitchen area and I protectively placed myself in front of Teren. "Please, let us go. We're just—"

He took another step to stand right in front of me, and I noticed the wide open door behind him. He crisply cut me off. "Don't even try and play innocent." He pointed a dirty finger at Teren, who weakly raised his head and looked up at him with defiance bravely etched on his face. "I know exactly what he is." The man glared at me. "And you too…vampire whore."

My mouth dropped. I'm not sure what shocked me more—him knowing that Teren was a vampire, or him calling me a whore. The scarred smile returned as he took in my shocked expression. "Didn't think I knew what he was?"

"What do you want with me?" Teren quietly asked through his tightly clenched jaw.

The man's smile left him and his dark, close-set eyes narrowed as he looked down on Teren, like he was nothing more than dirt the man had scraped off his shoe. "I want what God has commanded of me. I want to destroy all of your kind." His dark eyes flared with a zealot light. "I will end every abomination on this Earth."

Teren's clenched jaw loosened in shock at hearing the man's passionate words. I started shivering, as I blocked as much of Teren as I could.

"He is not an abom—"

I didn't get a chance to finish my brilliant rebuttal. The man reached out and fisted my hair with his massive palm. He jerked my head away from Teren and my body had no choice but to follow. He tossed me and my prickling scalp into the bench seat at the rickety table.

His finger landed on my chest with a force that I'm sure bruised me. "Your opinion on the matter doesn't interest me, whore." He motioned back to Teren. He was biting his lip to stop himself from crying out in pain as he attempted to move his body, to help me in some small way. "Your life became irrelevant the minute you let *that* feed off you." He leaned in close and his musky odor sickened me. His eyes flicked down my body. "And you let him inside you…an unholy beast…" He spat on the floor next to the table. "You disgust me."

Embarrassment and rage flashed through me. "Right back at you, asshole!"

He smirked, then slapped me. Hard. My head was suddenly facing the window and my ears were ringing. My jaw felt disconnected from my body and I could feel a warm trickle from a line of blood trailing down my chin. Apparently, I'd cut my lip on my teeth. Wonderful. I'd never been "bitch-slapped" before. I found I didn't like it.

I wiped the blood off with the back of my hand and slowly swiveled my head at the sound of Teren struggling and in pain. I turned to see the man watching in amusement as Teren unsuccessfully attempted to stand and defend me. Tears of pain were in his eyes as he tried to move his wrecked legs. He was breathing heavy, and soft whimpers were escaping him. His face paled to a sickening ashen color; he looked like he was going to pass out again.

The man let out a cruel laugh. "No fun when you can't heal yet, is it?" He leaned over Teren and placed his hands on his knees. "That's when you're easiest to catch, you know. When you're still mostly human…and weak."

"I will rip your throat out," Teren growled. Anger brightened his eyes and a deep snarl rose from his chest.

The man laughed again. Straightening, he kicked Teren's legs on the floor. So much pain instantly filled Teren's face that he couldn't even cry out. His mouth dropped and he gasped as he struggled for air. He seemed incapable of doing anything else. Eyes fluttering, his head dropped back on the chair.

"Teren!" I started to rise, determined to help him somehow, when the man stuck his finger on my chest again. "Stay," he commanded. I froze, pure hatred in my eyes as I glared up at him.

He smirked as he looked down on me. The scar on his lip made the move unnaturally menacing. He regarded me with cold eyes. "Do you love this evil thing?" He nudged Teren's toe, making him cry out.

"Stop it," I snapped.

"Do you?" he asked quietly.

A tear rolled down my cheek as I watched Teren start to come back to consciousness. "Yes," I whispered. My eyes shot up to the man. "And he's not evil. He's a good man."

Laughing, the man leaned over me. "He's not even truly human. He's not a man."

Wanting him to back up, I did something I never thought I would do—I spat in his face. The man didn't seem too shocked by the display, and calmly wiped his face with the sleeve of his army jacket. Straightening, he patted the knife on his belt. I froze as I remembered that this man was dangerous…and armed.

His rough voice dropped an octave. "Here is what's going to happen." He pointed at me. "You are going to help me move *this*," he kicked Teren's legs, and I flinched as he cried out in pain, "or I can do it all by myself." His lips curled into a cruel smile.

I swallowed as I imagined just how gentle he'd be with Teren's beaten body. I gave him a stiff nod and the man motioned for me to stand. Warily, I stood beside the table. My eyes never left the man's hard face. He bent down for Teren and I glanced back at the open door. Freedom was staring me in the face. I immediately ignored it, as Teren gasped in pain. The man had gathered his legs into his arms and was starting to lift him. Teren was struggling not to scream. I wasn't going anywhere without him.

"What are you doing? Let me take his legs!" I yelled, as I ran around to Teren's shoulders. I attempted to lift his upper body so he was more level. The icy rush of adrenaline coursing through me made it possible, and I lifted Teren securely, if not easily. Teren's head dropped back to my shoulder, as he passed out again from the pain.

The man roughly lifted his legs as he smirked at me. "Did you think I was going anywhere near his teeth? I'm not stupid, sweetheart."

"I disagree. He's gonna kill you, you know."

The man laughed and looked at Teren's limp form in our hands. "I doubt that...but it wouldn't surprise me if he tried." He looked back up to me. "He is evil, after all."

I bit back my angry retort as the man started to move backwards out of the camper. Teren groaned, and his head lolled side to side as we made our way down the couple of steps at the back of the vehicle. I tried to be gentle with my half of Teren, but the man couldn't have cared less about his bloody half, and we jarred him with every step down. Teren came to briefly at the bottom. He lifted his head off my shoulder and made a pained noise before dropping it down again. I kissed his head and whispered that it would be okay, as I felt a couple of his tears hit my collarbone. He was in so much pain...

I was so focused on keeping pace with the man holding Teren's legs, that I barely noticed the reddish-brown, dusty dirt under my feet. I started to struggle with Teren's weight, as my momentary rush of strength started to ebb. When my feet hit wooden steps, I looked up from where I'd been intently studying the circular pattern on Teren's t-shirt.

We were at an old farmhouse that looked like it had been abandoned in the early nineteen hundreds. The porch had missing floorboards, the front door was half off its hinges, and the windows were long gone. They had been boarded over with faded planks of wood in an X pattern. The man started up the steps, which looked about ready to cave inward, and I carefully followed him, trying to readjust my hold on Teren without shaking him too badly.

We finally made it around the missing planks in the porch, and through the half-destroyed door, and entered a small room with a rat-infested couch. I automatically started shifting to the couch, wanting to set Teren down, but the man turned down a side hallway. Teren groaned as his body went in two different directions. Cursing, I adjusted my grip and followed the asshole who'd abducted us. He led us to a lone door in a rickety hallway. The door had an iron bar padlocked across it. The lock was open and the bar was raised—awaiting its prisoners. He turned the doorknob after unceremoniously dropping one of Teren's legs. Teren screamed at that.

The man swung the door inward, exposing a pitch-black opening that seemed to devour all light that tried to touch it. I did not want to follow him in there. Everything in my body wanted to run while the man was preoccupied with flipping on a light switch, exposing a steep set of stairs that surely led down into Hell. But I couldn't run with Teren, and there was no way I was running without him, so I gathered my courage and made the conscious decision to follow the man when he picked Teren's leg back up and started down the steps.

He carefully backed down the poorly constructed wooden staircase. They were the kind of stairs that had large gaps between each step and no backing, so with every long drop you were just positive that a hand was going to reach out from behind and grab your ankles, making you fall and crash into the ground below. But somehow we safely made it down those long steps, Teren groaning with each one, and started walking through a cellar.

I hate cellars. My aunt had one in her house and when I was four, I was accidentally locked inside it for a few hours. She had an old furnace that groaned and whined periodically, and my child mind had transformed the noisy contraption into a monster that was searching me out to eat me. Now, at twenty-five, I was well aware that cellars were no different than any other room in a house…but a lingering childhood fear remained with me all the same. As we approached the far wall, I was already shaking with the prospect of being locked down here.

I struggled with gently lowering my half of Teren's body. The man simply dumped Teren's legs to the ground. Teren cried out as I propped him against the dank stone wall of the dirt-floor room. The air smelled rank—like mold and stale water. I could hear animals scurrying in the dark corners that the single, bare bulb hanging from a chain in the center of the room didn't illuminate.

Struggling with controlling my terror, I startled and screamed when the man touched me. He grabbed my hand, and just as I started to fight him off with every fear-empowered cell in my body, I felt cool metal slap around my wrist and cinch tight with a resounding snap. The man let go of me and confused, I followed the odd sound. I was shocked to see that my wrist was now handcuffed to a wrought iron bar attached to the stone wall.

Knowing it would do nothing, I reflexively pulled at my wrist. The bar didn't budge. Panic welled in me; now I was chained to the wall in this room that terrified me. Genuinely afraid, I grabbed Teren's hand. As he started to come back around, he loosely held mine back. He laid his head against the rough wall of the square coffin we were in, and tried to smile encouragingly at me, but his face was too full of fear and pain to successfully pull it off. At least Teren and I were in this together.

The man's chuckling returned my attention to him. He was smiling at the sight of Teren and me huddled on the dirt floor before him, holding hands.

I tried to appeal to whatever humanity this man probably didn't have. "Please, let us go. He's really hurt. He needs to be in a hospital."

The man laughed once and spat on the ground. "He'll be fine, once he changes. At least, until I stake him, of course."

I squinted as I tried to absorb what he was saying. "What?"

The man squatted down to look me in the eye. He reached out to touch my hair and I instinctively pulled away from him. "I don't relish killing humans, but you can't be allowed to live, vamp lover." He pointed with his thumb at Teren. "I'm going to let him finish you, and then I'll finish him." He brushed his hands off on each other. "All clean." He smirked at me. "You can think of it as me getting justice on your murderer, if you like?"

My body went ice cold with the confirmation that he *was* planning on killing us...and nefariously too. "Teren would never hurt me. Your plan will fail. He would *never* kill a human!" I felt Teren squeeze my hand a little tighter and I grasped his like a lifeline.

Weakly Teren muttered, "She's right. I'd never—"

The man brushed Teren's legs with his hands, making Teren stop talking and cry out in pain.

"Stop it!" I yelled at him.

He ignored my outburst and responded to my statement. "Won't kill, huh?" His dark eyes bored into mine. "Not even after he changes? Not even when he's...deathly hungry?"

Teren sucked in a sharp breath and I felt the blood draining from my face. That was the one time we were both a little unsure of. I frantically pulled at the cuffs again as I looked over at Teren. That was when I realized he wasn't restrained. Damn if my sister hadn't been right-on with her fear. Here I was, chained to the wall next to a vampire, just like some damn virgin sacrifice.

I sputtered in protest. "Weeks? You're going to keep us down here for weeks, waiting for him to..." My thoughts trailed off as my eyes ran over Teren's legs, soaked in blood. The man's jacket was streaked with it from where he'd held him up. "He won't make it for weeks." My eyes went back to the man's. "You've killed him already. He won't survive until the change!"

The man straightened and laughed at me. Shaking his head, he reached into his back pocket and grabbed a case. While I snuck a peek at Teren, who was scrutinizing every move the man made, our captor spoke in an amused voice. "I don't have time to wait weeks.

This one has nest-mates, who will eventually look for him." He opened the silver case and pulled out a syringe. Tapping the glass, he pushed some pink fluid out of the tip, removing the air bubbles. Smiling, his scar white against his pale lips, he knelt beside Teren and said, "I only need a day."

With that comment, he stuck the needle into Teren's thigh and injected the fluid. Teren screamed like he was being pumped full of molten lava. I tried to push the man back, but he was already finished. He stepped away from Teren, leaving him gasping in pain and clutching at his thigh.

"What did you do to him?" I hotly demanded, straining against my restraints in my desire to throttle the man.

Unimpressed by my display, he calmly held the empty syringe in front of him. "This…jumpstarts the conversion. He'll be dead by nightfall." My body went limp with shock and defeat while Teren clenched my hand with renewed strength.

"What? That's not possible…" I whispered, more to myself than the man.

He answered me though. "You both act like he's something special." He shrugged. "He's not. I've been chasing mixed breeds all up and down this country. They're all the same." He held the syringe up to me again, before putting it back in its case. "I cooked this up myself and it always works. It always forces the change, within hours. I even got this to work on a ten year old once." He said that with a look of cold pride, like changing over a child was an accomplishment.

My eyes were glued to the syringe being tucked back into its case. In that one instant, only a single thought echoed in my head and vibrated through my body: *The line was dead.*

Looking back at Teren clutching his leg in torturous agony, my first thought should have been for his well-being. I should have cared about his fear of dying, of crossing over into that unknown place. I should have cared about the pain that change was going to bring him, although with the pains he'd suffered recently, I was beginning to believe that the dying part might actually be the most relaxing thing he'd felt in a while. I should have cared that Teren's heart was about to stop and his skin was going to cool. I should have instantly cared about being anchored next to a man who was about experience insatiable blood lust.

But I didn't care about that yet. All I cared about, as the man coldly laughed at Teren's discomfort, was my empty womb; that one needle had instantly evaporated any hope of a child. I wasn't pregnant...and now I never would be. I'd never see a black-haired child in my home. I'd never hear Teren's laugh repeated in miniature. I'd never hear a tiny, musical voice say, "I love you, Mommy." My soul ached with the loss.

I knew on some level, that that shouldn't have been relevant right now. Somewhere in my head, I knew I'd never survive this night anyway, so being pregnant or not didn't even matter. But I'd been trying to have Teren's baby for a while now, and forcefully being made to let go of that dream ripped my heart to pieces. A sob escaped me and I sunk my head onto Teren's chest. His breathing had somewhat returned to normal, but his heart was beating wildly. His doomed heart was beating wildly. I sobbed even more.

Teren's hand came up to clutch my back as I mercilessly wept against his chest. The dying man in extraordinary pain was actually trying to soothe *me* because my uterus was barren. That thought snapped my head back to reality. Wiping my face off on my shirt, I turned to glare at the man standing a few paces away, watching us with a look of amused disgust on his scratchy face.

I was about to let out a stream of vile profanity that would surely be so scathing the man would instantly change his mind about our captivity and let us go. The man opened his mouth and began speaking before I could though. "You must be third generation at least." He reached behind him to grab a chair, then scooted to the edge of the pale circle of light. Half his face was in darkness, and the light half of him seemed all the more menacing because of it. I swallowed back my obscenities and glanced up at Teren. He was eyeing the man with a clenched jaw and lethal intent.

The man didn't seem to care that Teren wasn't participating in the conversation, and he continued to talk to him like he was— some men did so enjoy discussing their work. "Yeah, it's so much harder to spot you guys, when you can hide out in the sunshine." He shook his head. "It's rare to come across a fourth or fifth and I tell you, they are really difficult to tell apart from humans. You pretty much have to watch for them to feed."

I swear my stomach thumped with a phantom baby kick at the man's cruel words. My dry eyes threatened to spill back over with my heart wrenching loss, but I made myself keep full composure. This...*thing*...before me wouldn't get another second of my tears.

The man scratched his lice-infested jaw, okay, he wasn't lice infested, but the man was disgusting, and it helped stoke the fire in my belly to make him as physically gross as he was morally. "It was a lucky night for me that I went to that baseball game." He tilted his head and eyed Teren with a raised brow. "That was quite a catch...vampire."

My heart seized. Teren and I looked at each other and a moment of *Oh God* realization passed soundlessly between us. This evil Buffy wannabe had been there that night. He had seen Teren calmly pluck a ball from in front of my face barehanded. No one else in the stadium had made the connection but the one person who had some divine providence to do something about it.

We looked back over at him when his gravelly voice continued, "I followed you after that...just to be sure." Leaning forward on his hands and knees, he spat on the hard-packed dirt. "I followed you to your vampire nest. A ranch? Interesting." He ran a hand along his jaw while I paled at the thought of him anywhere near Teren's family. "I suppose I'll have to clear them out next."

"You son of a bitch!" Teren suddenly exclaimed. He jerked upright, like he was going to attack the man. Unfortunately his body wasn't up for the task, and he immediately crumpled back against the wall, as the pain shot through him.

The man let out a cold laugh as he watched Teren struggle. "Yeah...I didn't go near the property." He tapped a grimy finger against his ear. "I know what you can do. But I figure there are at least two other mixed...and the full vampire, of course." Teren's upper body went rigid as he breathed in and out with as much control as he could muster. I almost expected him to slip out his fangs and hiss at the man. I think if he thought it would do any good, he would have.

The man spat again before laying out his insidious plan. "I'll go in during the day, stake the mixed ones fast, and then torch the vampire while they sleep. Easiest way to rid yourself of a vampire—cleansing through fire while they nap." His lips started to spread into a smile, but then he frowned. "You got humans there? Breeders?" He shrugged. "I suppose I'll have to toss them in the fire too… I really don't relish killing humans, but, God's work must be done."

Teren dropped his mouth in speechlessness. My mind instantly went to my sister and her charred, blistered skin after the horrendous fire that had devastated our family. I couldn't believe someone would willingly impose that cruel fate on another. I pictured Halina's screams as she was awoken from a deep sleep. I imagined Jack's flesh melting, muscle sliding away from the bone…

I stood and nearly yanked my arm from my socket as I made a move for the man. He only turned his head a small fraction to glance at me in apathy. That disregarding look ignited my already flaring temper. "I'm going to fillet you! You will never touch them! Never!"

I futilely struggled against the cuffs; the iron bar scraped in protest with my furious movements. Finally, the man walked over to me. Teren tried to grab him, but he effortlessly scooted away from his grasp. Coming up to the other side of me, away from Teren, he clamped my throat in his big hands and harshly smacked my head against the wall. Dazed and seeing stars dance in my vision, I slumped down the wall in defeat. Teren immediately put his hand on the back of my head. I felt the wetness there and knew I was bleeding. My vampire would be aware of that too. He snapped his head around to the man calmly walking back to his chair. A low growl rumbled in his chest as his fangs slid out; he looked ready to tear the man to pieces.

The man only laughed again. "Ahhh…there's the beast. I was wondering if he'd show up to the party." He pointed at where Teren was still issuing a lethal growl from deep in his chest. "I've been biding my time, waiting to collect you and your whore. You provided me the perfect opportunity, by telling your friends and coworkers that you were going away for weeks…" He shrugged and a happy look crossed his hard face. "Thank you for that. No one is going to miss you for a long time. I'll be on the other side of the country before the police are even called…not that they'll ever find your bodies."

Feeling more in control of my vision if nothing else, I spat at the man, "Why are you doing this? They're not hurting anyone! They're innocen—"

He cut me off before I could finish my protest. "Innocent? Have they hypnotized you woman?" He spat again and curled his lip in disdain. "They're killers…each and every one of them." He indicated Teren huddled against me, fangs still bared, as if that proved his point.

"And what are you!" I yelled with a derisive curl of my own.

His back straightened and for a moment, I saw a soldier in that green army jacket. "I'm a holy man. I'm doing God's work. I'm ridding the world of anathemas." He narrowed his eyes as he snarled at me, "I'm not *adding* to them." Before I could respond he said, "They all kill…every one, so don't you say they are innocent, loving creatures. They aren't."

His voice rose and warbled. "My daughter was the innocent…" His eyes watered as pure, righteous anger filled him. "She was tricked by a monster. That thing got her pregnant, then devoured her and the baby in her womb, after he changed." His entire body shook and for a moment, I thought he was going to vibrate off the chair. He didn't though. Instead, he stood. Still shaking in a near epileptic fit, he walked over to stand in front of Teren. From the light of near madness in the man's eyes, I didn't even think he saw Teren anymore. He saw whatever poor vampire had harmed his child.

"He had the nerve to apologize, before I drove the stake through his heart. Apologize! For taking the life of my little girl!" He swung his foot and his steel-toed boot made contact with the bloody pulp of Teren's shins. The movement jerked Teren's legs towards me and his body followed suit. He slumped to the ground around my knees, crying out in pain before stilling, knocked out again from the sheer overwhelming power of agony.

I ran my free hand over his back and curled over him

protectively. "Leave him alone! He's already dying! You don't need to torture him!"

The man sneered at me. Ignoring my comments, he contemptuously said, "I watched you let him feed off of you at that restaurant. That's what made me positive I had it right." His eyes ran up and down my body, like I was the most perverted thing he'd ever seen. "You commanded him to drink blood from you and then you screwed him." My stomach dropped as I realized what he was talking about. I had thought we were perfectly alone that night by the dumpster. I didn't know anyone had seen that. Teren had been so focused on my blood, he must not have heard the man, and he'd seen…everything.

My face heated and I raised my chin in defiance. "Yes. I let him drink from me. I let him make love to me. I love him." My eyes ran up and down the creep's body with contempt. "He's more of a man than you'll ever be."

The man smirked again, brought his fist around again, and knocked me out cold…again.

Chapter 17 – Ya Tebya Lyublyu

I was officially not a fan of being knocked out. In fact, I was a little sick of it. Not being real big on the whole mind-nerve connection that was pain, I didn't want to be hit again in this life—ever. Of course, as I opened my eyes and a pale, hazy light blinded my irises, it occurred to me that my life wasn't exactly going to be a long and prosperous one anyway.

I groaned and placed a hand on the side of my head that had been clocked twice now…not to mention slapped. Oh, and shoved against a wall. I was fairly certain, by the sharp inhale I instinctively took as my fingers barely brushed my eye socket, that not only was I puffy, I was bruised as well. Great.

"Emma?" A soft, pain-filled voice brought me out of my pity party, and I lifted my head from the floor. I could feel a layer of dirt along the side of my face, but I was too sore to brush it off.

With a slow exhale, I carefully sat up on an elbow. A hand gently touched my shoulder and I turned my head to see Teren's light eyes inspecting me. I'd never seen such a look of worry and fear on his face. It made worry and fear surge through me.

"Are you okay?" we both asked each other at the same time.

He cringed and nodded as a twinge of discomfort passed through him. I forcefully made myself only look at his upper half. Seeing as how we seemed to be alone in our dungeon now—Buffy must have retreated upstairs to sharpen his stakes—I was sure that one glance at Teren's injuries would have me curled into a weeping, blubbering ball of worthlessness. And I couldn't do that. I needed to be strong for him.

I nodded that I was fine as well, and then I scooted my body close to his, careful to only touch his torso. I slung my arm over his chest and laid my head on his shoulder. His shirt was lightly damp, like he'd run a marathon, and his face was still a horrid gray color. I hoped he wasn't bleeding too badly…

His hand came around my shoulder and he clutched me tight; his other hand gently held my head against him.

"Do you know what he gave you?" I quietly asked into the fabric of his shirt.

"No," he replied, having heard me just fine, even through his fog of pain. He let out a ragged sigh. "Of course, I thought we were the only ones like us." His voice was low. It broke a couple times as a tremor of anguish made his body stiffen beneath me. "I had no idea there were others…"

Lifting my head, I cupped his cheek with one hand and made him look at me. He searched my bruising face and I felt his jaw tighten beneath my fingertips. "Are you in a lot of pain, Teren?" I knew it was a stupid question. I could see quite clearly in his rigidness and in the way his eyes focused and unfocused, that he was in a horrendous amount of pain. But sometimes, in bad situations, the stupid questions are the only ones you're left with.

"It's not so bad…if I don't move," he said in a breaking, restrained voice that made my eyes water. I blinked back the tears.

"Will you really heal from this?" My hand indicated his legs but I couldn't look at them again.

He knew what I meant, and his eyes also avoided looking down at his bloody extremities. He nodded once. "Yes…I think so." His face took on a seriousness that only comes when someone is about to utter something that will change your life forever. My stomach clenched at the intenseness of his eyes, and I knew exactly what he was going to say before he even said it.

"You have to run, Emma. You have to try and escape before…" His voice lost all its intense power and he swallowed a couple times before trying again. "Promise me you won't try and save me. I need to know—"

My eyes watered beyond anything I could blink away and tears streamed down my face as I cut him off. "I can't promise that…you know I can't." My voice had an awful pleading quality to it and I desperately wanted to give him an empty lie again, desperately wanted to convince him that, of course, I would run and leave him, when I had no intention of doing such a thing. I couldn't though. I was too scared and overwhelmed to lie at the moment.

His hand cupped my cheek and, gritting his teeth, he shook

his head. "You have to, Emma. You have to find a way to get out of here, before I can hurt you." His eyes filled with tears as well. "I don't want to hurt you…please." The tears ran down his cheeks, taking all my hope of staying strong for him with them. "I can't live if I kill you." His voice broke in emotion instead of pain, and he laid his head on my shoulder. "I can't take it if I kill you. Please, run…from me…" He started to sob on my shoulder.

I clutched him tight. Hearing him doubt his ability to not kill me, something he usually unwaveringly assured me of, was scaring me worse than being locked in this dank room. I swallowed and forced myself to answer him. "Okay, Teren…I'll run. I won't let you hurt me, baby." I had no idea how I was getting out of an iron bar locked room that I was handcuffed to the wall in, but my vampire needed a lie, and I found some small well of resolve in my body to give him one. After that, I turned into that weeping, blubbering ball of worthlessness that I'd wanted to avoid becoming. Together, we set a new world record for the most amount of tears dropped, in the shortest amount of time.

Eventually we regained control of ourselves. Teren laid his head on my lap, and I ran my fingers back through his hair. He started shaking, and I huddled as much of my warmth over him as I could. He relaxed, just the tiniest amount, as my heat seeped into him.

"I'm so sorry, Emma," he muttered into my legs.

I stroked his back and repeatedly ran a hand through his hair, trying to calm him and myself. "What? Why?" I didn't see anything about this that was his fault.

He sighed and a heavy shudder passed through him. "I never should have stopped. We'd be at my parents' place right now…"

I squeezed him tight. "Don't…don't you dare do that." He shifted beneath me and I felt him squeeze my thigh. I wasn't sure if he did that out of reassurance…or pain. "Don't you apologize for being a decent human being."

He laughed once, a mirthless sound that hollowly echoed through his chest. "If I were human…we wouldn't be in this mess."

Sighing, I pressed my head against his back and listened to

the steady thump of his still-beating heart. "Sometimes, Teren...being human has nothing to do with genetics."

He turned his head and carefully shifted his body to look up at me. Reaching out, he stroked my cheek. "I love you, Emma."

I clenched my jaw. "Don't do that to me," I choked out. He blinked in momentary confusion. "Don't you say 'I love you', like you're saying goodbye." Renewed tears stung my eyes as I spoke. I was a little surprised my body was still capable of making them. "There are no goodbyes here...we're both getting out of this." My voice broke on the end and I had to repeat my seemingly improbable statement.

Teren nodded and I could plainly see that he didn't really believe my line either. He smiled a weak, fake smile and brought my lips down to his. I softly kissed him before pulling back and losing myself in his calming blue eyes. "It goes without saying, but...I love you too."

****

Fifty-seven...fifty-eight...fifty-nine...

I was counting to five hundred. I was counting slowly and silently, biding my time to come up with a genius plan of escape that would get both Teren and I safely away from this mess. When I reached five hundred, I was going to act on that plan and be the superhero of my own life.

Ninety...ninety-one...ninety-two...

Now, I just needed that plan...

I ran a hand gently through Teren's hair. He was still lying on my lap, his body angled out away from me, so I couldn't see his face. I wasn't sure if he was just being quiet or if he'd passed out again from the agony. He'd been in and out of consciousness for most of our time down here.

I wasn't sure how much time had passed. It must have only been a few hours, but neither Teren nor I had a watch and there were no windows down here to judge time by the sunlight; just one bare bulb that illuminated the center of each of the four walls. The center, but not the corners. And I knew that in those dark recesses, rodents and other unpleasant creatures that I didn't want to think about were scurrying around. And of course, I couldn't stop the thought that those creatures would probably take a nibble or two off of me, once Teren had sucked me dry...

No. That wasn't going to happen. I was going to get us out of here.

One hundred and twenty-one...one hundred and twenty-two...one hundred and twenty-three...

Somehow.

The room itself was lending me no bursts of inspiration. It was mostly empty. A few broken chairs, a few empty bottles and a couple bags of what looked like fertilizer. No helpful items, like a shovel, or a shotgun, or a key to these damn cuffs. My arm was numb from being attached to this stupid waist-high bar, suspended in the air, while I sat on the floor with Teren. I was beyond the tingly *It's fallen asleep* stage and was in the full-on *My appendage is gone* stage. I was actually grateful for it. Maybe I'd simply gnaw my arm off, and if said arm was completely numb...maybe I wouldn't feel it. My stomach churned at the thought though.

One hundred ninety...one hundred and ninety-one...one hundred and ninety-two...

Teren twitched beneath me. He'd been doing that periodically, once his body had stopped shaking. I had no idea if that was a good thing, or a bad thing. Sometimes the twitch would elicit a quiet groan, sometimes they were silent. With that last one, he clutched my thigh. I flinched and bit my lip. He'd squeezed really hard and I was bruised for sure. I could take it though. His pain was so much worse. I ran my hand down his back until his body relaxed. He twitched again and then released his death grip on my thigh.

I'd thought about offering him some blood, but I honestly didn't know if that would help him at this point or not. And a part of me was worried that he wouldn't be able to sense when to stop, what with his brain on sensory overload. Plus, I needed all of my strength for when my brilliant escape plan went into effect.

Two hundred thirty...Two hundred and thirty-one...Two hundred and thirty-two...

Still blank. Apparently, I hadn't watched enough horror movies. I had no idea what to do about this little situation, and I was sure there had to be a movie out there somewhere with an ending similar to the predicament I was in now. Of course, the woman in that film probably had a bobby pin tucked up in her hair and would know how to use one to unclasp her cuffs. I neither had one, nor knew how to use one like that.

I exhaled in irritation and watched the barred door at the top of the wooden steps. The man hadn't come back. I supposed he wouldn't until Teren changed over. No point in watching it, really. We were securely locked in here. I was handcuffed to a wall for God's sake. Once Teren changed, and my demise was guaranteed, he'd drive a stake through Teren's beautiful, silent heart, before my blood had a chance to partially revive him. Then we'd both be dead and gone. Well, at least Teren didn't have to worry about a lifetime without me…just a few minutes really.

No…no more Negative Nancy. I was getting us out of here.

Three hundred and twenty-one…Three hundred and twenty-two…Three hundred and twenty-three…

Teren gasped as a large jolt through his body stirred him. He made a strangled cry and I soothed his back again. Once the wave of pain ebbed, he twisted his head to look at me. His eyes had a dreamy faraway look.

"Hi," he quietly said.

I smiled down at him on my lap. "Hey, baby. Close your eyes…rest."

He half-smiled in that crooked, charming way of his. "Since you gave up all your coffee for my shirt…maybe I could buy you another?"

I bit my lip and forced back the tears. He was slipping. The pain was making his mind look for ways around it, and he'd found a pleasant memory to linger in. Well, I'd play along. Delusion was better than screaming.

"I'd love that."

He gave me a wide smile, but then sudden panic filled his

eyes. For a moment, I thought his illusion had slipped and he was cognizant again, but when he spoke, he was still in the past. "Please don't leave if you find out what I am. Please don't hate me. Please don't run, like the others. Please don't think I'm a monster..."

A not-stoppable tear rolled down my cheek. I sniffled as I ran a hand down his face. "I won't leave, baby." I shook my head. "You're not a monster, Teren...you never were." My eyes flashed back to the door. There was only one monster in this house and he was upstairs. And he would pay...somehow.

Teren's eyes fluttered closed with a content sigh. I rubbed his cheek while his face relaxed beneath my touch.

Somehow.

Four hundred...Four hundred and one...Four hundred and two...

Teren jerked on my legs and his eyes flew open. He clenched his jaw and looked around the room, like he didn't know where he was.

"Baby...it's okay," I said in a soothing voice.

His eyes found mine and he exhaled a choppy breath. "Where are..." His thought fell off his tongue as his eyes closed in remembrance. When he reopened them, he met mine again. "We're still here?"

I weakly nodded and rubbed his cheek again. He clasped his hand over mine.

I wondered how long we had. I wondered if it was close to dark. The man said Teren would die by nightfall. Either way, our lives were completely different than they had been this morning. I flicked a glance at Teren's legs, and hoped he was right about them. I hoped he healed. They looked such a bloody, un-repairable mess; broken at the least, shattered at the most. I still wasn't about to take a glance under his jeans to find out. That sight would surely unhinge me, and I needed to stay somewhat focused on getting us out of here. I was pretty certain that if he hadn't been about to change, and I did get him safely away somehow, that his legs would probably have to be removed for him to remain alive. They looked *that* bad. I'd take him that way too, of course. I'd take Teren Adams any way I could get him.

Teren noticed me glancing at his legs. "It's not so bad anymore. It's almost like they're gone. I can barely feel them." He smiled when he said that, like it was a good thing.

I feebly smiled back, then a thought struck me as I remembered nightfall. "Will your family look for us?"

He was shaking his head as soon as the words left me. "No, I don't think so. Not tonight, anyway." He stroked my fingers with his thumb. "They'll only know we turned away from the ranch...they won't know why." He sighed a little as he stated, "We can't sense intentions." He shrugged as he searched my eyes. "Not even when we want to."

My head dropped as I considered that. I wasn't sure if I wanted his family anywhere near this madman, but it would dramatically improve our odds if they *were* here. Teren finished his thought in a soft voice, momentarily free from pain, "They won't worry until tomorrow, when they can't reach me on my cell. Then they'll probably wait until dark, so Great-Gran can go with them— she's the strongest of us. By the time they track me here..."

"We'll be dead," I quietly finished.

With a warm, peaceful smile on his face, he shook his head and looked at the wall over my shoulder, like he could see right through it to the outside world. "No...I'll be dead. You'll be free." His eyes seemed to glow with the hope of my freedom. I was positive that the only thing keeping him going right now was the thought of me escaping.

"Teren..."

His happy eyes shifted to take me in. "You'll be free," he repeated. "You'll run...you promised."

While technically I didn't *promise* that I'd run, now wasn't really the time to argue semantics...or the fact that I was still handcuffed to a wall. "Right, baby...I'll be free," I whispered instead. His grin widened, and his eyes fluttered closed again as he slung an arm around my waist.

I commanded myself not to cry.

Four hundred and ninety-seven…four hundred and ninety-eight…four hundred and ninety-nine…

Teren jerked below me and his eyes flew open again, but this time, it was different. Confused, I watched his face contort in pain and wondered if I'd somehow jarred his legs. I was being exceedingly careful to not move him. His mouth fell open in a silent gasp and I could see fresh pain cloud his pale eyes—a lot of fresh pain. He jerked on my legs a couple of times, like he was struggling against some unseen force.

I tried to still his body, so he wouldn't cause himself extra pain by banging his legs against the ground. "Teren…what is it?"

He couldn't answer me. He could only open and close his mouth and make horrid gasping noises, like he was struggling for air. Then his hand went to his chest. Then I understood.

Time was up…my vampire was dying. And this time he absolutely wasn't joking.

"No…stop it," I croaked out unintentionally. I knew it wasn't possible to stop this, but I wasn't ready. Aside from the not having a plan part yet, and the fact that within an hour I was about to be a snack, I just wasn't ready to say goodbye to Teren's humanity. It was such a selfish thought to have at the moment that I hated myself a little for it. But the fact was, I would miss that side of him that was like me: his fierce thumping heart, his warm probing hands, our long leisurely dinners on his patio with a glass of wine…

But that reality had ended the moment that bar had struck his shins. This would actually help him now. He'd heal and he'd be strong enough to get away from the lunatic upstairs…once he ate me, of course.

I pushed aside my selfish thoughts and focused on the dying, terrified man before me. He clutched my free hand and, still gasping in pain, sought my eyes.

I stared into his pale orbs, willing him strength. The whites of his eyes had been faintly glowing in the pale light of the bulb. They seemed to intensify as his body struggled to remain alive. I imagined that I heard his irregular, wet, thumping heart, pulsing unsteadily and uncertainly. Fighting for every last beat, before the weakness of its humanity claimed it, and the tired organ completely surrendered to the foreignness of his vampire blood.

"I'm here, Teren...I'm here. You're not alone." Not ever having comforted a dying person before, I had no other words.

While his body jerked in painful spasms, his eyes stayed locked onto mine, refusing to leave them. I knew he was soaking me in, trying to force himself to remember what I meant to him...to outsmart the thirst. I was pretty sure that was a losing battle.

A second later, he seemed to realize that too. His face hardened into stone concentration. He forcibly ripped his eyes from mine and lifted himself off my lap. With one hand still clutching at his chest, like its very presence was keeping that organ beating, he reached out with his other hand, took a deep breath, and letting out a scream of pain and frustration, ripped the iron bar that was anchoring me to the wall off its heavy support brackets. It clanked onto the floor a few feet away from us; my arm burned with fire as the blood suddenly rushed back into it.

Teren, his strength gone, collapsed back to my lap. I clutched him with both arms now, the empty manacle uselessly dangling from my wrist.

"Baby...?"

His hand reached up to stroke my face and a calm peace swept over him. Terror filled me as that peace spread from his face to his body. His shaking stopped. His gasping stopped. Looking up to my eyes with an expression so full of love, I thought my heart would burst, he whispered, "Ya tebya lyublyu."

I waited for the reciprocating inhale after the air from saying those words passed his lips. It didn't come. His hand dropped from my cheek to land by his side with a non-resistant thud.

My vision obscured and I blinked the tears down my cheeks, so I could watch his eyes, still locked onto mine, slowly lose their focus. The glow that painted the whites of his eyes vanished and his head drifted down, finally breaking our eye contact.

"Teren...?"

I shook his shoulder in a hopeless attempt to revive him. It was a joke...all of this was some elaborate practical joke, and any minute he'd jerk awake and say "got-ya" and I'd smack the shit out of him for scaring me. But he wasn't moving and he wasn't breathing. I shook him again, in the near maniacal way of someone trying to force a reality they wanted into existence. It still wasn't working, he still wasn't moving.

"No...please, no..."

I gave up trying to force my will into being. I gave up trying to pretend that the man I loved was only joking. I gave up trying to hold back the racking wails of sobs that my body demanded. I closed his eyes, so I wouldn't have to endure the lifeless stare any longer, then I hunched over his limp body and completely gave myself over into grief.

Teren Adams was dead.

****

I don't know how much time I spent huddled over Teren's lifeless body. I knew it was pointless. I knew I couldn't bring him back, and I knew that he would come back to me shortly, but it's not every day that you watch the light of consciousness fade from someone you immensely love. It affected me. I'd darn near say it wrecked me.

I even tried CPR. How ridiculous is that? I knew it was hopeless the moment I started the compressions on his chest. This was no sixty-year-old man with coronary failure. This was a vampire whose human heart could no longer handle the strain of his mixed blood. There was no artificial stimulation that could be done on his organ that would overcome that fact. It was simply...done. I still tried though. For a longer time than I cared to admit, I tried.

When that failed, or more appropriately, when my arms couldn't handle another forceful push, I slumped across his silent chest and cried some more of those useless tears. I knew he wanted me to run far away from him before he woke up, and I knew I was running out of time...but Teren had only freed me from the wall. I was still padlocked down here behind an iron barred door.

All I could do was wait for Teren to wake up and eat me. Then the man would hear my death and open the damn door. I sat bolt upright as my mouth dropped open. Oh crap. Did I just finally have an idea on how to get out of this hellhole? My mind tumbled over the details and I had to stop thinking for a second. I slowly exhaled for ten long counts before I tried again to think in a more organized way.

The man was waiting for Teren to kill me. After that happened, he'd have a very short window of opportunity, before Teren became too strong for him to easily stake. So he'd be listening closely after nightfall. Since Teren was lying dead before me, I was going to assume it was.

So the man was listening right now. In fact, he'd probably heard my heart wrenching sobs, I hadn't exactly been quiet. He was probably on the other side of that door, perched on a dirty little chair with his sharpened stake in his hand, waiting for a bloodcurdling scream. Once he heard that scream, he'd open the door and...

That was it.

Nervous butterflies swarmed my stomach by the hundreds as I considered everything I was going to have to do for this to work. I didn't know if I had the skill or strength to pull this off, but I knew it was my only chance. Once Teren woke up...well, I really didn't want to be anywhere near him when that happened. My only chance at freedom resided in that fanatic lunatic on the other side of the door.

Great. When did my life take such a drastic turn? Just months ago, I was plugging along at my tedious job, wishing something would come along to break up the monotony of endless days of copying and faxing, and endless nights of watching eighties sitcom reruns on the television. In truth, I'd been hoping for Clarice to retire, so I could have her more appealing job. And then maybe one of the firm's more prestigious clients would have taken an interest in me, and swept me off in his private jet to Paris, for an authentic French dinner and a romantic stroll down the Seine.

But instead, I'd crashed into a vampire.

I smiled, and my nerves settled somewhat as I thought over that day. The look of surprise and pain on his face as my drink had spilled down the front of him. His hands brushing mine as he'd taken my card and shoved it in his pocket. And now that terror was clearing my brain cells, I could clearly recall the crooked grin he'd given me, as I'd hurried away from him in embarrassment. I'd been awaiting an irate phone call that day, but he'd never been angry at me. Even back then, he'd been more amused by me than anything else.

I smiled wider as I looked back down at Teren's still body and stroked his hair. No, no bigwig sweeping me off to a foreign country could have measured up to the man that fate had forcibly led me to. My life with Teren was exactly what I wanted it to be, what I always hoped it would be...once we got past this little speed bump, of course.

I kissed Teren's forehead and scooted around his broken body as I stood up. I left him slightly turned toward the wall and facing away from me; he almost looked like he was sleeping that way. Silently, I grabbed the iron rod that Teren had pulled from the wall. It was contorted on one end, where the metal had twisted from the strain of wanting to stay attached to the stone wall. Teren's pure vampiric strength had disagreed, and brutally ripped it from its home. Luckily, the squeal of its removal hadn't attracted the vampire hunter upstairs; he'd either discounted it or Teren's loud yell had masked it. Either way, now I was free and now I had a weapon.

My nerves came back, and I inhaled and exhaled as slowly and smoothly as I could. One shot...no chance at a redo. Either the man or Teren would kill me if this didn't work. Nope, no pressure at all. Silencing the fear and doubt in my mind, I focused instead on the tiny things that I could control—my grip on the twisted end of the rod, my feet soundlessly crossing the dirt floor, retreating into the shadows under the stairs, and lastly...screaming.

"No, Teren...please...don't...please...no..."

Then I let loose all the terror and fear I'd been struggling to rein in for the last several hours, and I let out the loudest scream my body was capable of making. I was sure I was making every horror movie vixen very proud, as the scream rang throughout even my own ears. At the very highest point, I clamped a hand over my own mouth and shut off my vocals.

I was no actress, but I was appropriately terrified, and letting out that scream had been astonishingly easy and a little cathartic. Glancing at Teren's form, bathed in the soft light from the bulb, I took in his stillness as I stared at his back. He hadn't moved, hadn't reacted to my voice. Loud sounds didn't bother the dead. I tried to not reflect on how his skin had looked paler, sallower, and when I'd kissed his forehead, he'd felt cooler than usual. Now was not the time.

I firmly grasped my iron rod in both hands while I waited for sounds of movement upstairs. There was no way the man hadn't heard that. He would give Teren a few moments to finish his meal, and then he'd saunter down to stake my honey.

I went over everything Lita and Hot Ben had ever taught me in kickboxing class. True, it wasn't exactly the same as what I was about to do, but similar logic could be applied. Power comes from the hips—twist them, use the strength of your lower body. Aim for the soft spot of the temple. Commit to the hit and follow through. Abandon all fear. Breathe…

I heard the sound of metal scraping against wood and I knew the man was lifting the bar away from the door. Moments later, I heard the pop of the door unlocking. I closed my eyes and forced peace into my body. Ignoring my childhood fear of what monsters typically lurked there, I stepped further back into the shadows under the stairs. This time, the monster was walking *down* the stairs instead of lurking under them, and this was one monster I was going to deal with head on.

Heavy boots clomped down the long steps. I briefly considered just tripping him down the stairs, but I discounted it. That might only mildly hurt him, and I needed to *massively* hurt him. I only had one shot at this, and surprise was on my side, since he assumed I was hanging against a wall, dead.

His hoarse voice broke the stillness, "So, you finished her off, huh? Knew you would…they all do. Are you crying? Sometimes the bloodsuckers actually cry afterwards." His boot stepped off the last stair and he turned towards Teren's curled form on the floor. "Sometimes they even beg me to stake them. Don't worry…you won't cry long."

The man was too intently focused on the supposed threat of

the hungry vampire lying on the ground. He hadn't noticed that my body was nowhere to be seen. Well, he was about to see me. With the stealth of a stalking predator, I stepped away from the staircase and close to his side.

"Neither will you," I hissed.

The man startled and twisted to look at me. His eyes widened in shock at seeing me alive, and right next to him. He never even had time to realize I was armed. As soon as his head was facing me, giving me an ideal target, I focused all my pain, fear and rage at the maniac. I brought my arms around, twisting my hips and reinforcing the strike. Surprise and adrenaline gave me speed, and he never even moved to defend himself. He didn't have time. My hit was true, and the rod connected to his temple with a sickening thud that reverberated all the way up my arms.

The man's head snapped to the side. Just as I feared that I didn't have the strength to knock him out, his knees buckled and he dropped like a ton of bricks. The wooden stake fell away from his relaxed fingers and rolled onto the dirt beside him. I kicked the vile, symbolic thing under the stairs. The iron rod felt red-hot in my hand. Not wanting the metal touching my skin any longer, I dropped it to my side. It thudded to the ground and rested near my feet.

My vision swam as the adrenaline rushed out of my body and the realization of what I'd done, swept in. The man was very still and I really didn't know if he was alive or not. My stomach rose into my throat and I pressed on it to make it stop. Now wasn't the time to lose my last meal or stare at the downed man like an idiot. Now was the time to do what I'd told Teren I'd do...now was the time to run.

Just as I was mentally preparing myself for the flight away from this rickety farmhouse, and wondering how I'd get a hold of Teren's family in time so they could come help him, I heard it. A low growl was coming from one side of the room; an impossibly deep growl that sent shivers up my spine and dotted my skin with goose bumps. A growl that I'd heard a few times before, but never once directed towards me. An inhuman growl that made me afraid I'd lose control of my bladder.

Tracking the sound, I turned to stare over at the piece of ground where I'd left Teren's broken body. Only, he was no longer where I'd left him; only our ripped apart belts were lying on the ground. He was standing in a low crouch, his body lightly shaking as he wobbled on his feet. That wasn't what sent ice cold fear throughout my veins though. It was his face.

His skin was still ashen, and he had the sunken look of someone very ill. The whites of his eyes faintly glowed in the dim light, and his pale, light blue irises were locked onto me. They danced with a near frenzied excitement. His mouth was open in a vicious looking snarl and his teeth were extended to sharp points; his fangs were longer than I'd ever seen them.

He looked like a pure animal, nothing left of my Teren at all. And for a split-second sadness swept through me at the thought that maybe he *wasn't* my Teren anymore. Maybe that man really had died today. My sadness shifted right back to fear when the starving creature before me let out another deep, menacing growl, and took a step forward.

Chapter 18 – Shades of Gray

Now, here is the point where I clearly became a touch insane. A bubble of happiness ripped right through my core. Happiness you say? Wasn't I about to be Teren chow? Yes, I was, but the surge of joy I felt was from the fact that my honey had just walked—a clumsy I'm-going-to-topple-over-at-any-second walk, but a walk nonetheless. I was momentarily overjoyed that his shattered legs had indeed completely healed and he really would be fine. Not to mention the fact that he was clearly a reanimated being and I hadn't lost him to the other side. I was over the moon that he was sentient, if not alive.

My happiness instantly evaporated when he took his second step.

Pure prey-filled panic swept through me and I had the overwhelming desire to run. Every fundamental cell in my body was screaming at me to bolt for the stairs, screeching bloody murder the entire way, and plunge myself into the dark, barren landscape where our captor had taken us. I wasn't entirely an idiot though.

The part of my brain that, luckily, had firm control over my motor functions, knew that the surest way to get myself killed would be to act like the quarry I indeed was. Nothing would kick Teren's predatory nature into overdrive quite like me acting like a fleeing dinner. I instantly remembered Halina remarking how much she loved the hunt, and I knew that I couldn't do anything that a typical human would do in this situation. I couldn't run. I had to stand perfectly still and let him approach me. And let me tell you, fighting eons of pure instinct is difficult.

Teren straightened as he stiffly walked towards me; his blood-soaked jeans only emphasized the oddness of watching him walk in my direction. A small smile played at the corners of his wide open mouth and his extended fangs were so long they brushed against his lower lip. I imagined those teeth plunging into my neck. In my fear, I pictured them coming right out the other side.

A shudder passed through me and he paused, notating the movement with clear interest in his pale eyes. A stranger's eyes…not my Teren's. This was a creature of the night. This was hunger incarnate. This was a near-death, thirsty vampire and for the first time ever—I was terrified of him.

He resumed his stiff walk and when he had halved the distance between us, I knew I had to try to appeal to whatever human side was still in him right now, or else he'd kill me for sure.

"Teren…baby. It's me…Emma."

He cocked his head to the side and his brows scrunched, like he was hearing a language he ought to know but didn't currently understand. His shaky steps continued until he came to the unconscious man in front of me. Ignoring our captor lying on the ground, he walked around the still body, to come up to my shaking one.

Thinking my shivers were drawing him straight to me, I tried to control the tremors. But I couldn't control them anymore than I could stop my juicily pulsating heart from racing. I knew he would be able to hear my slushy, elevated beats. He could probably even sense the blood rushing throughout my veins in overdrive. Right now, I was irresistible to him and I couldn't do anything about it.

"Baby…please…it's me. You love me…remember?"

He stepped right beside me, his chest pressing against my arm. A low growl vibrated his ribcage and I felt it all the way up my body. I gritted my teeth to not move, to not scream. A tear rolled down my cheek, as the level of fear and concentration coursing through my body showed itself physically.

"Baby…you love me. Remember, Teren. Please remember."

He pressed harder into my side and a soft sob escaped me. Teren bent down and softly hissed in my ear. A huge shudder, which had nothing to do with how his body felt noticeably cooler, passed through my frame, and a pleased noise rumbled in his chest.

"Oh God, Teren…please. Baby, you promised…you promised. Please…please remember…you love me."

He ran his nose up my throat, inhaling the whole while. I bit my lip and mostly held back the scream. I couldn't stop how heavily I was breathing, though. I couldn't calm my heart. I couldn't ebb the terror in my veins. Teren shivered at my reaction and exhaled a cool breath across my skin. He lowered his head to the crook of my neck and I felt the brush of his rough stubble against my shoulder as he angled himself into position—for the last bite he would ever take from me. His cool lips caressed my skin as he pressed them against me. For a split second, my fear-soaked brain desperately wanted to believe that he was playing with me, teasing me, but I fully understood the situation, and I knew that nothing about this was a joke or an intimacy. He was going to kill me, because he couldn't help it, because the hunger was too strong.

I felt his mouth opening wider, taking my flesh inside. I felt his teeth grazing my skin. "Teren, please. I love you...I love you so much. Please don't do this. Please fight it...please. Ya tebya lyublyu."

I started repeating the Russian phrase over and over, like it was a lifeline and I was drowning. Teren hadn't clamped down on my skin, but his teeth were prickling my flesh like nails, waiting to be driven deep. Tears freely coursed down my cheeks as I mindlessly repeated the phrase. My body couldn't keep up this charade of pretending to not be food. I was losing the battle. I was losing my grip on my sanity. I was about to run. Even still, I knew the minute I moved, it would be my last.

That was when his black hair unexpectedly dropped from the edge of my vision. Confused, I took a stuttered breath and looked down. He was lying in a fetal position at my feet, clutching his stomach like it was an open wound and he needed to hold in his intestines to keep them from spilling out over the ground. He groaned and shifted to look up at me. My breath caught at the look in his pale eyes. I knew that look. That was *my* Teren returning my gaze.

"Emma..." The ache in his voice ripped me open...he was so hungry.

His eyes blazed with pain, a different kind of pain than before he'd died. His face was still a pale, sunken, unhealthy color and his fangs were still elongated. He closed his eyes and groaned again and I ignored every urge to kneel and comfort him. He'd resisted me once, twice was pretty much asking for it.

Suddenly, our captor moaned and moved. My terror-filled mind suddenly remembered that I wasn't the only meal bag in this room. Sickened by my idea, I whispered, "Teren, drain him." My tone was firm, sure, and showed none of the inner turmoil I felt over what I was asking my sweetheart to do.

Teren's eyes opened and flicked over to the man, who was now starting to rock his head slowly from side to side. Teren's hazy eyes returned to mine and he swallowed with great difficulty, like his throat was so dry he barely could.

"No." He croaked out, sounding like a man who'd been trudging through the desert for days with no water and could hardly still make speech.

I nudged the man's shoulder with my shoe; he groaned in response. "You will die unless you drink...so do it!" Heat entered my tone, as I began to realize that Teren might refuse *all* blood available to him.

His eyes steadily held mine. "No," he coarsely whispered.

Now I kicked the man, making him start to stir towards consciousness. "Drink, damn you! Don't you give up on me!" A different kind of panic seeped into my voice, giving it strength and volume.

With a resolved look in his pained eyes, Teren lightly shook his head. "No, Emma. I told you I'd never take a life. Not even his..." His eyes drifted back to the man, before returning to mine.

"Not even for me!" I yelled, nearly wanting to kick Teren now.

He gave me a soft, pained smile, and I instantly remembered that we'd had this conversation once before, back when we'd argued about him changing my sister. I knew exactly what his answer would be...what it had always been. "Not even for me, Emma," he whispered.

I shook my head in disbelief, when I realized what he was saying. "Please...I can't lose you."

He closed his eyes and slowly exhaled. A twinge of discomfort passed through his features, and I knew he was hiding how much he was really hurting from me, both emotionally and physically. When he reopened his eyes, it was with a visible effort, like they suddenly weighed a ton each. "I'm sorry, Emma...but no, I won't do it."

His hands loosened their death grip on his stomach, his face relaxed, then his eyes unfocused. They fluttered shut and with a long, shaky breath, his head dropped. Ignoring the maniac starting to revive next to us, and ignoring the instinct to stay away from Teren, I dropped to my knees at his side. He was dying…again, only this time he wouldn't wake back up.

"No! Please, Teren…please."

I shook his shoulders and he groaned. With a struggle, he reopened his eyes. His face was wan and anemic looking, and he couldn't entirely focus on me. The contrast was so different from the ferocious killer that had stalked me only moments before that it made it all the more terrifying. He was slipping so fast…

Smiling around his fangs, Teren repeated the Russian phrase that he'd said the first time he'd died, the phrase I'd used to eventually snap him out of his hunger-induced stupor. The way he said it this time, well, every syllable of it had the finality of goodbye.

I shook his shoulders even harder when his eyes started fluttering closed again. "No! You stupid, stubborn son of a bitch! No!" I started smacking his shoulders into the ground, but his eyes had successfully closed and he was no longer responding to me. "No…vampiric asshole! Don't give up on me now! NO!"

He was silent. He was still. I was more scared than when he'd inhaled me.

Another moan on the other side of me reminded me, yet again, that I wasn't the only human down here. Once the man recovered from my attack, he was going to be pretty pissed. He might not relish killing humans, but I was pretty sure he'd do it anyway, especially with the headache I'd surely given him.

I dropped Teren's shoulders and noted his still, gaunt face. I had no idea if he was dead-dead or just at a point where he could no longer move. I didn't exactly have the typical vital signs to check. Was he breathing…no. Did he have a heartbeat…no. He could be sleeping for all I knew. But he wasn't, he was dying, if not already dead.

Anger shot through me. No…this was *not* how my fairytale was ending. The Prince did not die and leave the Princess alone to get beaten to death by the villain. Every thought I'd ever had about myself shifted. Every line I thought I'd never cross blurred. What would I do to save someone I loved? Reality started dulling from the crystal-clear black and white world I'd previously known, to the hazy realm of varying shades of gray. What *wouldn't* I do to save someone I loved?

Nothing. There was nothing I wouldn't do to save him, and I suddenly knew exactly what I had to do.

Standing, I grabbed the iron bar still resting by my feet. I calmly walked over to our kidnapper, the fanatic who'd put us in this horrid mess. He'd regained consciousness enough to open his eyes and he looked up at me with a hazy, unfocused gaze. I could see his mind trying to fill in the gaps of the last few moments of his life. I didn't give him much longer to worry about it.

"You were wrong. I told you he wouldn't kill me." I flicked a glance down his dirty body. "He won't even kill you." My eyes found his again; his seemed more alert and I knew I only had seconds left before he could fight me off. I leaned forward over his body. "He's too good a man to kill you."

I raised the bar, and with one hard push, I shoved it into the soft spot at the hollow of his throat. The man jerked in surprise as the iron ripped through his flesh and hit his spine.

"I'm not so good," I growled.

I pulled the rod out and a fountain of blood followed it. The man sputtered and choked on the hot fluid. I took a step back and tossed the bar down again. The man's frantic eyes found mine as he tried to cover the wound with his hands. "He's better than us both," I whispered to him.

The man's eyes widened as he struggled to breathe, his hands clasped at his throat, but the move was ineffectual; dark, deep-red blood oozed between his fingers. Suddenly, a strong set of hands ripped the man's fingers from his neck and held them at his sides. A dark-haired head attached itself to his throat, and the man dropped his mouth open in what I imagined was a silent scream. I forced myself to watch the terror flash through the man's eyes as Teren stole his life-force from him. I had done this. I wouldn't avert my eyes from my actions. I would watch…and remember.

As I'd hoped, fresh, pooling blood had been too much for Teren's starved body to ignore and he'd instinctually leapt at the chance I'd offered him. I wondered if Teren was even aware of what he was doing right now. A part of me hoped he wasn't. He would eternally hate himself for this if he was making a conscious choice to kill.

I watched the man's face as he relaxed and stopped his futile struggling. His complexion started to pale from the pink, flush look of life, to a faded, dull gray color, as Teren adjusted himself on his throat and made a deeper wound with those sharp teeth of his. I forcefully ignored the happy noises Teren was making deep in his chest, and the audible swallows as he took in liter after liter of the man's blood. I focused instead on the man's eyes, hoping that the life soon faded from them. Even though he'd been actively planning our deaths, I had no desire for the man to suffer. I wasn't cruel, either. Instantly, I was glad we'd never discovered our captor's name. This memory would be bad enough. No need to personalize it even more.

Eventually, and in reality it had been thirty seconds at the most, the man's eyes lost focus and faded into the blank stare of nothingness that Teren had given me not all that long ago. Tears stung my eyes but I immediately forced them back. This man was going to kill me. This man had tortured and injected Teren with something that *had* killed him. This man had destroyed any hope I had of carrying Teren's child. I refused to feel anymore pity for this man.

A few moments later, Teren sat back on his heels and wiped his mouth off on his shirt. He looked at his fingers, slightly red from the man's bloody hands, and then wiped them on his jeans repeatedly. He seemed steadier, but he still had a sunken, unhealthy look about him. He was still hungry. He sat there with his head down for a long time as he took in the dead man before him. If he hadn't been aware of his actions before, he was now. I knew him well enough to know that he was beating himself up about draining this man…something he'd promised himself he'd never do.

Cautiously, I dropped to his side and put a hand on his arm. He turned to me and I clearly saw the turmoil in his eyes. I inhaled a deep breath and prepared myself to lie…for him. "I did this, Teren. Not you." I gave him a warm smile while he frowned. "You were strong enough. You turned away from me. You turned away from him." I cupped his cheeks, as tears spilled down mine. "You were so strong…you didn't falter." His eyes flicked to the corpse and he tried to turn his head back to the man. I kept his face firmly pointing towards me. Dropping my voice, I repeated, "I did this. He attacked me and I defended myself. I had no choice but to kill him and you had no choice but to survive." I searched his eyes. "Understand?"

He silently regarded me for a few moments while my lie sunk in. So, maybe it wasn't a full-on lie. Surely if I'd given the man enough time, he would have attacked me, and I would have had to defend myself. That wasn't what happened though. He'd still been frozen in confusion when I'd struck. But I knew that if I ever told Teren that, he would blame himself for not killing the man first. In his eyes, he would always think that he'd forced me into killing for him. He hadn't. Teren had made his choice to stay pure. I had made my choice…to save him. I didn't feel like either of us deserved condemnation.

He nodded as he accepted my version of events. I didn't know if he believed me or not, but he was going to let himself accept my scenario and that was almost more important than what he actually believed. He opened his mouth, his fangs tucked safely away, and spoke in a quiet voice that ached with residual pain, "I'm still hungry."

I put my hand on his cool shoulder. "Then let's get you more to eat. I'll take you to the ranch now. I'll take you to your family."

He inclined his head in a brief nod, and with my help, stood. He wobbled a little, and I put a hand on his chest to steady him. We both paused and stared at my hand. I flattened my palm and pressed it harder against his body. Nothing. No faint pulse, no slight thumping rhythm, just…silence.

"I'm sorry, honey…" I looked back up to his light eyes, "but I think you're dead."

I gave him a crooked grin and he finally truly smiled. He

laughed as he slung a weak arm around my waist and kissed my head. "Thanks to you, I'll be able to live my death without regret," he murmured. He looked back to the man's dry body and I knew he was adding in his head, *too much.*

His gaze returned to mine and his hand reached up to stroke my cheek. "I can't believe I almost attacked you." His voice was strained with exhaustion when he spoke again. "I can't believe I almost did it. I wanted to, so much." He looked down at the ground, avoiding any eye contact with me. "I've never wanted anything more…and…and I almost couldn't control it. I think for a moment, I stopped caring about everything…everything but quenching the thirst." He swallowed hard, and I could clearly see that the thirst was still with him.

I placed my hand over his on my cheek and he returned his eyes to me. "But you didn't attack me. You barely even touched me. Don't beat yourself up over things you didn't do." My tone implied that I wasn't just talking about him almost biting me. He seemed to understand that, as he nodded. His face was drawn and tired from his conversion, and I knew he hadn't had nearly enough blood for a full recovery. "Come on…let's go take care of you."

Supporting his weight under my shoulder, I somehow managed to get his shaking body up the stairs, out the damaged front door, and around the missing floorboards of the porch. Once we were outside on the soft dirt near where the man's rustic camper was parked, we both paused and took a deep breath, enjoying our freedom.

Then a tremor ran through Teren's body, so I started moving us forward again. I wasn't sure how far away the ranch was, but I was pretty sure we'd never make it walking. We shuffled up to the camper, the glow from Teren's eyes on this moonless, cloudless starry night leading the way. I helped Teren sit on the ground by one of the tires, and he looked up at me, confused. "I need to get the keys," I explained. He nodded, laid his head back on the vehicle, and shut his eyes, resting. I leaned over and kissed his cool forehead, making him smile. "I'll be right back," I said.

I carefully walked back into the shamble of a home, wondering where a madman might have thrown his car keys.

Realizing that the man wouldn't have just casually dropped them somewhere while he had victims tied up below, I made my way back down the wooden steps to reenter the cell that had changed Teren's life. And my own, I suppose.

I cautiously stepped up to the man. As I expected, he was still lying where we'd left him. My stomach lurched at the sight of his pale body, and I swallowed to keep back the bile. His throat was clearly torn open. It kind of looked like an animal attack. And even though I knew he didn't have an ounce of blood left in him, it didn't stop me from thinking that the man was going to spring to life at any moment and finish what he'd started.

Rolling my eyes, I pushed that fear aside, dropped down to a knee, and began rummaging through his pockets. Honestly, I had nothing to worry about. This man was very dead, and that fact wasn't changing. Apparently I *had* seen too many horror movies. I was switching to romantic comedies from now on.

I found the keys almost instantly. As I sat up, I noticed the bloody bar on the ground. I also watched a lot of cop shows with my sister—she was obsessed—and while his throat might look like an animal attack, the blood on the bar was a dead giveaway. I grabbed it and wiped away any fingerprints with my shirt. Some horrible fate had befallen this man, and even though we'd only defended ourselves, I didn't need Teren examined too closely by a group of curious policemen.

I looked around for anything else Teren and I might have touched, but besides our belts, which I picked up and looped around my hand, there really wasn't anything. I kicked at Teren's blood in the dirt, hoping to mask it, but not sure if I was doing a good job or not. I regarded the blood on the man's jacket, but didn't think I could remove the coat from the large man by myself, and Teren was still too weak to come back down here and help me. There was a lot of the man's own blood on it as well so I hoped it covered Teren's. Disheartened that I couldn't do more, I wiped off every door knob on the way out of the house, and then I turned my back on it and the horrid memories inside of it.

Teren's glow indicated where he was still waiting for me. Letting go of the residual fear of that house and everything that had happened there, I sprinted back to him. He was already looking my way and the glow of his eyes enveloped me. I relaxed into that tranquil gaze, then noticed that he was wiping his mouth on his shirt again. Curious, I glanced at the ground beside him and saw a couple of dead animals, including one that sort of looked like a rabbit.

My lips twitched into a smile as I pointed at them. "Did that help?"

He smiled briefly and then frowned. "No, not really. I feel like I'm being eaten from the inside out."

Now I frowned. I offered him my hand and he let me help him stand. Leaning back on the camper, he took a deep, steadying breath. His eyes closed, plunging us both into darkness. "Emma...you need to put me in the back." He said it so softly, I almost didn't hear him.

"What? No, I want to watch over you..."

His eyes reopened and the predatory look was back...along with his fangs. "I can't be in a small space with you right now." His eyes fluttered and the light shifted in and out. A low growl escaped his throat. "You smell too good. Don't tempt me, please..."

I swallowed and stopped my body from shaking again. "Okay...okay, Teren."

I left him against the side of the camper while I went around to the back. It was unlocked and opened easily. I turned around to go get him but he was right there behind me. I hadn't even heard him approach. He eyed me up and down, his fangs still fully extended, and then he slowly bent forward.

His breath increased as he came closer and I found mine increasing as well. He paused when he was almost within striking distance and with clear strain on his face, he retracted his fangs. Once normal, he finished his descent, moving to my lips instead of my jugular. I gave him a tender kiss while I marveled that we'd made it this far together, marveled that his cool breath and lips seemed to make mine even hotter...

A low growl escaped his lips and he yanked himself away from me. He stopped the noise and, lightly chuckling, said, "You really need to get away from me, Emma." I could see him raise an eyebrow as he studied me. "I'll have you in more ways than one if you stick around."

I flushed and he watched the color fill my skin with a small sigh of longing. Shaking his head, he forced himself to enter the camper. When he was at the top and about to shut the door behind him, I stopped him. "Teren, wait." He paused in shutting the door and his glowing eyes looked down at me with curiosity. I shrugged. "I don't know where I am." Sighing as I admitted that I was clueless, I rolled my eyes and asked, "Where's the ranch from here?"

He crooked a grin and pointed to where he could sense his family. "Find a road that heads that direction. When you find the main highway, you'll know where you are. If you get lost, just come back and ask me again." He frowned then. "Just don't let me get too hungry..."

"Right...no problem. Will you be okay for the trip there?"

What I really wanted to know was, *Will you die again on me, if I don't get you there fast enough?* but I couldn't quite bring myself to ask him that. He seemed to understand my real question though. "The dangerous part is over, Emma. I'm starving...but it won't end me." He twisted his lips. "I'm pretty sure anyway."

Ignoring that last part, I visibly relaxed and gave him an agreeable nod. With a tiny grin, Teren closed the door. I made my way to the front, unlocked the cab and slid inside, tossing the belts on the seat beside me. I fumbled through the keys on the ring and exhaled with relief when I found the one for the damn cuffs still hanging on my wrist. I popped them open and rubbed the red, irritated skin. Then I tossed the cuffs onto the seat, where they collided with the belts. Starting the camper, I mentally prepared myself for the long journey. Not only did I have to figure out where I was in relation to the world, but I had to find a nest of vampires that I'd never actually driven to. Should be fun.

It turned out to be easier to find the ranch than I'd anticipated. That doesn't mean I didn't get lost...I did. After driving back roads for what felt like an eternity, I'd finally given up and pulled over to ask Teren where his blood sense was directing him. Remembering his last words, I'd brought a peace offering with me.

I'd driven by a small stand that looked like it sold eggs during the day. Figuring they probably had chickens nearby, 'cause...duh, I stopped and darted over a small, wooden fence into a rundown yard that did indeed have a couple of henhouses in it. I reached inside one and felt around for a sleeping bird. Then, when I was pretty sure I was holding feet, I yanked my hand back and stole a chicken. Yep...that was what my life had been reduced to...stealing poultry, so my boyfriend wouldn't attack me.

I ran back to the camper, while the stupid bird flapped and flailed about, like it knew it was about to meet its maker. I stifled an *Oh my god, I'm holding a chicken by its feet* girly shriek and dashed to the back of the camper where Teren immediately opened the door.

I tossed the bird at him. He caught it, and drained it, all in one swoop. When he was done he tossed the bird's body outside and looked at me with scrunched brows. I studied his still sunken face, but noticed that his skin didn't look quite so ashen anymore. He looked minutely healthier...for a dead man at least.

"I can't believe you just stole a chicken for me." He shook his head in disbelief as his fangs retracted. "I could have gotten it."

I shook my head. "You would have eaten the whole flock and that's someone's livelihood. I just needed to know where to go, without you ripping my throat out."

He frowned as he pointed in the direction that we were already heading. I guess I hadn't been so far off after all. "I'm not gonna—"

Slamming the door in his face, I cut him off. "Okay...thanks."

He cracked the door back open. "Really?" He shook his head while I gave him a playful grin. "I'll bang on the cab if you start going the wrong way...okay?" I bit my lip and nodded and he, more gently than I had, closed the door again.

So, with only that one little pit stop, we finally made it to Teren's parents' massive spread of a home. They were all outside waiting in the parking area when I rolled up. They all had anxious looks on their faces. Alanna looked like she'd been crying and Jack, looking solemn, had his arm around her shoulders.

I wasn't sure why they looked so panicked already, before we'd even had a chance to tell them what had happened, but then I understood. From the blood bond they shared, they knew he was in the camper and from their unbelievably perceptive ears, they also knew he didn't have a heartbeat. What they *didn't* know was if I was bringing them a hungry vampire…or a corpse.

I immediately put the car in park, shut off the engine, and opened my door. "He's fine," I reassured them. My words didn't seem to ease their minds one bit; all three black-haired beauties flew to the back of the camper and ripped the door off its hinges to get at their son.

By the time I walked back there, they had already picked up his limp body and were herding him away from the vehicle. He weakly looked up at me as Halina and Imogen easily supported his weight. He seemed very tired. After his chicken snack, I'd found the highway, and we'd driven a couple more hours at least before making it to the ranch. He'd been silent in the camper the entire time. I'd carelessly assumed that that was because I'd been going the right way. He'd said before starting out, that he was pretty sure he would be okay for the trip, but as I studied his worn face, it was obvious to me that while the long drive hadn't killed him, it had definitely taken its toll on him. Silently, I berated myself for not finding him something else along the way.

"Thank you," he whispered, and then Halina and Imogen blurred him from sight. I had no idea which direction they went.

Alanna put a cool hand on my shoulder. I regarded her youthful face and thought she looked ten years older now, in her worry. New pink tears rolled down her cheeks as she pulled me in for a bone-crushing hug. "Thank you. Oh God, thank you."

She turned to flee to her son and I grabbed her arm. "Take me with you. I want to be with him."

Alanna looked back at Jack, who nodded to her after glancing once at me. Alanna scooped me up like I was no more trouble than a toddler and without another word, she blurred me to the pastures, where Teren was laying waste to their cattle.

The next thing I knew, she was setting me on top of one of

the tall, white fences that separated the different fields. I could hear the sounds of low growling and distressed animals, and a shiver went up my spine.

"Stay here, dear," she said while patting my thigh. Her tone was kind, but very firm.

I nodded and watched her flit away to where the sounds were coming from in the tall grass. I couldn't see much in the dark, but their eyes marked where they were in the night, gorging themselves on clueless cattle.

I watched their eyes in a near trance for a seemingly long time. I startled when a hand brushed my back. Turning, I saw Jack standing behind me with his foot propped on the bottom slat of the fence. His eyes were moist as he looked up at me. "Thank you for bringing back my son," he choked out.

I nodded and swallowed back the tears that wanted to fall. Jack looked out over the field, at the glowing eyes dancing in the night like fireflies. "I don't know what happened tonight...and I'm pretty sure I never want to know..." He looked back up at me, as I suddenly felt very self-conscious about my bloodstained clothes and beat-up face. "But we owe you everything. You're always welcome here...daughter."

Okay...that undid me, and the tears flowed down my cheeks. It had been a long time since a man had called me daughter. My father's own passing had left a void in my life that, until this very instant, I hadn't even realized was there. Warmth filled my body that this loving man before me could be a part of my life in ways I hadn't anticipated. He could be a father for me, as well as for Teren. I suddenly wanted Ashley to meet him...to meet the entire family. I wanted this ache that I'd just felt start to heal, to heal for her too.

Seeming unsure how to deal with my reaction, Jack awkwardly rubbed my back. Then he climbed over the fence and jumped down to the other side. Alarmed I spouted, "Where are you going?" I was pretty sure he was walking into the lion's den in the middle of a feeding frenzy.

He gave me a crooked smile that was so much like Teren's, I had to swallow back tears again. "I thought I'd lost my son tonight.

I'm going to go watch him be reborn." He held out his hand to me. "Want to come?"

Steeling myself, I nodded and jumped down to land beside him. I clutched his warm, dry hand and followed him into the night, to watch my honey live in the only way he could now.

Chapter 19 – Fire and Ice

Cool arms slid around my body the next morning and sighing contently, I stretched. Various aches and pains reminded me of the previous night's adventure. Everything that had transpired in the past twenty-four hours still seemed a little unreal to me. We'd been kidnapped, Teren had been killed, and then he'd been reanimated. We'd killed our attacker and we'd managed to escape, more or less intact.

A twinge of revulsion rose in my stomach at what we'd had to do to get out of there, but I pushed it back. I was sure I'd have nightmares over plunging a rod through that nameless man's throat, but now wasn't the time to dwell on it. Now was the time to cherish that we'd made it, that we were alive. Well, we were safe at least. Only one of us was still technically "alive".

I snuggled back into the cool, bare chest behind me. Grabbing one of his hands, I applied his cool, soothing touch to my aching face. I was pretty sure I had a black and blue eye. I felt like I had a black and blue brain too.

Teren pulled me in close. I shivered a bit under his touch. "Am I too cold for you?" he whispered.

"No," I murmured. "You feel wonderful…everything is sore."

Kissing my head, he pressed his body along the length of me. I sighed in contentment again as he comforted my aching body and my heart. Jack and I had watched him and the girls feed last night for what felt like hours. It had been mesmerizing to watch them silently move between the Wagyu, the special cattle his family had brought in, just for his awakening. Teren had said that he didn't like hunting, but he still had a predatory way of moving as he'd circled an animal and brought it down in one flawlessly smooth maneuver.

The women had let him get his fill before they'd moved in as well. Between the four of them, they'd gone through a half dozen cattle. There would be plenty of steaks in the freezer for a while.

When Jack and I had wandered amongst the vampires hand

in hand, I'd been afraid for just the briefest moment that they'd turn on us. But Teren had only looked up from his meal, smiled uncertainly at me, and then resumed eating. The sight had rattled my stomach some, but that was who he was now, and at the moment, that had been what he'd needed. My fragile stomach was just going to have to deal with it. And really, after watching him devour a man…cows were a welcome sight.

Eventually, the emotionally charged evening had caught up to me. With drooping eyes, I'd nearly dropped like a sack at Jack's side. That was when cool arms had encircled me and swept me up into a tight embrace.

"I've got you, Emma," Teren had whispered into my ear, before flitting me back to the house and putting me into our bed. At least I'm assuming that's what happened. In all honesty, I vaguely remembered him speaking my name before the exhaustion overtook me and I fell fast asleep.

A pale ray of morning light fell across his arm as he held me tight to him in our massive bed here at the ranch. I noted how his skin was a little paler than it used to be, but he was still a touch darker than mine. I also noted the absence of his heart thumping against my back. I supposed I'd just have to get used to that too. And I would.

"Are you all right?" he whispered.

I twisted in his arms to look at him. Concern was in his sky blue eyes as his fingers against the side of my battered face began stroking my cheek. I put a hand on his chest, which was slightly warmer where my skin had heated it. "I'm okay, Teren. Actually, I'm better than okay…because you're okay."

Smiling, he leaned in to timidly kiss me, like he was suddenly afraid he'd break me. I tried to deepen his hesitant kiss, but he resisted and continued moving against my cut, swollen lip in a soft, temperate way. I ran my hand up his neck, through his dark hair, and forcibly pulled him into me. He was being slow and gentle and that wasn't the assurance I needed right now. Eventually my insistence paid off. With a low groan, he kissed me back, hard. I groaned too and he instantly pulled away.

"Did I hurt you?" His worried eyes flicked over my bruised face.

I shoved his shoulder back. "Stop it…I'm fine. Stop worrying about me and kiss me like you mean it. You don't need to hold back."

He raised an eyebrow at my command, then grinning, he leaned in and ardently kissed me. His cool tongue stole my breath for a second, until I got used to the new sensation. His mouth moved to my neck, and I let out a blissful sigh as heat rushed in to replace the chill left by his lips, tongue and breath.

His hands slipped down my shoulders to the cotton tank top I was wearing. It was only then that I realized I was in my pajamas, pajamas that had been packed away in Teren's car, the car that had been abandoned somewhere between our house and the ranch.

"Ummm…where did these come from?" I asked.

My voice came out a little husky, and a low growl escaped Teren's throat before he answered with, "What?"

"My clothes…our stuff?"

He stopped placing kisses along my throat and looked up at me. His eyes were smoldering, and I had to bite my lip. "Gran and Great-Gran got my car last night, while I tended to you." His eyes flicked down to the mattress and his voice softened. "They also took care of…the farmhouse and the camper."

A shudder passed through me that had nothing to do with Teren's body. "Oh," I whispered. His eyes returned to mine and he searched my face, concerned. "I'm fine," I said immediately, before he could ask. "Are you?"

He took a moment before answering. "I am."

His soft lips returned to mine, before following the path his hands had taken down my tank top. He lingered on my chest, feeling my body react to him through the fabric of my light shirt. Scrunching the material up, he began trailing kisses down my ribcage to my stomach. Groaning, I ran my fingers through his hair again. With a swift, cool lick in-between each kiss, his lips traveled across my stomach. After he went past my belly button…he paused.

I was about to beg him to keep going, when he softly spoke into my skin. "I'm so sorry, Emma." I lifted my head to look down at him. He raised his head to look back at me and pain was in his eyes. "I'm so sorry I couldn't give you a baby. I know how much you..."

Sitting up, I grabbed his face; my sore joints protested the swift movement. "You didn't fail, Teren...that was stolen from us." I searched his sad face. "It was taken from us, okay. You have nothing to feel sorry for." I kissed him as he started to nod. Lying back, I pulled him over my body. My hand ran to his shorts and started pulling them down.

Breathing heavy, he broke away from my lips. "They can hear." He shook his head. "They won't be leaving me out of earshot for a while...sorry."

I brought his lips back to mine. "Then they can listen...I don't care." I stopped kissing him and stared at him intently. "I had to watch you die...almost twice. I'm not letting a little thing like modesty get between us again."

He matched my intense gaze with one of his own. "I can't believe what you did for me."

I realized then, that he did indeed know exactly what I'd done for him, even if he was choosing to play along with my version of events. I rubbed his cheek with my thumb. "There's nothing I wouldn't do for you, Teren...nothing."

His intense gaze softened into one filled with love, and he slowly shook his head. "You were wrong about one thing."

"Hmmm?" I ran a finger along his strong, stubbly jaw.

"I'm not better than you. No one's better than you." I gaped at him as I realized that not only did he know exactly what I'd done...he'd heard me do it. He'd heard everything. He knew everything.

He started to open his mouth, with what looked like an apology on his lips, but I cut him off. "Don't you apologize for my choice. I don't need it or want to hear it...ever. If I had to do it over again, I would change nothing." I grabbed his cheek. "Nothing, Teren."

He kissed me then, and for a moment, I let myself forget that we'd just been through a horrid ordeal. That, while I put on a brave act for him, I was deeply remorseful for having taken a life, even a twisted one like that man's. That my life was now a touch more complicated with a dead boyfriend. That my body hurt everywhere. That we weren't entirely alone here at this ranch, or even in this room. I let all of that go, and all that I let touch my mind, was everywhere this amazing man in my bed was touching my body. And for the rest of that morning, a morning that I had been so sure last night I'd never get to see, Teren did his best to make me forget everything but him.

And he succeeded…over and over again.

****

We stayed at the ranch, recovering and adjusting to Teren's new lifestyle. His family sent the help away, claiming a family emergency was shutting them down for a while. I was sure they'd cleaned up the Wagyu slaughter before sunrise, and none of the hands were even remotely suspicious of the family, but, as we'd painfully learned, you can never be too careful.

Well, I wasn't entirely sure about none of the hands suspecting. I'd happened to be coming down the staircase when Peter had been saying goodbye to Jack and Teren. Teren had shaken his hand and Peter had looked at their shaking hands the whole while, with an expression on his face like he was doing math in his head.

When they'd released, he'd clapped Teren's shoulder and left his hand there for a long time as he'd searched Teren's face. Teren had looked a bit uncomfortable under the scrutiny, and Jack had even coughed once into his hand, but Peter had only continued searching Teren's face.

Finally, he released him and smiled. He glanced at me as I hit the bottom step and then back to Teren. Peter's voice was rough, but very kind, when he told him, "I'm sure everything will work out just fine." Teren tilted his head and was about to speak, but Peter turned and left the home.

I'm not sure if Peter suspected anything, but he was no dummy, and he'd worked for the Adams for a while, I'd been told.

Teren also told me that Peter rotated the men he brought in with him and kept them under a tight leash while they were on the property, never letting them stray into the fields after dark. I'm no genius, but it seemed to me that Peter Alton knew exactly what the Adams family really were...and he protected them the only way he could.

Once Peter and the hands were gone, and we were alone here on the ranch, his family was morose around me. Sure, they threw on we're-glad-you're-alive smiles, even Halina, which surprised me at first, but there was an air of sadness that filled the home. Their dreams of future children had died that day, right along with mine. No one mentioned the loss to me. I think they sensed that I'd burst right into tears if they did. But I saw the occasional sweep of their fingers under their eyes, or a body blurring from the room, if I entered at the wrong moment. They were mourning right along with me and I appreciated that at least I wasn't alone in my grief.

After a couple of days, the need to call my sister and let her know about the ordeal I'd just survived was too great. I called her early in the evening on a phone in the library, where I felt like I had some semblance of privacy...even though I didn't. I promised myself that I'd be strong and not cry. I didn't make it past, "Hey, sis."

Brokenly, I told her the story of how we'd been kidnapped and how we'd gotten away. I told her as much detail as I thought she could handle, only telling her that, in the end, Teren didn't touch me and we'd gotten away from the man. I was pretty sure the women in Teren's family knew the truth about our escape, especially Halina and Imogen, who had cleaned up the mess. I'd forgotten, in my haste to get away from that nightmare with no trace of us left behind, that a couple of the vampire women in the family had experience in cleaning up crime scenes. Halina in particular had a lot of experience.

My sister listened to my story in shocked silence and just as I was sure she was no longer on the other end of the phone, I heard the sounds of someone rustling around. "How do I get there?" she calmly asked.

"Ash...I'm fine, you don't have to—"

"Some jackass just tried to kill my sister! I'm coming over to see you, even if I have to drive around aimlessly to do it!"

I was about to tell her that we could get together in a few days—I was still really black and blue and I'd rather be healed a little more before she saw me—when Teren poked his head into the room. I twisted my lips at the intrusion and he quickly said, "I'll go pick her up."

I blinked and automatically repeated that to Ashley, without thinking too much about it. Teren blurred from my sight before I had a chance to even say "wait" and Ashley, sounding both pleased and nervous, said "okay" and hung up the phone. I hung up the empty line and wondered how that conversation had gone so much differently in my head.

Almost two hours later, the family and I were standing in the parking lot, watching the lights of Teren's car bounce along the driveway. Filling myself with confidence, I walked over to where Halina was leaning against her sports car.

She looked over and smiled crookedly when she noticed my approach. I harbored no ill will towards Halina, but she wasn't exactly the most comfortable person to be around and she had an odd sense of humor. Nothing made her grin more than scaring the crap out of me and I was pretty sure she'd love to make my sister wet her pants.

In my most menacing tone, I firmly told her, "I will drag your sleeping ass out into the sun, if you so much as drop a fang at my sister. Play nice."

She gaped at me, surprised, and as I looked around, I saw that the other vampires were gaping at me too. I straightened my shoulders and focused my eyes only on Halina's. She started laughing suddenly, and slung a cool arm around my shoulder. "I like you more and more every day."

The rest of the vampires laughed. Jack even joined in, after Alanna leaned over and whispered in his ear. So, when Teren's car finally stopped and he stepped out to walk around and let Ashley out of the car (such a gentleman...even dead), it was understandable that he was shocked to see Halina's arm still draped over me.

Laughing at the look on his face, I walked over to his car and waited for him to help Ashley out. Then I engulfed her in a ferocious hug. She hugged me back just as tight. "Don't ever get yourself almost killed again," she whispered into my hair as she sniffled.

I pulled back to examine my horrifically scarred sibling. She was the most beautiful sight I'd ever seen. "I won't...I promise."

Ashley traced the outline of the bruising around my eye with a broken sigh and a slight shake of her head. A tear dropped down her cheek as she looked over at Teren. At the same time, they both smiled at each other. I was sure my sister had had some words for him in the car, both complimentary and admonitory, but they seemed to have come to a mutual level of love and respect for each other. Whatever fears my sister had for him and me, had hopefully dissolved with the knowledge that even facing death, Teren hadn't hurt me. He'd never hurt me.

I introduced my sister to my extended family. They each took her in with a warm embrace and no outward show of fear or disgust for her appearance. These were people who were used to out of the ordinary and they had a threshold for weird higher than most. My sister's disfigurement was nothing worth more than a cursory glance; noted, then forgotten. Even Halina gave her a genuinely warm smile and something seemed to pass between the two women when they hugged. It was almost like they shared an instant connection; two women who'd had a horrible fate thrust upon them at too young of an age—outcasts from the world, trying to find their places in it.

I truly relaxed as I watched them embrace. If my sister could bond with Halina, then the rest of the Adams family would be a snap. And it did appear to be that way. Never leaving my side for long, Ashley conversed breezily with Alanna, talked at length with Imogen, and gazed at Jack in such a way, that I suspected she was aware of what role he could play in her life as well. She even spent some time laughing with Halina, and learning some Russian phrases—phrases that I was absolutely positive were Russian curses that would have made the KGB blush.

Teren drove her back home an hour before dawn, after lengthy goodbyes and promises to return longer when she had a break with school. Halina looked disappointed that she was leaving, and told Ashley to let her know if anymore foolish boys bothered her. I hoped my sister was aware enough of Halina's nature to not take her up on that offer. I was pretty sure that any frats who crossed Halina would get more than a light nibble and a mind wipe.

A few nights later, Teren and I were curled up on the couch in front of the massive living room fireplace. His family was relaxing outside in their massive hot tub. Apparently the vampires enjoyed the near-searing heat on their chilly flesh even more than humans did, and from what Jack had told me, their skin was a much hotter temperature for a while after leaving the tub. I'd tried not to think about the intimate implications of that, as I nodded at the man who was practically a father to me.

Teren and I talked about some of the things our captor had told us. My memory of that night was hazy at best—I had been smacked around a lot—but Teren remembered quite a bit, even with the fog of pain he'd been dealing with at the time.

"So...you're not alone," I told him, as we lay side by side on the couch; the heat from the fire caressed my back, while the coolness of my boyfriend's chest gave my arms goose bumps. "You're not the only mixed vampires."

Teren looked over my head into the flames of the fire. His eyes danced in the changing firelight as he thought about that. "Yeah...and all this time we thought we were the only ones." He returned his gaze to me. "Who knows how many of us are out there?"

I bit my lip as I searched his face. "Will you try and find them?"

He looked back to the flames and pulled me tighter. I laid my head on his silent chest. "I don't know. It's tempting. Maybe...someday."

"You know I'm coming with you, right?" I murmured into his chest.

He laughed and kissed my head. "You know I'm not leaving you behind, right? We vampires tend to stick close to what we like, remember."

I peeked up at him with a crooked grin. "Does that mean you like me?"

Without missing a beat, he answered, "Sometimes."

I playfully poked his arm and he laughed. He held me close in silence and just as I was about to flip around to warm up my chest and cool off my back, he spoke. "He mentioned fourth and fifth generations. He said that they were rare, and hard to spot, but if we could find some of the older generations, maybe we could see if diluting out vampirism is even possible."

I pulled back to look at him and a sad smile lit his face. "I know it's too late for us…but it would be interesting to know if it could have been possible for our line to remain…alive." He shrugged and looked sorry for mentioning it.

I swallowed back the surge of grief, and felt pleased that only one tear escaped my eye. Teren tenderly stroked it away. "Yeah, it would be interesting…"

"I shouldn't have brought that up. I'm sorry." Remorse tightened his face as he stroked my cheek.

I shook my head. "It's okay, Teren. It's okay to talk about children. We should talk about it. We both lost…" I brushed another stubborn tear off my cheek. "Besides, maybe one of these older generations has tried to turn someone. We could find out if it's possible…"

He pursed his lips at me and I let it drop. He still didn't want to talk about it. I didn't want full vampirism for me, or even for my sister anymore, but if we could find a way to become like Teren? Well, that would be considerably more tempting…although, drinking blood still seriously grossed me out.

I flipped over and snuggled my too-warm back into his cool embrace. My arms and chest heated in the glow of the blazing fire. Slightly turning my head, I whispered over my shoulder, "You and your family will need to be extra cautious from now on, now that you know there are people out there…hunting you."

He sighed and kissed my head. "I told you not everyone is a fan." I stroked his arm and pulled him tighter, savoring him being close; I'd been so sure I was going to lose him. He kissed my head again. "You're right…we'll be careful, more so than usual." I rested my head on the crook of his arm and nodded. "And besides…we don't know for sure that he was working alone." He said that last part quietly, like he meant for the others to hear it, but not me. I had heard it, though, and I clutched his arms tight to me. He was right; we didn't know that for sure. The man's life had seemed solitary…but we had no real way of knowing. And if he'd told someone about the nest of vampire ranchers that he'd found…

A low growl vibrated against my back and I twisted around to look at Teren. He was staring into the fire, his eyes intense. "Let them come, they'll regret it," he said, his voice as intense as his eyes. "I'm not so weak anymore and I won't be taken by surprise again. No one will ever touch my family."

I swallowed and a shiver ran through me. I hated the thought of Teren's family being in danger, of Teren being in danger. Twisting back around, I closed my eyes and let that fear burn out of me with the heat of the fire on my face. Right at this moment, I was safe with Teren and he was safe with me. Everything else would just have to be worried about on another day.

After a while, my face and body felt healed enough to leave, but the ranch was so comforting and welcoming, not to mention packed full of bursting-with-blood bovines, that we delayed returning to the city. We delayed returning for the full six weeks, and before we knew it, November arrived…and Teren's twenty-sixth birthday.

On that night, the girls surprised him with an elk. I had no idea where they got it and the idea of them hunting the countryside for one and then lugging it back to the property, made me insanely happy. I was giggling near uncontrollably when they showed it to him. Teren laughed at my reaction and then the rest of his family joined in too. Well, everyone except Halina; she was eyeing the Elk with interest, and I was pretty sure that if Teren didn't drain it soon, she'd take a bite while his back was turned.

Eager to give him my own present, which required far less clothing, I pulled him into the house when he was finished with his birthday meal. His family stayed outside, only watching us flit indoors with amused expressions on their faces. I supposed they'd become a little accustomed to our physical relationship, and while I wasn't going to let it stop me, it did still sort of ick me out.

Walking backwards down our hallway, I started pulling off Teren's shirt while we kissed. I successfully removed his shirt and flung it over my shoulder; it landed just on the inside of our door. Teren laughed and started unbuttoning my top. Inside our room, the fireplace was burning away and a merry, orange glow danced across Teren's chilly flesh. I backed him into the door a second after he closed it and ran my hands up his body.

He made a low growl deep in his throat and finished blindingly fast with my shirt, throwing it on top of his. His hands ran up my back and I shivered. His skin felt like he'd momentarily walked into the freezer in the kitchen; cool, just on the verge of being cold. It was enough to send goose bumps racing along my skin, but not enough to be completely uncomfortable. And after his skin left mine, I felt all the hotter for its absence. We were the perfect blend of fire and ice.

Teren pushed us away from the door and started making quick work of my jeans. I started in on his as well. "Happy birthday, baby. I hope you didn't fill up on that elk," I whispered in his ear. All I got from him was another low growl in response.

His lips trailed down my body as he sank to his knees. He started pulling down my jeans. When he reached my hips, he stopped and looked up at me, a little irritated. "What *is* that?"

I tried to control my heavy breath, as I pushed his head back to my skin. "What's what?"

He looked back up at me, like I was intentionally doing something to annoy him. "That noise? I've been hearing it for a few days and it's really distracting right now…"

Irritated myself now, I stepped closer to him, so he'd refocus on the task at hand. "God, Teren, I don't know…you could be hearing a moon landing with those ears of yours."

He sat back on his heels, further frustrating me. I put my hands on my hips as he stated, "No…it's coming from you."

Embarrassed, I crossed my arms over my body. "I did eat a lot today…" Alanna had been outdoing herself with gourmet food for Jack and me; one of her greatest joys was cooking, and she loved having some humans around to do it for. I'd been eating way too much and had definitely gained weight this time—my clothes were even getting a little tight. I was kind of scared to step on a scale, and maybe just a touch happy that we'd be leaving our love nest soon—so I could start eating more moderately.

He dismissively waved his hand at me. "No...I know those sounds." He brought his fingers to his chin, while he sat there thinking. "This is different...it's almost like—"

I cut him off, my face heating. "You know those sounds? Teren! You do not have permission to listen to noises that my body makes. We need to talk about boundaries."

He shot to his feet and took two steps away from me. "Oh my God, Emma."

I looked over his shocked face with scrunched brows. "I'm just saying I don't want you eavesdropping on my digestive track. It's nothing to freak out about."

His face broke into a strange expression. He took a step towards me, cocking his head, like he was intently listening. "Oh my God, Emma," he said again, almost reverently.

My heart started racing at the odd look on his face. "You're freaking me out, Teren."

He looked down my body and then looked back to my eyes; a crystal clear tear fell down his cheek as he regarded me in awe. "Oh my God..."

He took another step towards me and I stepped away from him, until the backs of my legs hit the bed. Confusion added to my trepidation. My heart felt like it was going to burst right out of my chest. I was about to yell at him to tell me what the hell was freaking him out, when I finally noticed where his eyes were going when he looked at my body. The realization hit me at the exact moment his hand came up to rest on my abdomen.

My eyes flashed up to his. "Teren, do you...hear a heartbeat?" A tear rolled down my cheek at the very idea.

His eyes flicked back and forth between mine as he nodded. "Yes...I think so..."

My hands flew to my mouth as I physically held in a sob. A baby? With the horror we'd been through, and the lasting grief I'd felt over the past few weeks, I hadn't been paying too close of attention to my body. We'd been so sure that that future was lost to us that I hadn't let myself consider the fact that I could have been pregnant before Teren's change and not known it. Heck, he could have very feasibly gotten me pregnant the morning of the attack, and I wouldn't have known it for weeks. It was such a long shot, and it hurt so much to think about the possibility that I hadn't let myself.

"A baby?" I whispered through my fingers.

Instantly, the door to the room burst open. I didn't even care that three, crying, eager women were staring at Teren and me, half-dressed in our bedroom, with both of our jeans undone and his hand still caressing my stomach. A baby…

Teren held out a hand to hold back his family and surprisingly, they gave us space. The room buzzed with excited energy though and my heart raced even higher. Teren brought his hands to my cheeks.

"Emma…I need you to calm down, so I can hear the heartbeat again. It's too faint to separate from yours, when you're so worked up. Can you try and relax for me?" Instantly, the light was shut off and the fire was doused. Engulfed in darkness, Teren's eyes glowed at me intensely, and I allowed myself to relax into his gaze, allowed his soft light to ease my surging heart and calm my breath.

"Good…that's good, Emma."

Someone flicked a light back on and I watched him drop to his knees again and put his ear against my stomach. He looked up at me and frowned, before returning his head to my belly. Whatever he could hear, it was too quiet for the others to hear without skin-to-skin contact. They held hands and silently watched Teren. None of them were even breathing.

Suddenly, he sat back on his heels and gazed at me in adoration. He slowly shook his head. "You may want to sit down."

A grin spread on my face at the relaxed look on his. "Why? Aren't I pregnant?"

His corresponding smile lit up his entire beautiful, dead face. "Oh yes, you definitely are...but..."

My grin faltered slightly. "But?"

He smirked at me. "I hear two separate heartbeats."

I didn't sit so much as fall.

There was a mad rush of crying, excited women swarming around my body, like I was suddenly sacred to them. Not bothered one tiny bit that we were still half-naked, they hovered around us, congratulating and offering advice, for a good twenty minutes before exiting our bedroom. I think the only reason they left us at all, was the fact that Jack had tromped into the room and kicked them all out, after giving me a warm, congratulatory hug, of course.

Finally able to stretch out on our bed alone, I snuggled into the crook of Teren's cool embrace. Our bodies entwined, and I smiled as Teren's finger drew lazy circles around my bare abdomen. "I can't believe we're really going to have a baby. I can't believe we're going to have twins, Teren." I smiled up at him. "You don't do anything halfway, do you?"

Laughing, he kissed my head. "I hope you were sure that you wanted this. Raising vampires isn't exactly the simplest job."

I smirked at him. "Raising any sort of child isn't a simple job...and yes, I've never been surer." I kissed him and then pulled back with a frown on my face. "There is one thing we should talk about now."

"Oh?" He smiled peacefully at me.

I propped myself up on an elbow; my hair brushed over his shoulder. "Well, besides the fact that I'm taking over your closet when we move in together..." he smiled wider at that, but didn't argue, "are you finally going to ask me to marry you?"

He snuggled into the pillows and raised an eyebrow. "I don't know, Emma..." he started chuckling, "that's a pretty big commitment."

I smacked his chest. Smartass. I raised my own eyebrow in a very clear indication that he didn't have much choice on the subject—he *was* marrying me. If I was going to be having his vampire twins…then my dead boyfriend could at least make an honest woman of me.

He kissed my hand on his chest. "Whenever you want a ceremony, you just let me know, but in my eyes, we were married the day I died. The day I somehow managed to refuse your sweet, intoxicating blood…and even turned down that psychopath's vile stuff." He paused and looked at me. A thoughtful expression was in his eyes as they roamed between mine. "Even though the memory of taking his life will haunt me, I've found that I'm…grateful." He smiled with one corner of his mouth and reached up to cup my cheek with his cool palm. "I'm grateful to you, for not allowing my stubborn conscience to ruin our chance at a life together."

His smile suddenly switched to a frown and his hand dropped from my face to trail down my arm; a line of goose bumps followed it. "I put you in a position I never should have." I started to object, but he cut me off. His small smile returned. "But you…you saw to the heart of the matter, and did what you had to do, to save us both, and I love you so much for that, Emma." He rolled me on top of him and brought both cool palms to my cheeks, firmly holding me. His eyes were suddenly intense. "The moment you spilt his blood for me, to save me, you became my wife."

I blinked back the tears several times. Darn romantic vampire. "Teren, that was beautiful…and a touch creepy." We both softly laughed and the intense mood around us, lightened. His palms trailed down both of my arms, coming to my hands resting upon his chest, where he lovingly stroked my fingers. I smiled as I watched his content face absorb me.

"I love you endlessly, Teren…but, I want the whole kit and caboodle." I looked down at his chest as I interlaced our fingers together. "I want to spend the rest of whatever life I have left with you, and I want it official. I want the cheesy music and the horrid bridesmaid dresses and a sea of flowers and my mother crying hysterically and my sister standing beside me…" I looked up at his calm face, his small smile matching mine. "I want the whole thing…and I want it here, at your amazing family's amazing home."

He was starting to nod, when as an afterthought I added,

"Plus…and this is almost just as important to me…" I looked him squarely in the eye as he cocked his head in question. "I know we've kind of done things backwards, but I really have no desire to be an unwed mother." He grinned and softly laughed as his eyes drifted down to my bare stomach pressed against his. I laughed as well and added, "I also have no interest in getting married in a dress from a store called 'Just in Time', so let's do this quick, okay? How does a December wedding sound to you?"

He laughed in earnest, swept his cool arms around to my back, and pulled me down to his chest. "It sounds perfect." He brought me all the way down to his lips and the word "perfect" echoed in my head as we kissed.

Yes, somehow we'd made it through and we were going to have everything we'd dreamed about having—a home together, a strong marriage, two wonderful families…two children. I was sure there would be some difficulties ahead of us, and more "big" issues for us to tackle. We'd have to hide his secrets from our friends, coworkers, and my mom. We would all be on constant alert now, watching out for anymore psychos who might wish Teren and the rest of his family…my family…harm. Plus, someday, Teren would have to come to terms with the looming threat of my mortality; I would be separated from him one day, that was just life. And on top of all of that, was the unknown element of carrying, birthing and raising mini-vampires.

But for now, for this one moment, none of that mattered, because everything was indeed as he'd said…perfect.

The End

About the Author

S.C. Stephens is a *New York Times* and *USA Today* bestselling author who enjoys spending every free moment she has creating stories that are packed with emotion and heavy on romance.

Her debut novel, Thoughtless, an angst-filled love triangle charged with insurmountable passion and the unforgettable Kellan Kyle, took the literary world by storm. Amazed and surprised by the response to the release of Thoughtless in 2009, more stories were quick to follow. Stephens has been writing nonstop ever since.

In addition to writing, Stephens enjoys spending lazy afternoons in the sun reading fabulous novels, loading up her iPod with writer's block reducing music, heading out to the movies, and spending quality time with her friends and family. She currently resides in the beautiful Pacific Northwest with her two equally beautiful children.

Titles currently available for purchase:

The Thoughtless Series (Published by Gallery Books):
  Thoughtless
  Effortless
  Reckless

Collision Course (Published by S.C. Stephens)

The Conversion Trilogy (Published by S.C. Stephens):
  Conversion
  Bloodlines
  'Til Death

Connect with S.C. Stephens

Email: ThoughtlessRomantic@gmail.com

Facebook: https://www.facebook.com/SCStephensAuthor

Twitter: https://twitter.com/SC_Stephens_

Website: authorscstephens.com

CPSIA information can be obtained
at www.ICGtesting.com
Printed in the USA
LVOW01s1032050317

526180LV00009B/689/P